UNBRIDLED HOLIDAY

A novel

by

Kristin Dow

Other fiction by Kristin Dow:

LIBERTY & MEANS

CHAPTER ONE

Like a school of minnows being swallowed by a whale, Brook Holliday meshed with the throng of travelers pushing their way up the gangway into the gaping mouth of the cruise liner. She had made it this far, had gotten through two flights without losing her composure, but her spirits could still use a jolt of electricity to snap to life. If it weren't for the press of the crowd, she'd consider slinking away and hailing a cab back to the airport, but there was no turning back now. Brook was committed to going through with this trip. With each step she took, her doubts about the next few days washed over her with increasing intensity. *The ocean will do you good*, she assured herself for the thousandth time, hoping that the repetition of such a notion would achieve results. *Time to breathe in the damn sunshine.* Brook paused to gaze up at the bright sky and drew in a whiff of moist warm air. The tease of tropical weather to come was at least a welcome change from the chilly October rain she'd left behind in Kansas City.

"You're holding up the line!" an irritated voice shouted a few people back. Dragging her baggage along behind her like a heavy shackle, Brook ascended the remaining incline of Astroturf and crossed over into a world of gleaming deck boards, sherbet colors, ample merchandising, and controlled chaos. She scanned the mob jammed into the reception area, searching for her other half who'd charged ahead and disappeared amongst the muddle.

Families of both the nuclear and blended variety scampered about the ship, struggling to keep their wits and units together. Clusters of friends greeted each other with hugs and high-fives. Old-timers puttered along the fringes of the action, in no rush, in their element, seasoned pros. Brook caught an adoring couple devouring each other with bedroom eyes and quickly averted her attention elsewhere. At last, she spotted Melissa.

"About time you caught up."

"Sorry. Thanks for snagging us a place in line." As a Child of the '80's embarking on her first cruise, Brook couldn't help but reference *The Love Boat*. "So where's Julie with her clipboard and Colgate smile? Or Gopher with his corny jokes?"

"Forget them, where's Isaac?" Melissa added. "I need a daiquiri pronto. The sooner we get to the pool, the better." She brushed off the top of her shoulder as if removing a layer of crumbs. "I've got public transportation all over me."

Brook agreed that they could both use a cold, potent cocktail and gathered her tangle of corkscrew curls into a loose ponytail, San Juan's humidity winding her hair tighter by the minute. They progressed at a painful crawl, and when she and Melissa at last stepped up to the counter, an agent with an outdated Rachel shag and pencil-thin eyebrows greeted them. "Hello! Paramount Cruise Line welcomes you aboard the Paradise!"

And there's Julie, Brook thought. *Polished perkiness at your service.*

"Hello," the two replied in unison.

"Name?"

"Holliday." Brook held up her fingers as if to give the peace sign. "Two l's."

"What a fitting name," the woman chirped.

Brook nodded before reaching into her tote and retrieving a blue plastic pouch. She ripped open the Velcro closure, slid out the contents, and fanned the collection of papers out on the counter—tickets, birth certificates, passports, confirmation numbers, medical information, emergency contacts...the works.

The agent blinked at the display. "I, uh, only need your tickets and one form of identification, please." Brook siphoned out the requested documents and filed the rest back in her pouch as the agent began to work her terminal with furious keystrokes. "Holl-i-day," she said, piecing out the name as if it were complex and foreign. "This will just take a minute. The system's slow today." Just then, the tapping on the keyboard came to a stop, and the woman's hands froze in mid-air like a pair of claws. One of her skinny eyebrows arched up to the shape of a pyramid.

Don't say it, Brook pleaded in her head. *Please, don't make a big deal about our cabin.*

"This is interesting," the clerk noted, her eyes darting back and forth between Brook and Melissa. "Looks like there's been a mistake. The system says you two are staying in a honeymoon suite."

"That's correct," Brook clipped.

The agent fluffed her shag. "Oh. Okay. I get it." She leaned over the counter and lowered her voice. "No need to hide here. You'll find we're a very cosmopolitan ship. Our staff is mostly European. And I think you two make a darling couple."

"We're sisters," Brook clarified.

The clerk's forehead bunched up in confusion. "I don't understand. Why would the system put you in the honeymoo-"

Brook thrust her left hand forward and spread her naked fingers wide. "Wedding didn't happen." She paused for emphasis. "So there you have it."

The woman clucked her tongue and tilted her head in sympathy. "Oh. I'm so sorry. Wow. You must be in a world of hurt."

Brook swallowed, but couldn't form a reply. Pity from others was almost as painful as the situation itself.

"I'm here in place of the groom," Melissa elaborated, donning her authoritative lawyer voice. "Since my sister wasn't going to get a refund with such late notice, we stuck with the suite. Now the travel agent assured me the change had been made. I am in the system, aren't I?"

"You are in the system."

"Then what's the problem?"

The agent continued with her typing. "No problem. We're here to make your stay as pleasant as possible. And in your case, Miss Holliday, we'll be sure to take extra special care of you while on board." Brook presumed that this was an empty promise, but even if it were true, she didn't want any fuss on her behalf. She just wanted this mess to go away and to feel whole again. "And kudos to you for going through with the honeymoon," the woman continued. "You're a brave girl, a real inspiration. You know, I once saw a news piece about a bride getting jilted at the altar. You know what she did? She threw the big party anyway, turned it into her own celebration. I mean, you might as well, right? It's not like she was getting her money back at that point."

"That's where I was," Brook said. "Point of no returns. Gifts I can take back, but not this cruise."

An awkward silence followed which seemed to eclipse the din.

"Our room keys," Melissa prompted.

With a nod, the agent returned to business and slid their access cards into a paper jacket, scribbling the room number on the outside and handing it over with a cheery smile. "You're all good."

Far from it, Brook quipped in her head. *How could you say such a thing?*

As they headed out of the lobby, a leather-faced man in a tangerine Hawaiian shirt intercepted the sisters and ushered them over to a cardboard cutout of a sunset on the beach. "Squish together, please," he instructed, his weather-beaten features now concealed behind a camera.

Melissa frowned at the cardboard scenery. "Why do this when we're about to get the real thing?"

"Smile!"

Wilted from a long day of travel, Brook would rather capture a great white shark than this particular moment. "No than-"

CLICK! "We like to take a before picture," the photographer said, shooting them a greasy grin. "After a trip aboard the Paradise, you will never be the same. The photos will be on display right outside the gift shop. Just $5.95 a piece. Now scooch aside, please. Let the others have their turn."

The sisters went on their way, navigating a maze of hallways and taking more than one wrong turn before locating their room. Brook set her things down and ran her finger over the door's brass placard, the words "HONEYMOON SUITE" etched into its surface in tasteful block lettering.

"You can do this," Melissa said.

"Sure." Brook pumped her fist in the air. "I will survive."

"That's the spirit, but please, don't start singing that song. I'll have it in my head the rest of the day and I just got rid of that damn *Love Boat* theme." Melissa squeezed her eyes shut in a grimace. "Shit. Now it's back."

Brook squared herself in front of the door, swiped the card through the security slot, waited for the green flicker of light, and entered. The scene she beheld astonished her.

The room should have been classified more as a nook than an inhabitable space. A full-sized bed had been crammed in the corner with a dresser wedged in between it and the other wall, leaving only about four square feet of fleur-de-lis patterned carpet for them to bump about. Brook's old dorm room at Corbin Hall had been palatial in comparison.

"*The Love Boat* didn't look like this," Brook observed.

Melissa shrugged. "Camera adds ten pounds, right?"

Brook stamped her foot. "No! This isn't how it's supposed to be at all!" She rummaged around in her tote and whipped out a pamphlet, holding it out in front of them like a treasure map. "See? There's supposed to be a Jacuzzi and a king-sized bed." She pointed to the glossy photo in the Honeymoon Haven section picturing the amenities.

Her sister moved in for a closer look. "Ah, there's an asterisk. As a lawyer, I know to always look for the fine print. Check it out."

Brook brought the pamphlet up to her nose and squinted her eyes. Sure enough, below the picture was a starry symbol the size of a pore. At the bottom of the page, the notation read, "Features not included in all rooms. Captain's Guest Quarters pictured." Brook stuffed the brochure back in her tote. "This is so typical," she spat. "The one job Chip had, booking the honeymoon, and he screwed it up."

"I hate to defend the louse, but we are in a honeymoon suite."

"I would have gotten us a much better deal," Brook groused as she squeezed through the entryway with her belongings, noting the miniscule bathroom to her left where the toilet seat hovered over the stand-up shower. Brook tossed her bags onto the bed and set her hands on her hips. "You know, I wanted to do Europe. I've always wanted to go there, but nooooo, *he* insisted on the Caribbean. And during hurricane season!"

"Why didn't you do a Mediterranean cruise?"

"You still have the culture, Mel. Chip didn't want to take a vacation where he'd have to think."

Melissa rolled her eyes. "Hey, bright side of all this is that you don't have to compromise yourself for him anymore."

"I didn't...nevermind." Brook plucked the bottle of bubbly from a plastic gold bucket sitting on the dresser. The label had pruned from too long of a soaking, but she could still make out the word "Champaigne" in fancy slanted cursive. "This is a joke!" she blurted, dunking the bottle back into its tepid bath.

Melissa muscled in beside her and flicked the cellophane wrapping of the complimentary fruit basket. "Here's what you get for your money," she noted, "A hat of Carmen Miranda's." Melissa detached the congratulatory card, crumpled it up, and lobbed it into the thimble they had for a trash receptacle.

Brook steadied her hands on the edge of the dresser. "It's okay," she said. "I've gotten used to disappointment."

"I see you've gone from shock to the bitter phase of your recovery."

Brook gave her sister a wan smile. "Hey, it's still progress."

Melissa clapped and rubbed her hands together. "You've got five minutes. Let's change and grab those tissues they've given us for towels. The pool is calling our names."

"Aye, aye captain," Brook replied with a salute.

Melissa zipped open her suitcase and rifled through her belongings. "And if we're lucky, maybe we can get you laid," she muttered.

"What was that?" Brook asked.

A coy grin spread across Melissa's face. "I said if we're lucky, maybe we'll have a good maid."

CHAPTER TWO

Scott Webster squeezed a lime wedge and as it dripped into his bottle of Tecate, a rivulet of citric acid trickled down his finger into a forgotten papercut. Shaking off the sting, he reclined back in his lounge chair and gulped down the frosty goodness. This was just what he needed—a cold beer, a refreshing breeze, and some peace and quiet by the ship's pool. No computer. No e-mails or phone calls. No back-and-forth battles with ad reps over numbers and dollars.

As ironic as it was, Scott had his company to thank for his free passage to the Caribbean. After spending three years chained to his desk as a media buyer for Pendleton Scrubb Advertising, he had been rewarded with an incentive trip for placing the most ad dollars in his department for two consecutive quarters. Scott tried to overlook the fact that Pendleton handled the cruise line's advertising and the trip had come at little, if any, cost to his employer. He would have actually preferred a pay increase and promotion for all his grunt work, but wasn't about to pass up the opportunity to get away, although he wouldn't be able to leave the office completely behind him. Scott willed himself to forget about Pendleton, wishing he had an off-switch for the part of his brain that insisted on stewing over his mundane frustrations.

"You brood too much," Rebecca had recently told him back home. Scott's older sister served as his chief confidante and wise counselor, and her voice had a way of seeping into his thoughts, either encouraging or needling him, depending on the circumstances and his frame of mind. "Take advantage of this chance to escape," she'd advised. "A change of scenery can work wonders."

Wonders. A tall order, but Scott went ahead and placed it. He aspired to write the Great American Novel someday and dared to hope that the islands might bring a story to life. He had some ideas floating around in his head, enough to keep the dream alive, but none had taken root and grown into anything substantial enough to dedicate to paper. Plus, he could never find the time and energy to write. With so many late nights at the office, his mind was too often scrambled from numbers and paperwork to form a complete sentence, much less create compelling prose. Scott dreamed about quitting his day job so he could develop his craft full-time, but no way could he afford to do so, especially since he lived in a pricey apartment on the Country Club Plaza. And money wasn't the only issue. He first had to prove himself worthy before taking such a dramatic leap.

Scott gulped more beer and shut his eyes, enjoying the reggae band's rendition of "Here Comes the Sun" drifting across the pool deck, an appropriate tune as the late afternoon beams warmed his body and melted away his cares. If things could only stay like this on the boat, Scott would be completely satisfied. But he knew this trip would not be free of trouble. Scott's life was bound to catch up with him, and there would be no escape.

CHAPTER THREE

After an invigorating dip in the pool, the sisters agreed that their "champagne" had to be mixed with something for consumption. Brook flagged down one of the many uniformed servers scuttling about the deck and ordered pineapple juice. The man smiled and nodded, appearing to have registered the request, yet stayed rooted to the spot as his eyes became transfixed on Melissa's own pineapples spilling out of her bikini top. "Thank you," Brook added. The waiter snapped out of his trance and dashed off.

Brook adjusted her own push-up bikini top, feeling about as voluptuous as a carrot stick next to Melissa and all her curves. "Who knows where she got the chest," their mother would say whenever Brook sized up her piddly lemon halves against her sister's melons. "You're like me and the other women in our family," she'd console. "Flat as ballerinas." Brook had also inherited Olivia Holliday's round face, green eyes, fair skin, and a right foot that angled out when she walked, an idiosyncrasy she had to remind herself to correct. About the only thing Brook didn't get from their mother was Olivia's terrific memory. Like their father Jack, Brook required notes and lists to keep the details of her life in order. Others called it organization. She called it a necessity. Melissa, on the other hand, had a razor-sharp memory, walked with a perfectly normal, confident gait, and got the olive-tinged skin, tall frame, and regal jawline of their father, all of which served her well at the firm of Herzog,

Brinkman, and Pfeiffer. Brook knew better, but she sometimes felt like Skipper trying to catch up to Barbie. Her wedding had been no exception. Melissa might have had a starter marriage with its share of battles, but at least she made it down the aisle.

Brook flipped back the lid to her jug of sunscreen and slathered on a layer of SPF 45 while Melissa cracked open a hardcover of *The Testament*. "A lawyer reading Grisham?" Brook chastised. "A pathetic choice for a vacation read."

"Hey, for an estate attorney, Grisham is pure fantasy."

The server returned with their pineapple juice and Melissa signed for the drinks, setting her book on her chest and blocking any further ogling from King Leer. Brook lifted the impostor champagne from its replenished ice bucket and with the neck pointing away from her, began to coax out the cork with her thumb. Despite her caution in dislodging it, however, the cork shot out of the bottle and hit the thigh of a passenger whose strut across the deck came to an immediate halt.

A pair of unnerving ice blue eyes rimmed in smudged charcoal glared at Brook from underneath the wide brim of a straw hat. The woman's skin had a glaze to it that looked about as natural as her coconut shell boob job. White leather Daisy Dukes were shrink-wrapped to her hips. "Watch what you're doing," she snapped.

"Sorry," Brook called out. "It was an accident."

The woman sneered at her before continuing with her swagger in her two-story platforms.

"Geez," Brook said, wiping off the sticky liquid that had spilled onto her leg. "The cork couldn't have been much more than a tap. Talk about your drama queen."

Melissa lowered her cat-eye shades. "Those shorts give new meaning to Tighty Whities," she commented, shaking her head in disapproval. "That's just a yeast infection waiting to happen."

Brook chuckled as she added the bubbly to their juice.

Melissa raised her glass in a toast. "To our sisterhood."

"Sisterhood," Brook echoed. "Just remember, I will not be donning a tiara and howling at the moon at any time during this cruise."

"You read too many chick books," Melissa replied.

Brook sipped her concoction, drinking on the behalf of not only her and Melissa, but any bride who'd been denied her big day, on the behalf of jilted lovers everywhere determined to triumph over adversity. That's why she had agreed to go through with the honeymoon after much cajoling from her sister. If Brook could get through the cruise without feeling the urge to jump overboard, then she was going to be all right. Someday. "Thanks for coming with me, Mel. Thanks for everything you've done."

"Well, you did the same for me during my divorce. And Mom and Dad performed damage control. I got the easy part."

"I still think they should have taken this trip. They lost a lot of money."

"It would have been too weird for them. And you've got to stop fretting about the money. You can't-"

"Put a price on my happiness," Brook finished, repeating what their mother had said dozens of times since this nightmare began. After a moment, she added, "But I was happy. Why wouldn't I have been? I was getting everything I wanted."

"What about the fights, Brook?"

"Every couple argues when facing a big life change. It's no reason to…" she couldn't finish.

"The Jumboscreen should have told us something," Melissa said. "The Royals stadium was no place for him to pop the question. You don't even like sports."

"It wasn't like it took place during a baseball game. It was a New Year's Millennium benefit at the club. Y2K was kind of a big deal."

"The proposal was broadcast for everyone to see. *Très* tack-ay. And Chip did it on the one night that surely had the most engagements in recorded history."

"He wanted it to be memorable."

"Memorable, maybe, but not original. And I think he exploited the moment to promote his family's business in front of all that money."

"Chip wouldn't do that."

"Wouldn't he? He shocked us all with what he's capable of. I still think we should sue the little shit. Emotional distress, time away from work, financial loss, not to mention-"

"Stop. Enough talk about him." Melissa said nothing more and returned to reading her book.

As Brook nursed her drink, she noticed a twentysomething couple clasping hands as they passed by, the display of attachment evoking images of Brook's alternate universe where everything had gone according to plan. The scenes she pictured in her mind, however, had been altered to reflect the recent turn of events. As she and Chip posed for a picture to cut their wedding cake, he'd place his hand behind her head as if to bring her in for a kiss, only to end up shoving her face down into the topping of sugared flowers. SPLAT! And when Brook envisioned the tossing of her bridal bouquet, one of the single girls would volley it right back to her, yelling, "Think again, sister! You're still one of us!"

In want of a distraction, Brook reached for the *Real Simple* magazine she'd bought during their layover in Dallas, a fairly new publication with practical advice on enhancing and organizing the lives of modern women, a magazine that spoke to her on so many levels it was spooky. She leafed through the pages, stopping when she came to an article about preventative car maintenance. It wasn't the topic that interested Brook, rather the colorful illustration of an ultra-thin, chic woman posing next to a Volkswagen Beetle, twirling a set of keys around her finger as her scarf flirted with the breeze. *I can do that*, Brook thought. *I can do better than that.*

Realizing she wasn't in the mood to process useful information, Brook set the magazine aside and drained the remainder of her drink. "I can't sit here anymore," she told Melissa. "I'm going for a walk. How about I sign us up for massages in the morning? We do have an entire day to kill before we get to our first island."

"Won't have to twist my arm," her sister replied, her nose still in her book.

"There's also a pirate ship cruise when we get to Antigua. Steel drums, rum punch, we can even walk the plank."

Melissa raised her glass. "Ahoy, matey."

~

After securing the reservations for tours and pampering, Brook found a secluded spot for that essential soul-searching gaze out over the water, resting her elbows on the polished wood railing as the wind roared past her ears and dried out the remaining dampness from her curls. She found solace in the great expanse of the ocean blue, a reminder that her troubles were insignificant in the grand scheme of things. Brook told herself that a love gone wrong was as old as time and others had been treated much worse than she had. Nonetheless, a fresh ache developed in her chest.

Words floated to the surface of the water like the letters in a bowl of alphabet soup, spelling out fragments from a note full of infuriating clichés that would forever be seared in Brook's memory.

>I'm sorry.
>I can't marry you.
>It's for the best.

I can't marry you. That was the line that bothered Brook the most. He could have expressed himself in dozens of ways—*I can't get married, I'm having second thoughts, It's not you, it's me.* No. It was, *I can't marry* YOU. Vinegar on the wound. One would think Chip would have put a little more thought into his words. Then again, what did she expect from a man who had bolted just two weeks before they were to be husband and wife? Two weeks that seemed to have lasted two centuries, time that Brook spent waiting by the phone, checking her e-mail, praying for a response to her dozens of messages. Desperate for any sign or clue to Chip's whereabouts, she'd ransacked his loft, studied photographs, and lingered about their favorite hangouts. She had come up with nothing.

"Where did he go?" Brook asked, addressing the sea. She'd posed the same question to herself and Chip's family more times than she cared to think.

"If we knew, we would tell you," his mother had claimed during one such conversation. Brook didn't know whether or not to believe Maryanne Kincaide. Her loyalty naturally resided with her son, and the two women had never formed a close bond as Maryanne often made Brook feel as if she came from a tin can trailer in Hicksville, Oklahoma instead of a two-story Tudor in Tulsa.

"I deserve some answers," Brook insisted. "Did he get scared?" She took a gulp before continuing. "Is there someone else?" Although it wouldn't diminish the pain, Brook almost wished there was another woman. At least that way, she'd have a simple explanation and could place the blame on the male libido. "Please, Maryanne, just tell me. I can cope. It's the mystery that's killing me."

"We don't know anything, Brook! Chip has only called us once on his cell to let us know that he's okay. He won't talk to us or listen to reason. You know, he quit his job." Maryanne said this as if it were the more pressing matter, trivializing Brook's heartache. Truth was, Brook could care less if

Chip left the family business. He hated selling commercial property, although he never would have admitted it.

"We think he might be in Chicago with an old college buddy," Maryanne added.

"Kevin Rockhill? But they don't talk anymore. We didn't even invite him to the wedding."

"Well, when we checked Chip's e-mail at the office, we found a message from Kevin inviting him out for a stay."

"Wherever he is, Chip needs to call me. He can't just leave me in the lurch like this and not face the consequences." Brook stopped, feeling as though her words were falling on deaf ears since the Kincaides tended to regard themselves above reproach when it suited their needs. "You pressured him," Brook wanted to add. "Chuck was always giving him hell over his sales quota. Chip probably felt trapped. Why else would he flee like this and cut himself off from everyone he knows?" But she had said none of this. Instead, she fought back another waterfall of tears threatening to spill.

"I can't imagine how you must feel, Brook. You worked so hard on the wedding. I've never seen anyone tackle a to-do list like you. And my friends raved about the invitations you designed."

"Is that supposed to make me feel better?" Brook croaked. "I've been hurt and humiliated, Maryanne."

"We all have, dear."

Brook didn't feel an ounce of sympathy for Chip's parents. They were too wrapped up in how their son's disappearance would affect the family business to even bother addressing the deeper issues at hand. For instance, how could Chip feel as if he had no choice but to leave town? And if he'd been unhappy or gotten cold feet, why hadn't he confided in anyone, most of all, Brook? They didn't keep secrets from each other. Regardless, any inner turmoil her fiancé might have been experiencing did not excuse his actions. Chip Kincaide certainly had his faults and Brook had been prepared to accept them, for better or worse. Never did it cross her mind, however, that he could be such a fucking coward.

The words from his note sank to the bottom of the ocean. Brook wished she could tie her sadness and confusion to a block of concrete, toss them overboard, and watch them do the same.

CHAPTER FOUR

Scott didn't know if it was the clomp of wooden heels or the flounce of the enormous floppy straw hat that first alerted him to her presence. If those weren't enough to get one's attention, her dental-floss bikini top and white leather boys shorts certainly were. As she progressed down a row of lounge chairs, men straightened their postures and sucked in their guts, admiring the view and ignoring the cross looks of their female companions. "The Girl from Ipanema" had been written for women of her kind and most guys would kill for the company of such a creature. Scott didn't have to.

"There you are," Waverly said, tossing aside her zebra-print bag, its bamboo handles clacking together. "I've been circling the deck to find you and got pelted by a champagne cork."

"Alert ship security," he teased. "Did you get a close look at it? What vintage was it?"

Although she fought it, a smile tugged at the corner of Waverly's mouth. "Don't be a smartass. Flyaway corks have been known to kill people." She rubbed the back of her thigh. "It'll leave a mark. I bruise like a banana."

"Then you should eat more of them, get some potassium in you."

Ignoring his remark, she twisted her torso around to examine the injury. Something flickered off her skin and Scott moved in for a close inspection.

"Are you wearing…glitter?" he asked.

"Body shimmer," she replied. "It'll give me some color before my tan has fully developed." The bronze shellack gave her skin the appearance of a Krispy Kreme donut. Scott half expected her to start dripping.

Waverly spread out a plush beach towel, removed the flying saucer from her head, smoothed her jet black hair, and slipped on a pair of dinner plate Jackie O. sunglasses, executing each move in a deliberate and assured manner. After wriggling out of her tight shorts, she at last took her seat, windmilling her long legs like a Nair model. Scott resisted the urge, but stole a look at Waverly's chest, a pair of round bubbles that had magically appeared last year after her "spa retreat" in Arizona. He wondered how they would feel to the touch, even though he supposed he'd already groped them during the one night they had together. He forced himself to look away. Scott had yet to form a solid opinion about his travel partner and didn't want her physical attributes to cloud his reason.

An accomplished Account Manager with striking good looks, Waverly Marks was known at his office for not only her strategic politicking, but also her nosebleed heels, tight pencil skirts, and snug tops. Scott's interaction with her had taken place mostly at Pendleton's obligatory happy hours and involved pedestrian conversation, including the night when she kept buying him Jägermeister shots. Having had a stressful day, he pushed aside common sense and downed them with abandon. The next morning, Scott woke up with a nauseous stomach and Waverly in his bed. When she started bombarding him with questions about the cruise he'd supposedly asked her to take with him, all he could do was race to the bathroom to hurl. With no other options, however, Scott had to trust Waverly's word and went ahead with their travel plans. Besides, he didn't have the time or luxury to be picky.

A server rushed to Waverly's side and she ordered a dirty martini with extra olives. Scott had to shout his request for another Tecate as the server scurried off and could only hope he'd been heard. After a minute or two of quiet, rather common between him and Waverly as they didn't have much to talk about, she spoke. "You sure left the cabin in a hurry."

"I wanted to get outside. Those walls in that broom closet were closing in on me."

"You could have waited."

"It looked like you had a lot of unpacking to do. I was just getting in the way. And it's not like we have to spend all our time together."

Waverly sighed before taking out a Zippo lighter and a pack of Virginia Slims from her zebra bag.

"Uh, once again, I'd prefer it if you didn't smoke around me," Scott said. "It's one of my biggest pet peeves. I'm kind of freaky about it."

She tapped out a cigarette and lit up. "Relax, we're outdoors."

Scott was tempted to snatch the coffin nail out of Waverly's mouth, but refrained from doing so, following the advice of Tug McTyde, his best pal at Pendleton. "Forget the smoking and all your weird hang-ups. You get to score with the Office Hottie!" That's what baffled Scott the most about Waverly, why she would show any interest in him instead of the rising superstars of the office. Perhaps she saw him as a pet project ripe for a corporate grooming. Or maybe his ambivalence towards her was the attraction. Some girls came wired that way.

The waiter had evidently heard Scott and brought them both their drinks. Scott signed for them, telling himself that he was on vacation and shouldn't worry about the perpetual sucking noise coming from his bank account. When he handed back the bill, he asked where he could find the climbing wall he saw featured in the ship's brochure.

"Qué?"

"Rock wall." Scott mimed climbing.

The server shook his head. "No wall to climb. Only on boat mas grande."

"A *bigger* boat? This thing is huge!"

"Es pequeña." The server pinched his fingers as if holding a fly by its wings. "This ship adios in dos años."

"It looks brand new."

"Si, si. We have disco, hot tub, a comedian, you know, like Señor Seinfeld."

"But no climbing wall."

"Sorry."

"Gracias."

"Just as well," Waverly said. "I don't get all these activities. I'm here to unwind." And with that, she opened an issue of *Vogue* as thick as an epic novel and in between sips of her dirty martini and drags off her cigarette, moved her lips as she read. Tifani Diamond, an actress whose stage name seemed more fitting to the porn industry than mainstream Hollywood, graced the magazine's cover, posing in a white corseted top with a peek-a-boo lace-up front, her auburn mane of hair cascading over her shoulders. A modern Harlequin heroine. The movie star seemed to taunt Scott with her smug smile. "I am fabulous and you are nothing."

Scott gulped a few swallows of Tecate and excused himself to find a restroom. After taking care of business, he took the scenic route back to the pool. He stopped at a buffet table and loaded up a plate with cheese and fruit, snacking as he strolled, drawing in the sea air and hoping a moment like this might bring about a creative spark of inspiration. What Scott encountered though brought him just as much pleasure.

She gripped the railing with both hands and had her eyes fixed on the ocean in such a probing manner he couldn't help but move in for a closer look. She had a stoic elegance about her, possessing the milky skin and soft lines of a goddess carved out of marble. The only part of her that moved were her blonde curls blowing in the breeze. There was nothing special about a good looking woman catching a man's eye, but Scott felt as if this particular instance had significance. His feet had turned to stone and he couldn't take his eyes off her. Judging from the woman's serious expression, it looked as if she had important, possibly troubling matters on her mind. Scott knew that look, had been in that place many times, and although he wanted to set his hand on her shoulder and ask if she was okay, he dared not to disturb someone so engaged in her thoughts.

He didn't know how much time had passed when she turned and headed off in the other direction. Scott noticed that as she walked away, her right foot turned out at a forty-five degree angle. The quirky walk reminded him of his mother's duck waddle, the telling mark of Katherine Webster's ballerina days. Scott stayed put and watched her until she turned a corner and disappeared. It went against his better judgment, but he knew he'd be on the lookout for those wild curls and off-kilter gait until he saw her again.

And it would happen. The server had said it himself. This boat "es pequeña."

CHAPTER FIVE

Their first night on board, Brook and Melissa feasted on escargot, lobster tail, basil pesto potato puree, and crème brulée, all washed down with a bottle of Pinot Grigio. Sluggish with such rich food and drink, the sisters slouched in the ship's lounge, taking in the Ivanka and Hershel Broadway Revue, a married duo Brook supposed had been kicked out of the Vegas scene years ago, no longer able to keep up with the high caliber celebrities, skimpily-clad showgirls, and mind-boggling performances of Cirque de Soleil.

Ivanka swished across stage in a red-sequined mermaid dress which looked like it had been sewn on to her hourglass body. Brook was amazed the woman could even breathe, much less pay homage to Ethel Merman. Her husband looked like a suave prom date from the seventies with his waxy mustache and powder blue tuxedo. Not a sophisticated pair, but they went together. Ivanka and Hershel provided living proof that there was someone out there for everyone, maybe even for Brook. But she reminded herself that she was not in the market for love, lust, or even like right now. She wanted nothing to do with any "l" word tied to affection towards a man.

"This isn't entertainment," Melissa griped. "This is a *Saturday Night Live* sketch."

Brook chuckled. "Yeah, it's pretty old school." But the duo sang their medley with such blind devotion and verve, Brook couldn't help but be amused. Shame on her and Melissa for being so jaded and critical. "They have passion," she added. "And you can't deny Ivanka's got a set of lungs on her."

"Let's hit the disco."

"We need to digest."

Melissa crossed her arms. "You're turning more into Mom every day."

"I don't want to hurl that fabulous dinner all over the dance floor," Brook said, directing her attention back to the show.

After the act finished their medley, a spotlight zeroed in on Ivanka center stage. "Folks, we're going to bring the house down for a moment," she announced in a breathy, subdued tone. Ivanka then clutched a hankie to her chest and began a teary, over-the-top rendition of *Evita's* "Don't Cry for Me Argentina."

Melissa groaned. "Much more of this and I'm going to hurl, disco or no disco." She motioned to one of the nearby servers. "Vodka tonic, please."

"Same for me," Brook said, straightening up and pulling her frilly chiffon top down over her stuffed gut, the band of her skirt digging into her waist. If others had been right and Brook had lost too much weight during the last few months of strict dieting, recovery seemed just a couple of more meals away. She didn't even know how she was going to get down her drink on such a full stomach, but when in Rome…

Ivanka finished her solo and took a bow. She and Hershel then launched into another medley, sampling crowd pleasers from *Cats*, *Grease*, and *West Side Story*. Brook smiled when she noticed Melissa tapping her finger against the sweaty glass of her highball.

~

Scott had been distracted all evening and after no sign of the intriguing woman, forced himself to pay more attention to Waverly. Across the table, she mouthed the words to the Broadway tunes being belted out on stage, bopping her head and jiggling her foot to the beat, shedding her normal pretense and vanity. The Ivanka and Hershel show was a bit hokey for Scott, but he was glad their act kept his companion entertained. What was also refreshing was the absence of Waverly's usual application of war paint, gel, glitter, and goo. Since they had stayed so late on the pool deck and lost their way back to the cabin, Scott and Waverly had scrambled to make it to dinner on time. She emerged from the bathroom wearing a fancy satin black strapless dress, but had to step out with wet hair and barely a trace of makeup. With the change, she seemed not only more human, but softer at the edges.

Scott shifted forward and tapped Waverly's arm. "You look like you're having a good time."

She kept her eyes glued to the stage. "Yeah, so?"

"I'm just surprised. This doesn't seem like your thing." Ivanka and Hershel clutched each other as they depicted the star-crossed lovers singing "Somewhere" from *West Side Story*.

"These songs take me back to my pageant numbers and school plays," Waverly said, meeting his eyes. "I was the lead in *West Side Story* in high school." She spoke as if she had taken home the Tony, but then her boastful expression hardened. "For once, it paid *not* to be the blonde."

Scott opened his mouth to speak, but she shushed him. He scooted back in his chair and sighed. Learning about Waverly's theatrics should have impressed him, but coupling that with the attention she strived to generate for herself only stirred up the memory of a past love who had eaten his heart for breakfast. Scott then wondered what the hell was wrong with him. Why did he compare every woman to Her? It had happened years ago. He should stop using her as a crutch and move on already. But sometimes it was impossible to forget, especially when the world provided him with constant reminders, triggers beyond the ordinary scraps of a serious relationship.

Scott came to a decision. He would forget his past, as well as the captivating blonde he stumbled across that day. After the show, he would take

Waverly back to their cabin and put the moves on her. It's what any warm-blooded, straight American male would do. It didn't matter that he didn't see a future with Waverly; she hadn't indicated that she wanted one with him. She was the no-strings-attached fling guys longed for, the Holy Grail of casual dating. And it wasn't as if the experience would be miserable. They had slept together once before and although Scott was too drunk to remember it, he assumed he enjoyed himself. It was settled. For once, he would stop over-analyzing his life and seize the moment.

When the show appeared to be drawing to a close, Scott crept his hand across the table, ready to take action.

~

Ivanka and Hershel basked in the applause. "Thank you, and welcome," Hershel said, his velveteen voice melting into the mike. "Ivanka and I are delighted you could be here with us this evening to kickoff your stay aboard the Paradise." He loosened his bowtie so it hung around his neck like slick black seaweed. "We hope you enjoyed the show. It was a thrill and privilege to perform for you. But my wife and I have hogged the spotlight enough for the evening. We'd like to end tonight with a game for you."

Brook cringed as she guessed at what Hershel proposed: group participation. She hoped it wouldn't be something lame like a sing-a-long or the way out-dated Macarena. "We're going to need some volunteers," Hershel continued. Brook wanted to duck out, but didn't dare suggest that she and Melissa leave as surely they'd be singled out as participants. She shrank in her chair. A student willing the teacher not to call on her.

The rest of the crowd must have been just as reluctant to volunteer because Hershel received little response. "Come on now," he urged. "Don't be shy." Ivanka weaved her way through the tables, recruiting a handful of guys from the audience and dragging the poor fellows to the stage. "Let me rephrase this," Hershel added. "Who wants free champagne and rum cake?" A few hands shot in the air, including Brook's that had been forced up by her sister. She wrenched free of Melissa's grasp and slapped her palm down on the table. "You!" Hershel beckoned, pointing in Brook's direction.

She put her hand to her chest and mouthed an innocent, "*Moi?*"

"Don't try to hide, sweetheart," Hershel said. "Get that gorgeous face up here."

Brook stood and scooted out her chair. "Tonight. While you sleep," she told Melissa before making her way to the stage.

~

Scott's hand closed in on Waverly's. *Five, four, three, two*—just then, someone grabbed his arm, foiling his plans. Ivanka stood over him, flashing him a smile that had more wattage than the Broadway lights themselves. She pulled him out of his seat and before Scott could protest, he found himself center stage, the spotlight blinding him. He looked to the other shell-shocked recruits for some explanation, but the guys just shrugged. Downstage, Hershel whispered to a cluster of women as if he were Ziegfield giving a pep talk to his showgirls. Ivanka arranged the grumbling group of men into a circle with their backs to each other. She then instructed them to get down on one knee. "Like you're proposing," she said.

Not the best way to get our cooperation, Scott thought, but the troop did as they were told.

Hershel then stepped out front and center. "Ladies and germs, we're going to play a game of Musical Men. It's just like Musical Chairs except, well, you get the picture." Hershel turned towards the circle of kneelers and sent them a devilish grin.

A flush of heat spread across Scott's face as the women swarmed in around the men. Wanting to avoid eye contact, he studied the scuff marks on the floor.

Ivanka then warbled "I'm Gonna Wash That Man Right Outta My Hair" and the ladies began marching. Scott could feel their greedy eyes boring into his thigh, but he kept his own peepers focused on the ground. "Brace yourself," his neighbor said. Scott stiffened his body, preparing himself for the moment of impact.

~

Brook took her first step, not only in Musical Men, but also as a single person mingling with the opposite sex, rushing to quick, unfair judgments of people based solely on appearances. The men/chairs included the following: Pudgy, Slimy, Droopy, Crabby, Gangly, and…YUMMY. A handsome man with rumpled, sandy-blonde hair gazed down at the floor with intense concentration. Brook hoped Ivanka would cut the singing when she made her way over to him as he was the only one in the bunch not licking his chops. "I'm gonna wash that man right outta my hair, and send him on his-" the girls scurried for a spot, knocking over a couple of guys in the process. Brook parked it on the closest lap, that of Droopy who reeked of tiger balm. But she was safe. One girl out. Six left.

Brook survived the next four rounds, the audience bellowing with laughter every time Ivanka stopped her singing and the players made a rush for the laps. The competition was fierce and the men took a beating, all except for the good looking one who remained still during the collisions. Brook, on the other hand, got her arm clawed and foot stomped on in the process. Never one to take a lackadaisical approach to games, she gave it her all and made it to the final round, having one more chance to land in the lap of Mr. Yummy who remained the last man kneeling.

Ivanka started in with "I've Got Rhythm," belting it out at a frenetic pace. Up against an Amazon woman, Brook's shorter legs gave her an advantage as they spun around in a tight circle. Brook cued in on Ivanka's voice, waiting for a nuance or inflection in tone. After having to endure close contact with Slimy, Droopy, and Co., she'd be damned if she was going to miss out on the grand prize. When the singing stopped, both she and the Amazon stood on either side of the coveted lap. Brook darted into position, pressing her hand against the man's back and planting her feet on the ground to keep her full weight off of him (although she hadn't taken this precaution with the other "chairs"). The man didn't budge. No wonder Hershel had kept him in the game. Mr. Yummy then looked up at her and their eyes locked. Blood rushed to Brook's cheeks and her heart boomed like a bass drum.

"We have a winner!" Hershel proclaimed. Realizing that she had stayed on the guy's lap for longer than necessary, Brook rose and smoothed her skirt. Ivanka brought her a bottle of "champagne" and then stepped aside to assist the man to his feet. Hershel sidled up next to Brook and curled his arm around her waist. "What's your name, sweetheart?" he asked.

She smiled into the mike like a game show contestant. "Brook Holliday."

"And where are you from?"

"Kansas City."

Hershel nodded and brought the mike over to Mr. Yummy who looked at Brook as if she had said she came from the planet Zorgon. "And how about you, sir?" Hershel asked.

"Scott...I'm also from Kansas City."

Brook felt her eyebrows lift to her hairline.

"Reee-aa-llly?" Hershel said. "And you two don't know each other?"

They both shook their heads.

"Well, how's about that," Hershel continued. "That's what Ivanka and I love about working on a cruise ship. You can be out in the middle of the ocean and run into a neighbor." He turned towards his wife. "I think that calls for a song, don't you?" Ivanka nodded, apparently not about to pass up a chance to ham it up.

"Everything's up to date in Kansas City," Hershel sang and Brook immediately recognized the song from *Oklahoma!*, a childhood and of course, Tulsa favorite. "They've gone about as far as they can go," Ivanka joined in. The couple swayed side-to-side as they continued on. "Ev'rythin's like a dream in Kansas City. It's better than a magic lantern show!" Brook and Scott just stood there, exchanging shy smiles during the serenade.

~

Scott had to remind himself to breathe. It had happened. The Jolt. His sister claimed such a thing only occurred in the movies, but when the woman took a seat on his lap and he realized who she was, a current ran through Scott's body that brought him to life. And he felt certain it wasn't just the intimate contact of their encounter.

Scott hadn't even been paying attention. Instead, he had concentrated on steadying himself like a block of concrete to survive the slamfest whenever the singing stopped, cursing Hershel every time he left him in the ridiculous game. The sandaled feet were nothing but a blur moving past him until the last round when he noticed a player walking with one foot out at an angle. And then there she was, pressed against him, her curls brushing his face.

Scott must have turned to jelly because Ivanka had to help him to his feet. She patted his back and handed him a box of Tortuga rum cake for being such a good sport. But Scott wanted a different prize, the woman's name. Then he got it. *Brook Holliday.* And she didn't wear a wedding band. He almost performed a back flip when she revealed they were from the same city. He was amazed he could even speak his own name.

Ivanka and Hershel's tribute to Kansas City sounded like gibberish. The entire room had turned into a swirl of nothing, except for Brook. Scott would have liked to say something, but didn't want to shout over the singing. At last, the Broadway birds said good night and took their leave. The spotlight dimmed and Scott and Brook stood in the soft lighting of the stage as the crowd began to disperse.

"Good job at the game," he finally managed to say. "Glad to see you're doing our hometown proud."

She smiled, her vibrant green eyes lighting him up inside. "Thanks. I will be expecting a parade upon my return."

"Naturally. I'm sure the mayor's on top of it." They shared a slight chuckle. "So, uh, where do you live?" he asked.

"In Brookside. With my sister."

Scott nodded, delighted that she not only lived with her sister, but also volunteered the information. "So it's Brook in Brookside. That's easy to remember."

"Exactly. How about you?"

"I have an apartment near the Plaza. Just me. Don't even have a dog. But I like dogs. I hope to get one someday, but I want a house first." So much for clever conversation. Scott always stank at small talk.

Brook opened her mouth to respond when a tall, buxom blonde with razor-sharp features joined her side. "This is my sister, Melissa," she told him.

He greeted the newcomer who seemed to eye Scott with trepidation. "So you're from our neck of the woods."

"Not too far from where you live."

"Huh." The sister didn't appear exactly thrilled about the connection. Her smile was forced and tight.

To make matters worse, Scott's reserve of wit and intelligence seemed to have run out on him. He racked his brain for something to keep the conversation alive, but just then, an arm slithered around his shoulder, coiling around his neck like a snake. Waverly slinked up against him, her dense breasts flanking his tricep. He had forgotten all about her. Scott tried to pull away, but Waverly tightened around him, placing a hand on his stomach as if she owned him. He knew he was behaving like a fickle bastard, but he wished that she would vanish.

"I see you have more champagne," Waverly said to Brook. She then shifted her icy gaze to him. "Better keep your distance." Scott knitted his brow. "She's the one who bopped me with the cork this afternoon."

Brook tucked a springy curl behind her ear. "Sorry about that. Again. It was an accident."

Waverly didn't respond.

Scott tilted his head towards the sisters, the only part of his body that could move under Waverly's hold. "Can you believe they're from K.C.?"

Waverly shrugged with indifference. "Funny, we come here to get away from home and look what happens."

The four of them stood there in awkward silence until Brook held up her prize bottle. "How about we all split the spoils?" she suggested. "Although I'm afraid it's not the real deal." She tapped the label with her finger, but when she looked down at it her eyes widened and she nudged her sister. "Hey, this is actual champagne, not the fake stuff we got with our room."

"Wait, you got champagne with your room?" Waverly asked.

Brook looked at them like she had accidentally revealed that she had a stash of cocaine in her cabin. "Um, yeah. I, uh, arranged it beforehand, you know, a treat for our arrival. But it turned out to be a rip-off."

"Hmm, too bad," Waverly said without a drop of sincerity. "Anyway, we'll have to pass. We've had a long day of travel."

Scott's face felt on fire.

"Us, too," Melissa said, tugging on Brook's arm. "Maybe another time."

Brook managed to throw Scott a quick good-bye over her shoulder as her sister pulled her away. Although disappointed to see Brook go, what else could he expect? No self-respecting woman wanted to hang around a man wearing Waverly Marks as a stole. He broke free of her vine-like arms and they headed back to their cabin, only speaking to each other when they disagreed about the best way to go.

CHAPTER SIX

The following morning, the phone rang in the honeymoon suite at the crack of yawn.

"The castle!" Melissa yelled. "Make for the purple castle!" She jerked and kneed Brook in the thigh. Melissa talked almost as much in her sleep as she did awake. Albeit entertaining at first, Brook had hardly slept a wink. She rubbed her thigh and fumbled for the phone with her free hand.

"This is your wake up call," a digitized voice stated. Brook placed the phone back in its cradle, wanting to cancel their morning massages for more shut-eye, but since they were the only slots left when she made the appointments and they'd be charged for them anyway, she pulled back the covers.

"I'll be in my funnel," Melissa mumbled dreamily.

Brook gave her a shake. "Get up!"

Melissa sprang to life and grabbed Brook's arm. "Where are we?" She spoke with the urgency of someone who had just traveled through time.

"On the ship, you rambling freak. Now get dressed."

Even though Brook and Melissa had emerged from their cabin at a respectable hour, the ship was already alive with activity. The retired Florida contingent launched pucks across the shuffleboard deck while passengers of all ages mixed company on an oversized chess court, the checkerboards painted on the ground like a game of hopscotch, the squares occupied by gnome-sized queens and bishops. A group of yogis stood on one leg like a flock of pelicans, their self-possessed serenity keeping them still and in balance. On the flip side, a class of cardio junkies jumped rope, their licorice whips lashing at the air. And of course, sun worshippers lazed about their stations, svelte felines basking in the morning rays. As Brook inventoried the varied surroundings, *Alice in Wonderland* sprang to mind and she couldn't help but think that when she and Melissa loaded up plates with fruit and mini-muffins, one nibble might alter her size.

The ship's spa served ladies on one side, gents on the other. The girls undressed in teak cubicles with linen privacy curtains, slipping into lightweight white waffle robes. They then stepped out onto a private deck lined with massage tables, the ocean serving as the backdrop. No orchestrated chants or forest sounds needed here to simulate a serene atmosphere. Behind a bamboo partition, Brook dropped her robe and slipped her naked body in between the cool sheets draped across the table. She lay on her stomach, positioning her face on the cushy ring of the head pillow when a pair of dainty feet appeared in beaded flip-flops. A woman's airy voice from above said, "Good morning," and the pink painted toes wiggled as if waving hello.

"Morning," Brook murmured.

"Any problem areas?" the masseuse asked.

Where to begin? Brook wondered. "Neck and shoulders," she told the toes. "And back. Also my arms and legs. I'd just get everything."

"Okay, then." Brook heard the shaking of liquid in a bottle, followed by the sound of hands rubbing together, and the smell of sandalwood soon mixed with the salty sea air. Her muscles gave way to the massage which was pure bliss and long overdue, but as the harder, stubborn kinks were kneaded out of Brook's body, she tensed under the pressure. "Relax," the masseuse urged in her gentle tone. Brook inhaled as deeply as she could while resting on a full stomach. *Innnnnn…Oooouuuut. Breeeeeeathe sunshine.* She repeated this mantra over and over, and before long, the sleep deprivation from not only last night, but also the last two weeks, hell, the last few months, caught up with her and she slipped into a welcome slumber.

~

Brook stood alone on a beach, wearing nothing but the spa's waffle robe. A crown of ivy encircled her head and her hair hung in long spiral tendrils that hit her halfway down her back. Posing like the Statue of Liberty, she held her bridal nosegay up towards the sky in one hand and had the large platter from her china set resting in the crook of her opposite arm. Just a few yards away, was an artist's easel, layers of tulle draped over the canvas on display. It appeared to be sinking in the sand as the surf rumbled at its feet. A huge wave then crashed on a formation of rocks in the distance and Brook sensed a shift taking place. She now clutched a bouquet of paint brushes instead of her nosegay and the platter had turned into a paint palette covered with oily swirls of bright, saturated colors.

Outfitted with the supplies to create a masterpiece, Brook started for the easel, wanting to unveil it and get to work, but the stretch of sand in which she traversed seemed to widen with her every stride. Panicking, she started to run until finally she closed in on the easel, breathless. Upon ripping off the gauzy tulle, she beheld something she didn't expect…her own face. Instead of a painter's canvas, she stood before a rectangular mirror mottled with age. Her image was fragmented and blurry, but Brook could see enough to know that her appearance had been altered. She zeroed in for a closer look until a figure over her shoulder caught her attention.

Brook turned around and spotted a man standing on top of a sand dune. He was too far away for her to make out any distinct features, but close enough for her to see that he wore a Shakespearean costume—white puffy shirt with a velvet doublet, jewel-toned pantaloons, and tights. He removed his feathered cap and bowed. The man then straightened up and stepped forward, but as he did so, he lost his footing and disappeared behind one of the sand knolls.

Fog moved in and a ship's bell sounded in the distance.

~

The tinkling tones of a triangle instrument signaled the return to reality. "All done," the masseuse announced. Brook cracked open her eyes and a droplet of drool fell from her lips, just missing the masseuse's feet as it hit the deck boards. "Take your time to get up," the woman continued. "Enjoy the sensation. But before I go, I recommend you try one of our yoga classes. It'll help alleviate all that tension."

"M-kay," Brook said, the rubdown transforming her mind and body into such a state of mush she would have agreed to try spelunking had the masseuse suggested it. After a few minutes of immobility, she somehow gathered enough energy to peel herself off of the table and shuffle back into the spa.

Melissa had bumped up her session to ninety minutes (lawyer money) so Brook floated back to the cabin alone, sipping on a fruit smoothie. Her body tingled as if it was full of fizz and she couldn't recall the last time she felt so good.

Brook's mood lifted even more when she saw Scott jogging her way. He slowed down when he spotted her, scuffing his sneakers on the deck. "Hi, Brook. I was hoping that was you." He bent over to catch his breath, his wet hair licking his flushed face, and Brook's heart beat quickened as if she had been the one engaged in vigorous exercise. She reminded herself that Scott was taken, but didn't see the harm in being friendly.

"You're making me feel guilty," she said. "Here I just got done with a massage and you're training for the Boston Marathon."

"Hardly. Anyway, I'm glad I ran into you."

"Oh?"

He wiped his glistening forehead with the back of his hand and smiled. "You're a good excuse to finish my workout. Do you mind if I walk with you?"

"Not at all," she responded, wanting to leap in the air and click her heels. A man wanted to spend time with her. But Brook maintained her composure as they moved along and didn't allow herself to forget how things stood. "Won't your girlfriend mind us walking together?" she prodded once they'd gotten past the usual pleasantries.

"Waverly? Nah. And she's not my girlfriend."

"She seemed pretty attached to you."

"We're not together," he claimed. "Well, we are on this trip, obviously. But we're coworkers first and foremost."

"I see." There was a stretch of silence.

"I got the cruise through my job," Scott elaborated. "And…I work long hours. Let's just say I didn't have the option to be choosy when it came to dates." He looked down and fiddled with the hem of his t-shirt.

Brook guided the conversation in another direction. "Where do you work?"

"I'm a media buyer at Pendleton Scrubb Advertising."

"Really? Maybe you and I shouldn't be talking."

"That impressed, huh?"

"No, it's not that. I'm the Research Director at KCXT."

He nodded. "Right. We could spill company secrets. Well, I guess I should just come out and confess. I'm Scott Webster, corporate spy. You think we met by coincidence, but it was all by my design. That game of Musical Men…rigged."

Brook pretended to frown. "And I thought I found my calling."

"Sorry to dash your dreams. But I have my mission."

Another beat passed. "You know, it's refreshing not to get a blank look when I tell someone what I do," Brook said. "Most people at the station don't even know."

"I get the gist of it," he said. "You help others make sense out of the ratings, especially those sales reps who, from my experience, don't always operate with the best of scruples. I've had a rep fudge numbers and then blame a computer glitch when I called him on it."

"That doesn't surprise me," Brook said. "I've seen how working on a commission can bring out the ugly side. But my closest friend at the office works in sales and she's great. I don't know if I could stand to work there if she wasn't around." Brook paused. "KCXT doesn't exactly foster a cozy atmosphere. It's very compartmentalized and corporate. Not to mention cheap."

He punched her lightly on the arm and the imprint of his touch melted into her skin. "No wonder you needed a vacation."

"I probably shouldn't have told you all that."

"Hey, I could say the same thing about Pendleton. Besides, I don't buy the Kansas City market and as far as conflict of interest goes, I know a ton of media buyers who have dated their reps."

"But we're just talking," she said.

"Right. Yeah. Perfectly innocent. I didn't mean to imply…I just meant…we're not treading in tricky waters."

She smiled. "I know."

Scott raked a hand through his sopping hair, creating a sea of cowlicks. "I see your station tower all the time."

"It's hard to miss. I call it The Needle."

Scott laughed. After a moment, he asked, "So, it's just you and your sister on this trip?"

Heat blossomed on her cheeks. "Yes."

"Is there…someone special back home?"

Brook swallowed the last of her smoothie before replying. "No, I'm single." The word sounded odd as it rolled off her tongue. *Single.* It was the first time Brook spoke the s-word out loud, and the first time the concept didn't make her heart feel like a hardened clump of mud. Brook brought their stroll to and end, however, when they came to her corridor. "I'm down this way," she said, not about to let Scott walk her to the honeymoon suite just to extend their time together. She had divulged enough for one day.

He nodded his head in the opposite direction. "I'm on the other side." Brook realized it would have been quicker for Scott to have crossed over on the main deck to get to his room. He had gone out of his way to walk with her. "It was nice running into you, Brook."

"You, too."

"Maybe I'll see you around."

"Maybe." Brook watched as Scott backed away, failing to notice the fire hose box behind him before he ran into it.

THUNK!

Scott rubbed his shoulder. "I'll look where I'm going now," he said. And off he went.

~

Brook pressed up against the inside of her cabin door, grinning to herself and marveling at how she could feel such a spark with someone she barely knew. Always a woman of action, a girl with a plan, it killed Brook to do nothing about her budding attraction, at least for now. Nothing could happen between them on this trip. It wouldn't be right. Brook would have to exercise patience, not one of her stronger attributes. It seemed like such a waste of the setting, though. What better place to explore a romance than a cruise, lovers' paradise?

She shook her head in amazement as she was getting way ahead of herself. Even if Scott was interested in her, she'd probably quelled those feelings when she unloaded her work issues on him like he was her shrink.

Why had she done that? Was it nerves? But he had kept walking with her. He could have left at anytime. Perhaps she was assigning too much meaning to Scott's friendliness and glances. Brook had been out of the dating game for so long, she didn't know how to interpret the signs. Plus, she didn't know what to make of the whole Waverly business.

Brook stepped over to the dresser and rested her hands on its surface. When she flicked her eyes up to the mirror though, she was seized with horror. Her hair looked as if she had styled it with Crisco shortening, and the massage pillow had crinkled her face into that of a crone. As her mouth hung open, Brook also noticed a shred of blueberry peel caked to her front tooth, along with a few raspberry seeds lodged in between the cracks along her gum line. And Scott Webster had seen it all up close. If he did have any interest in her, she'd probably nipped that in the bud.

"Why aren't you showered yet?" Melissa asked. Brook was so upset at her reflection she didn't even notice the return of her sister. Melissa, of course, looked refreshed and resplendent, her hair pulled back in a sleek ponytail. "I expected the bathroom to be free by now."

"Look at me. I'm a disaster."

"Hence, the shower. What have you been doing all this time?"

"I ran into Scott."

"Who?"

"Scott Webster. The guy we met from home last night. He saw me like this. This is horrible."

"You're right. It is horrible. You're getting all worked up over a guy you shouldn't be bothering with. That Ban de Soleil bitch was on him like a leech. I'm surprised the look she gave us didn't freeze our blood. Clearly, she wanted us to know he's with her."

"She's threatened," Brook said.

"Maybe, but that doesn't matter."

Brook picked at the corner of the dresser. "He says she's his coworker, not girlfriend, not date, not even friend."

"Don't be so naïve. Of course he said that. He's a guy. Listen, even if he was available, he's a local. You need a rebound. No attachments. No mess. I suggest you find someone from another land. It'll be an exotic tale to tell everyone back home."

"Maybe so," Brook said in a flat tone.

"I'm only trying to protect you, Brook. Remember, Chip was supposed to be a rebound."

"So."

"Sooooo…you have a habit of going from one boyfriend to the next with no resting period in between. It's not healthy."

"And you're an expert? You haven't had one meaningful relationship since the divorce."

Melissa's expression hardened. Brook sat down on the bed. "I'm sorry. That was a cheap shot. I've seen up close how guys resent your success. Especially that husband of yours." She paused before continuing. "You know, I'd forgotten that Chip was a rebound. It seems strange to think of him that way."

"That's my point. You never did."

Brook shot up to her feet. "You're right. I don't why I'm even entertaining the thought of Scott. It's silly." She collected her shower bag and change of clothes. "Besides, this is a big boat and we'll be spending most of our time out on the islands," she added. "What are the chances that I'd even see him again?"

"Exactamundo." Melissa snapped her towel against Brook's backside. "Now hit the shower."

~

Brook had meant what she said and had no intention of gushing over some guy. In fact, she found plenty to keep her occupied during the rest of the day at sea. After going for a swim, she and Melissa dozed under the shade of an umbrella for a good portion of the afternoon. Brook then found a solitary spot to add a few characters to her sketchbook, illustrating the yogis, the giant chess match, the tan and toned sun worshippers. By the time the day drew to a close, Brook had not even caught a glimpse of Scott or any other man to tickle her fancy and felt cleared of any complications. The rekindling of her spirit was the intention of this trip and she seemed to be on the right track.

The next morning, however, as the sisters climbed aboard a Land Rover for a safari tour of Barbados, Brook thought a tropical spell was playing a trick on her. Out of all the tourist traps the island had to offer…out of the entire fleet of SUVs lined up and ready for departure… she would pick the one with Scott Webster on it.

CHAPTER SEVEN

When Brook and Melissa joined the Barbados tour, Scott's heart broke out into a jig. Someone upstairs liked him. He had been attracted to Brook from the get-go and now fate seemed to be backing him up. These chance encounters had to mean something.

Sit by me! Sit by me! he thought, taking him back to his school days on the bus, willing his crush to sit next to him so he could pull her hair. Unfortunately, Waverly chose this time to lean over the cab and grab his hand, positioning her rock-hard knockers on his knees.

Brook froze, standing stooped under the canopy. She gave Scott a stiff smile and then turned to her sister. "Let's take the rear seats so we can see out with no obstructions."

"Good idea," Melissa responded. Waverly backed off, looking like the cat that had just chomped on the canary. The sisters took their places next to the tailgate and Scott's dancing heart fell flat. Although the distance was only a few feet and Brook sat within his line of vision, she felt very much out of reach.

Four guys then filed in, prepsters with Julius Caesar haircuts who seemed to have coordinated their look—Tommy Bahama shirts, cargo shorts, Teva sandals, and Greek letters tattooed on the insides of their ankles. *Sigma Cheeseballs*, Scott thought, wishing a friendly family had joined them instead.

The Frat Pack picked their spots, the pudgier ones taking seats next to Scott and Waverly while the other two exchanged a look of consultation before switching sides and sitting down next to the sisters. They all smirked amongst themselves as they noted the Hollidays, their eyes drawn to Melissa's large chest in particular and Scott knew all too well what filthy thoughts were going through their minds. The one sitting next to Brook focused on her though, gawking at her legs when she wasn't looking. He introduced himself as Mason and flashed her some orthodontist's opus. Scott's face burned as if the bright sun beat through the protective canopy.

A khaki-clad guide approached the vehicle carrying an Igloo cooler and a stack of plastic cups. "Afternoon," he greeted in a sunny British accent. "Name's Nigel and I'll be the leader of this adventure. How is everyone today?" The passengers muttered their "fines" and "goods." He then slapped the side of the Igloo. "Very well. Who wants to be in charge of the Jungle Juice?"

"The what?" Waverly asked.

"Rum punch," Nigel explained.

"You do it, Mason," the baby-faced frat boy said. "You were social chair."

Mason obliged his friend, took the cooler, and began filling up cups. Nigel hopped in the cab up front and passed out lids and straws through the open window. "You'll thank me later," he said.

Once drinks were in hand, Mason stepped up behind the guide and gave him a slap on the back. "We're good to go," he announced, acting as if his drink service made him official speaker of the group.

Nigel nodded and scratched a note on his clipboard before slipping it into a zippered pouch. Turning around to face the passengers, he asked, "Everybody buckled?" The group nodded. "Jolly good. Because as Bette Davis said, it's going to be a bumpy ride." He shot them a wide grin before the Land Rover lurched forward.

Equipped with a headset, Nigel began his spiel over the speaker system. "Independent since 1966, Barbados remains part of the British Commonwealth and its influence can be seen everywhere from elegant resorts, four-star restaurants, chi-chi shops, and charming guides such as yours truly." The passengers chuckled. "Of course along with traditions like afternoon tea and cricket, the island also harbors a bit of the famous English reserve and formality." He spoke his last several words with a posh accent as he stuck his nose up in the air. "But you will find that for the most part," he continued, switching back to his happy-go-lucky mode, "the locals are friendly, polite, and helpful."

As the vehicle plodded along a dirt road, Waverly spat out a round of complaints. It was too hot, too humid, too windy, too dusty, too rough. She couldn't understand the guide and he drove like a maniac. Her disgruntlement was broadcasted for all to hear, but the chattering Nigel seemed oblivious to her, having probably grown accustomed to the occasional sourpuss. For Scott though, her every word was like having a coconut knocked against his head. Waverly refused to acknowledge or appreciate any of the scenery: the quaint churches, the lush landscape, the quivering palms, the beautiful Brook Holliday.

Every now and then Scott would glance back at Brook and in more than one instance, he caught her looking at him as well. Meanwhile, Mason talked her poor ear off, bragging about all the tropical getaways he'd graced with his presence.

"You mean you haven't been to Belize!?" he cried out. "That's criminal. You have to go. It's a must."

"I'll get right on it." Brook replied, but she sounded bored with his travel tales. When there was a break in Mason's diatribe, Brook addressed the fratsters sitting next to Scott and Waverly. "So, where are your wives?" she asked. The two exchanged surprised looks and Brook pointed to their hands which had tan lines on their left ring fingers. Scott supposed women were trained to look out for such things. Men could be slime.

"This is a guy's trip," Mason said. "We're from the same pledge class at USC. Go Trojans!" The Frat Pack whooped and high-fived each other. Mason continued, "Every year we take a vacation, no girls allowed. Of course we bend the rules when we stumble across exceptional women like you and your sister."

"So why not wear your wedding bands?" she pressed and Scott noticed Melissa knocking her foot against Brook's ankle.

The baby-faced one spoke next. "We don't want to lose our rings, with all the activities and excursions. Our wives would kill us. Plus the heat makes the fingers swell."

"Well if your fingers are so swollen how could you possibly lose your rings?" The married ones shrugged in response.

"I like you," Mason told Brook with a cocky smirk. "You've got bite." He gnashed his teeth together and growled.

Just when Scott didn't think he could stand another second, the Land Rover stopped at Andromeda Gardens where the group would take in the exotic plant life and have their lunch.

~

The stone footpath hardly looked treacherous, the sun-bleached flagstones even had a pleasing aesthetic in their design, but Brook found the terrain tricky to negotiate as she strolled with her sister. Mason and his cronies had left them to find a restroom, a welcome break in Brook's opinion. She only hoped they weren't using the gardens as their pisspot.

Melissa broke the silence. "You could be a little friendlier," she suggested.

"How about you play harder to get?" Brook retorted. "You were all over that Cameron."

"Camden."

"Same difference." Brook paused to take another swig of her Jungle Juice.

"And about Scott," her sister said. "You said you were going to forget him."

"I didn't plan on winding up on the same tour."

"Maybe so, but what was this?" Melissa turned around, peeked over her shoulder, and fluttered her eyelashes. She then put a finger to her lips, giggled, and looked the other way. "It was Scarlett O'Hara a la Caribbean."

Brook turned away to study a hibiscus plant. "Maybe I wanted someone to rescue me from Mason. He came on too strong for my taste. I could feel his eyes on me the entire time. It was unnerving."

"You're just not used to it. Take Mason's interest as a compliment, and a triumph. You've landed your rebound."

"I don't know, Mel. Those guys are a bit much. Did you see those frat tattoos? How lame can you get?"

"We all did stupid stuff in college."

Brook guzzled more Jungle Juice before replying. "If you're referring to Chip, I'm well aware of that mistake."

"No, I didn't mean-"

"Best dating pool in my life and I wasted my time with him."

"You were happy with him back then."

"And look where it got me. I wish I could do it all over again. Do you know how many opportunities I passed up because I was with Chip? Kevin Rockhill even made a pass at me."

"Who's he?"

"The one Chip might be hiding out with in Chicago. But I shouldn't count Kevin because he slept with everyone, including half my sorority. But there were others, good guys I should have given a chance. Just think of what could have been."

"Hindsight's twenty-twenty. It doesn't help to pine after the past."

Brook nodded her head downhill where Mason and Co. clambered up the stone steps. "Then why are you so ga-ga about these guys who are trying to relive their USC days?"

"We're just hanging out, Brook. It's a vacation. There doesn't always have to be a purpose and reason to everything. And I think Camden is cute."

"Yeah, I like how he just happened to mention his family's restaurant chain, ski lodge, and beach house."

"He's proud of his background."

"I can't stand it when people drop assets, especially when they belong to their parents. Chip used to talk about his family's lake cabin like it was a European chateau." Brook drained the last of her punch and crumpled the plastic cup in her hand.

"No more dwelling about Chip," Melissa commanded. "And watch the drinking. I know how you can get when you're upset."

They ended the conversation when the guys came into earshot. Camden snapped a picture of the sisters with his digital camera, waving them over to come look at the results. Brook didn't know if it was the shrunken size or pixelation of the display, but she appeared to be grinding her teeth.

"I'll e-mail you my pics," Camden told Melissa.

"You better," Melissa replied, punching him lightly on his bicep.

Mason seemed disinterested in the action, but then brightened when he spoke. "I stopped by the restaurant and got us the best table on the veranda. It's filling up fast so we've got to get a move on." He slipped an arm around Brook and guided her up the path. She would have insisted on walking on her own, but the rum punch had diluted her resistance.

~

Savoring the Barbados fare, Scott washed down his mouthful of fried flying fish with a Banks beer, the best part of his lunch with Waverly which had so far been marinated in silence with only a peppering of meaningless chit-chat. Thank goodness for the restaurant's calypso band to pad the conversation and fill in the awkward gaps. Scott cringed, however, whenever the chortling from the Frat Pack carried across the terrace.

"They are so obnoxious," Waverly said, noting the commotion. "You'd think they were fresh out of college. And those girls are hanging all over them like they're rock stars."

Scott peered over Waverly's shoulder. He could only catch a glimpse of Brook through a potted palm, but it was enough to read her expression which had the appearance of having just eaten a rotten oyster. "I don't think Brook likes them," he said. "She seemed annoyed on the tour. And it was more like that guy was all over her."

Waverly rolled her eyes and in the process, dislodged one of her false eyelashes. It dangled from her lid for a second, like a caterpillar hanging on for dear life, and then fell into her cucumber soup. Scott tried to suppress his laughter, but failed.

"Shit!" she said, fishing the lashes out with her spoon. "It's not funny, Scott. These aren't cheapos from the drugstore. They're top of the line, worn by Sarah Jessica herself. All that damn wind must have loosened them." She peeled off the other set, stretching out her upper lid and exposing her eyeball, a sight which gave Scott the willies. Waverly then tucked the lashes into her purse and let out a pitiful sigh.

"I don't know why you mess with all those…enhancements," Scott said. Waverly pressed her lips together and tears began to trickle out from the corners of her ice blue eyes as if they were melting. Scott didn't know if the false lashes had caused an irritation or if she was crying. "Everything okay?" he asked.

She mopped the tears with her napkin. "This isn't going how I had envisioned."

"What do you mean?"

"Us."

"Oh."

A fresh round of guffaws erupted from the Frat Pack. Scott wanted to shoot out of his chair and yell at them to keep it down, but kept his attention on Waverly.

"I don't think you're giving us much of a chance," she said. "You know, there's more to me than meets the eye." She pointed to her own pair and gave him a weak smile, as if to make light of her cosmetic mishap.

Scott shifted in his chair.

"I know what people say about me, especially at the office. They think I'm a high maintenance bitch."

"I've never heard that," Scott lied.

"Don't try to cover for them." Her expression turned rigid. "It's the price a woman pays for asserting herself in the workplace. I've caught people in my own department bad-mouthing me to high heaven. It's almost like they want me to hear."

Scott set down his fork. "I'm sorry. We work with some nasty people."

"Yeah, but I've dealt with this junk all my life. My mom calls it jealousy." Waverly let out a snort. "My mother. She always wanted me to show up everyone else. The woman wouldn't let me leave the house without passing her inspection. Even when I was a kid, my hair had to be brushed smooth, the part in my pigtails straight and centered." A relaxed tropical setting hardly seemed like the place for Waverly to delve into family issues, but she continued. "When I was a teenager, if my outfit didn't match perfectly or made me look slightly dumpy, I was sent back upstairs to change. Most kids were tardy because they slept in. I came to school late because of costume changes, at least that's what they felt like." She sipped more of her soup. "My mom wanted me to carry myself as if I were always competing in a pageant."

"You should have dyed your hair bright purple or something," Scott said.

She shrugged. "Funny thing is, I liked pleasing her. She worked late nights so her morning inspection was sometimes the only time I saw her. I enjoyed being her precious doll. But I did go through a granola stage in college. No makeup, ratty hair, patchouli. I wore nothing but hemp clothing and Birkenstocks."

"I can't picture that," he said.

"It was just an experimental phase. Hippie chick didn't work for me. Plus, I prefer XTC over marijuana when it comes to serious partying."

This last piece of information didn't surprise Scott. Numerous Scrubbs at Pendleton dabbled in recreational drugs. If management ever screened for narcotics, they'd have to reprimand half the staff.

Waverly went on about the pressure to make the cheerleading squad, land the lead in school plays, and survive the cutthroat world of the Texas beauty pageant circuit. Although her mom sounded like a monster and Scott sympathized with Waverly, it annoyed him when a person pinned everything that was wrong in their life on a parent. He could certainly play that trump card, but Scott chose to pretend his father never existed, blocking out what few memories he had before the prick ran off to Boston with a cellist. Besides, the man died three years ago. Heart attack. Justice had been served. None of Scott's family had attended the funeral.

As far as Waverly was concerned though, a well had been sprung and she treated the lunch as her own personal therapy session. Scott sat back and indulged her, sipping his Banks beer, his fragmented view of Brook Holliday providing him with much needed consolation.

~

According to Nigel, Mount Hillaby was the highest point on Barbados and perched on top with the bright, clear afternoon, Scott could see dots of windsurfers cutting across the glassy turquoise water in the distance. He brought up his camera, a hand-me-down from his mom, a 35mm held together with duct tape but still capable of producing crisp, clear pictures. His clunker of a camera clicked and advanced. The counter indicated that he'd only used three exposures of film.

Scott inhaled the fresh air and continued to admire the spectacular view. There was so much more he wanted for himself out of life; creative fulfillment, accomplishment, and stability would be nice, not to mention someone special to share it with, but in a moment like this when he could get swept up in nature, his current station didn't seem all that bad. Moments later, Scott heard the crunch of gravel as someone approached and thought that Waverly had returned from her cigarette break, but to his delight, it turned out to be Brook Holliday coming in his direction.

"It's something else, isn't it?" she asked, joining him at his side. "Can't get this view back home." Her words slurred together and she swayed like one of the palm trees blowing in the breeze.

"Are you all right?" he asked.

She gave him a beatific grin. "I'm fine," she said. "How could I not be fine? It's a gorgeous day and my cup runneth over with Jungle Juice." She hiccuped and it seemed to knock her off balance. Brook had obviously had too much to drink and Scott was furious that she was wandering about on her own.

"Where's the rest of your crew?"

Brook came closer and cupped her mouth. "I shook them off at the pass," she whispered before breaking into a fit of giggles. She then slipped on the uneven ground and lost her footing.

Scott moved in and steadied her, bracing her upper arms. "Whoa, watch yourself. We don't want you tumbling down the hillside."

"I'm feeling funny," she said. "Must be the attitude. I mean *altitude*."

"How about I walk you back to the truck?"

Brook looked down at her arms, as if she just realized he was touching her. Scott kept his hold. She then fixed her hazy eyes on his. "I know I just met you, but I like you, Scott."

"I like you, too," he replied, humoring her.

She frowned though, hardly the response he would have liked. "I don't like your friend. She's like a cat." Brook formed a claw as she hissed and Scott struggled to keep a straight face. "Cats turn on you like that." She snapped her fingers. "I'm like you, Scott. A dog person." She studied him for a brief duration before continuing. "And you know what else? You're like a dog. A friendly, scruffy dog." Then, Brook did something that Scott would never have expected. She planted both hands on his cheeks and gave him a kiss, the kind you'd give a cherished pooch on its head, but on the lips. When she was done, she kept her hands on his face. "You are so damn cute! Can I put a bandana on you and take you home?"

Scott was speechless.

Brook blinked hard and appeared as if she didn't know where she was for a moment. She then stumbled towards him and grabbed his arm. "Help me," she squeaked before collapsing against his body. Scott caught her, feeling like he was trying to straighten up the leaning tower of Pisa. He'd never imagine such a petite woman could be so heavy.

"I had waaaaaay too much Jungle Juice," she mumbled. "And wine. Good wine. I like wine. Fine wine."

Before Scott could get a handle on Brook's limp and heavy body, he spotted Mason marching towards them. "There you are," he barked out to Brook. "Why'd you run off like that?" Mason regarded Scott as if he were covered in festering boils. "What's going on here? Brookie, is this guy bothering you?"

She pulled back from Scott and addressed Mason. "I told you before, don't call me Brookie."

Mason held up his hands. "Okay, okay. Don't be so touchy."

"I think you're the touchy one," Scott almost spat, but kept silent.

Mason swooped in next to Brook and hoisted her arm around his shoulder, tearing her away from Scott. "I believe you are wasted, sweetie pie. Let's get you back to the car."

Despite the disdainful looks Mason shot over his shoulder every now and then, Scott shadowed the two down the hill to the Land Rover. He joined them in the cab as well, claiming that he was waiting for Waverly to return. Brook guzzled bottled water as if she had just spent a month in the Sahara and Mason talked down to her as if she were a child. "There, there, now that's a good girl." Scott thought he should be the one taking care of Brook. She had flat out asked him to help her, not Mason. And she liked Scott. She had kissed Scott! He only wished she had been sober at the time.

Waverly had apparently warmed to their guide as she and Nigel shared a companionable smoke under the shade of a tree. During a break in their conversation, however, she spotted Scott in the cab, glanced over at Brook, and then sent a glacial gaze back in his direction. Turning her attention back to her new buddy, Waverly blew out a cloud of smoke, moved in close to Nigel, and then tossed her head back in a peal of laughter.

The journey back to the boat was much quicker and smooth than the ride out, a shortcut route to shuttle weary tourists to their home base. Brook sat up front and rested her head on her sister's shoulder while Mason sang dirty drunken songs with the Frat Pack.

"Brook, do you want more water?" Melissa asked during a break in the revelry. "Or a Coke? It'll coat the stomach."

"Nuh," Brook replied, keeping her eyes closed and her arms wrapped around her midsection. After a minute or two, she stirred and stared at the floor of the cab. "What went wrong, Mel? What did I do wrong?"

"Uh, nothing," Melissa replied, patting Brook's knee. "You've just had too much to drink. Happens to the best of us."

Brook brought up her head and gave her sister a grave look which Melissa either didn't notice or chose to ignore. The Frat Pack began another song and Brook continued with her nap, batting away an errant curl tickling her nose. Even trashed, she was adorable.

"Stop staring," Waverly hissed in Scott's ear, but he couldn't help himself because now Brook intrigued him on a whole other level. For some reason, he didn't think she was talking about that afternoon. What had Brook been referring to? What had gone wrong?

CHAPTER EIGHT

Brook woke the next morning feeling as if she'd slept in a vise. The fluorescent lighting above flooded the cabin with a harsh glare and penetrated her eyeballs. It took a minute for her to establish her bearings. "Uuuuuhhhhhh," she moaned, her voice raspy and raw. "What happened?"

Melissa was already up and wearing her bikini and a sarong. "Morning, sunshine. We have arrived in Martinique."

"Why does it smell like a McDonald's in here?"

"I brought you biscuits and breakfast meats. No better way to cure a hangover than to get some starch and grease in you." Melissa sat on the bed and offered Brook a plate of good ol' country heart attack with a side of Evian. "Here. Eat."

Brook's stomach felt so hollow she would have devoured a hockey puck had it been covered in gravy. She swallowed a biscuit almost whole and gnawed on the bacon. "This is delicious," she said, speaking with her mouth full.

"I thought it'd hit the spot. How are you feeling?"

"A dose of Tylenol and a shower and I should be okay."

"I should think so. You passed out as soon as we stepped on the boat. You missed a fantastic dinner, by the way."

"How can you be so lively? You drank your share."

"It's called pacing yourself. Plus, I'm used to keeping up with the lushes at the office."

"I can't believe I wasted the entire evening. I'm never drinking again."

"Sure. I've heard that one before." Her sister lifted her brow. "Mason asked about you at the disco last night."

Brook's forehead tightened. "I forgot about him. The day's a bit cloudy. I remember eating calamari at lunch and Mason ordering expensive wine. And then we were at some park. We could see the ocean…"

"Mount Hillaby," Melissa clarified. "Where you took off like a bolt of lightning."

"Did I almost fall down a hill?" Brook asked. "I think so. But Scott caught me." She smiled to herself until more of the encounter came back to her. "I was stumbling all over the place like a drunken fool. I think I called him a dog." Brook also wondered if she had kissed Scott, but surely that had been a dream. She wasn't one to give a new acquaintance a bold smack on the lips.

Melissa stood and set a hand on her hip. "I don't know if you accused Scott of being a canine, but you certainly weren't that nice to Mason. I'm surprised he's still interested in you. He must like a challenge."

"I wish he'd give up."

"I don't get you, Brook. Mason's totally your type. Cute, preppy, ambitious."

"That's just it, though. He's Chip 2000, another version of what I'm supposed to be leaving behind."

"Mason is much more worldly than Chip," her sister countered. "I can't believe all the places he's been."

"I can't believe how much he talks about it."

"Oh, he's just showing off. You know how guys get, especially around their married friends. They like to rub their freedom in their faces."

Brook reached for the Tylenol bottle on the dresser and shook out a couple of tablets, popping them into her mouth.

"Give Mason a chance," Melissa went on. "It's only a fling."

Brook chased the tablets with water and swallowed. "I've never been the fling type."

"We're going to change that." Her sister took the plate away and whipped back the covers. "Now get out of bed. We're meeting the guys at the beach in half an hour."

~

Brook and Melissa trudged along the stretch of compacted sand, carrying their snorkeling gear in their totes, although Brook's felt as if it were full of rocks instead of plastic implements. "I'd prefer it if we spent the day together," she grumbled. "Just the two of us."

"I heard you the first hundred times," her sister said. "We're not flaking out. It'll be fun. The guys know this great spot for snorkeling."

"It better be damn magical after this trek."

"That's your hangover talking. You'll feel better after a good swim."

"Snorkeling is not a pretty pastime, Mel. Your hair gets tangled and mashed. You have to spit in your mask to keep it from fogging, hardly ladylike and attractive."

"I know. I only taught you how to do it."

"And your bum is sticking out of the water the entire time. Don't think the guys won't be checking that out, especially those married ones."

"Why should you worry, Miss Skinny Minny?"

"I'm thinking of you. I know how sensitive you are about that area."

Melissa stopped and gave Brook a pointed look. "I'm fine with my body. You're the one who can't let go of your junior high insecurities."

Brook sighed and accepted that there was no way to get Melissa to change her mind. She anticipated a day full of annoyances, but then grew angry with herself. Having already ruined one night with too much drink, it would be silly for her to let unwanted company spoil her day. She would enjoy this snorkeling excursion no matter what. And if the USC gang became too much to handle, at least they'd be underwater most of the time and she could literally drown them out.

To Brook's relief, only Mason and Camden greeted them at the designated hotel umbrella stand, their smarmy married friends nowhere in sight. "I'm afraid our pals are out of commission today," Camden explained.

"Too many shots at the disco?" Melissa asked.

"Looks like it," Mason said. "They're off worshipping the porcelain god."

Her sister held up a hand. "We get the picture. Say no more."

"Shall we?" Camden asked, offering his arm to Melissa. She threaded hers through his and they strolled away. Brook and Mason exchanged awkward smiles and followed.

"Can I help you with your bag?" he asked.

"No, thanks. I got it."

"Glad you're feeling well enough to make it out today. I was worried about you."

"Guess I can't party like I used to. Lesson learned."

"Hey, it's only natural to get carried away on vacation," he said. "That's part of the idea, right?"

"I guess."

"So this spot is supposed to be a real find for snorkeling. The bartender at the disco recommended it to us. It'll be a good warm up for my scuba dive tomorrow in Antigua, although it will be hard to top my trip in the Caymans last year. Are you licensed to scuba?"

"No, it's too adventurous for me. I'll stick with the shallow waters thank you very much."

"Oh, you gotta do it." Mason dipped his head as if to check himself. "I've been saying a lot of that since I met you. God, I must sound like such a braggart. Some get jazzed about travel in Europe, but for me, it's the tropics. Guess it's the California boy in me."

Brook noted Mason's five o'clock shadow and disheveled hair, preferring his current surfer dude look to that of yesterday's stiff country-club golfer. And although he still seemed bent on impressing her, he had toned down the suave single guy act, forgoing the cheesy lines and salesman smile. But perhaps the circumstances in general improved her impression of him. Seeing Scott with Waverly on the Barbados tour had put Brook in a foul mood and she might have displaced her irritation onto Mason.

"You know, sometimes I want to say to hell with entertainment law and pursue marine biology," he added. "But I've gotten too used to the money."

"This snorkeling will be like child's play to you," she said.

"It'll do for now. I'll get my fix."

A break in the conversation followed. "I'm sorry if I acted standoffish yesterday," Brook offered.

"Don't sweat it," he replied with a wave of his hand. "We all have our moments. Besides, I know about your situation."

She came to a stop. "My situation?"

"Melissa told me about your…recent breakup." He whispered the last two words like it was an embarrassing medical condition. Your "recent breakup." Your "case of herpes."

Brook felt the color rise in her cheeks. Melissa and her damn blabbermouth. She figured if she aimed just so, she could swing her bag and knock her sister right on the head. "What did she tell you?" she asked.

"She said you just got out of a relationship which didn't end well."

Brook waited for Mason to mention the wedding, even the nature of its undoing, but he said nothing more. Apparently, Melissa had exercised some discretion.

"She's right," Brook admitted, continuing forward. "My life has been out of sorts recently. I haven't been myself."

"But you seem to be in better spirits today."

"Yes, I am."

He sent her an earnest look that caught her off guard. "Someone would have to be crazy in the head to let you go." His words sounded like a symphony to Brook's ears and provided her with an assurance she hadn't been aware she needed. Mason Whatever His Last Name Was…definite rebound potential.

The foursome came to a secluded part of the beach where a handful of other snorkelers-in-the-know explored the water. They set down their gear and Brook rifled through her bag for her jumbo bottle of sunscreen. Locating it, she beckoned Melissa to rub the lotion on her back.

"But you already have on two coats."

"Third time's a charm," Brook said with a smile, handing her the bottle and backing up close to her sister.

"How about Mason do the honors?" Melissa whispered in her ear.

Brook held her hair up off her neck. "Baby steps, Mel. Baby steps."

They all waded out with their fins in tow, masks and snorkels dangling around their necks. Apparently chomping at the bit, Mason snapped on his fins in a flash and swam off before Brook was even knee-deep in the water. She moved out further and crossed her right leg over her left thigh, slipping her foot into the fin without incident. She struggled, however, with the other one, unable to get her foot positioned just so, toggling to keep her balance. Why was one side a cinch and the other hard? The same thing happened to her whenever she put on socks. Perhaps getting into yoga would help improve her balance. Seeing Melissa and Camden float away together, Brook hastened to catch up, but a wave knocked her over and she fell into the water.

"Need some help?"

The voice belonged to Scott Webster and Brook marveled at how he always happened to pop up just as she was ready to forget him. He was alone and looking very handsome and fit in his swimming trunks. No washboard abs, but they hadn't gone all soft either like a lot of men her age. Brook nodded for some assistance and he waded over, offering his hand. She took it and, filled with a sudden surge of nervous excitement, shot out of the water with too much force, knocked up against him, and they both toppled over with a splash, their bodies tangled up as if they were playing a game of Twister. It took a few awkward maneuvers for them to right themselves and whatever dexterity and grace Brook possessed seemed to have abandoned her with Scott's presence. "Sorry about that," she said, shaking the water out of her fin. "You probably wished you hadn't come over here."

"Not at all. Here." He held the fin steady for her and Brook rested her hand on his shoulder as she squeezed her foot in, experiencing another pulse of excitement with the contact on his slick, bare skin. She noticed Scott had a dusting of sand-colored freckles on each shoulder, just like her.

"Brook, you coming?" Melissa yelled. The gang stood on a sandbar, hands planted on their hips to express their impatience. Brook held up a finger, wishing the others had forgotten about her.

"You're in for a treat," Scott said. "There are some amazing fish out there."

"Would you like to join us?" she asked, feeling like an idiot the instant the question left her lips. Nobody wanted to be a fifth wheel. But a selfish part of her wished Scott would come.

"Thanks, but I'm turning into a prune." He showed her his shriveled fingerprints before putting on his mask. "See you around, Brook." He swam off just as quickly as he had appeared. Brook sighed, donned her own mask and mouthpiece, and headed in the opposite direction towards Mason. The other fish in the sea.

As she drifted through the water during her snorkel, Brook could feel the sun's rays shine on her back and she was thankful for the extra layer of sunscreen. Her breathing sounded like Darth Vader's, minus the menacing undertones. *Hooooo-paaaaah, hooooo-paaaaah.* The fish pretty much minded their own business, impervious to human intruders. Brook supposed they were used to being watched. She took in the wonderful alien sea creatures as if they were art pieces in a museum, smiling at them with her eyes, committing their distinct shapes and bright-colored patterns to memory so she could draw them later. *Hooooo-paaaaah, hooooo-paaaaah.* A sense of peace and calm came over Brook while immersed in the underwater playground, sheltered from all the ugliness back on land. If this wasn't breathing in the sunshine, then she didn't know what else would qualify.

~

Scott carried his fins and gear to shore, refreshed from the swim, but also distressed after seeing Brook still hanging out with that Mason clown. Although she didn't seem much into him on the tour, it now appeared as if they had officially paired off and Scott was just going to have to accept it. He might have shared a couple of moments with Brook, even a kiss, but Mason now had the upper hand, not to mention the freedom to pursue her.

"You're dripping on me!" Waverly snapped, bringing Scott back to his present situation. He shook his hands over her, giving Waverly a sprinkle of saltwater and she sheltered herself with her *US Weekly* magazine. "Stop messing around!"

"It's so hot out here. Don't you want to get in the water? It's incredible."

"I saw *Jaws* when I was a kid."

"You're not going to get attacked by a shark," he said. "They don't feast on each other," he added with a mumble.

"Pardon?"

"Nothing."

She waved him aside. "You're blocking my sun."

Scott plopped down in his lounge chair. "You might want to put on stronger protection. You're starting to crisp."

Waverly pulled down her Jackie O. shades and rolled her eyes at him. "I don't burn. I bronze."

"The rays are stronger here than at home."

"Scott, please." She pushed up her specs and returned to her magazine. "Don't pretend to care."

"I don't!" he wanted to shout. Scott simply didn't want to hear Waverly bitch to high heaven when her skin bubbled up and blistered.

He sat back and opened up his copy of John Irving's *A Widow for One Year*. As big a fan as he was of the writer's work, however, he couldn't get past the first sentence on the page. The words simply wouldn't sink in. He shut his book and looked over at Waverly cooking in the sun, flicking her cigarette so the ashes fell in the sand. Scott didn't even bother to ask her to not smoke around him anymore. The more she sucked on her ciggies, the less irritable she was.

Waverly had grown so unattractive to him it had become a joke. The first night on board, she'd told him to forget sex because it was her time of the month. But Scott had spotted a box of Monistat in a plastic bag from the gift shop. No wonder, considering the tight shorts she always wore. But even if a yeast infection hadn't deterred physical intimacy, he doubted that anything would have happened between them. They hadn't even come close to kissing which spoke volumes when people of the opposite sex were sharing a confined space. Unfortunately, it didn't look like that would be the case between Brook and Mason.

A cloud of anger swelled within Scott's chest. He grabbed the end of his drenched towel dangling over the back of the chair and brought it down over his head.

CHAPTER NINE

Mason cast a fishing line and began to reel in his catch. Brook played along and pretended to swim towards him like a fish, only to get body-slammed by a guy spinning out of control on the crowded dance floor. Mason caught up with her and sent the body masher a dirty look and it appeared as if they might exchange blows, but when Soft Cell's "Tainted Love" began to play, the nastiness subsided, replaced with a schizophrenic switch to delight, matching the crowd's general mood of nostalgia and saucy attitudes. One couple looked as if they had choreographed an entire dance to the song, striking dramatic poses during its famous jarring beats. Mason broke away from Brook and performed some Fred Astaire/James Bond moves, improvising fancy footwork and then suddenly freezing to point a fake gun at an imagined enemy. It tickled Brook how dancing allowed adults to be kids again, to show off, be in the moment, and not care what other people think. The inhibitions had peeled away with each drink and the alcohol was flowing. The song tapered off, but BONUS!, it was the extended mix of "Tainted Love" and the music moved into the band's remake of "Where Did Our Love Go?". Brook looked around for Melissa and Camden, but they had disappeared and probably wouldn't be returning. Although Mason had grown on her during the course of the day, Brook preferred having the buffer of another couple to ease her back into the single life. She supposed if something were going to happen with him though, they needed some alone time. But how cozy could they get in a noisy disco? He grabbed her hand and pulled her in close, answering her question. Brook could feel his hot beer breath on her neck.

It was then that a forgotten memory surfaced in her mind. Brook and Chip had once danced like this to the exact song. He had taken her to a fraternity pajama party where the tradition was to douse everyone with as much cheap beer as possible. Silly college stuff, yes, but it was that night, soaked to her core in Natural Light, her body suctioned to Chip's, that she knew he was hers. Sadness began to surface as well. Brook not only mourned that special feeling she once had for her ex-fiancé, but also the confidence she had back in those days. In the cocoon of university life, the world had felt like it was hers for the taking. All she had to do was study hard for a killer GPA, and the rewards would come. To her astonishment, once Brook had her diploma in hand, she began to feel hollow and aimless. She had worked so hard for her grades, but the last thing she felt was accomplished. Chip was there to help fill that emptiness, at least on the personal front. Everything would be okay because she had a handsome, well-do-to boyfriend with potential, because she had a social calendar jammed with outings and activities. She had tricked herself into thinking that her life had substance and meaning.

"My feet. They're killing me," Brook said, having to yell in Mason's ear to be heard. "Can we sit down?"

He pouted, but then nodded and led her away from the hustle and bustle of the dance floor to settle into a booth. Brook slipped off her heels and sank into the cushy upholstery. Mason ordered a round of drinks and although neither of them were having wine, this sparked a recounting of his trip to Napa Valley with his pledge brothers. "Nothing beats California," he claimed. "It's the only place to live."

"Well, not the *only* place," she replied.

"Yeah, I guess there's Florida."

"And plenty in between."

He leaned across the table. "So dazzle me then, what's the big deal about Kansas City?" Brook thought the question out of sequence considering the time they had spent together, but then realized he had asked her nothing about where she lived. "I mean, what do you do for fun there?"

"Oh, you know us Midwesterners," she began. "We go out cow-tipping and then line dance until we've worn the heels off our shitkickers."

"No, seriously."

"I don't know, the usual stuff. Restaurants, movies, parks, shopping, museums. Mel and I love to go out for sushi."

"You're kidding, right? I would only eat sushi on the coasts where it's fresh and clean."

"Clean?! Geez, it's not like we eat out of troughs. In fact, the one time I got food poisoning was when I had some bad fish in Florida during a business trip. It depends more on the restaurant, not the city."

The server arrived with their drinks and Mason took a slurp of his whiskey sour before saying, "You're not going to convince me that you can get a decent cut of fish in Kansas City. Steak, maybe, but not sushi."

"You've never even been there."

"No, I stick to California when traveling stateside. It has everything. The ocean, mountains, vineyards, big cities…"

"Traffic, smog, earthquakes, fires," Brook added.

"It's worth it."

"For some, yes. It's all relative depending on what you want. But you shouldn't dismiss places you know nothing about."

"I've heard enough."

"Arrogance. Attractive."

Mason scowled at her before knocking back his drink and scooting towards the end of the booth. "You know, I think I might call it a night. I liked the challenge at first, Brook, but you're just too much work."

"You insulted my way of life based on nothing but stereotypes. Do you expect me to just sit here and not take offense?"

He rose and gave her a smirk. "I was just looking for a bit of fun on this trip. If I wanted to be given a hard time I would have stayed at home with my girlfriend."

Brook grabbed his arm before he could leave. "Hold it. Did you say...GIRLFRIEND?"

He shrugged. "Yeah."

"Yeah? Is that all you can say? How can you be so flippant?"

"Why do you care? Anyway, it doesn't matter."

"Yes, it does. Just so you know, my fiancé ran out on me. That was how my relationship ended. Betrayal's the worst feeling in the world."

"I'm not engaged."

"It's not the degree of the relationship that matters."

He shook off her hand. "You need to lighten up. And I'm gone so don't you worry your pretty little head about me."

"It's not *you* I'm worried about!" she yelled as he left.

But Mason didn't call it a night. Instead, he headed back out to the dance floor and worked his way into a knot of women who immediately started bumping and grinding against him. Disgusted with the scene and how much she'd lowered her standards in the name of a rebound, Brook picked up her shoes by the straps and stormed out of the disco as fast as her bare feet could carry her. The night air did little to cool her down as she wandered the ship. She felt stunned, bemused, and just plain pissed.

How could this have happened? Was she absolutely clueless when it came to matters of the heart? But Mason had pursued her! Everything about him had indicated that he was up for grabs. And how could his friends stand by and watch him come on to her? Had they formed a pact—what happens at sea stays at sea? It made her blood boil that her sister was off sucking face with one of the accomplices, just as guilty as the perpetrator as far as Brook was concerned. Camden could be a cheater as well. She considered combing the ship to find Melissa, but knew it'd be a fruitless effort.

Brook continued down the side of the lower deck, encountering a heavyset man leaning against his scrawny wife, or mistress, who could tell? He let out a moan and wiped his brow with the back of his hand.

"I don't get it," the woman said in a southern drawl. "This came out of nowhere."

The man put a hand to his stomach and made a gagging noise. He then ran to the railing and retched overboard. His companion rubbed his back and made sympathetic noises.

"Seasick?" Brook asked, expressing concern for her fellow man, but also maintaining a safe distance.

The woman shook her head. "I doubt it. He was fine until about an hour ago. I'm wondering if it was the lobster he had for dinner. Sometimes fancy food doesn't sit well with him. He's a meat and potatoes kind of guy."

"Kill me," the man said, straightening up. A string of spit dangled from his chin and Brook felt her own stomach churn.

"Come on, hon," the woman cajoled. "Let's get you to the infirmary. I hope Marty's not sick as well. He looked a mite green after dinner. Did he have the lobster?"

"Uuuuuhhhhhhhhhh," the man groaned as the couple shuffled away.

Brook carried on with her aimless stroll, coming upon the stern. Passengers were scattered about the deck, taking in the starry night. A couple of kids who were up way past their bedtime pointed to the diamond-encrusted sky and rattled off the constellations' names while their yawning parents struggled to keep awake. A man nestled up behind his sweetheart and fanned out their arms together in a "T," probably trying to reenact the famous scene from *Titanic*. A bevy of rowdy women then entered the scene, hanging on each other as if one were to let go, they'd all take a tumble. They had feather boas draped around their necks and wore cardboard glitter tiaras that read

"Fifty & Nifty." With each toast of their plastic champagne flutes, they praised one another with relish. "You're the best!" "No, you are! You're fantabulous!" Brook remembered the first day of the cruise when she told Melissa that she refused to wear a tiara and howl at the moon in honor of their sisterhood, creating a ruckus just like the one taking place. Her sister was not the sappy type, but definitely the empowerment type. There was no danger, however, in them going overboard on the bonding. Brook had hardly gotten in any quality time with Melissa. Even when they were together, they seemed to bicker more than anything else. She watched the women with curious amusement as they staggered past her. It wasn't until after they had cleared out that Brook noticed a figure standing by the railing across the way. With the moonlight, she could see that he was keeping an eye on her. Scott Webster.

"I'm surprised to see you alone," he said.

Brook inched forward, gradually closing the distance between them. "I don't need company to keep myself entertained," she said.

"I'm not saying that. It's just you and that guy seemed pretty chummy on the beach today."

"Maybe, but why would you care?"

"You're too good for him. I know his type. He's a snake."

So Scott had seen through Mason. Good for him. What did he want though, a gold medal? He was a guy! Men automatically didn't trust one another because they're all after the same thing. One only had to look at Waverly to know why Scott had brought such a miserable creature on this trip. "So where's *your* friend?" she shot back.

"Waverly?"

"No, Mother Teresa. Of course I mean her. Now that I think about it, I better get out of here before she pounces on me and claws my face."

Scott rested his elbows on the railing behind him. "Waverly is in bed with a killer sunburn. The only body part she can move is her mouth. As you can imagine, I had to get out of there."

Brook sealed her lips to keep from smiling. She had seen how time with Waverly could rattle one's nerves, but she wasn't about to let Scott off the hook. "I don't get how you ended up with her," she said. "Wait a minute, yes I do. She comes with her own flotation devices, very handy in case of an emergency."

Scott looked away and raked a hand through his windblown, sandy-blonde hair. "I know it appears to be as simple as that," he said. "But there's more to our story."

Brook joined him at the railing and gazed out at the inky water. "I'm listening," she said, her tone ironic and teasing. She could feel him looking directly at her, but she kept her eyes on the ocean.

"She's here because I got drunk," he explained.

"Okay..."

"I told you before that I got the trip through work."

"Right."

"Well, for weeks people grilled me about who I was taking. I wanted to postpone it, especially since my sister's about to have her first baby."

"Congratulations."

"Thanks. So you can see why I wanted to wait. But the date was non-negotiable. I exhausted all my options—family, my buddy Tug, no one I wanted to take could get away. And I had no one special in my life which some of my coworkers thought should disqualify me for the trip."

"Sounds like you work with some real champs," Brook said.

"They were just envious, but the pressure was there. Truth be told, I wanted to go alone. But the hawks at Pendleton might have asked me to give the trip to someone else, or worse, bring someone from my department." He paused. "So I was searching for a date not three weeks ago."

Brook recalled where she was three weeks ago, curled up in the fetal position on her bed, reeling over the wedding that would never be.

He continued. "I got wasted one night and I guess I panicked. Waverly just happened to be around when it happened. Next day at work, she's telling everyone about the trip. I don't even remember asking her. I'm not making excuses. It's my own fault she's here." Another pause. "Nothing's going on between us," he added.

Brook faced him. "You don't have to explain yourself to me."

"I know. I just wanted you to know the whole story."

"Why?"

He shrugged and smiled at her.

Brook put her back to the ocean. She didn't know what to think or feel. Here Scott was, taking responsibility for his actions, owning up to a mistake, making it clear that he cared what she thought of him. Her attraction towards him grew stronger and she was glad to be in his company.

Just then, a woman zipped past them, carrying a toddler in her arms, begging him to, "Hold on!" Brook had forgotten all about the other passengers. With the roar of the wind and ocean, it was easy to block out the rest of the world. Scott's good looks also had a way of holding her attention.

"Hmmm. Getting drunk and behaving out of character," Brook said. "I can't imagine such a thing," she finished with a holier-than-thou tone.

He gave her a good-natured nudge. "Yeah, you must think I'm such a…DOG."

Brook looked down at her shoes dangling from her wrist. "I was hoping I dreamt that part. I'm sorry. I shouldn't have called you a dog."

"You meant it in a nice way." A twinkle alighted his eyes.

"And I kissed you, didn't I?"

"Just a friendly peck. You know in Europe, that's nothing, but I think in some cultures it means you're married."

In spite of her blazing cheeks and the mention of the M-word, Brook laughed. "I'm not usually like that," she claimed. A beat passed. "I normally start drinking early in the morning, not the afternoon."

Now he laughed. "Hey, dealing with Waverly, I'm surprised I'm not boozing it up at breakfast."

"So I take it you two won't be picking out china patterns when you get back home."

"Uh, that would be a big N-O."

She clucked her tongue. "What a waste of a vacation."

"It hasn't been a waste," he said. "I met you."

Brook's insides fluttered with giddiness, and the last of her remaining anger or thoughts about Mason, or any man, vanished. "That guy…from the tour…he's out of the picture," she confessed.

A slight smile formed on Scott's face. "Good," he said. "Now how about we have a seat?"

CHAPTER TEN

Only Tug McTyde and Scott's immediate family knew about his desire to write fantasy stories, yet not long after he and Brook kicked back in a pair of deck chairs, he was telling her all about his secret ambition. He even went as far as to go into his idea about the horsemen statues at the J.C. Nichols fountain on the Plaza. Scott always made a point to circle the landmark whenever he went for his jogs and one day, he assigned names to the iron warriors mounted on their valiant steeds and pledged to bring them to life. "I call them Granier, Falsafett, Brewshire, and Lockheed," he said.

Brook spent some time absorbing the information. "I like the names. They have a nice ring to them."

"You think so? They don't sound too much like decrepit villages?"

"No. Why would you think so?"

"I don't know. I guess I'm unsure about the whole idea. The names are about as far as I've gotten. I'm still waiting for the story."

"I wouldn't force it. Sometimes an idea sprouts in one place, but comes to life in another form. And don't let that blank page intimidate you."

Scott raised a brow. "You sound like you've been there."

She nodded. "In a way. I love to draw."

"You mean TV ratings don't stir your soul?" he asked, mocking astonishment.

"I know, it's shocking. Actually, my job was a fluke. One day I'm fresh out of school and temping at the front desk of the TV station, next thing I know I'm covering for the Research Director while she's out on maternity leave. When she didn't return, and who could blame her, management approached me about the position. The rest is history."

"Sounds like you impressed them."

"I think it's more like they got me at a bargain price. I liked it at first, even found it interesting, but it's not leading anywhere. And I'm starting to think that just because you can do something, even if you do it well, doesn't mean you should be doing it."

A kindred spirit, Scott thought. Brook was another artist trapped inside Corporate America.

Brook continued. "I almost studied art in school. But it seemed like they sucked all of the fun out of it."

"The Establishment has a way of doing that," Scott said.

"Exactly. The art majors in my sorority looked strung out and miserable most of the time. I don't think they ever slept. And most of them ended up doing pharmaceutical sales anyway so what was the point?"

"What medium do you prefer?" he asked.

"Charcoal, pencils, and pastels mainly. But I don't kid myself. I'm not good enough to make a living at it."

"Who says?"

She hesitated before answering. "Mr. Sweeney, for one. Or as I liked to call him, Mr. Meanie."

"And who is this heathen?"

"My high school art teacher. He *hated* me. According to him, true artists are misunderstood neurotics who operate on the fringe of society. They don't keep orderly work stations, serve on Student Council, or associate with cheerleaders. He used to actually pat me on the head and say 'cute' when evaluating my work."

"He sounds like a patronizing jackass."

"That he was. His grading system wasn't about creativity, composition, or form. It was completely subjective and biased. He favored the stoner clan who never turned in their work on time. His class was the only "C" I ever received. When I approached him about it, he flat out told me that I lacked an edge and it would be foolish of me to think of art as anything more than a hobby. He dismissed me as mediocre, but offered no guidance when I asked him for help."

"Someone like him shouldn't be allowed to influence young people's minds," Scott said.

"Yeah, but I shouldn't have listened to him."

"You were a teenager. He was the adult and should have known better."

Brook nodded. "It's stupid how that one naysayer can stick with you. He had this bizarre voice that will forever haunt me. It always sounded like he had a bubble in his throat. I wanted to take my painting knife and puncture it." She stopped and seemed to check herself, picking at a plastic strip of her chair. "Do you ever feel like people hold your strengths against you?"

"What do you mean?"

"Like with Sweeney. He faulted me for being tidy and organized. It's just how I function. Some people thrive on chaos and drama, but I need a system to process and understand things. I've never expected others to operate the same way. Even those who praise my organization seem to do so with a bad taste in their mouth, like it's an achievement, but also a flaw that I should learn to overcome."

"People like to begrudge others for something they don't understand or can't do themselves," Scott said, loving that Brook was being so open with him and that he finally found an intelligent woman who could hold a meaningful conversation. "You have an artistic side, yet have tendencies and a lifestyle that go against the grain of that image. Some people don't get that.

They want you to fit into a mold so they can categorize you, as if people can be sorted and stacked in Tupperware containers. Society sizes people up with shorthand, but too many times we end up shortchanging one another."

Brook's face lit up and it seemed as if Scott's words had an impact. "You certainly sound like a writer," she said.

Scott felt his face flush and hoped it went unnoticed in the darkness. "I don't know about that. By the way, thanks for not pointing out the obvious."

"What's that?"

"That someone like me working at an ad agency should get into copywriting, you know, cut my teeth. It's what Danielle Steel did."

"Oh? Big fan of hers?"

"She's not my cup of tea. I read about her in a writing article."

"I get the idea," Brook said, "but writing for someone else isn't the same. Plus, copywriting sounds pretty dull, like the ratings analysis I have to do."

"That's what I like to tell myself, but any writing would be good practice. Anyway, it's a tough gig to land and pays next to nothing. Copywriting is the way into Creative Services and everybody wants to work in that department. Including me. I think."

Brook met his eyes and studied him for a moment. "We're getting into some weighty topics here," she said. "Aren't we supposed to be talking about our favorite colors and top ten movies?"

Scott shook his head. "No way. Now tell me more about your drawing."

Brook propped herself up on her elbow. "I've never been able to give it up. I design greeting cards and stationery in my spare time."

"Yeah?"

"They're just silly doodles."

Scott wagged a finger at her. "Now that's Mr. Sweeney talking."

Brook dropped her gaze before meeting his eyes. "Well...I have this one series about this svelte, sophisticated city gal. Her name is Sadie Paskahonie." So Brook also named her imaginary friends. Scott felt like she'd been put on earth especially for him. "I draw her doing everyday things like sitting in the coffee shop, walking her schnauzer, reading a book in the park. She looks especially good on a thank you note."

"I'd love to meet her sometime."

"Would you?" Brook put a finger to her lips and considered him with an affected air of stern scrutiny. "I don't know. Sadie's selective about the company she keeps, being such a jet setter and all. But I might be able to put in a good word for you."

"Who knows, maybe you could design my book covers someday." Scott worried he was jumping light-years ahead, but relaxed when Brook smiled.

"You haven't even seen my work," she said.

"I know, but I can tell you have excellent taste. You exude it."

"Exude? Begrudge? Such fancy words."

"Call it a pathetic attempt to at least sound like a writer."

"Don't be so hard on yourself."

"Okay, but the same goes for you."

They regarded each other as if they now shared an understanding and Scott wished he could freeze time. Brook then parted her lips as if to say something, but must have changed her mind because she looked down at her lap and smoothed her skirt. "It's late. I should be going." She picked up her shoes and got to her feet.

"Come on, let's hang out until sunrise."

"I would, but I can't. We're going on the pirate ship cruise tomorrow, today I mean, and I should get some sleep."

Scott rose as well. "I hate to see you go."

"I'd ask you to join us, but the excursion was almost full when we first came on board. I doubt there's an opening."

"Maybe we can meet up later," he suggested.

She nodded. "I'd like that."

Scott walked her back to her cabin and their conversation resumed with ease, but Brook wrapped things up at the end of her hallway. "Good night. I hope I didn't talk your ear off."

He gave both his lobes a tug. "No. Still attached."

Her radiant smile made it all the tougher for him to say goodbye. A silence fell upon them. *Do something! Make a move!*

Scott pecked Brook on the cheek, giving her a sweet, G-rated farewell, but for now, it would be enough.

~

Brook paused before entering the honeymoon suite and traced her cheek where Scott had kissed her. She then brought her fingers to her lips and pressed.

Upon entering the cabin, she was surprised to find Melissa awake in bed with John Grisham. "I thought you'd still be with Camden," she said.

Melissa snapped her book shut. "I gave him the boot. Did you know Mason has a-"

"Girlfriend? Yes. But how did you find out?"

"Camden invited me back to his cabin to see the trip pictures on his digital camera. It was just an excuse to get me alone, I know, but we went through the motions anyway. Well, he scrolled through the memory card the wrong way and accidentally came across a party where Mason's girlfriend was drooling all over him. Camden tried to cover for him, but I was out of there."

"Mason and I had a falling out as well."

Melissa set her book aside and hunkered down into the covers. "I'm sorry I kept forcing things with him. No more. We are so done with those losers." She turned on her side. "But you seem pretty calm. I would think you'd be fuming. If anything, you look happy."

Brook shrugged. "It's no big loss. I was never that into him. And I've been out exploring. It gave me some time to cool down."

"I know we haven't had much alone time together," her sister said. "It's my fault. I just wanted you to have some fun, find someone to help you put Chip in the past. But starting now, it's just you and me, Little Sis."

"That's all I wanted," Brook said, speaking the truth, but now she felt torn. Melissa finally wanted to focus on their sisterhood, the true purpose of this trip, and all Brook could think about was the next time she might see Scott Webster. She took out her nightie from the dresser drawer and began to shed her clothes.

Melissa lay on her back and shut her eyes. "So, anything exciting happen on your walk?"

"Nothing special," Brook replied, slipping the nightie on over her head, the cool, silky fabric skimming her body. "I was just hanging out with the stars."

CHAPTER ELEVEN

Scott spent the next morning drifting about the ship, observing how the place seemed less lively than usual, but he was too preoccupied with recapping his night with Brook to give it much thought. He recalled the wind playing with her curls, the moonlight reflecting off her opalescent skin, the way her emerald eyes connected with his, engaged in thought. He should have gone for a real kiss. He could be such a wuss sometimes.

"Excuse me, sir?" Scott cringed at the intrusion into his daydream. He had wandered into the ship's lobby where the excursion agent motioned him over in an urgent manner. Although annoyed, Scott obliged the man and approached the station. The agent, Bob, according to his name tag, tilted his head to one side. "And how are you this morning, sir?"

"Doing pretty good."

Bob scanned Scott's face as if checking for markings. "Feeling all right?"

Scott thought the question peculiar, but responded, "Yes, I feel fine."

"Do you have any special plans in Antigua today?"

Was that where they were? Scott couldn't keep track. The ports had started to blend together with a repeating pattern of liquor stores, t-shirt shops, fine jewelers, and perfumeries. "No, nothing special planned," he told him.

Bob's face brightened. "Perfect! I've got just the thing for you, sir."

Scott expected to be bullied into some high-priced activity with no appeal to him—parasailing, bungee jumping, feeding chum to sharks. He opened his mouth to say he wasn't interested, but Bob didn't give him the chance.

"How would you like to sail on the Merry Merchant?"

Scott perked up. "You mean the pirate ship?"

"The very one. It's a huge party."

"But I called a few hours ago and they said it was booked."

The agent cleared his throat. "Sometimes the late shift isn't fully informed. And we've had some last minute cancellations." He motioned Scott forward in a private confidence. "Between you and me, Antigua ain't all that special, not nearly as pretty as the other islands. The Merry Merchant is the way to go. I can get you on for half price."

Scott didn't need convincing. He would have paid a month's salary to get aboard that pirate ship with Brook Holliday. Fate was back on his side. He slapped a hand down on the counter. "Sign me up!" Scott didn't even bother to question the cancellations, steep discount, or Bob's desperation.

"Super. How many, sir?"

"One."

Bob's face fell. "Just one?"

"Just one."

The agent took Scott's information and handed him a ticket. "You better hurry, sir. The Merry Merchant leaves in ten minutes."

Scott dashed out of the lobby and sprinted back to his cabin. There, he scribbled a note to Waverly explaining where he would be and tossed his stuff into his backpack as quietly as he could, not wanting to wake the sleeping beast. To his dismay though, Waverly stirred and sat up in bed, her face still as red as a tomato, all except for the cucumber slices around her eyes where her Jackie O. shades had been. "Where the hell are you going?" she demanded, sounding alert for someone who had just woken up.

"I'm going on the pirate cruise."

"You're deserting me?"

"You refuse to go out in public with your burn."

Waverly touched her scorched, swollen face and winced. "Yeah, but I thought-"

"You thought I'd hang out here all day? It's silly for both of us to miss out on the fun." Scott experienced a twitch of guilt. "I told you to wear sunscreen. I'm not going to be punished for your poor decision. And I bought you tons of magazines and a gallon of aloe vera. You should be set."

"You are so transparent. *She's* going to be there, isn't she?"

"Who?"

Waverly huffed. "That blonde chick from home."

"Yes, she'll be there."

Scott didn't think it possible, but Waverly's face turned a deeper shade of red. "So that's it. You've written me off."

"Give me a break, Waverly. We're kidding ourselves here. You never even showed much interest in me at the office until I won this trip."

"It was an excuse to get to know you, Scott. You keep to yourself at work, except when you're hanging out with Tug McTyde. But I guess what people say about you is true. You're unavailable."

"No, I just can't force feelings that aren't there. I'm sorry to be so blunt, but I want to be straight with you. I know we had that one night together, but that doesn't mean-"

"Don't flatter yourself," she interrupted. "Nothing serious even happened."

His body went rigid. "What? Wait a minute, I thought we-"

"You passed out as soon as we got back to your place."

He pressed his fingertips against his temples. "There was an empty condom wrapper in my bedroom trash. I saw it with my own two eyes."

"Yes, I thought of that while you were hurling in the restroom that morning. It was obvious you remembered nothing about the night so I thought I'd...authenticate the story."

Scott imagined that his face had turned as scarlet as Waverly's. All this time he thought they had slept together; it was the only reason he had put up with her! "Did I even ask you on this cruise?"

"Wouldn't you like to know," she said with a smirk.

He shook his head in disbelief. "You're a fine piece of work. No wonder you do so well at Pendleton."

"You could stand to learn from me, Scott. You can't just put your best efforts forward and hope life goes your way. You've got to shape circumstances to your advantage. I saw an opportunity and seized it. But if you take off today, I won't hesitate to ruin your rep at the office, what little exists that is."

Scott zipped up his backpack and hoisted it over his shoulder. "Spare me the dramatics, Waverly." With those parting words, he turned his back on her and left, hearing an object hit the door after he closed it behind him.

CHAPTER TWELVE

Although impressed with the authentic look of the Merry Merchant, Brook thought the atmosphere on board resembled more a ghost ship than a party cruise, bringing in numbers that came closer to a small, exclusive tour. What also surprised her was that Melissa, a woman who liked to be where the action was, didn't seem to care about the poor turnout.

"More places for us to sit," her sister noted.

"You seem kind of subdued today, Mel. You hardly spoke a word during breakfast. Feeling all right?"

Melissa pivoted her hand in a so-so gesture. "I'm dragging today. Maybe all the eating and drinking is catching up with me. Must be getting old."

"Ancient," Brook teased. "But are you sure you're up for this? We can go back." Considering how lifeless the boat appeared, Brook thought returning to the mother ship might not be a bad idea. She might even be able to track down Scott. There was probably still time to catch him before he headed out for the day.

"I'll get my second wind," Melissa insisted. "We paid extra money for this. It'd be stupid to miss it."

They ascended the steps to the upper level where a Long John Silver impersonator greeted them, complete with hat, eye patch, wooden sword, and a stuffed parrot mounted on his shoulder. "Arrrgh!" he roared. "Sit on me timbers." He nodded towards the wooden bench that ran the length of the deck. The sisters did as they were told and when they took a seat, a nearby wench offered them rum punch. Brook helped herself, but Melissa declined.

"*You* turn your nose up at a free drink?" Brook asked incredulously. She set her hand on Melissa's forehead, only joking around, but the clamminess she felt concerned her.

Melissa whacked her hand away. "Booze just doesn't sound good to me right now, okay? You don't have to make a big production out of it. And you better watch yourself. I don't want to have to babysit you like the other day."

"No worries," Brook said after taking a sip. "This is more Kool-Aid than anything else, not nearly as potent as the Barbados tour. I don't know if you've noticed, but the ship waters down its mixed drinks. With all the vodka tonics I drank last night, I barely got a buzz. But in this case, that's fine."

As more passengers trickled in, delaying their departure as there seemed to be quite a few stragglers, Brook gazed out at the aquamarine water and basked in the sea air. After a few cleansing breaths, a voice said, "Give me all your gold," and her heart stood still. Brook turned around and found none other than Scott Webster sitting by her side.

"How did you-"

"I held Long John Silver at knife-point and demand he give me passage."

Brook checked the area to see if the enemy was in close proximity.

"I'm alone, if that's what you're wondering," he assured her. "Waverly is still out of commission and has officially declared war on me." He gave her a good-natured smile. "But let's forget about all that. We're here to have fun." And now, as the ship at last pushed off from the harbor, it seemed as if the cruise might turn out to be as lively as promised. The crowd had swelled to a respectable size, but Brook only cared that it now included Scott.

Tropical tunes played on the sound system and after a few warm-up songs, a crew dressed in peppermint-striped boatneck t-shirts and khaki shorts popped up on deck, pitchers of rum punch in hand to replenish any empty cups.

Brook found that as she talked with Scott, the words once again flowed out of her with great ease. During a pause in their conversation, he leaned in and dropped his voice to a lower register, "Is Melissa okay? She's not half as festive as she was in Barbados."

Melissa sat quiet and still, sipping ginger ale like it was the elixir of life. "I think the heat might be getting to her," Brook surmised. "I offered to go back to the ship, but she wouldn't hear of it."

"Call me selfish, but I'm glad you didn't."

"Me, too," Brook said.

After a beat, Scott stood up and set a hand on Brook's shoulder. "I'll be right back." Before she could ask where he was going, he dashed off.

"Geez, you two are chatting up a storm," Melissa said.

Brook faced her sister. "I feel bad. I'm breaking our pact. It was just supposed to be the two of us today."

"Don't sweat it. I violated our code many times on this trip. And I'm not in a social mood right now."

"I know you don't think I should bother with Scott, but I can't help it. I like him."

"I can tell. And I'd venture to guess that he feels the same. He can't take his eyes off of you." Melissa reached into her tote, brought out her crushable straw hat, and crammed it on her head. "Do what you want, Brook. I'm done interfering."

"Really? I'll be sure to mark the date."

When Scott returned he had a wet hand towel folded up in the palm of his hand. "Here, Melissa, I thought this might cool you off."

"I'm fine. Why are you two making a fuss?" Nonetheless, she took the towel and dabbed her face and neck. "Thanks, Scott." He sat back down, having earned huge points with Brook. He'd given Melissa no choice but to accept his offering and be more comfortable.

A dark-skinned man in a crisp, Clorox white uniform then appeared and blew into a whistle which looked like a miniature flute, signaling that the party was about to get cranked up a notch. His limber hips swiveled to the calypso beat, inviting everyone to dance. The passengers sat glued to the benches at first, tapping their feet and moving their heads like a collection of bobble dolls on the dashboard of a car, but no one was ready to take the plunge. If Melissa had been in top form, Brook knew she'd already be out on the dance floor, but now she had the damp towel underneath her hat, draped around her like a nun's headdress. The first brave souls to break the ice turned out to be the Fifty & Nifty gang, only instead of wearing their cardboard tiaras from the night before, they donned brightly colored doo-rags. Brook wondered if they had a theme for each day of the cruise and got a kick out of watching them twist and shake their thing, not caring about keeping up with the beat or what anyone thought of them. She supposed that such carefree abandon came with age and experience—marriage, children, careers, death, divorce, cancer. Whatever cards they had been dealt, it seemed as if they had made the most of it and were here to celebrate life and friendship. Eventually, pockets of dancers sprung up and brought the deck to life. Brook and Scott joined in as well and she was glad to find that he possessed both form and rhythm. Someone had taught the boy how to dance.

Once the crowd got going, Whistle Man produced a bamboo pole and recruited a couple of dancers to hold it about a yard off the ground. He then bent backwards as if he had been born without bones and passed under the stick. Everyone cheered and he raised the pole, motioning for folks to line up.

Scott nudged Brook. "Okay, Miss Champion of Musical Men, do you think you can win this contest?"

She grabbed Scott by the hand and led him to where the line had formed. "Let's limbo. Just like the pirates used to do." The electricity she experienced from holding Scott's hand made Brook feel as if her body could do anything.

The first couple of passes were a cinch, a simple tilt of the head. After that though, the game got interesting. Scott was out in the third round, claiming that he hadn't had a groin injury since playing junior high basketball and planned to keep it that way. Brook, however, lasted until it was just her and two other players, a lithesome teenager and a member of the Fifty & Nifty club. As she prepared for the next attempt, Brook sucked in a deep breath as the stick was dropped to a level that only a gymnast could pass under without permanent injury. Nonetheless, she widened her stance, arched her back, and scuffed her flip-flops on the deck as she went under, thinking this was one of the few instances in life where having a small chest gave her an advantage. Although her thighs, abs, and back objected to every movement, Brook thought she might have it. But before she could complete the pass, her legs buckled and she pitched backward, falling flat on her backside, the heat rising in her face. The audience applauded her for her effort though as Scott helped her to her feet. Whistle Man gave Brook a consolatory smile and a snack-sized rum cake. Predictably, the teenager won the contest, the prize bottle of Bacardi Gold going to her parents.

Brook and Scott shared her rum cake, what consisted of about three bites each, and when they finished, Long John Silver came over to them and held up a camera. "Argh! Let's take a picture before we feed you to the sharks!" Scott slipped his arm around Brook and drew her in close. She nestled up against him, their bodies touching as if they had known each other for months instead of days, but she liked it. Long John took the shot, lifted up his eye patch, and winked at them before moving on.

Before long, the ship dropped anchor in a secluded cove and the passengers scattered about, most of them climbing down the ladders to swim to the white sandy beach. Brook and Scott agreed that walking the plank was a must. "Mel, you coming?" she asked.

Her sister waved them away. "Nah, you kids go ahead."

"Are you sure?"

"Definitely. You jump, I'll watch."

Brook and Scott lined up for the plank and moments later, she spotted Melissa dog-paddling away from the ship, her straw hat skimming the water as she moved along. Her sister turned around and waved as she waded in the water before heading for shore.

"Aaargh!" Long John Silver growled at Brook when she failed to step up at her turn. He edged her up the ladder and down the plank with the threat of his blunted wooden sword. With her feet dangling off the edge of the diving board, Brook fanned out her arms like an Olympic diver, bounced off, and hugged her legs to her chest for a cannonball. The impact on her lower back stung, but she emerged from the water as giddy as a kid. *Again, again! I want to go again!*

And she did. Brook and Scott jumped overboard probably a half-dozen times, performing all kinds of twists, turns, and tricks. All the swimming and activity should have worn Brook out, but her energy didn't waver. After the plank, they swung from the rope swing on the other side of the ship a couple of turns before hitting the beach.

On the shore, they came across Melissa napping on a standard-issue beach towel, her straw hat covering her face. Brook bent down and removed the hat as if checking on a stew. Her sister's eyes fluttered and her lips twitched. "Camels spit peppermint turds," she mumbled.

"That can't be a good sign," Scott said. "She sounds delirious."

"No, that's normal for Melissa," she told him, replacing the hat. "She's a sleep talker, usually in the style of a Beatles song from the LSD years. Let's hope that when she wakes up, she'll be back to her old self."

Brook and Scott meandered along the shoreline and even when gaps came about in the conversation, she didn't experience the normal panic to fill it with empty dialogue. During one such instance though, Scott ran ahead of her to pick up a stray Frisbee in the sand and tossed it her way. Caught off guard, Brook scrambled to catch it. When she threw it back, the disc wobbled in the air and landed in the ocean. "Sorry!" she called out as he chased after it. Instead of another toss, Scott came over and moved in behind her. He wrapped his arms around hers and positioned the Frisbee in her hand, his resting on top. "You want to flick your wrist," he instructed, demonstrating the motion.

Forget form, Brook thought. If her ineptitude got Scott to cradle her like this, then she didn't want to learn.

He continued with the lesson. "On the count of three. One. Two. Three." He flicked his wrist, but the Frisbee didn't fly. "You've got to let go, Brook. Again. One. Two. Three." She let him guide her through the motions and they both released the disc. The Frisbee sliced the air and then landed as soft as a feather.

Scott retrieved it and sent it sailing back. Brook jumped up in the air to reach for it, barely catching it on the tip of her finger. When she landed, a surprising image popped into her head, that of the bride she had drawn leaping for joy across the front of her thank you notes for her wedding showers. Right then, Brook felt like that bride, happy and carefree. To better capture her recent engagement, however, she should have drawn a stressed out lunatic running around in circles, tearing her hair out. Planning the wedding had been like having a second job and although Brook missed the idea of walking down the aisle, she didn't miss the hours spent scurrying across town running errands. She'd like to think that someday, she'd be engaged again. If so, how would she act the next time around? No way would she allow herself to be the frazzled, out-of-control whirlwind that she was. She didn't like that bride one bit. And her fiancé had wound up feeling the same way.

Brook snapped out of her musing when the bell aboard the Merry Merchant clanged, carrying across the cove and reverberating off the jagged rocks. She looked at Scott and he nodded towards the water. It was time to return to the ship.

~

The fun and frolicking had apparently zapped everyone of their energy as the passengers seemed like a different bunch back on the Merry Merchant. Parents carried tired, crabby children, lovers sat in comfortable silences, the doo-ragged fiftysomethings leaned against one another in contentment. Even Long John Silver seemed to have lost the wind in his sails, kicking back and removing his captain's hat and buckled boots. The sound system no longer blasted energetic party tunes. Instead, a steel drum band offered them slower, more soothing numbers. Melissa lay sprawled out on the bench, continuing with her nap under her straw hat. Brook wasn't so concerned about her now; the dip in the ocean had seemed to cool her off, and her mellow mood matched the general spirit of the trip back to the cruise liner.

Scott led Brook out to the center of the deck where a few couples swayed to a sleepy, rolling version of "Guantanamera." He twirled her around, took her in his arms, and she placed her head on his shoulder, feeling at ease and in sync with his every move. A gentle breeze strained to find its way through what space remained between their bodies.

The world melted away and it seemed as if the steel drums played just for them. Brook lifted her head and glanced up at Scott, just to make sure he was real, and he gave her that endearing look which made her feel like the most intriguing and important creature on earth. Then his face grew serious. He tipped his head down and kissed her.

Brook lost all awareness of her movements and her body, but at the same time, never felt so in touch with herself. Kissing Scott was thrilling, yet came natural to her, like she was born to do it. She could have locked lips with him all day, but the dreamy sound of the steel drums echoing in the background came to a stop and Brook remembered where they were. It pained her to do so, but she pulled away…eventually. They smiled at each other and she returned to the comfort of his strong shoulder as the band resumed their playing.

Taking a peek at the horizon, Brook wanted to capture the full beauty of the moment and lock it away in her memory. Out of the corner of her eye though, she couldn't help but notice her sister across the way. Melissa sat buckled over on the bench, her arms hugging her stomach, a look of utter disgust on her ashen face. She then threw a hand over her mouth and her chest convulsed. When Melissa sprung out of her seat and ran off toward the stairs, Brook broke away from Scott's embrace.

"What's the matter?" he asked.

"It's Melissa. I think she's sick. I should go check on her."

"I'll go with you."

Brook flew down the stairs to the lower deck where she found her sister's tropical-patterned, heart-shaped behind sticking out on display. Brook caught up with Melissa at the railing and heard retching sounds, followed by sloppy splashes. She held her sister's hair back away from her face and Scott grabbed the straw hat just as it was about to fall off into the ocean.

A pot-bellied man who had no business wearing a Speedo stopped and peered overboard. "Another one bites the dust," he said, clucking his tongue and shaking his head. "I'm telling ya, it's not just booze and seasickness. Something's going around." He turned and waddled off. "I hope you have Pepto," he sang over his shoulder.

"Big help he is," Scott said.

Melissa whimpered and Brook rubbed her back.

"I'll go get another cool rag," Scott offered.

"Good idea," Brook said as he left. "Feeling better?" she asked, donning her Florence Nightingale voice.

"I want to die," Melissa squawked. And then more slop hit the surface of the ocean.

~

Scott accompanied Brook and Melissa back to their cabin, carrying their bags as she assisted her ailing sister. When they reached the room, Brook relieved him of her stuff. "Thanks for all your help," she said, disappointed in the direction the day had taken.

"Not a problem."

Melissa slammed her body against the wall and slid down to the floor. "Ooooooooohhhhhh."

"Melissa, get up," Brook ordered. "That floor's filthy."

"Don't care. Uuuuuuuuuuhhhhhhhh."

Brook rifled through her bag. "Hang on. We'll call the ship's doctor and you'll be feeling better in no time." She searched for her key card and as she did so, Brook could sense Scott moving towards her. She assumed he wanted another kiss and felt this was hardly the time, but when she looked up she noticed his brow crinkled in confusion.

He pointed at the door. "Uh, I think you have the wrong room. This is a honeymoon suite."

Brook froze for a second and then continued with her rummaging. "No, we're in the right place." With the distraction of her sister's condition, she had forgotten that Scott wasn't supposed to see the suite. Brook positioned herself to block the brass placard. "Now where is that freakin' key?"

"Oooooooo. Eeeeeeeeee."

"But I don't get-"

"Here it is!" Brook proclaimed, cutting Scott off and holding the key card up as if she had found lost treasure. She swiped it through the slot and pushed in the door. Scott then helped her lift Melissa off the floor and get her to bed, not an easy chore with the confined space and dead weight.

Minutes later when the patient was put to bed, Scott crossed his arms and surveyed the room. "This doesn't look like much of a honeymoon suite. It's not that much different than my cabin."

Brook picked up the miniscule wastebasket and set it next to the bed. It would hardly contain any accidents, but it was better than nothing. She put a finger to her lips and motioned towards the hall. There, she kept the door propped open with her foot. "Let's hope she has the worst of whatever it is out of her system," she said.

Scott again noted the placard on the door. "Why are you guys staying in a honeymoon suite?" Brook let out a nervous laugh and tucked a curl behind her ear, averting her eyes away from him. He took a hold of her hand. "What's going on here?"

Brook let out a resigned sigh and met his gaze. She supposed there was never going to be a perfect time to tell him about her past, so why not now? She opened her mouth to let it all out when a ding sounded over the ship's intercom system.

"Ladies and gentlemen, this is your captain speaking." The disembodied voice coming from the ceiling had a hollow, grave tone to it. "I regret to inform you that a number of our passengers and crew members aboard the Paradise have fallen ill with a stomach virus."

Brook dropped Scott's hand.

"In the interest of the safety and health of all those on board, and in cooperation with the Center for Disease Control, we will be docking the ship a day earlier than planned."

Disappointed moans could be heard down the hall.

"Instead of going to St. Thomas, we will be heading back to San Juan, arriving late tomorrow morning. We regret having to cut your vacation short. You will be refunded for the missed portion of the trip. Details and instructions will be dropped off at each room. The ship is in the process of being sanitized, but to prevent further outbreaks, we ask that everyone please wash their hands thoroughly and frequently, especially after using the sanitary facilities. It has been our pleasure to serve you aboard the Paradise and we apologize for any inconvenience."

Brook and Scott shared a look of disbelief.

"I guess we know what Melissa has," she finally said. Brook then got an idea. "Wait right here." She snagged a plastic bag off the dresser and offered it to Scott.

He held it up and examined the contents. "Horse pills and condoms?"

"No, echinacea and alcohol wipes. Who knows if herbal remedies work, but it's worth a shot. We've probably both been exposed."

"Don't you need this?" he asked.

"I've got plenty to go around."

Scott stuffed the bag in his pocket and thanked her. He then shifted his stance. "I was looking forward to spending more time with you."

"I know. This is rotten luck."

"Broooooook," Melissa called from the cabin.

"I should go," she said.

Scott nodded, but once again, his eyes flicked over to the brass plate.

"Oh, that," Brook said, following his gaze. "It was a mixup. The ship's mistake."

"Oh?"

"Not much of a bonus, is it? I feel sorry for the poor lovebirds who shell out the extra bucks for this so-called suite." A crash came from the cabin and she winced.

"BROOOOOOOOK!"

"My sister hardly ever gets sick, but when she does…it ain't pretty."

Scott took a couple of steps back down the hall. "I'll call later to see how you two are doing."

She smiled. "That would be nice. Bye. I had a great time today."

"Best pirate adventure I've ever had," he said. "And I played a lot of Treasure Island as a kid." Scott's good humor then seemed to fade and he once again furrowed his brow, looking as if he had something to add, but then he turned to leave.

Brook watched him until he was out of sight. She then backed into the room to tend to her patient.

CHAPTER THIRTEEN

After a lukewarm trickle of a shower, Scott got dressed and took another one of the echinacea pills Brook gave him. He stepped out of the bathroom and began packing, his spirits lifting when he realized that an earlier return home would mean he could take Brook out sooner than later. Once in Kansas City, they could date under normal circumstances and who knows what could happen.

Continuing with her bed-in at the cabin, Waverly had herself propped up on pillows, mouthing the text of her *Entertainment Weekly*, another celebrity rag featuring Tifani Diamond on the cover, this time posing in a black leather catsuit. Waverly's sunburn had faded from a tomato red to a raspberry sorbet, but she still looked raw and shiny. It hurt him just to look at her. It hurt him to look at her, period. Since his return, they hadn't exchanged a word, but still some matters needed to be addressed.

"You heard the announcement?" he asked.

Waverly kept her eyes on her glossy magazine and briskly flipped a page. "Uh huh. Couldn't happen soon enough as far as I'm concerned."

You and me both, Scott thought. "Well, I'm pretty much packed," he told her, zipping up his duffel bag. "You look like you're still in pain. Do you need help with your stuff?"

Her eyes shot a spray of icicles his direction. "I don't need anything from you," she spat.

He clenched his fists. "Okay, then. But someone's got to see about the arrangements. We can't expect everything to just magically fall into place once when we get to San Juan."

"I'm not going anywhere," she said, her voice set and final. Scott shoved the key card in his pocket and marched out the door.

Angry passengers crowded the lobby and yelled at weary, rumpled desk clerks.

"I want my money back!"

"I'm not sick, why should I have to cut my trip short?"

"My kids are HEARTBROKEN!"

"No, I won't do a layover in Atlanta!"

"Get a hold of yourself!" Scott wanted to yell. If the clerks felt the same way, they hid it well behind their congealed smiles and empathetic voices. They worked so furiously Scott almost expected the computers to catch fire from all the activity. He took his place in line and during his wait, occasionally stood on tip-toe to search the sea of heads for Brook's honey-blonde curls and piercing eyes. But he found nothing except cross faces.

After taking care of the new flight reservations, Scott stepped away from the chaos to call Brook's room on one of the lobby's phones. He paused, however, as he reached for the receiver. *Honeymoon suite.* He still couldn't get the image of that brass plate out of his head, what might as well have been a neon sign. Brook had called the arrangement a mixup. It seemed odd though, that two sisters should end up in the suite instead of a couple, but he supposed computer glitches didn't make such distinctions. Still, Scott wondered if there wasn't another explanation. Brook had looked like she had a confession to make before the captain's announcement came on and pandemonium broke loose. And what she had said on the Barbados tour about something going wrong…it seemed to mean more than her having too much to drink. Scott also recalled how sad she had looked that first time he spotted her on board. Could there be something she wasn't telling him? Or was his overactive imagination giving him the wrong idea? Whatever the case, just getting to know Brook satisfied him enough at the moment. It had been so long since he clicked with someone, he didn't want to pry and risk making her uncomfortable or upset. Brook had explained the suite and he had no reason not to believe her.

Scott picked up the receiver and dialed the room number. He got a busy signal and debated whether to go back to their cabin and make sure everything was all right, but dismissed the thought as he didn't want to insinuate that Brook couldn't handle a crisis. In the short time he had known her, he could tell she was a capable woman.

Leaving the discord in the lobby behind, Scott located the piano bar, the inside of which felt like a cave in comparison to the bright lights and cheerful colors of the rest of the ship. The piano man, rather woman in this case, played a low-key mix of jazz standards and oldies for a sparse audience, a refreshing breather from all the hyper activities and recent disruption aboard the Paradise. Scott took a seat and ordered a Beck's. The dim lighting and flickering candles created such a romantic setting, his heart ached that Brook couldn't be there with him.

Scott chuckled to himself as his grisly, pessimistic view towards love and romance seemed to have jumped ship, replaced with a longing he hadn't felt in years. Scott's dating life had too often felt like a series of grueling interviews for the position of Potential Husband, his every response scored and weighted against other candidates on a scale he couldn't even begin to comprehend. Not so with Brook. With her, he experienced an inexplicable connection that went beyond their similarities and artistic interests. In a short span of time, she had brought the feeling of possibility back into his life.

Where to take Brook on their first official date? It had to be somewhere memorable and special, not just your run-of-the-mill dinner and a movie. Scott pondered the options until the set finished. He emptied his beer, got up, and dropped a ten dollar bill into the jumbo snifter on top of the piano. He couldn't afford to give such a generous tip, especially after settling the room charges with which Waverly had taken many liberties. *It's an investment in the arts*, he rationalized. He hoped that someday, someone would repay the favor when his first book stood on a shelf, begging to be bought.

  Scott didn't return to the cabin. Instead, he reclined on a lounge chair with another beer and studied the stars twinkling in the night, smiling to himself as his lids grew heavy. Just as he began to drift off, however, the ship seemed to have sailed under a blanket of clouds, leaving the previous sparkle behind to dangle over the waters.

CHAPTER FOURTEEN

When Brook stepped off the elevator on Monday morning, the mayhem of KCXT's administrative offices assaulted her with brutal force. Workers dashed down the drab gray halls, uttering hurried, false pardons as they dodged one another. Coffee guzzlers gathered with their oversized mugs, stepping on each other's words as they summed up their weekends. As Brook passed by, they stopped their conversations to give her perfunctory nods, a couple even welcomed her back, but nobody invited her into the fold or pressed her for details about her trip. They simply returned to the business of not listening to one another. Phones rang, assistants answered, bosses barked, doors slammed. The air smelled like rancid coffee.

Brook's shoebox office shared a paper-thin wall with the copy room where a Canon behemoth hummed and churned all day. She plopped down in her mustard-colored chair with peeling veneer armrests, a 1970's relic that didn't know the meaning of back support. Brook had submitted a requisition form for a new chair once, filling out more paperwork than she did when she applied for her job. Over a year later, still no chair. She reclined back a fraction of an inch and shut her eyes, imagining herself back in the Caribbean and riding horseback on a beach with Scott, the scene taking place in slow motion of course. Brook wished she could have seen him one more time before they had to leave. She popped open her eyes, forcing herself back to reality. Brook had learned better than to get caught up in fantasies. She had also began to wonder if what Melissa had implied was true. Could she be latching on to a new romance before getting over the old, thus never having to deal with what went wrong in the past?

But it was too early for such deep thoughts so Brook set them aside for now and pressed the button on her computer, the machine whirring and sputtering as it came to life. She held her breath and crossed her fingers, hoping her beige box of bytes wouldn't crash on her as it tended to do, especially on Monday mornings. Fortunately, she processed the ratings without incident and printed out the reports to be hand-delivered to upper management, a handful of execs who refused to embrace e-mail distribution and had the power to refuse it. KCXT—a company being dragged into the millennium kicking and screaming. She feared that one day, local television stations would be relics, extinguished with advances in technology.

As Brook navigated the news room down on the first floor, Hector Rodriguez, the numero uno sportscaster, intercepted her path like a stalwart linebacker. With his uni-brow creased in a bothered manner, he shoved a cardboard box at her. "This needs to be shipped right away," he demanded, speaking in a stern version of the plastic voice he used on air, except when Hector signed off and pronounced his name with Mexican bravado.

She handed the box back to him. "I think you're mistaking me for someone else."

"You're one of the new interns, aren't you?"

"Actually, no." She struggled to keep her voice polite. "I'm Brook Holliday, the Research Director."

The strip of carpet above his eyes lifted. "Ah, yes. The Ratings Girl. Tell me, how many people watched me last week?"

Brook felt a growl building within her. "Uh, I don't know off the top of my head."

"Sure you do. It's your job."

"We have seven newscasts a day. It's a lot to keep track of."

"Come on, just ballpark it for me."

The growl threatened to escape. Brook didn't like being put on the spot and refused to give out a guesstimate as it always came back to haunt her if she was the least bit off. "Really, I'd have to look it up. And I'm swamped right now. Just got back from vacation. Gotta run." She stepped away from him and held up her papers. "Urgent numbers to deliver."

Although Hector had some pull at the station, Brook didn't worry about blowing him off. She had introduced herself to him at least a dozen times before and yet he still asked her to ship packages, fetch coffee, and make copies.

Back in her office, Brook straightened her desk, noting the files she had spread out on the corner so each printed label could be seen and not forgotten. MORNING NEWS AUDIENCE COMPOSITION, 10PM NEWS RATINGS ANALYSIS, YEAR-TO-DATE SWEEP TRENDS. They were pet projects she'd been meaning to get to for weeks, all of which fell under the category of "going the extra mile." For now, she stacked the files and set them behind her on the credenza. She had a backlog of e-mails to tackle first.

As Brook read through a Nielsen notice touting improvements to their software which were years overdue, her mind began to wander. So many things didn't get said when she and Scott last saw one another. No phone digits had been exchanged, no plans set in place. Having an unlisted home number, Brook kept telling herself that Scott couldn't get a hold of her until they had returned to work, but a part of her wondered if he had caught on to her secret and wanted to stay clear. He was a smart man and she doubted she'd sounded convincing when she lied about the suite. She still felt terrible about deceiving him, but Brook didn't have the time to unload her baggage. She had slapped a Band-Aid on the truth and it would have to come off if she and Scott continued to see each other. *If.* Had their connection been real, or did they simply get caught up in the romance of the cruise? Now would be the test. And Scott Webster knew where to find her.

"A watched phone never rings."

Perry Sinclair seemed to materialize out of nowhere and leaned against the doorjamb with an air of entitlement. The fluorescent lighting accentuated both the orange hue in his fake tan and the grays in his swoopy ocean-wave hairstyle. Perry had surely been hot stuff back in the early '90's when he first became an Account Executive and seemed to have stuck with the yuppie look of the time. He grinned and hooked a thumb through one of his suspenders. "Look at you, Miss Thang." His eyes rolled across Brook's chest. "Ga-roooovy outfit."

Instead of going with one of her traditional neutral pant suits that day, Brook opted to wear a shift dress with a bold print of chocolate brown flowers on a cream background. A pumpkin cardigan added a punch of color and layer of warmth. To top off the look, she had pinned her curls into a loose pile on top of her head and glided pumpkin spice lip gloss across her lips. But Brook began to regret her choice in outfit as Perry eyed one of the flowers like a bee zoning in on its target.

"You look like you belong on the set of *Laugh In*," he continued. "Sock it to me!" He inhaled some coffee before his next comment. "You know, you don't look like you just got back from the tropics. Where's the deep dark tan?"

"My skin doesn't-"

"When I went spear fishing in Cozumel, I spent a month at the salon to get ready."

"And did you ever stop?" Brook felt tempted to ask, but bit her tongue.

Recently divorced, Perry was on a quest to return to dating form and spent his lunch breaks at the gym most days, using the tanning booth as much as the treadmill. Apparently, his efforts were not in vain. Last spring, he got caught having a late-night rendezvous with a field reporter on the conference room table, forgetting the cardinal rule that there was no such thing as dead time at a TV station. But when management got wind of the incident, Perry received nothing but a slap on the wrist and strutted about as if he should be congratulated. The poor field reporter, on the other hand, walked through the halls with her head bent down, started stumbling during her news reports, and eventually transferred to a station in Topeka. Brook still found it hard to look Perry in the eye. He'd forever be "the one who got caught doing it in the conference room." Of course she now had her own stigma to live with. She was "the one who called off her wedding." As if she had a choice in the matter. Thank heaven her coworkers didn't know the full story.

Perry stepped into her office and tugged at his tie. "Hey, I know you've been having a rough time lately. That's why I've been laying off on my research requests, you know, giving you some space. But if you need to talk, Brook, I'm your man."

"Um, I'm feeling better."

He nodded. "Good to hear. Good. To. Hear." He rubbed his lips together as if to see what remained of his Chapstick. He smacked them together before continuing. "So, I'd like to take you out for coffee sometime, or tea in your case. What's that stuff you drink?"

"Chai tea."

"Right. That's it. Guess the java don't jive with you."

"Gives me the shakes."

"Probably because you're so damn skinny. Anyway, I'd like us to get acquainted outside of work."

"I don't think-"

"Now hear me out." Perry moved closer, shifted into a lunge position, and planted his hands on the edge of her desk. "I know you play it all buttoned up and serious here at the office." He lowered his voice. "I looked up your sign. You're very much the Capricorn, Brook. Ambitious, but reserved, some would even say standoffish."

Brook squirmed in her seat and her poor excuse for a chair sounded as if a spring had popped.

Perry went on. "People have to chip away at the ice to get to the core of who you are."

Bad choice of words, Brook thought. Chip *away at the ice*. Distracted with the reminder of her ex, she forgot to take offense at his remarks.

"But Brook," he went on. "I see the fire inside you, ready to be ignited."

"I've met someone!"

He backed off. "What? So soon?"

She shrugged. "I didn't plan it."

"It can't be serious though, not yet at least. You've gotta play the field. What harm could there be in going out for a drink?" It was no wonder why Perry had such a stellar sales record. He refused to be refused.

"I'm a one-guy type of woman," she said. "You know me, I like to focus." It bothered Brook that she was using Scott to avoid Perry's advances. It seemed to cheapen her feelings for him.

"Well, if it doesn't work out, which rebounds never do by the way, my offer stands." He slurped more coffee. "Oh, before I forget. I want to run an income profile on all our newscasts."

"You already have one. It's in your quarterly news packet."

"You know, I think I misplaced mine."

Brook reached into her drawer and produced one of the many spare packets she kept on hand. Her presentations seemed to sprout feet and scamper away on her colleagues, often ending up in the communal recycling bin.

"Thanks. You always deliver." Although Brook returned to her queue of e-mails, Perry lingered, even after the phone rang.

"This is Brook," she answered.

"Patricia here. Got time for a quick pow-wow?"

"Sure thing. Be right there."

"Boss lady?" Perry asked when Brook hung up. She nodded. He cracked an imaginary whip and belted out a, "Hee-ah," before finally taking his leave.

~

Patricia expected lickety-split responses to her summons so seconds later, Brook found herself sitting in her boss's cavern of an office where the blonde wood desk seemed to separate superior from subordinate by miles. The door slammed shut by itself, as if an angry ghost had just stormed out of the room, and Brook jumped. Even though she knew all about the button under the desk that triggered the catch on the door, Patricia's parlor trick gave her the spooks every time. Brook couldn't help but imagine another hidden button, one to a trap door in the floor that would open up and swallow her if she acted out or said anything displeasing.

Patricia tossed back her hot-rolled, copper-colored hair and Brook suppressed a smile as she thought of her boss's nickname, Copperhead. Brassy and harsh from too much processing, the hair color clashed with Patricia's tomato-red suit jacket, one of an endless collection of nautical blazers in gaudy colors. Brook once kept track of the jackets for a month to see if there were a pattern to the colors, like teal on Tuesdays, or eggplant on Fridays, but the choices appeared to be random.

"How was your trip?" her boss asked.

"It was great. A much needed getaway."

"Feel refreshed? Ready to take on the world?"

"Um, I'm still playing catch up."

"Right. That's why I never take long vacations. I have to put out so many fires when I return that it defeats the purpose. But that's just me." She drummed her fingers on her desk blotter, her manicure flaking at the edges. "I wanted to speak to you, Brook, before you're swamped with projects. And please be open and honest with me. How are you doing?"

Her boss's attentive gaze expressed sincere concern and a pang of guilt hit Brook as she recalled all the times she griped about Patricia's unpredictable and demanding management style. "I'm doing all right."

"You've experienced a big blow. Now, I don't want to stick my nose where it doesn't belong. Having said that, what happens in your personal life spills over into work and that does involve me." She paused, as if daring Brook to object. "You've kept the reason, or reasons, behind the cancellation to yourself and I respect your privacy, but keeping your emotions contained can be harmful. Your mind becomes jumbled with troubles and it's easy to lose focus. So if you have anything to get off your chest, you can confide in me. I'm not just your boss, I'm a person. Your friend."

Brook didn't say anything at first, not because she had yet to figure out the reasons why her fiancé had left, but because Patricia was one of the biggest gossips in the office and Brook had to search her brain for a response that was vague yet satisfactory. "We went in different directions."

"Different directions," Patricia echoed, gazing out the window with a cluck of the tongue. "Lord, does that sound familiar. That was the case with both my husbands, neither of which could hold on to a steady job." She shifted her attention back to Brook. "I learned the hard way to stick to our kind, A-types who have their act together, those who are able, accomplished, aggressive."

Abrasive, anal, and annoying seemed more fitting to Brook.

"We aren't like those temperamental brats over in Graphics and Promotion," Patricia continued with a disdainful snort. "They think their creativity gives them license to be difficult. They know nothing about what it takes to run a profitable business. But back to my point." She pressed her palms together under her chin as if to pray. "I want to stress how much we're all behind you, Brook." Patricia tipped her hands every couple of beats as she spoke. "We're a team here. When one of us hurts, we all hurt." She spread her arms wide. "I consider everyone in my department to be family." Patricia's expectant look indicated that she wanted Brook to say the same.

After an interval of silence, her boss folded her arms. "I know how much time and effort you put into planning the wedding. And let's be frank here, work hasn't been the number one priority for you lately." Patricia swiveled back and forth in her cushy leather captain's chair, letting the accusation sink in. Brook conjured up her poker face, giving away nothing. She wasn't going to *admit* to her long lunches and personal phone calls. Patricia would need to produce hard evidence, a document citing the date and time of every offense.

"A major life change provides us with an opportunity for evaluation and growth," her boss went on. "Brook, now's the time to channel your energy into renewing your commitment to this station. I encourage you to take your job to the next level, soar above and beyond the expected." She extended a hand as if to direct Brook towards a path of righteousness. "Let me be your guide. For starters..." she chewed on the inside of her mouth for a moment. "Don't be so serious all the time. Smile more." Copperhead demonstrated, bearing her bleached fangs. "Have fun with your job. Plus, it never hurts to bring in donuts every now and then."

"Is that it?" Brook asked, not sure how to process this advice. "Smiles and donuts?"

Patricia sniffed as if she'd expected more gratitude. "For now. I don't want to overwhelm you on your first day back. And I'd like to get your input as well. I want this to be an exchange." She waved Brook towards the door as if to sweep her away. "So give my advice some thought. We'll save the rest for later."

The rest?, Brook wondered as she rose to leave. But she didn't dare stick around to find out.

~

Brook returned to her office with her head in a spin, her boss's speech the crescendo of annoyances from that morning. Sure Brook had been distracted during her engagement, but she still got her shit done at the end of the day. She delivered her reports on time and did quality work. What else did Patricia want? Was management trying to milk more work out of her? If so, where would the extra effort get Brook?

Back when she started her job, Brook's life at the station seemed full of potential. She never knew exactly where she would go after she put in her time, but the Research Director position had proved difficult to fill in the past and if she succeeded, it only seemed natural that she'd be rewarded with something more exciting and lucrative. Now, she felt stuck and what options the station offered held little appeal. She had zero interest in selling air time, an intangible product with fluctuating revenue that seemed to bring out the worst in most of the sales force. News always had openings, but that in itself raised a red flag. Plus, Brook would have to start at the bottom of the ladder, work unfathomable hours, deal with impossible egos, and make about a third of what she took home now. Once, a key Marketing position opened up and it looked as if a chain reaction of promotions might create some opportunities. Brook got excited again about work, pumping people for information and polishing up her résumé. But instead of promoting within, management brought in an outsider to fill the vacancy. The tried and true employees, those who had picked up the slack in the interim, stayed put. On the plus side, Brook did have her pay increase to look forward to at her annual review, but she got the standard raise no matter how she performed, what barely offset inflation. It was absurd that Copperhead suggest she step it up without any incentive. No wonder Brook's pet projects sat dormant in her office, collecting dust.

The phone chirped and Brook answered it in a distracted and agitated state, the benefits of her vacation already beginning to wear off. Her spirits lifted, however, when she heard Scott Webster's voice on the other end.

"Rough morning?" he asked.

"The return to reality. It's never pretty."

"I hear you there. I'm missing those islands too. But cheer up. It's supposed to be forty degrees and cloudy today."

"And here I thought I was done with my bikini."

Scott laughed before speaking again. "I missed you." Brook didn't know how to reply to such a bold statement. "I mean, I missed you on the boat, before we left. I tried to get a hold of you, but I got a busy signal."

"Yeah, I spent most of that night listening to Chicago's greatest hits while on hold for the ship's staff."

"I also went to your cabin in the morning, but you had already left. And we obviously didn't end up on the same flight home. You spell your last name with two l's, right? I looked you up, but couldn't find you in the phone book."

Brook liked all that she heard. He had definitely made an effort to get in touch. "We're unlisted," she said. "That's my sister's doing. She doesn't want her clients bothering her at home."

"How is Melissa?"

"She's fine now, but things were a mess. I'll spare you the gory details. Let's just say Melissa finally lost those few vanity pounds she's been griping about since law school."

"Yikes. I hope you didn't catch it."

"No, I was spared."

"We both got lucky then. Must have been those hippie pills of yours."

Brook wrapped the phone cord around her finger. "Then you owe me," she teased.

"Is that how it is? Well, are you free this Sunday?"

"Sunday? You want to take me to church or something?"

"I guess you could call it a kind of church. A bunch of people gather to worship a higher power."

"Oh?"

"I've got tickets to the Chiefs game," he elaborated. "Would you like to go?"

Although relieved Scott didn't want to take her to a revivalist affair, Brook wasn't exactly thrilled about attending a football game. Was this his idea of a proper first date?

"I've got great seats," he continued. "Hello? Are you there?"

"Oh, sorry. Sure. I'd love to go."

"Even if you're not that into football, I promise you, it'll be a blast. The tailgating alone is quite a scene, a Mecca for people watching."

"Sounds like fun," Brook said, hoping she came across as a good sport. She told herself it was an honor to be asked to a Chiefs game. She had never been to one, but knew that decent tickets were a hot commodity in this town.

"Great," he said. "I'll pick you up Sunday morning about nine."

"Nine?! Isn't that a bit early?"

"Not if we want to tailgate."

"Oh, right. Should I bring anything?" She began scratching down a list on her notepad: sunblock, sunglasses, bottled water, antacid…

"Don't worry about a thing," he told her. "I'll take care of the details." She set her pencil down and rested against the back of her rigid chair. "I'll call you later this week to get directions to your place. Could you give me your home number? To be honest, I don't like making personal calls at work."

"Sure." Brook gave him her digits, happy that he left the directions for later, giving them an excuse to talk again before their date. After telling him goodbye, she hung up the phone and closed the door to her office. Brook didn't pay much attention to football, but she had seen enough to know how to perform a victory dance.

CHAPTER FIFTEEN

Scott hung up the phone, pushed himself away from his desk, and spun around in his chair. He had a date with Brook Holliday! The mountain of paperwork to catch up on no longer seemed as monumental as building a skyscraper out of matchsticks. And work could wait a while longer. He had to share his good news. Scott practically skipped over to Tug McTyde's cube and knocked on the metal frame of the partition. His friend turned around and despite having a rather tired appearance, welcomed Scott back with gusto, giving him a mind-jarring slap on the back. Although bursting to talk about Brook, Scott knew another matter had to be addressed first. "How did your dad's knee surgery go?"

Tug pushed up his wire specs. "It was a picnic. There's nothing like seeing a stocky old Irish man in a hospital gown. And as usual, my little sister conducted her own melodramas. I never thought I'd say this, but I'm glad to be back at work."

"Can I do anything?"

His friend stroked his rust-colored goatee. "You don't happen to have Ashley Judd's number on you?"

"I'm afraid it's at home."

"Another time then." Tug took a seat and fiddled with his staple remover. "My dad will be all right. He's a tough guy and he's got a physical therapist who won't take any of his crap. It's just at a time like this, he really misses my mom. We all do. She kept everyone in line." Scott gave Tug a sympathetic pat on the shoulder. Mrs. McTyde had passed away a few years back. Breast cancer.

"So be a pal and cheer me up," Tug continued. "Tell me all about your Caribbean getaway." He raised his brow. "And what happened with Waverly? I hear you two aren't speaking."

"How did that get around so fast?"

"Two words. Water. Cooler. But say it isn't so."

"Can't. It's one of the few rumors around here that happens to be true."

Tug lowered his head. "Such a pity."

"No, it's not. She's devious and shallow."

"She says you ditched her for another girl."

Scott shook his head in disbelief. "This place is more like high school than a place of business. It's a wonder any work gets done."

"Did you ditch her?"

Scott supported himself against the file cabinet. "Ditched is a strong word." He lowered his voice. "Not that she wouldn't have deserved it. Nothing had even happened between us that one night. She tricked me into thinking we'd slept together."

"You better be careful, Scott. Waverly's making herself out to be the victim and she's got friends in high places."

"I don't care. I'm not going to let her rain on my parade. Yes, I met someone. Someone I like. And she's from here, if you can believe that."

Tug straightened his posture. "Yeah? She got a friend?"

"A sister. And she's just as good looking, but I have to make it through the first date before thinking of a fix-up. We're going out this Sunday to the Chiefs game. I've got killer seats."

"What? You bastard! You should be taking *me* to that game."

"Sorry, but you don't have soft skin and sparkling green eyes."

"I've got Irish attitude and an ample supply of testosterone. I'd say I'm much more qualified." Tug then pointed an accusing finger at Scott. "Wait a minute. I know what kind of money you make. How did you score good seats?"

"My brother-in-law. He's on house arrest until my sister has the baby."

"And you're taking this woman you barely know." He clucked his tongue. "That's just wrong."

"Maybe next time. I wanted to jump at the chance to do something besides the tired dinner-movie combo."

"You should have come to me. I've got a whole bank of ideas. There's the jazz district, the gangster tour…" Tug counted the options on his fingers, "or you could take her to one of those extreme haunted houses. 'Tis the season. She'll cling to you for dear life."

"I'll keep those in mind for the future."

"You're not thinking here, Scott. A Chiefs game is an all-day affair, a risky venture that could make or break a date. Call her back and tell her there's been a change in plans."

"No way. I don't want to throw her for a loop. I'm going to be careful this time."

Tug tilted his head. "You seem pretty into this girl. Has your vow of solitude come to an end?"

"I think it was more of a dating slump."

"No, a slump is when you try to date to no avail. *I'm* in a slump. *You* were in a funk. So who is this lucky lady to be bestowed with my Chiefs ticket?"

Scott could feel the smile stretch across his face. "Brook Holliday."

His friend shook his head. "Man, you're already a goner. Now get outta here. You're a disgrace."

As Scott made his way back to his cube, he passed a billowing flower arrangement left unattended at the reception desk. He backtracked and after establishing that the coast was clear, plucked one of its daisies, adjusting the flowers to fill in the hole. He then headed towards the east section of the floor.

Waverly appeared to be mesmerized by her computer, moving her lips as she read the display on her screen, absentmindedly picking a flake of peeling skin off her face. Noticing Scott, she shifted her eyes in his direction, narrowed them to slits, and flicked the scaly fleck at him.

Not to be deterred, he spoke. "I see your sunburn's getting better."

"Yeah, I'm expecting a call from the Olay people any minute."

It was a good thing Scott had the daisy concealed behind his back; otherwise, Waverly's venomous glare might have wilted it. He wondered why he was even bothering to put the animosity between them to rest, but went ahead with his proposition. "Listen, how about we bury the hatchet?"

Waverly pivoted in her chair. "All the gossip getting to you?"

Scott moved in closer, keeping the volume of his voice in check. "Hey, you didn't exactly behave well in all this, but I'm not going to broadcast it. I'd like to forgive and forget."

"What happened, Scott?" she whispered. "Did you finally clue in to the clout I have around here? Trying to protect yourself?"

Although tempted to shove the daisy up Waverly's nose, Scott offered it to her instead. "Let's be friends," he suggested. "Or at least civil coworkers. After all, we do have to breathe the same recycled air five days a week."

Waverly put a hand to her heart and dabbed pretend tears from her smoke-rimmed eyes, but the false sentiment soon shifted back into a scowl. She snatched the daisy, sniffed it, and bit the flower off its stem. She then spat the mangled petals into her trash bin.

Taking the not so subtle hint, Scott backed out of her cubicle. When he turned to leave, however, he ran smack dab into Leslie Stoneburner scurrying by as if the building had caught on fire. "Watch it," she snapped.

"Sorry, Leslie." He helped his boss pick up some of the files she had dropped, noticing one labeled "R-ORG," what he assumed to be a new account, more work for her to dump on him.

She straightened up and patted her dishwater-blonde hair fashioned in the shape of a mushroom cap. Her boxy gray suit concealed any trace of femininity and washed out her sallow complexion. Leslie became more conservative drab with each passing quarter, making it difficult for Scott to believe that he'd once been attracted to her back when they had their brief dalliance. He should have never given in to the impulse, but he supposed that after realizing just how dull his job would be, he longed for some workplace intrigue and excitement. Scott had gotten it all right. He was still being punished for what had happened with his boss. "Actually, I'm glad I ran into you," she said. Leslie extracted several files and handed them over. "More stuff from down the pipeline. Best get crackin'. I know you're still behind after being out last week."

A snort came from Waverly as she watched the handoff with smug satisfaction. Just give her a Himalayan cat to stroke and the picture would be complete.

Leslie stepped up to the partition, peering over the wall with her beady eyes, and Scott waited for the cutting remark his boss was sure to make, Waverly's crisped complexion providing an easy target. Since her last promotion, Leslie conducted herself in a hostile and intimidating manner, a deluded campaign to assert her importance. When she ended up speaking to Waverly in a honeyed tone to ask if they were still on for lunch, Scott about dropped his stack of files. It couldn't be. Leslie and Waverly despised each other. Their bickering around the office was legendary.

"Business meeting?" he asked, fishing for information. Both women shook their heads.

"Just us girls getting together to chit-chat," Waverly said with a coy grin.

They were an odd pairing, like a schoolmarm hanging out with a vixen, and Scott found their sudden alliance deeply unsettling. He did not need Leslie, his first botched office entanglement, commiserating with his latest. If only he had met Brook Holliday months ago, his life would not have these complications. Scott excused himself, hoping he displayed an air of indifference as his insides curdled with trepidation. And unlike most days at the office, he was glad to have a mound of paperwork to occupy him.

CHAPTER SIXTEEN

"I can't believe Perry made a move on you!" Danielle said with incredulous disgust. Wanting to save the discussion about the cruise until they were seated for lunch, Brook and her friend spent the ride to the restaurant venting about work. "I always knew he had a crush on you, but you'd think he'd have some tact."

"You're talking about Perry," Brook pointed out. "The guy who left his butt print on the conference room table."

Danielle shivered. "You know, it's people like him who give us sales reps a bad image. That used car salesman vibe of his has got to go."

Even in her perturbed state, Danielle Swan looked polished and chic at the wheel in her hand-tailored pant suit. Half-Korean and half-Caucasian, she was without a doubt the most gorgeous person Brook knew, possessing an uncommon, no-fuss beauty—radiant skin, shapely eyes the color of a strong cup of tea, glossy chestnut hair. Brook often told her friend she should be strutting down the catwalks in The Big Apple instead of working in Sales at a TV station in Kansas City. Danielle would wave away the suggestion and argue that she could never give up food or the exotic edge she had in the Midwest. She'd insist that people like her were a dime a dozen in New York City. "But here, I stand out." Indeed she did. A refreshing change from the in-your-face sales exec, Danielle's good looks and amiable personality served her well in her line of work. The gap in their respective incomes was wide for sure, but Danielle never lorded her success over anyone.

"And then you had to be subjected to one of Copperhead's lectures," she continued. "I think there's no question that you need a beer with your barbeque."

Brook would have preferred the relaxed setting of a bistro or brewery for their meal, but Danielle had a craving for Gates Bar-B-Q and since she offered to buy, Brook went along with the plan, even though their customer service made her bristle. Herded through the doors like cattle, the two joined the other ravenous carnivores corralled into Gates's holding pen as the girls behind the counter took orders with a disdainful air of impatience. What super-sized honkers were to Hooters, sister attitude was to Gates. "Hi, may I help you?" would be yelled in one's general direction. Patrons were then expected to sound off their order with both command and volume. No polite exchanges, no hesitation, no indecision. Often though, customers were still a few people away from the counter when being addressed and with the congestion, it was unclear as to whose turn it was, eye contact not being a part of the greeting. It was when someone didn't speak up at their turn that they received a pointed look and another irritated, more emphatic, "HI, MAY I HELP YEEEEWWWW!" As rude and chaotic as the system seemed, it worked. Orders came out fast and correct, even with substitutions and additions. One just had to know the correct way to say it.

As they crept forward in line, Danielle smoothed back her hair and Brook noticed something was missing from the picture. She gave her friend a poke. "Where is it?" she asked.

"Where's what?"

"It's okay, Danielle. You don't have to hide it."

A moment passed before Danielle slipped her hand under the collar of her blouse and brought out a necklace. Brook let out a dramatic gasp and shielded her face. "The light! It's too much! I'm going blind!" Her friend blushed as she glanced down at her sparkly engagement ring dangling off the end of the braided chain. "Seriously, why isn't that on your finger? Not because of me, I hope."

"No. It's just that since Steve and I already live together I want something to signify the change. So for now, I wear it around my neck. When we're married, it goes on the finger."

"Huh. Interesting concept."

"And I hate to admit it, but my sales are better when people think I'm single so I'm going to take advantage of it while I can. I know that's wrong, but it's reality."

"What does Steve think?"

"He's not crazy about the idea."

"Can't say I blame him. You should be showing that thing off."

Danielle stuck out her chest and gave her shoulders a wiggle, but then her good humor faded. "Hey, are you okay talking about this stuff?"

"I can handle it. I refuse to have people tiptoe around me, especially you."

Her friend tilted her head. "I have to say, you seem back to your old self, Brook, in fact better than I've seen you in months." Her eyes widened. "Did you get some action?"

Brook thought back to the Merry Merchant and smiled.

"You did! I knew that trip would be good for you."

"HI, MAY I HELP YEEEEWWWW!" someone boomed. The two stood at attention and Danielle took charge of shouting out the order. "Mixed plate, hold the ham for turkey, with a B-B on the side!"

Once installed in a booth with their tray of food, the first thing both women did was take a sip of their Boulevard beer, a popular local brew. "You know, they do this all the time in Europe," Danielle noted. "Having a drink with lunch is no big deal over there. It's considered a condiment."

"I'd love the chance to find out for myself someday," Brook said. "That's one thing I regret about college, not studying abroad or backpacking across Europe. I didn't think I could stand being away from Chip for so long." She sighed and shook her head. "Pathetic."

"It's never too late."

"You're right." Brook held up her pint. "With you as my witness, I pledge to conquer Europe before my thirtieth birthday." They toasted.

"Salud! Santé! Cin cin!" Danielle replied.

Brook pushed up her sleeves, grabbed some napkins off a stack as thick as a deck of cards, and tucked one into the neck of her dress. She figured she looked ridiculous, but barbeque was messy and dry cleaning was expensive. Her friend armed herself in a similar fashion.

"Okay," Danielle motioned with her hand as if to ask for cash, "you now have my undivided attention. I want details." Brook began to describe the boat, the gourmet food, and the beauty of the water and the islands. "I can get all that from a commercial," Danielle interrupted. "I want to hear about the guy."

"He has potential," Brook admitted. "And get this, he lives in Kansas City. We're going out this weekend."

"No. Way. That's spooky. What's his name?"

"Scott Webster."

Danielle's french fry made it only halfway to her mouth. "Not Scott Webster from Pendleton Scrubb."

"Yes…"

"Oh."

"What's that for? What do you know?"

Danielle popped in the fry and chewed. "He has a history there."

"I know all about Waverly if she's who you're referring to."

"Waverly? Never heard of her. I'm talking about Leslie Stoneburner."

Brook gulped. "And she is…"

"She's one of my contacts over at Pendleton. I recognized Scott's name immediately because she obsessed about him for months and always called him by his full name which I thought was pretty wacko. 'I'm training this cute guy, Scott Webster. Scott Webster walked me to my car. Scott Webster kissed me.' Then he ended things in an e-mail. Oh, she was livid. Anyway, she's his boss now and I'm sure she's made him suffer. Leslie has a combative nature. She's certainly made me dance for her dollars on more than one occasion."

Brook took a couple of gulps of beer to cope with her mounting disappointment. Scott had dated *another* coworker? Did Pendleton ever let him out of his cage? Or maybe he was one of those habitual office daters like Perry Sinclair aspired to be. Maybe Scott was interested in Brook because he had gone through all the women at his office and had no choice but to look to the other side of the business.

"He dumped her in an e-mail?" she repeated.

"According to Leslie."

"Terrific."

"Now wait. Let's give him the benefit of the doubt. We only know her side of the story and Leslie is the type to distort things to her favor. She never mentioned them going on a date so they probably kissed just that once. It was a little office fling. They happen all the time."

"Apparently so."

"Leslie tends to blow things way out of proportion," Danielle added. "I've lost count how many times she's threatened to pull her ads off the air when she hasn't gotten her way. She used to be nice. We'd even go out for the occasional drink. But over time, she's developed a nasty attitude. I hate calling on her now. My guess would be that she smothered him. That would make any guy run."

"Still, no one deserves to be dumped in an e-mail," Brook retorted. The din of the restaurant seemed to amplify and rattle her nerves as Brook couldn't help but form a connection between an e-mail ending an office romance with a note ending an engagement.

"No guy is perfect," Danielle argued. "And people change, learn from their mistakes. What matters is the present and how he treats you. Besides, this is your first date after Chip the Drip." Brook chuckled at the nickname Danielle had assigned her ex. "It's not like you'd want this to go anywhere."

"Right," Brook agreed. "I'm just getting my feet wet."

"So tell me, where is he taking you?"

"The Chiefs game."

Danielle's face fell. "Oh. How romantic."

Brook picked up a rib and began to tear at the meat. After a couple of bites, Danielle resumed with the conversation. "I don't know if I should bring this up right now…"

Brook tightened her grip, bracing herself for more unwelcome news.

"It's a bold thing to ask, but it's a pressing matter."

Brook met her friend's eyes, but continued to pick at the meat.

"If this is too much of a sore spot for you, I'll completely understand, but you seemed okay with this stuff earlier so I'll just come out with it." Danielle paused. "Steve's mom wants to throw us an engagement party and…well…I was wondering if you'd design the invites." She winced as if she expected Brook to throw her rib across the table.

Despite the nature of the request, Brook experienced a tinge of excitement about the idea and wiped her hands as she contemplated it. She found it comforting that Danielle had faith in not only her art, but also her ability to handle the subject matter.

"I'd like you to do all my stationery, invitations for the showers, the wedding, thank you notes, everything."

"Don't you want a professional?"

"You are a pro, Brook. I've said it before, you should be designing cards instead of analyzing ratings."

"And how would I pay the bills?"

"You could make it work. It's not like you're a frivolous spender."

"But I don't want to live in my sister's house forever. Now that I'm single, I should start saving to buy a place of my own."

"Have you even worked the numbers?"

"No, but the economy isn't what it used to be. People are cutting back."

"You don't see everyone giving up their designer coffee, do you?" Danielle countered. "Boutique cards are the same, an affordable splurge. E-mail cards are a fun novelty, but they're not personal. People long for a more intimate connection, something special, tactile, and organic." Danielle rubbed her fingers together as if she were handling fine silk, although the ends were stained with barbeque sauce. "I got a card from a girlfriend once for no reason. It made my day. There's a huge market for cards."

"Which has already been bled dry. Remember, we're sitting about a mile away from Hallmark's headquarters."

"But your cards make a statement, tap into people's personalities. Hallmark's too big for that."

"I don't have the right degree."

"What are you talking about? You studied Business."

"Exactly. Not Art."

"Who cares? What you have to offer is your own unique taste and style. You can't teach that."

Brook thought back to the last time she sat in an art class, being subjected to the harsh criticism of Mr. Sweeney. "Your colors are too bright, Miss Holliday," he had said in that bubble voice. "Your work looks cartoonish. Do it over." Why did the negative feedback needle Brook's brain? Plenty of people like Danielle have lavished praise on Brook's work, including Chip. Why did she have such a hard time believing them?

"I can help you with any sales pointers you might need," Danielle offered. "If anyone could run their own business, it's you, Brook."

"We're getting away from your original question."

"Okay, okay, I can take a hint. I'm backing off. I shouldn't be lecturing you, especially since you had to endure one of Patricia's talks this morning. So, what do you say?"

Brook swallowed the last of her beer. "I'll do it."

Her friend's face lit up. "Thanks. It would mean so much."

"Who knows, it could be therapeutic for me."

"Good attitude. I know you'll make it so special and memorable. All your work is."

"Hey, I'm on board. There's no more need for flattery."

CHAPTER SEVENTEEN

Scott stepped out of his brick apartment complex and inhaled the crisp autumn morning. He relished this time of year. The air had oomph and hardly a day went by without getting a whiff of a barbecue grill hard at work. Forget the spring with all its rain and allergies. Fall was the best time of year to begin a romance. Scott stretched, warming up his muscles for what he planned to be an extensive jog, the goal to clear his head of all the muck from work that week and be in top form for his date the next day.

Scott headed down the quiet, tree-lined street still vibrant with the golds, oranges, and reds of the changing leaves. His block had a collegiate atmosphere to it—plain vanilla dorms, stately red-brick Greek houses with fluted columns, dilapidated wooden structures ripe for demolition. Most residents were transient twentysomethings who wanted to be near the nightlife action of both Westport and the Plaza. And one paid a pretty penny for such convenient access to both. Scott knew he was out of his league when he had met his neighbors—a software programmer, a couple of lawyers, a pharmaceutical sales rep, and a biostatistician (whatever that was)—people who probably made double what he did as a media buyer. But he convinced himself that with a few sacrifices, he could make the rent. It was too late to change his mind anyway. The lease had been signed with what felt like his blood.

Scott rounded the corner and followed his normal route. The Plaza was one of Kansas City's top draws, an elegant shopping and dining district modeled after Seville, Spain, a shrunken replica built in the 1920's. Along with the Old World architecture, works of art dotted each block—fountains and statues of mythical gods, symbolic creatures, and blithe children. The Plaza had its Gap, Victoria's Secret, and Starbucks, of course. It seemed impossible to escape the conglomerates nowadays no matter how charming and exclusive the locale. But the quaint European atmosphere at least set the chains apart from their cookie-cutter indoor mall counterparts. It was all about location.

The streets began to blossom with activity. Dogs led their owners toward the Three Dog Bakery for a gourmet canine treat. Stylish singles sat at push-pin tables and sipped lattes, their unwashed hair and tired eyes indicating a rough Friday night. Preppy suburbanites had driven in and looked more polished and alert, their hair groomed and faces fresh with a good night's sleep. They have come here on an outing, many of them mothers pushing strollers, drooling as much as their infants as they eyed a construction sign reading "Pottery Barn Kids Coming Soon." Couples moseyed along hand-in-hand, but Scott didn't mind them like he usually did as they dawdled about and took up more than their share of sidewalk.

He passed Barnes & Noble, drawing in the aroma of paper pulp mixed with coffee, reminding him of the rare instances when he could steal away from the office and drift about the bookstore. He would prefer to frequent the local book shop on State Line instead, but Barnes & Noble was closer to Pendleton Scrubb and offered prices kinder to his paycheck. Once Scott was making real money, then he could shell out the bucks for full-priced books and support the little guy. While he jogged in place, waiting for a break in traffic to cross the street, a nearby oboe player in a wheelchair croaked out an unrecognizable tune. Scott backed up and dropped a fiver into the man's beckoning hat, money he had brought for his own fancy coffee, a post-jog reward. The oboe player nodded in gratitude.

Scott left the retail stores behind to do the mile loop around Mill Creek Park. But first, he had to say hi to his boys. The J.C. Nichols fountain was dormant during the cooler months and the statues had a splotchy green patina to them. Without the action of gushing water, the horses, front hooves batting the air, and their skilled riders appeared restless, as if dying to come to life and continue their adventures. Scott slowed down to catch his breath and circled the outer edge, sending a mental salute to each one—Granier, Falsafett, Brewshire, and Lockheed. Those names. They didn't even match up with all the sculptural depictions, especially the Native American spearing an alligator. Why had he grown so attached to the sound of them? And why did this spot have such a hold on him? He'd done some reading on its history. The fountain was sculpted in Paris in 1910, spent some time on an estate in New York, but after a fire destroyed the grounds, it fell victim to vandals. The Nichols family salvaged the pieces and brought them here, dedicating the fountain to its patriarch in 1960, honoring the man who had helped shape Kansas City's urban landscape, including the Country Club Plaza. What the figures stand for isn't certain, but it's generally believed that they represent four prominent rivers—the Seine, Rhine, Mississippi, and Volga. Having learned this, Scott still couldn't get a handle on the story trying to surface in his mind.

Picking up the pace, he continued on his way, tuning in to the rhythmic pounding of his Reeboks on the rubberized trail. He counted on times like this, when he was focused on physical activity, to create a channel for inspiration. It was when he wasn't thinking about writing that ideas and clarity would come to him. But nothing happened. His creative juices felt dried up, just like the fountain.

Scott's upcoming date with Brook boosted his spirits. Even after stepping off the rubbery trail and returning to the hard, less forgiving surface of the sidewalk, he found that he had just as much spring to his stride.

~

Brook worked in vigorous, determined strokes, trying to keep her mind on technique over content. She kept her tackle box of art supplies within arm's reach, her materials sorted and categorized since hunting for the perfect tool could be a valuable waste of creative energy and flow. Needing some hair color, Brook assessed her collection of brown pencils bundled together with a rubber band, picked the one that matched Danielle's shade, and began to fill in the sketch. She'd been drawing her friend's wedding designs for a couple of hours now and although absorbed with her art and wanting to approach the project with professional detachment, playing around with wedding motifs conjured up snippets of unpleasant flashbacks Brook couldn't suppress.

The professionals and their less than stellar service.

"Your china pattern is being discontinued. Surely we told you that when you registered."

"Fine, we won't have everyone recite the Lord's Prayer if that's what you want, Miss Holiday. But let me remind you that this is not a secular service!"

"Trust me, baby's breath is making a huge comeback! It will look great!"

Then there was Brook's mom. Olivia had felt so left out.

"Why not have the wedding in Tulsa? As it is, I don't even feel like the Mother of the Bride. Let me do something!"

And Chip—

"I need to add more guests to the list. New clients and yes, we have to include them."

"Your invitations look nice, but shouldn't we send out something more formal and traditional?"

"Let's do a karaoke machine at the reception. The guys will love it!"

Brook's pencil strokes became more harried as she darkened in the area. There had been so many decisions with the wedding, so many unsolicited opinions. It had her chasing her tail all over town. "Slow down, Brook! You're going ninety miles an hour!" With her hand now zipping across the paper, the point on the pencil broke from too much pressure and Brook realized she'd marred her bride with the coloring of a three-year-old. Perhaps it was time for a break. She went into the kitchen to fix herself a mug of chai tea latte, yet as the water heated in the microwave, her musing picked up where she had left off.

People had been telling Brook to slow down ever since Chip slipped the ring on her finger. Easy for them to say. They didn't have to coordinate the whole affair on a deadline. Chip had insisted on a wedding by the end of 2000, not only for its important place in time, but also because anniversaries would be easy to keep track of. Plenty of other engaged couples had targeted the same year, and the competition was fierce to secure venues. In the race to keep up, Brook had to operate in full commando mode from the get-go. She didn't have the luxury of time for the engagement to even sink in, much less reflect on the significance of the commitment she was about to make. But her life had come to a dead stop that day she found the note. *I'm sorry. I can't marry you.* Now, Brook had plenty of time to ruminate on her nuptials.

She shook off the memories of her botched relationship and turned her thoughts to Scott Webster. In doing so, however, Brook began to wonder if she could be getting carried away again. It had been less than a month since the satin aisle runner had been yanked out from under her, yet she was already getting worked up over another guy. And who to turn to for dating help and guidance? Melissa cut someone loose as soon as he developed any sort of attachment, and Danielle lived in Wedding Land. Brook needed a confidante in between those extremes. *Sex and the City* seemed to be the modern woman's guide to dating nowadays, but Brook didn't subscribe to HBO. Then there were *The Rules* and all that Mars and Venus mumbo jumbo. Everyone had their theories and advice on dating. Brook felt completely out of touch, but she had an inkling of what the experts would be telling her: *IT'S TOO SOON TO BE GETTING INVOLVED. YOU STILL HAVE TO HEAL.* And she thought they might have a point.

CHAPTER EIGHTEEN

Eric Clapton sang about cocaine while Scott sat in his Civic and tried to calm his hyperactive heart. *It's just a date,* he reminded himself, *not a walk on the moon. Get a grip and get out of the car.* He wiped his sweaty palms on his jeans before releasing the latch on the door.

Brook's house had a cozy Seven Dwarves cottage look to it, typical of the smaller homes in the fashionable Brookside neighborhood, built back in the day when the facades of middle-class abodes were made out of brick and stone instead of stucco and siding. The front door was painted a glossy chocolate brown and was such a dense and solid piece of wood that it seemed to absorb the sound of Scott's knock. Doubtful that he'd been heard, he was searching for a doorbell when the door swung open and Brook stood before him. She had on a mossy green fleece jacket over a t-shirt with jeans and sneakers. Although a tad disappointed that Brook didn't sport any red in support of the Chiefs, the unusual shade of green flattered her light complexion and accentuated her eyes. She greeted him with a warm smile, steadying his jitters. "Hey there," she said, motioning for him to come inside. "Looks like a beautiful day for a game. I hope you haven't been waiting long. We don't have a doorbell."

"Just got here," Scott replied as he stepped forward, the floorboards creaking underneath his Rockports. The inside of the house was tastefully done in understated taupe, but was a tad cramped with overstuffed furniture and an array of pillows. It smelled like freshly blown out candles and coffee. Melissa sat across the way at the dining table wearing a pink terrycloth robe, sipping a beverage from a ceramic head of Fozzie Bear as she read the paper. Scott liked that Brook's sister had no qualms about being seen in her robe without makeup. Of course, on the trip, he had watched her tossing her cookies over the side of a ship in a skimpy bikini.

Melissa nodded at him and flicked the sports section of the paper with her finger. "Are the Chiefs going to do it today?"

"Let's hope so."

"Their offense is going to have to step it up. Gunther better figure something out or he's going to be out of a job."

"Melissa's the sports expert in the family," Brook said, picking up a mini backpack and hanging it on her forearm. "I might have grown up in Oklahoma, but football still escapes me. But I promise, I won't bombard you with annoying questions the whole game."

"Yes, she will," Melissa said with a knowing, playful wink. Such a friendly exchange surprised Scott. Brook's sister seemed mostly indifferent to his presence on the cruise, maybe even annoyed at times. "I wish I was going to the game," she said in a pitiful, childish tone.

"Mel doesn't think I deserve to go," Brook told him.

Melissa rolled her eyes. "She thinks special teams are for the more slow-minded players."

Brook hit her sister on the arm. "I do not."

"Hey, watch the coffee," Melissa said, guarding Fozzie with her hand.

Scott laughed, relating all too well to the teasing of an older sister. He would have liked to hang out longer, but knew they should hit the road. "Are you ready?" he asked.

Brook seemed caught off guard for a moment but held up a fist, "Sure. Go Chiefs," she cheered.

Scott kept a clean car, unlike someone else Brook knew who had treated his Ford Expedition like a garbage truck. *Stop it,* she accosted herself. *You will not compare Scott to Chip. Be in the moment, damn it.* Brook knew that if things continued to progress with Scott, she'd have to tell him about her canceled nuptials, but such heavy news was no way to begin a date.

"Good tunes," she said, acknowledging the Clapton playing on the stereo.

"Thanks. I'm afraid it's just a plain old-fashioned 'Best Of' collection. I haven't gotten into the whole CD burning phenomenon yet. My home computer is a dinosaur, but it's got a word processor and that's all I need."

"Any progress with the writing?" she asked, immediately regretting her question since they had only been home for a little over a week.

"Nah. Work has been a nightmare." Brook wondered if Waverly or Leslie Stoneburner were the source of his woes at the office but didn't pry.

The car descended a hill on Wornall, giving them a postcard view of the Plaza. The Spanish clock tower above Williams Sonoma caught Brook's attention in particular and seemed to be sending her a message. *Time. You need more time.* But she had to start dating again someday so why not now? It's not like it would get any easier. Sometimes it was best to dive right in. She thought back to her cannonball off the plank of the Merry Merchant. Yes, it had stung, but she'd also felt elated.

"So where do you live around here?" she asked.

"In one of the brick boxes on Roanoake."

"I always thought it'd be fun to live off the Plaza. I love its energy and charm."

"Brookside has its share as well. It's a highly coveted neighborhood."

"Yes, but you get little house for a lot of money."

"The same goes for the Plaza. Of course I'm just a renter."

"Me too, only I'm related to my landlord. I was close to buying a little place of my own in Prairie Village, but when Melissa got divorced, it made sense to move in with her. Plus I was waiting..." she stopped herself.

"Waiting for what?"

For a stupid ring. "For that big fat raise," she said. "And I'm still waiting."

"That makes two of us. I love the Plaza, especially since I can walk to work, but I pay a lot for an apartment without modern conveniences and parking is scarce. It can be a pain."

Brook smiled. "So can living with my sister. She's a hard worker except when it comes to housekeeping. But I don't mind tidying up. I find it rewarding at times." She clamped a hand over her mouth before dropping it at her side. "Whoa. Did I just say that out loud?"

"I get what you mean. It's instant gratification."

"Exactly. I like results."

"So you and your sister seem close."

"We are, when we're not bickering. Mel can be bossy and meddlesome. No matter what, she's always at the ready with her arsenal of advice."

"I think it comes with the territory," he said. "Mine is the same way. I can't wait for her baby to arrive."

They drove a while in silence, passing the shuttlecock sculptures arranged on the lawn of the Nelson-Atkins Museum. The pieces stood as tall as the trees, fit for a game of badminton among giants. "Where are we going?" Brook asked, surprised they weren't heading downtown to get on the interstate.

"We're taking a scenic route to avoid the highway traffic. It's not too bad for a Royals game, but for the Chiefs, it's a mess."

Brook's nails dug into the armrest. How could she have forgotten about the twin stadiums? Kauffman Stadium, home to the Royals, the Stadium

Club, and of course, the Jumboscreen on which Chip's proposal had been televised, was located next to Arrowhead. During her entire date, Brook would have a colossal reminder of her past. She was furious at herself for not realizing this sooner and insisting on other plans.

The Clapton CD ended and looped back to the first track. "Hey, I appreciate you getting up early on a Sunday morning," Scott said. "There's a whole group who gathers to tailgate before the game. I call them the Tribe of Lightpost 32, strategically stationed near the porta potties."

"You guys think this through."

He held up his index finger. "Tailgating is both an art and a science. *Sports Illustrated* itself coined Arrowhead Stadium the top tailgating scene in the NFL."

"It must be something else."

"You're in for a treat," he said.

With the backstreet route, they indeed avoided any major traffic jams and before long, rolled through the parking gate of the stadium. Just then, Scott gunned the Civic, racing a pack of cars across the asphalt as if chasing after gold. Brook clasped her hands and pressed her foot on an imaginary brake. "Sorry," he said. "One has to be aggressive here. It's every man for himself." He stooped over the steering wheel, exhibiting the intense concentration of a criminal on the run. The teenage boys directing traffic might as well have been invisible, even with their day-glo vests and fevered motioning. In the distance, Brook could see two pickup trucks charging towards each other, swerving in the nick of time to avoid a collision. Scott careened towards a row of spots quickly filling up with cars from every direction. Brook couldn't watch. When the car jerked and came to an abrupt stop, she peeled open her eyes now level with the dashboard. "We're here," Scott announced in a breezy manner, as if they had arrived via an enchanted carpet ride instead of catapulting through space. He popped the trunk and hopped out of the car.

Brook gradually lifted herself up in her seat, noting the two massive concrete bowls in front of her. She turned her gaze away from where the Royals played, but couldn't get rid of the memory of the New Year's Millennium party at the Stadium Club. The big band music swirled in her ears like the echoes of a ghostly dream. Brook had been blinded that night. Both literally and figuratively. First, it was the camera light shining in her face, filming the proposal for all the bluebloods in attendance to see. Brook had squinted during the entire broadcast. Then, as her former beloved got down on one knee and slipped a ring on her finger, she had slipped on a pair of blinders. All she could see was the light at the end of the aisle. A vision of perfection. A hallucination. Thinking back, Brook wondered why Chip had to make such a spectacle out of the proposal. Was he afraid she might have refused him otherwise? Had a part of her wanted to decline his offer? No, it couldn't be possible. If they hadn't wanted marriage, then why would they have stayed together for so long? Brook returned to the present when she heard the trunk slam shut. She got out of the car and asked Scott what she could carry.

"Just this." He handed her a collapsible, nylon chair-in-a-bag. Brook slung the cylindrical tote over her shoulder and walked beside Scott as he pulled his cooler along like a red wagon, its plastic wheels rumbling across the blacktop.

A convention of tribes had gathered to feast, dressed in their native garb of Chiefs merchandise—football jerseys, sweatshirts, caps, jackets, anything that could be exploited for retail consumption. It was not a fashion show, but a show of dedication, a sea of red and Brook felt out of place in her mossy green fleece. The cooking equipment ranged from simple Hibachi grills to stainless steel monsters. Brook was amazed at some people's investment in the team and pointed out a Chiefs arrowhead on the door of a sedan. "Someone actually painted the logo on their car?" she asked. "Now that's devotion."

"That's a magnet," Scott clarified.

"Oh." Brook imagined that although she didn't wear a speck of red, her face probably added to the team spirit.

They arrived at Lightpost 32 where a white pop-up tent had been set up with Chiefs flags stationed at each post. Just off the tent, a barrel-chested man wearing a red apron and chef's toque waved a stick at Scott before turning around to poke at a mound of charcoals. He then did a double take, propped his stick against the legs of the grill, and made his way over. "Scottie!" he belted out in a gravelly voice before giving him a slap on the back.

"Uncle Al," Scott replied.

Brook's chair bag slipped off her shoulder. Did he say *uncle?* She was meeting *family?* What was Scott doing to her? Family required research, preparation, and most of all, time to get used to the idea.

"And who is this?" Al asked, removing his mirrored aviator glasses.

"This is Brook Holliday," Scott said.

Brook willed herself to relax and extended her hand. "Nice to meet you."

Al wiped his hand on his apron before shaking hers. "Likewise. Very likewise." He pumped her hand with a crushing grip.

"I like your hat," Brook said, breaking away from Al's firm grasp and pointing to his head.

He reached up and patted the white puff. "Yes, I leave no question about who's in charge of the grill."

"My aunt and uncle run the whole tailgating operation," Scott said, bringing out a couple of bills from his back pocket. "Here, Al. Something for your trouble."

Al waved him away. "You know your money's no good here."

Having probably gone through this routine before, Scott pressed no further and stuffed the money back in his pocket. He then rubbed his hands together. "So what's on the menu today?" he asked.

"The usual. Burgers and bratwurst. Your aunt also brought some sun-dried tomato chicken sausage junk." Al rolled his eyes.

A squat woman with rosy cheeks squeezed in between the two men. "God forbid we try something new and healthy for a change," she said. She kissed Scott on the cheek, wiped away the lipstick she left there, and smiled at Brook. "Hi, I'm Helen, Scott's aunt."

"I'm Brook. Thanks for having me here."

"Oh, the pleasure is all ours. We always bring plenty of food for…special guests." Helen threaded her arm through Scott's and beamed at him. "It's been so long since-"

"How about we set our stuff down," Scott suggested. He shrugged out of his aunt's hold, placed his hand on the small of Brook's back, and guided her towards the tent.

"Need any help?" Helen called after them.

"Thanks, but we've got it," Scott replied.

Brook smiled back at the couple over her shoulder. Al and Helen gawked at her as if she had shown up walking on stilts. And they weren't the only ones. Brook could feel many eyes on her as they entered the tent, and the chatter died down so that the pre-game radio show was the only talk to be heard. It had obviously been some time since Scott brought a date to one of these parties.

After the introductions, Scott led Brook to an empty patch where he unsheathed the chairs and set them up side by side. "My chairs are child's play compared to the fancy ones they make now," he said. "They're hand-me-downs from Al when he upgraded." Scott tilted his head towards an unoccupied ruby-red nylon loveseat, complete with armrests, drink pockets, foot props, magazine pouch, everything but a toilet. It looked like a throne situated at the head of the roundtable of outdoor comfort. Scott dug into his cooler and retrieved two Boulevard Pale Ale beers. "I assumed you aren't the Budweiser type," he said.

"You guessed right," she replied. "Microbrew snob." Although Brook wasn't accustomed to having beer before ten in the morning, she was grateful for the drink as the curious looks and hushed whispers were making her terribly self-conscious. Fortunately, the excitement of her presence seemed to wear off after a while and football talk filled the air. The tribe critiqued the roster, threw out stats, and engaged in heated debates. Brook tried her best to keep up, but the numbers and names meant little to her.

"Fascinating, isn't it?" It was Brook's neighbor, a burly, square-jawed man named Chris who reminded her of a hunky lumberjack with his blocky build, five o'clock shadow, cleft chin, and red-checked flannel shirt. He had considerably kind eyes, and she immediately warmed to him.

"I'm afraid I don't know much about the sport," she told him. "I get the general idea of course, but all the technical stuff is lost on me."

"Oh, you'll never be in doubt about the mood. We're the rowdiest fans in the NFL."

"So I've heard."

"All you have to do is just follow the crowd."

"But my mom taught me to never follow the crowd," she joked.

He tapped her beer with his thermos. "Touché. I guess that explains your green jacket." He tugged at her sleeve and smiled.

"I know, I'm committing a cardinal sin—no red."

"You do stand out. But by the looks of you, I'd guess you don't need to go against the grain to turn heads."

Brook felt her cheeks flush. Was this guy coming on to her, or was it just innocent flattery to put her at ease?

Helen came up next to Chris and rested a hand on his shoulder. "Where's Brad?" she asked.

"In Wisconsin. He had a death in the family."

"I'm sorry to hear that," Helen tutted.

"It wasn't a close relative. He hadn't talked to his cousin in years. Still, he thought he should be there." Chris paused. "Sometimes it's just easier if I don't go with him. His family…can be difficult." Chris turned his attention back to Brook. "Brad's my, how do you like to put it Helen? Special friend."

Brook nodded that she understood, relieved that Chris was for sure not hitting on her.

"Well, I'm sorry to hear that," Helen said, patting his shoulder. "It won't be the same today without his Ramen noodle cole slaw."

"Oh, I brought the slaw," Chris said. "He made it before he left."

Helen grinned. "He's a keeper."

"I think so, too," he responded.

"Do you need any help?" Brook asked, wanting to be polite.

Helen's face brightened. "Actually, that would be great." Brook had hoped to be turned down, but got to her feet. She glanced back at Scott as she followed his aunt out of the tent, catching what appeared to be a pinched look on her date's face.

A rectangular table lay upside down on the asphalt. The two women unfolded the metal legs on either side and flipped it over together. Helen then opened a trunk-sized Rubbermaid container and took out a square of red gingham tablecloth. "So, tell me how you met our Scottie."

"Uh, we met on a cruise."

Helen snapped the tablecloth open and Brook helped her smooth it out across the surface. "Oh, are you the one he took with him from work?"

"Um, no. We met on the ship."

His aunt paused as she brought out a stack of napkins. "Oh. Okay." Helen seemed to be calculating the square root of an astronomical number in her head. "So, you two just met."

"Yes. Scott did take a coworker with him on the trip, but things didn't work out between them." Brook didn't like having to explain matters and longed to be back in the fantasy world of the cruise, as opposed to the reality of Kansas City, but now that she thought about it, they'd had their share of complications at sea as well.

Helen handed her a tower of cups. "Well, we're glad to have you here. It's good to see Scott with someone for a change. He can be such a loner sometimes."

A gust of wind blew a cloud of charcoal smoke their way and the two women stepped aside, fanning the air with paper plates. "Helen!" Al shouted from somewhere beyond the smoke. "Five minute warning!"

Helen planted her hands on her hips. "Al, you're supposed to give me more notice!"

"Sorry. I was distracted, sweetie."

"Yeah, yeah. You were yapping football." Helen shook her head and rushed over to a cooler.

Scott emerged from the tent and helped his panicked aunt set out the food. Brook continued to help as well, picking up a packet of bendable straws and pulling at the plastic to open it. The industrial-strength packaging was tough to tear, however, and when it finally gave way, the straws scattered, showering an austere, white-haired woman with a spray of peppermint-striped sticks. "Sorry," Brook squeaked, amazed at the distance the straws had traveled.

Barely missing a beat, the new arrival glided over, plucked an errant straw off her red cashmere sweater, and handed it to Brook with the obliging and graceful smile of a queen humoring a clumsy plebe. The woman had perfect posture, and the upturned collar underneath her cherry-red sweater was crisp and Clorox white. Her hair was pulled back in a tight bun at the nape of her neck. Her supple complexion could qualify for a Dove commercial.

Brook bent down to gather the straws.

"Mom," Scott said, greeting the woman. With that one loaded word, Brook froze, fighting the urge to scamper away on all fours. "I, uh, didn't think you'd show," he added, a tinge of nervousness in his voice. With some assistance from her date she now wanted to kill, Brook managed to stand on her wobbly legs which felt as if they were full of applesauce.

"I'm not here by choice," his mother said. "I couldn't get out of work. What's the point of having an assistant when she can't fill in for you when you need her?"

"Mom, I'd like you to meet Brook Holliday. Brook, this is my mother, Katherine Webster."

"Hi, sorry again about the straws."

Katherine gave her a polite nod. "Hello."

Scott raked a hand through his hair. "Uh, my mom works for the Kansas City Ballet," he said. "She used to be the prima ballerina back in the day, but now she's in charge of fundraising. The company sets her up in a suite so she can butter up the high rollers for donations. But she always tailgates with us common folk, isn't that right, Mom?"

Katherine shrugged.

"It's a perfect day for a game," Brook said. "Brisk, but sunny."

His mother pulled at her sleeve. "I suppose. I'd rather be at the hospital."

"Sorry?"

Scott put an arm around Katherine. "My mom's anxious to be a grandmother. My sister's due date is just days away."

Katherine turned to Scott. "Have you heard from Rebecca today?"

"No, Mom, relax."

"I wish she'd do a better job at keeping me posted. You know, both you kids were early."

"I'm sure if there were a development, you'd be the first to know." Katherine frowned, reached into her purse, and checked the display on her mobile phone.

Helen joined them, her hair now mussed and her sleeves pushed up to her elbows. She looked thick and homely next to the slender and imposing Katherine. "You have perfect timing as usual," Helen told her. "Right when the food's about to be served." Brook sensed a trace of animosity here, but the two women exchanged cheek kisses. "Did you meet Scott's friend?"

"Yes," Katherine responded, turning her focus back to her phone and pressing a few buttons. "I hope this thing works out here. The stadiums could be interfering with my reception." She let out a deep, dramatic sigh. "I asked off for one day. You'd think the ballet would give me a break after last week's event. Sometimes I wonder why I still do it. It certainly isn't for the money."

"You do it because you think it's critical to support the arts, remember?" Scott said.

"I shouldn't be here. I should be with Rebecca."

"That's what Paul is for," Helen said. "And if you're so worried about your phone, why don't you call Rebecca and have her ring you back?"

Katherine looked away. "She stopped answering," she clipped. "Dreadful caller ID."

Helen turned her head and coughed, what sounded more like a laugh to Brook.

"But you're right," Katherine continued. "I should test my phone. Where's Christopher? He always has his cell on him. You know how the gays love to stay in touch, even a scruff like him. Oh, don't give me that look, Scott. I danced with puffers for years. I of all people know what they're like." Katherine peered about and then hurried off when she spotted Chris.

Helen blew a wisp of hair away from her face. "Sometimes she still acts like she's the prima ballerina."

"Sorry, Brook," Scott said. "My mom's not wearing her best colors today."

"Well, at least she's wearing red," Brook replied. The three of them shared a weak chuckle at her joke before Helen excused herself to get back to work.

Brook unzipped her fleece and peeled it off, suddenly feeling as if she had dressed too warm.

"I guess I've broken about twenty laws of dating etiquette," Scott said. Brook didn't respond as she tied her jacket around her waist. "To be honest, this doesn't feel like a first date," he continued. "I'm more comfortable around you than that." His words failed to put Brook at ease, and she continued with her silent treatment. "And I promise you, my mom was dead set on staying home today. I was just as surprised to see her as you."

She let out a bark of a laugh. "Somehow I doubt that." Brook crossed her arms. "Will anyone else be joining us? How about Leslie Stoneburner? I hear she's delightful company."

He cringed. "You heard about her?"

"You know what they say about Kansas City, it's just a big small town. And girls talk. More importantly, they listen. You broke up with her in an e-mail?"

Scott stuffed his hands in his pockets and kicked at the ground. Now, he looked uncomfortable. Served him right for springing his family on her like this. "Listen, there wasn't much to break up," he explained. "We kissed once, that's all. Then she bombarded me with e-mails and all this affection at the office. She even decorated my cube for my birthday and baked me this complicated cake which she couldn't stop talking about. I didn't read my employee manual, but I knew her behavior was inappropriate and it had to stop." He paused before continuing. "Maybe I should have gone to Human Resources, but I didn't want to make a big fuss, especially since I was partly at fault. Instead, I replied to one of her e-mails saying that we should keep our relationship strictly professional."

"So, it's true."

He hung his head. "Yes. I know I should have handled the situation face-to-face. I learned my lesson. She's my boss now and our interaction is always defensive and awkward."

"Dating at work can be tricky business."

"Amen to that."

"It's interesting that you did it twice."

"Hey, I thought I cleared up the whole Waverly issue. This isn't a habit of mine. Dating isn't even a habit of mine." He reached out and gave Brook's shoulder a reassuring squeeze. "It's a good thing you came along. It's not everyday that I hit it off with someone special."

Brook began to soften.

"I'm sorry about surprising you with my family. It was inconsiderate of me."

"It's nothing I can't handle," she said.

"There's one more thing you should know," he added and Brook held her breath. "As far as my family…my father's been out of the picture for years."

"Well, kids, the grub's on," Helen announced. "Help yourself."

Brook wanted to follow up on what Scott had just told her, but a buffet line hardly seemed like the place. Besides, if he wanted to elaborate further on the subject, he would. It was his call. Scott loaded up a burger and Brook had a sun-dried tomato chicken sausage in honor of Helen and all her cordial hospitality. The tailgaters passed through the line and had a seat, munching in contentment as the coach's voice, Mr. Good Ol' Boy, droned on the radio. After clearing his plate, Scott got up, announced he was going for seconds, and asked Brook if he could get her anything. She told him she was fine and indeed felt that way until Katherine appeared and sat in Scott's empty chair. Brook's stomach then contracted and she set her food down on her plate.

"What's the matter?" his mother asked. "Is it the tomato sausage? That didn't sound appetizing to me. I like the plain old-fashioned brats myself. They're full of fat, yes, but nothing beats the flavor." Katherine took a bite of her bratwurst and smiled with satisfaction.

"Everything's delicious," Brook said. "I'm just not used to eating this much so early in the day. Guess I'm still digesting my oatmeal." She picked at her potato salad before speaking again. "So you danced with the ballet?"

Katherine swallowed her food and dabbed her mouth with a napkin. "Yes. Before I hung my slippers to have kids."

"Then you must be the one who taught Scott to dance so well. He's got great rhythm on the dance floor."

"It helped with his gawkiness," Katherine said. "And shyness. Dance can work wonders for a child's self esteem. I saw it all the time when I ran my own studio. But all kids should be taught the basics of different forms of dancing, not just the ones who can afford lessons. They should make it a required course in school." Katherine swallowed her next bite before asking, "And what do you do, Brook?"

"I work at KCXT," she said. Nod of approval. "I'm the Research Director." Followed by blank expression. "I process and analyze the ratings."

"I once got one of those Nielsen booklets in the mail," Katherine said. "I didn't participate. I don't watch much TV except for public television. And the paperwork seemed like too much of a hassle."

"That's what we keep telling Nielsen. It's a very out-of-date process. I compare it to those food journals we kept in Health class back in school. You blow off the assignment until the day it's due, then just fill in what you can remember and make up the rest. But Nielsen has no competition so they take their time catching up with technology." Although worried she might be boring Katherine, Brook went on. "There's a lot of room for human error. And cable and satellite TV don't make anything easier."

"It's absurd," Katherine said.

"I agree. It measures the way people watched television back when there were only three networks and remote controls were considered a luxury. It's amazing that millions of ad dollars are spent based on the results. Anyway, my job is to come up with a positive spin on the ratings so our sales staff can get the best rates for ad space."

"And then people like me come along and talk them down," Scott told Katherine. "We both pretend to believe in the system."

His mother looked up at him. "I've said it before, Scott. You're wasting your talent at that agency. You're an artist at heart."

"So is Brook," he said.

She lifted her brow. "Is that so?"

"Not really. I dabble in greeting card design."

Scott gave Brook's foot a flirtatious tap with his hiking boot. "She just might put Hallmark out of business some day."

Katherine put a hand to her chest. "Don't say such a thing. They support the ballet every year."

"You have nothing to worry about," Brook reassured her. "It's just something I do in my spare time, mostly for friends and family."

"Do you have a website?" Katherine asked.

"I'm afraid my operation isn't that sophisticated. But maybe someday if I get serious about it."

Katherine regarded her son with an affectionate, yet also charitable expression. "You'll never change, Scottie." She turned back to face Brook. "My son's always had a soft spot for creative types." Nobody spoke as Scott's face turned the same hue as his cranberry red turtleneck sweater.

Checking her watch, Katherine rose and addressed her son. "I hate to eat and run, kiddo, but I've got to get to the suite, put in some face time with our sponsors before the game begins." She pecked him on the cheek, and he took her plate. "Brook, it was a pleasure meeting you."

"You, too. Enjoy the game."

After Katherine took her departure, Scott plopped down in his nylon lawn chair and pulled at his turtleneck. "So…that was my mom."

"So it was."

A silence fell between them. "We should help pack up," he said. "It's getting close to game time."

CHAPTER NINETEEN

Scott shimmied his way down the row of fans, careful not to spill the hot chocolate he carried. The Chiefs were ahead and the game was going well so far. He didn't know if he could say the same about his date. Brook was hard to read. Although her mysterious reserve had attracted him to her in the first place, right now he could use more open expression to gauge how things were going. Was she keeping track of all his penalties? If so, was he in danger of getting tossed out of the game?

"What do you have there?" she asked when he sat down.

"Hot chocolate."

"Yum. I was just thinking that sounded good. It's gotten chilly since the sun went behind the clouds." Scott gave himself a mental high-five. It seemed like he had finally scored a touchdown. Brook sipped her cocoa, but quickly drew back as though she had just consumed arsenic. "Ouch, that's hot."

"Is it? I'm sorry."

"It's not your fault." She noted the cup and then showed him the side reading "WARNING: CONTENTS MAY BE HOT!" in bold lettering. "Guess I can't sue," she said.

Scott blew into the hole of his lid before taking a tentative sip. He about gagged. The drink had the grainy texture and weak taste of Ovaltine.

Why did something else have to go wrong? "This tastes terrible, Brook. Don't feel obligated to drink it."

She blew on her drink and took another sip. "Oh, it's fine, once it's cooled off."

Liar, he thought, but Scott appreciated Brook pretending to enjoy the four dollar cup of crap.

When halftime arrived, the Chiefs cheerleaders pranced onto the field for some "wholesome" entertainment, braving the cold in nothing but sequined halter tops and hot pants. Scott was mindful not to pay too much attention to their gyrating hips and high kicks during the routine. Instead, he focused on a man in a red and yellow superhero getup mimicking the cheerleaders' dance. His bulging beer gut jiggled over his utility belt and he gave his mullet the occasional toss over his shoulder. "Now he could teach those girls a thing or two," Scott joked, nodding his head in the man's direction.

Brook laughed. "You know, my superhero costume is at the cleaners. I'll remember to plan better next time."

Scott liked what he heard. *Next time.* At the end of the cheerleaders' routine, Brook turned to face him and placed her hand on his arm, sending a ripple of electricity through his veins. "You know what? This is your book."

"What, Captain Mullethead over there?"

"Everything. Just look at your crowd alone. Your mom is a former ballerina. I'm sure she has hundreds of interesting stories to tell. And Chris, he's not your typical gay man. He looks like he could snap a tree in two. You said it yourself on the cruise. People don't fit neatly into labeled packages."

Scott shrugged. "I don't know. I like making stuff up about good conquering evil in faraway lands."

"But why deny yourself material that's right in front of you? There's still plenty of room for creativity and imagination."

"So you're a writer now?" he asked, his tone more defensive than he intended.

"No," Brook replied. "It's just that you are trying to write about dragons, knights, and wizards, but the stories don't come. And I imagine since Harry Potter came along, publishers are flooded with fantasy material."

"I'm not a copycat who chases after trends."

"I'm not saying that. I just think that if you're not getting anywhere, maybe you should look in your own backyard."

Scott stared off into the middle distance. He loved that Brook had opinions and stood her ground, but he didn't know how to react to her advice without shutting down or coming across as a sulking child. She had brought up a valid argument, one he often thought about himself, but she didn't know what it would require of him to draw from his own experience.

"I'm sorry," Brook said after a couple of beats. "I'm stepping over a line here. I shouldn't be telling you how to write. I don't like people telling me how to draw."

"There's nothing to apologize about," he said. "You were expressing an opinion, and I like that. If I'm going to ever be a writer, I'll have to develop a thick skin."

"Maybe, but it wasn't my place to-"

"No, I appreciate your honesty. Anyone can tell me what I want to hear. Maybe you're telling me something I need to hear."

"Maybe I should keep my big mouth shut," she said. "My way is to throw myself into projects with full force, sometimes without thinking things through or taking a step back to look at the big picture." She seemed to get lost in her thoughts for a moment before continuing. "My way isn't necessarily the best way."

"Well, I tend to think *too* much," he admitted. "And it's not like what I'm doing is working all that well. Maybe I should take a different approach."

Brook smiled and Scott wanted to kiss her, to relive what happened on the Merry Merchant, but he held back since they were surrounded by screaming football fans who'd probably cuss them out for any sappy displays of affection. He settled for putting his arm around her and brought her in close to his side. The crowd roared as the players spilled forth from the stadium's archway, charging onto the field for the second half.

~

The Chiefs won, but it came at a cost, at least to Brook. Although she enjoyed the game and Scott's company, her head hummed from the deafening crowd noise and classic rock blaring over the sound system. She had her fill of spectator sports and was ready to go home and take a nap. As she and Scott traipsed across the parking lot, however, it didn't look like they'd be leaving anytime soon. Cars were already lined up bumper-to-bumper and going nowhere, horns honking as if that would help alleviate the congestion. She didn't even want to think about how many drunk drivers were behind the wheel growing surly and impatient by the minute.

Back at the tent, most of the Tribe of Lightpost 32 had gathered again, slapping each other on the backs and celebrating the victory. Scott retrieved his cooler from Al and Helen's Suburban and wheeled it over. "You don't mind if we hang out a while longer, do you?" he asked. "We hold a chili party until the traffic clears. It beats sitting in the car."

"Can't argue with that logic," she said. Although anxious to leave, Brook thought getting some food in her stomach might ease her mounting headache, and a hot bowl of chili sounded perfect for a day that had grown progressively cloudy and cold.

Scott lifted the lid to the cooler. "Would you like another beer?" he offered.

"No, thanks. Water sounds good."

"Excellent idea," he said and handed her a bottle.

Brook put her back to him and popped in some Tylenol she had stashed in her pocket. When she turned back around, Scott had gotten sucked into a play-by-play discussion of the game so she snuck away to join Helen at the pair of pots cooking over butane flames. "Smells delicious," Brook observed.

"We've got your traditional beef chili," Helen told her. "Al makes it nice and spicy. I also made veggie green chili for those of us watching our figure."

"Will Katherine be coming back?"

"No. She always leaves after the third quarter unless it's a nail-biter. Katherine believes in showing up fashionably late and leaving the party while it's in full swing."

Brook felt a little snubbed, but also relieved as she was much more at ease around Helen. Scott's aunt had a welcoming mother hen quality about her which Brook found ironic when Scott told her that Al and Helen never had children of their own, at least not the human variety. He said their kids were various mutts they'd rescued over the years.

Helen set a hand on Brook's arm. "I know Katherine wasn't exactly all smiles today. Don't take it to heart. She was upset about work and has a one-track mind nowadays with her first grandchild on its way. Plus, she takes a while to warm up to new people."

Brook looked down at the tin lid of one of the chili pots. "Oh, she was okay."

"Their family's a tight bunch. My brother had no clue how good he had it."

"You mean Scott's father?" Brook asked.

Helen tutted. "Yes, the rotten apple on our family tree. He was a brilliant and talented pianist, but terribly selfish and temperamental. He left when the kids were still young, thought his britches were too big for Kansas City and wanted to hang with the heavy hitters in Boston. In my opinion, his ego held him back more than his family ever did. He eventually found the success he wanted, but he was always a disappointment to me."

Brook thought of Scott's questionable dating history. Was it simply misguided bachelor behavior, or deep-rooted family psychosis?

"But don't you worry," Helen continued. "Scottie's *nothing* like his father. He's as loyal as a Labrador." She lifted a lid and stirred the beef chili. "This is a big day. Scott hasn't introduced us to anyone since…" she searched the sky, "well, since Tifani Diamond I guess."

The name hit Brook like an errant football falling out of the sky. "I'm sorry," she began. "Did you say…Tifani Diamond? As in the movie star?"

Helen nodded. "Yes, but *I'm* no fan of hers. You have to be able to do more than strut about in skin-tight clothing to win me over. And I'm not about to pay good money to go to any of her movies, not after what she did to our Scottie."

Brook couldn't speak, but didn't have to as Helen offered the story.

"They dated back in college. She was Tiffany Peterson in those days, spelled her name the normal way. She was something else. Thought she was hot stuff even before she made it big. Had Scott jumping through hoops. Not the healthiest of relationships, in my opinion. Al and I had mixed emotions when he bought her an engagement ring."

Brook swallowed back a lump. *Engagement ring?*

"He was so proud of that speck of diamond, bless his heart. And then she had to go off to Hollywood and change her last name to Diamond, as if to rub her rejection in his face. He offered to go with her, to help support her, but she said marriage was poison to a budding actress's career. Selfish, selfish girl."

Brook sat down in the nearest chair she could find. As soon as Waverly was out of the picture and the mess with Leslie Stoneburner explained, Tifani Diamond had to be added to the mix. Tifani Diamond! Brook became so overwhelmed with information that she forgot all about her own relationship bomb she had yet to drop.

"Aunt Helen, what are you doing?" Scott interrupted. "Spilling the family secrets?"

"No!" Brook blurted. "I mean, Helen was just telling me what goes into the chili."

Scott looked to his aunt as if to confirm this, but Helen avoided his gaze and occupied herself with another stirring of the pots. He then shifted his attention back to Brook. "Well, some in our family would consider that a secret. I hope you're prepared to take it to your grave."

Brook gave him the best smile she could and crossed her heart.

~

Scott played a Bill Evans jazz CD for the ride home; Brook kept mostly to herself as she listened to the mellow jams. The cloudy sky had sped up dusk's arrival, and thunder rumbled in the distance. When Scott pulled into her driveway, he killed the engine and shifted in his seat to face her. "Here you are."

"Thanks for taking me to the game."

"Thanks for going." He studied her during a break in the music. "Is everything okay? You've been quiet the whole way home."

"I'm fine. Just tired."

"I know, it's been a long day, and you got more than you bargained for. My aunt's a talker."

"I liked Helen. She was nice." *And informative*, Brook thought.

He smiled and after a beat, moved towards her. Brook realized that kissing Scott would be dangerous, and not just because her chicken sausage-beer-cocoa-chili breath could peel the paint off his car. She jerked her head the other way. "I can't do this!"

"What's the matter?"

Brook turned back around. "I'm not ready for this, Scott. It's too much for me right now."

He tilted his head. "Listen, Brook, I know this date wasn't ideal. But we still had a good time, or is it my imagination?"

"That's part of the problem. I like you."

"I like you, too, but I don't see that as a problem. I think we might have something here."

"It has nothing to do with you. It's me."

"Don't feed me that line."

"I'm supposed to be married!"

Scott's eyes became the size of Oreo cookies, and they sat in silence as fat raindrops began splatting on the windshield and roof of the car. After a bit, he shook off his expression of shock. "What? You're married? How-"

"No, I was going to be married. My fiancé bailed out on me two weeks before our wedding day. And I mean that in the literal sense. He took off without any explanation, and no one seems to know where he is. The cruise was…" she couldn't continue.

Scott smacked his palm against his forehead. "Your honeymoon suite wasn't a mixup with the ship."

Brook nodded. "Melissa took his place."

"I had a feeling there was more to the story. Don't I feel like an idiot."

"You shouldn't. You only believed what I told you. I'm sorry I lied."

"Why didn't you tell me the truth?"

"The moment never felt right. But I'm telling you now so you can see where I'm coming from. I'm not ready to get wrapped up in someone's world right now, not until my own is back in order. I've pretended that I'm strong, even convinced myself that I'm okay, but I'm not. I've been kidding myself, and I can't move on until I've gotten some answers." She sighed and swiped a curl out of her face. "Timing is everything in relationships. I wasn't supposed to meet you. Not yet."

He faced her and grabbed her hand. "Then put me on hold. This doesn't have to end."

She pulled away from him. "Yes, it does. I'm still hurting. It's not fair to ask you to fill the void. I need to be alone."

Scott stared out the windshield blanketed with a sheet of rain. "I'm an expert at being alone," he said in a grim tone. "It's highly overrated."

Brook didn't expect Scott to see her side. She couldn't tell him that his past had triggered a sudden mode of self preservation. And he wouldn't understand her need to break free of her pattern of jumping into relationships. The fact that she'd been dumped right before her wedding should provide enough of an explanation.

"Why does it have to be all or nothing?" he went on.

"This is just what I need to do. I need to be me. Just Brook."

"Not all guys are jerks like your ex."

"Scott, let's say I was a friend of yours, or your sister, wouldn't you advise me to be on my own for a while?" He opened his mouth, but nothing came out. Brook grabbed her backpack. "I'm sorry. Maybe-"

"Goodbye, Brook." He reached across her and opened the passenger door. "Have a nice life."

Brook stepped out into the downpour, and Scott slammed the car door shut. She rushed up the crumbling brick path as fast as she could and fumbled with her keys at the door for what felt like an agonizing stretch of time. Once indoors, she looked out the front window and wiped the moisture away from her eyes, a mixture of tears and rain. As Scott pulled out of the driveway, Brook hoped she wouldn't regret letting go of a man who had been angry with her, but still waited around to make sure she made it safe inside the house.

CHAPTER TWENTY

The elevated train sped along the track, its steady rumble accompanied by a clacking at rhythmic intervals. *Ka-chunk, ka-chunk. Ka-chunk, ka-chunk.* As it began its loop through downtown, it dropped its speed to a more leisurely progression, giving Chip Kincaide a glimpse into the office buildings floating past him where nine-to-fivers sat slumped at their desks, pecking away at computers, jabbering on the phone, snacking on processed food. They were encased behind the glass windows as if on display in a natural history museum. *Corporate Life at the Dawn of the Millennium,* what used to be Chip's life, a stifled existence he was glad to be rid of. Shifting his attention over to the map posted just above the doors, he searched the street names for one that intrigued him. Chip had no specific destination in mind. Today, he wanted to roam—whimsy and public transportation his only guides. *Ka-chunk, ka-chunk. Ka-chunk, ka-chunk.*

If Brook had been there with him, she'd have out her *Frommer's* book, pocket map, and detailed notes outlining their itinerary and route. She would know exactly which stops led to which destinations and the best time to hit each place. Not a minute would go to waste. She would be exhausting. Brook Holliday operated at full throttle, a hum of activity buzzing within her at all times, and Chip had no longer been able to keep up. No shrink required to tell him that his recent behavior was an act of rebellion against her, in addition to everyone and everything that had ruled his life. Order. Structure. Deadlines. Obligations.

Quincy. LaSalle. Adams. Madison. The choice was his. *Ka-chunk, ka-chunk. Ka-chunk, ka-chunk.*

Chip glanced a few rows back and spotted a man with droopy, distant eyes sitting slouched and despondent, jaded to his surroundings. Chicago seemed to drain the life out of some people, but not Chip. The city had an energy that fed him. And he relished in the anonymity. Here, nobody observed his every move and the Kincaide name wasn't posted all over town advertising commercial space. Here, Chip could lose himself in the hustle and bustle of a big city, a *real* city with both grit and glitz, a place that had too much attitude to bother with him. And he liked it that way.

Back home, Chip had always had to put on a show, playing the dependable son, the chummy business associate, Brook Holliday's doting lover. Wherever he went, someone seemed to know him or at least know about him. Brook had even complained about it at times. "Can't we go out for a nice quiet evening without any interruptions?" Chip used to like the attention, the connections, the familiar feel of his hometown. But after a while, the recognition had stopped feeding his ego and instead made him feel as if he had gone nowhere, accomplished nothing because it had all come too easily. He had chosen a predictable path, one that had been paved with gold and marked with clear directions.

After graduating from the University of Kansas, Chip's father had "suggested" he explore opportunities beyond the family business, but it was nothing but lip service. Chip knew what was expected of him. He was an only child, the sole heir to the throne, and he wanted to please his parents who had given him everything. Besides, most of his friends had hated their first jobs and were broke all the time so Chip didn't see why he should pass up a lucrative opportunity just because his pride resisted nepotism. And if he hadn't intended on joining the family business all along, why did he major in history with no plans of seeing it through to grad school? His degree had been an indulgence he allowed himself before succumbing to the inevitable.

If only he had been good at his job. No matter how much time he put in, strategizing, networking, and schmoozing, Chip struggled to make his sales quota. It also didn't help that he had to move generic institutional space which lacked the high-profile luster of a revitalization project or prestigious locale. "Paying your dues," his father had called it. "As the boss's son, you have to work twice as hard." Commercial real estate was a bitch of a business to begin with, and Chip didn't need additional impediments working against him. Then the economy started showing signs of decline; companies put the brakes on their expansion plans and tightened their purse strings. Supply became much greater than demand and Chip's sales figures turned into his worst nightmare. And since he was being groomed to guide Kincaide & Associates into the next millennium, his colleagues scrutinized him under a microscope. Some even seemed to watch him with bated breath, ready to pounce the instant he screwed up. Chip did not disappoint. Losing the Krueger deal had been a major blow. If anyone else in his department had his track record, they would have been let go without a second thought and everyone knew it. Chip had kept Brook in the dark about his mistakes and failures at the office. Nobody wanted to marry a failure, especially one that had been given his advantages. So he fired himself and left town.

Sometimes, deep in his conscience, Chip could hear what people were saying about him back in Kansas City.

"What a chicken shit!"

"Who does he think he is?"

"How could he let us all down like this?"

"He must have someone on the side."

Poor Brook. The rumors must be flying all around her. And all she had done was say yes to a wedding proposal from her college sweetheart. Wanting to sweep Brook off her feet, Chip had popped the question at the

Royals Stadium Club. He even arranged for it to be broadcasted on the stadium's Jumboscreen so his family and peers could share in the celebration. When the clock struck midnight and the crowd welcomed in the year 2000, he assumed the position and Brook accepted. She had acted thrilled, jumping up and down with joy, but once the camera left them, Chip saw it. The spark left her eyes. Despite his grand gesture, her expression seemed to say, "This is it?"

And then all that wedding nonsense took over their lives. Appointment after appointment. Decision after decision. Shower after shower. The amount of attention, energy, and planning involved for this one day seemed obnoxious to him. Take their wedding song. He and Brook had discussed for months what to play for their first dance as husband and wife. Chip wanted to go with one of the standards, but Brook balked at the idea, claiming they'd all been done to death, insisting on the unique and unexpected. It eventually became a running joke of theirs to suggest either inappropriate songs with raunchy lyrics like "Erotic City," or syrupy love tunes of the Celine Dion variety. One night, Brook had danced around his loft to "I've Had the Time of My Life," performing moves from the finale number in *Dirty Dancing*, her goofiness providing him with a brief reminder of how carefree and fun she used to be, one of the reasons why he'd fallen in love with her. Chip had played along, imitating Patrick Swayze to the best of his ability, but then she collapsed on his couch and began to sob. "What is wrong with us?!" she screeched. "Why can't we come up with a fucking song?! And YOU! You dance like you're a marionette!" Brook's mood swings had become more erratic and extreme with each occurrence, as if she was in a constant state of PMS. And Chip could now see that her outburst wasn't about their wedding song. Something was amiss in their relationship and neither had the guts to acknowledge it, much less fix it. So they soldiered on, posing as the perfect couple, and as the big day closed in, Chip felt like little more than a checkmark on Brook's to-do list for life. One suitable husband. Check!

Regardless, he shouldn't have treated her like he did, and there were times when his desertion made him nauseous with guilt. But if he'd voiced his concerns and broken off the engagement in a mature, adult manner, they might have convinced themselves to work it out, to go through with the wedding as planned. If not, she would have hated him no more than she surely does now, and even if they had parted on somewhat good terms, it would have been no less painful. It was the amicable breakups that tortured people, the lovers who tried to stay friends, struggling to redefine their relationship, never able to make a clean break. Brook Holliday had good reason to cut him out of her life and despise him forever. In a twisted way, he had done her a huge favor.

Ka-chunk, ka-chunk. Ka-chunk, ka-chunk. Chip had yet to feel the pull to get off the train. The clouds blanketing the city threatened rain with their dark undersides, and he thought it might be better to visit one of the museums that afternoon, wander through a sheltered exhibit instead of the streets. Funny, Brook was always trying to get Chip to go to art galleries and museums back home, and he'd put up such a fight. Now, he couldn't get enough of them.

She would bounce back. Brook would have a good cry, curse his name, rally her spirits, and carry on. Pampered pretty girls like her never stay single for long. Soon, she'd find someone else to be her checkmark, a stable provider with a bright future. She would then wait out her days at the TV station until she had a kid, just like they had once planned. Yes, Brook Holliday would turn out all right in the end. He was sure of it. Someday, he'd call her to apologize properly, and she'd be so involved with her new life she wouldn't even want to hear his explanation.

Chip shifted in his seat and pulled at his skull cap so it covered the tops of his ears. In the window's reflection, he could see tufts of his dark hair sticking out underneath the cap. He had never had long, scraggly hair before. He liked it. And his goatee…it was starting to fill in quite nicely. No more All American Boy. No more pretending.

Kevin Rockhill has been a good influence. The two had drifted apart after school, but Chip got back in touch after seeing Kevin's information listed in a mass e-mail from one of their pledge brothers. Kevin replied the next day, raving about his life in Chicago. He loved his job, dated an array of women, and there was always something to do. It sounded like heaven. The exchange in e-mails continued, and when Chip mentioned, much to his surprise, that he'd like to live in Chicago, Kevin invited him out and offered him a place to crash. When he arrived at his buddy's doorstep, Chip fashioned his story so that the breakup sounded mutual and fortunately, Kevin didn't press him for details. "I always thought Brook had a stick up her ass," he'd commented. Chip aspired to be like Kevin—independent, assured, satisfied. It was time for him to carve out his own path, no matter how selfish it seemed. He wasn't going to be anyone's checkmark. He would be his own exclamation point!

    A nearby passenger howled with laughter as he read the satire of *The Onion*, and a woman glowered at the man before returning to her scribbling in a journal. Chip had been so lost in thought he hadn't realized the train had left downtown and passed the stops for the major attractions. It was just as well though since plump raindrops were now dampening the city. Chip wished he had brought his own diversion, one of his historical biographies to pass the time, but he was happy enough to just take in the city, committing its details to memory as he headed back in the direction from which he came.

CHAPTER TWENTY-ONE

As Brook put the final touches on her design for Danielle's engagement party invitations, Regis Philbin's voice pierced her ears. She looked up at the television set situated on top of the file cabinet in her office, a perk management allowed so its employees could keep apprised of the business. Brook only turned it on to help pass the time and had forgotten all about it until an outburst from Regis broke down her barrier.

The television gods were still hunting for that special perky someone to replace Kathy Lee and that morning's fill-in for the gabfest was a B-list sitcom actress, Simone Something. She had starred in a *Friends* knockoff a few years back which had been cancelled after five episodes. In an obvious attempt to revive her career, Simone went overboard on her co-hosting gig, slapping Regis on the thigh as she cried out, "That is just too much! Too much, Reeg!" Brook actually sympathized with the guy. Regis's pained expression indicated that he longed for the days of hearing about Cody and Cassidy.

Simone flipped back her shiny, flat-ironed hair as if Pantene could be on the lookout for their next spokesperson. "Our first guest today," she said, her eyes moving across the teleprompter, "is one of Hollywood's hottest leading ladies. Her new movie *Über Spy* opens this Friday. Please give a warm welcome to…Tifani Diamond!"

Brook felt her stomach roll over. Even before learning about the connection with Scott, she had never respected the actress's work much. Tifani Diamond's movies represented everything wrong with Hollywood: stereotypical characters, gratuitous sex and violence, corny, uninspired dialogue like, "Let's do this thing." Although she wanted to switch the channel, Brook stayed tuned, curious to learn more about the woman who had once captured Scott Webster's heart. As the audience cheered and the theme music played, Tifani appeared from backstage and strutted towards the hosts as if making her way down the catwalk, criss-crossing her stiletto boots, jutting out her bony hip, sucking in her cheeks.

"So, Miss Diamond," Regis began once air kisses and pleasantries had been exchanged. "You have been one busy lady. This is your fourth movie out this year. Now tell us a bit about *Über Spy*." Regis said the title with a hint of dramatic intrigue.

"Well, Reeg," Tifani cooed. "As Simone mentioned, *Über Spy* opens this Friday, only in theaters."

Regis turned to the camera. "Only in theaters? ONLY IN THEATERS?" His voice raised a few octaves. "Where else would a movie be opening, in a car dealership?"

Tifani let out a forced giggle. "Of course not, but with so many movies going straight to video nowadays, you just want to clarify-"

"Of course you do," Regis interjected, waving her away for taking him too seriously.

Simone placed her hand just above the crease in her cleavage. "As an actress myself, I would kill for a plum role like this. It's such a strong female character. And to work with Chaz Finglehausen..." Simone said the name as if he were Spielberg, "you must have been pinching yourself. I know I would be. It would just be too much to take."

"Yes, when Chaz asks you to be in his movie, 'no' isn't an option," Tifani said.

"And you and Chaz have become a hot item," Simone crowed.

Tifani kept a stoic expression as she rearranged herself in her seat. "I admire Chaz for his creative vision," she said, skillfully sidestepping the nature of their relationship. "Some critics argue that he's a director who puts style before substance, but I promise you," she stiffened her posture, "my character's not just a hot chick running around in leather, beating up the bad guys."

"Sure," Brook quipped.

"It's an action adventure comedy with a feminist twist," Tifani added. "And the fight sequences are pure art. Both women and men will get a kick out of it."

Regis stroked his chin. "Speaking of kicks, I understand you underwent hardcore training for this role."

"Yes, I worked for months with a Kung Fu master and did all my own stunts."

"Yeah, right," Brook mumbled.

"Amazing!" Simone proclaimed. "No wonder you look so incredible. You certainly are cut like a diamond," Simone elbowed Regis and shrieked at her play on words. Tifani gave the co-host a tight smile. After Simone composed herself, she continued. "Seriously though, I remember the media blitz for my TV show and how ker-azy all the hype was. How do you stay grounded with such a circus all around you? Does it ever get to be too much?"

"Well, I'm a Midwest girl at heart," Tifani said. "When I need a reality check, I hop on a plane and go home. But that won't be any time soon. For my next project, which Chaz Finglehausen is also directing, we'll be shooting in London." Brook clicked off the TV, no longer able to bear the sight of Tifani or the rehearsed plugs that comprised daytime talk shows.

She turned her attention back to her notebook of drawings, the only pastime which quieted her mind nowadays, and flipped the pages to a sketch of Sadie Paskahonie reading a book on a park bench, the sophisticate's beloved schnauzer napping at her feet. Sadie had the life. She loved her job designing women's footwear, practiced yoga on a daily basis, knew how to combine the funky with the refined when it came to her clothes, and spent her free time steeping herself in culture. Men didn't leave Sadie Paskahonie. Her admirers worshiped her because she didn't need them to feel complete.

The bleating of Brook's phone interrupted her thoughts. "It's me," her boss sang. "Got time for a pow-wow?"

~

Patricia sported her teal nautical blazer that day and had her flaming red, hot-rolled hair pulled back on one side with a barrette. Brook heard the electronic buzz come from underneath her boss's desk, and the door slammed shut just as she cleared the entrance. She took a seat and perched her pen on her legal pad.

"You won't need to take notes," Patricia said, but Brook kept her pen at the ready as her boss could spit out demands at a frenetic pace and expected her subordinates to keep track. "Seriously, relax. Today we're only here to have a discussion." Brook relented and set her pen down.

Patricia drummed her nails on the edge of her desk. "So, have you taken some time to mull things over?"

"I've, uh, been doing a lot of thinking."

"I don't doubt it. Sometimes you seem like you're off in another land. Makes me wonder what's going on in that brain of yours." Patricia narrowed her eyes as if to bore through Brook's skull with x-ray vision. Even after the moment passed, it left her feeling squeamish. "I asked you in here to continue our dialogue, and today I'd like to address how we can redefine your job."

Brook straightened up. "Really? That's great. I'd love to expand my role and think I could incorporate my skills into more of a marketing function."

Patricia held up a hand like a traffic cop. "Whoa, I can't do that. Marketing isn't a part of my department." She brought back her hand and gave her Breck-styled curls a tousle. "Let me be more clear. We're here to redefine your *approach* to your job." Brook's enthusiasm drained out of her. As if to manufacture some suspense, Patricia swung around in her leather throne and grabbed her Royals baseball from its stand on her windowsill. George Brett, National Baseball Hall of Famer and local sports hero, had signed it himself, and her boss tossed her prized ball as she spoke. "Now, I want you to know that in general, we are very pleased with your job performance. Even during your engagement, you delivered your reports and analyses with efficiency and accuracy. We value your contribution, Brook, but there's always room for improvement and growth."

Brook's forehead began to pound with each smack of the baseball in Patricia's palm.

"Communication is a critical component of any job and…" Patricia paused. "This is not easy for me to say, but it's an area in which you need work. I've listened to how you talk around the office. I've even had a complaint from one of our assistants."

"A complaint about what?"

Patricia stopped tossing the ball and cupped it with both hands. "You tend to come across as…condescending. Clipped. Curt."

Out of all the problem areas Brook could possibly have, a superior attitude would have never crossed her mind. She felt an uneasiness swell inside her as the words rang in her ears. *Condescending. Clipped. Curt.* Another "c" word popped into Brook's head, one she couldn't shake no matter how hard she tried. Just change the "r" in "curt" to a…

"Now these are strong words, I know," Copperhead continued. "But I don't know how else to put it. It's my job as your manager to address both your strengths and weaknesses. Otherwise, I'm doing you a disservice." She set the baseball aside and whipped out a piece of paper with typed bullet points listed on the page. "I've developed some pointers to help soften your demeanor." She handed it over with a self-important air.

Brook glanced at the text, but the tears welling in her eyes made it impossible to read. She wanted to speak, to defend herself, but it felt as if a knot of rubber bands clogged her throat. *I will not cry*, she told herself. *I will NOT cry.*

"If you'd like, I could even arrange to have a consultant come in to coach you."

Somehow, Brook managed to clear her throat, dissolving the lump in her windpipe. "I don't mean to come across that way," she began, her voice teetering on a tremble. "I see myself as someone who works with people, not above or below them. But I do get frustrated when I have to take time out of my day to show one of our assistants how to format a document or where to locate a file. It's their job. They should know that stuff like the back of their hand. I did when I held that position and I was only a temp."

"You're a tough act to follow, Brook. There's no denying that. But you can't expect people to pick up on things as quickly as you."

"I have no problem helping people out. Others have done the same for me. It's when people aren't willing to listen and learn that I lose my patience. Take Harry, for instance. He's a manager and he calls me into his office every other day to ask me how to attach a file to an e-mail. It's a simple point and click function that I've shown him countless times. And why doesn't his own assistant do it for him if it's so tough?"

"Not everyone is receptive to technology. Some of us, including me, remember the days when a desktop meant a block of wood, not a computer screen."

"Don't we have to adapt? And it's one thing to lend a hand every now and then, another to feel taken advantage of. I'm the Research Director. Administrative support is not in my job description."

Copperhead ran her tongue across her bleached fangs. "We're all part of a team here, Brook." She eyed her baseball, picked it back up, and tossed it back and forth between both hands a few times, her actions orchestrated and nauseating.

Brook drew in a shallow breath before speaking again. "How am I supposed to feel like part of a team when I still get mistaken for an intern? Maybe that's why I come across as clipped. It's aggravating to have to clarify who I am and what I do. And it never sinks in."

"Brook, you must learn to assert yourself without damaging people's egos. We all have to do what we can to get along with others." Copperhead failed to catch the baseball this time and it landed in a nest of paperclips, scattering them about the desk. She set the ball back in its stand and swept the area clean. "I know this must be hard to hear. No one likes criticism. But my goal is to help you, to develop you. I want to address this now, while you're still young and shaping your career. To be honest, I could see you running your own business someday. You certainly have the brains and organization for it."

Brook was too upset to appreciate the compliment. Her boss might have good intentions, but she could use her own set of bullet points on effective management techniques. Copperhead continued to ramble on for what felt like an age, her words running together into a stream of ribble-rabble. When she at last dismissed Brook, she closed with one last piece of advice. "Remember, in business, the "us" comes before the "I"."

~

Later that day, after the shock had dwindled, Brook read the dreaded bullet points.

IMPROVING COMMUNICATION AND OVERALL WORK ATTITUDE

> * Rollercoaster your voice. Your tone says more than the words themselves. Tape record yourself, analyzing and modifying your inflection.

* Be aware of your body language. Uncross those arms! Smile! Gesture emphatically to show how passionate you are about your job!
* Once a quarter, do something spontaneous to build relationships with coworkers. Organize a Crazy Hat Day or potluck lunch.
* Step out of your comfort zone. Learn magic tricks and share them with others. Tell a good joke (work appropriate of course). Halloween's coming up, wear a wacky costume!
* Drink coffee instead of tea. It will boost your excitement level!
* Never allow yourself to rest or rust.

Brook blinked a few times and read the words again, the last tip seeming like an out-of-place afterthought, not that any of it made sense. But one thing was for certain. Copperhead wanted Brook to become some hysterical office cheerleader/clown and this so-called advice hit home in a way in which a tornado would. Brook wanted to run to Danielle's office for comfort and consultation, but the whole matter was too embarrassing for her to share with even her closest workmate.

As injury continued to sink in, Brook began to recall more serious work infractions which had taken place within her department. A couple of years back, a senior Account Executive had snuck in a station-restricted ad in the late night rotation, selling air time to a phone sex operation and taking the money under the table, what should have been grounds for an immediate dismissal. And just months ago, Perry had been caught doing the nasty in the conference room. Brook's tone of voice seemed trivial in comparison to these two offenses, yet both sales execs were "top performers" and therefore, subjected to nothing but a stern scolding behind closed doors. Perhaps on a subconscious level, Brook did think she was above all the nonsense at the station. She wadded up the sheet of bullet points and chucked it in the trash.

Right then, none other than Perry Sinclair himself peeked into Brook's office. "Hard at work, or hardly working?" he asked and although he cracked this tired joke all the time, Brook let out an unnatural, bordering on psychotic laugh. Perry appeared surprised at her reaction, but apparently interpreted it as an invitation and stepped in, rocking back and forth on his tasseled loafers. "Hey, you know what I realized?" he asked.

That I'm a total bitch? Brook thought.

"You drink chai tea…" Perry pointed to the empty mug on her desk, then back at himself. "I do tai chi." He bent his knees, leaned to one side, and moved his hand slowly through the air as if wiping it with a sponge. "Funny, huh? What do you call that, you know, when the sounds are switched? Chai tea, tai chi. Is it onomonopeeeya?"

"I don't think so, but I don't dare correct you. I don't want to sound…*condescending*."

Perry cocked his head. "Huh?"

"Nothing."

"Anyway, I didn't know if I had told you I'd taken up tai chi. It's all about being in the moment, Brook. You know, slowing down. You should try it. Maybe you could join me in my class sometime."

Brook was in no mood to go down this road today. "Perry, I don't-"

"Hey, before I forget, what are you going as for Halloween next week?"

"I haven't given it much-"

"I'm thinking of going as Clyde Barrow. People have always told me I look like Warren Beatty, and I love the whole gangster look. But there's got to be a Bonnie to go with Clyde..." he wiggled his brow, "You'd look great in a beret."

"Actually, I know what I'm going as, but I want to keep it a secret." This was a lie, but the image of Brook dressed up as a cheerleader with oversized shoes, painted face, and red rubber nose popped into her head.

"Oh. Okay. Whatever. I was just throwing it out there." He ran his hand underneath one of his suspenders. "Soooo...are you still seeing that guy?"

She hesitated before replying. "Perry, I'm really busy."

"I'll take that as a no."

"Take it however you want." Brook could hear Patricia's words. *Clipped. Curt.*

"I hate to say I told you so, but rebounds never work out," Perry said.

"Then why would you even want to go out with me?"

Perry shrugged. "Just for a good time. Hell, I'm not looking for anything serious. I don't ever intend on getting married again. Death. Trap."

"Okay, but I don't think it's wise to date coworkers," she said.

He stretched out his suspender. "Then quit. Problem solved." Brook couldn't find the words for a response as awkwardness crowded her tiny office. "Come on, I was only joking," Perry added after a few beats. "You know me, always fooling around."

"Yes," Brook replied. "Everyone here knows how you like to fool around."

Perry's assured demeanor evaporated, and he let go of the suspender so it snapped against his starched shirt. Now he was speechless, and it gave Brook pleasure to put him in his place. Served him right for being so damn pushy all the time. But when he left with his tail hanging between his legs, Brook became overcome with wretchedness.

This place seemed to bring out an ugliness in her, and although Brook hadn't meant to patronize her coworkers, she speculated why she might have come across in such a gruff manner. She hated her job. This was no newsflash, but Brook had decided at one point to bite the bullet and stay put, squirrel away her income until she and Chip started a family. She could stick it out because it wouldn't be forever. Even before her plans had changed course, however, her disgruntlement and boredom seemed to have gotten the best of her and affected the way she conducted business. And unlike her boss, she doubted that crazy hats, lame jokes, or coffee would provide a remedy.

CHAPTER TWENTY-TWO

Scott swirled the Guinness around in his pint, the dark stout's lingering cap of foam clinging to the sides of the smudged glass. Although he lived on a Budweiser budget and the cruise had stretched his resources to new limits, Scott treated himself to an import. Despite what all the commercials told him, no watered down domestic could wash away his cares. He took a swig and set the glass down on the bar, using the back of his sleeve to wipe away the trace of froth on his upper lip. If Rebecca were with him, she'd shake her head and hand him a cocktail napkin, preaching that such sloppiness was no way to attract the opposite sex. But his sister had no business being at a smoky Irish bar like O'Dowd's that evening. Rebecca was where she should be, at home with her newborn son. She had more pressing matters on her mind than her younger brother's disappointing love life.

Tug nudged Scott in the arm. "I have good news," he announced.

Scott turned his barstool to face his friend. "Unless you've discovered the secret to time travel so I can redo my date with Brook, I don't want to hear it."

"Man, when you fall for someone, you fall hard. Snap out of it."

Although work and family kept Scott busy, Brook Holliday occupied his thoughts more than he cared to admit. "I'm fine," he said with a dismissive wave of his hand.

"Yeah, your zest for life is infectious." Tug clucked his tongue and shook his head. "I feel for the girl, Scott, I really do. And I was looking forward to meeting that cute sister of hers. But botched wedding aside, I say if she couldn't appreciate the Chiefs game, then good riddance."

Scott rotated his pint on the bar. "It wasn't about the game. I overwhelmed her."

"Give yourself a break. You had no idea what was going on."

Exactly, Scott thought. Some novelist he would make. Writers were supposed to be observant, keenly attune to people's emotions.

"And you were out of practice," Tug continued. "Think how long I've been trying to get you out there."

"So, what's your news?" Scott asked, steering the conversation back to its original subject.

Tug rubbed his hands together as if to warm them. "I've got some big-time work scoop." He glanced over his shoulder, surveying the bar filled with polished mahogany, soft lighting, and hard bodies. With Pendleton Scrubb's offices only a couple of blocks away, it wasn't unusual to see their coworkers out at the Plaza bars right after quitting time. Even though no Scrubbs were in sight, Tug hunched in close and lowered his voice. "This is strictly hush-hush. Kyle Harding is leaving Creative Services. You've always wanted to work in that department and now it looks like there might be an opening."

Scott appreciated the lowdown, but wouldn't allow himself to get excited. "Come on, Tug. You know how the system works. Those jobs are given to the partners' sons and all their pot-smoking, Gameboy-addicted friends. They breed more resentment than ideas." He picked up a matchbox and flipped it around in between his fingers. "Pendleton is a joke. Ad agencies are nothing but jazzed up sweat shops."

"True, but here's the chance to move up from the assembly line and make a difference. And you never know what can happen unless you try.

Your dream job's not going to fall into your lap." Scott recalled the night he met Brook. She had fallen into his lap. Literally. "Hey," Tug said, snapping his fingers and bringing Scott back from the Caribbean. "Listen, agencies are starting to cut back on their media departments. It's like an epidemic. We could get the axe." He dragged his finger across his neck and made a squawking noise. "You should check out this lead. I might even pursue it myself."

"Really?"

"Don't act so shocked. I've got a few ideas brewing in my head."

"No, I just thought you were thinking about going back to school someday."

Tug sighed. "I don't know what I want to do. But I could definitely use a change."

"People are going to be all over this job," Scott said. "The competition will be fierce."

"Somebody's gotta get it. Why not one of us?"

Scott could think of many reasons, but suppressed his cynicism. In actuality, Tug probably stood a better chance at getting a Creative Services job than he did. Although his friend griped about work as much as anyone else, he hadn't pissed off some key players like Scott had. "Thanks for the heads up," he said. "You're a true pal."

"No problem. But my generosity ends here. Have to watch out for my own interests. Let's just hope there is a position and not a..." Tug didn't finish as his eyes drifted upwards. Scott turned around to see what had captured his friend's attention.

It was her, striking a pose in a black leather catsuit. Tifani Diamond then gave a swift kick to a bald guy wearing a floor-length fur. Of course it wasn't Scott's former beloved kicking ass, it was the character from her latest movie, another classic titled something like *Chainsaw Chicks*. After the clip, the E! Channel cut to various shots of the actress fanning her feathers on the red carpet, her auburn hair always pulled back to accentuate her dimpled cheeks and chiseled jaw. "Yeah, suck in those cheekbones, sweetheart," Scott mumbled. He flagged down Arnie the bartender and pointed to the television stationed above the bar. "What's with this crap?"

Arnie glanced up at the TV and shrugged. "I thought it was on ESPN."

"It's not. Change it," he barked.

"In a minute," Arnie shot back, suddenly overtaken by a barrage of women demanding Godiva martinis.

"Easy there," Tug told Scott. He leaned forward and adjusted his eyeglasses. "I'm digging her."

"She's such a bad actress," Scott spat.

They watched as Tifani Diamond sat in front of a life-sized cardboard cutout of herself performing a high-kick in the catsuit, the animated version of her talking and gesturing with the self-importance of someone who had just discovered the cure for AIDS. "You see," Scott continued, "this is the part where the actress comes off as all smart and savvy about her movie, regurgitating garble her publicist fed her. Then she tries to convince us, Mr. Joe Public, how down-to-earth she is, that in spite of her glamorous life, her favorite thing to wear is just a plain t-shirt and jeans. That's supposed to keep her accessible to us commoners."

Tug downed the last of his Black and Tan. "Don't care. She's hot," he said, dabbing his goatee with a napkin. "And look how high she can kick. Man, I bet she's dynamite in bed."

"Hardly," Scott said with a snort. Tug shot him a puzzled look, and Scott was tempted to spill the beans on his history with the actress, but knew if he did so, his friend would bombard him with questions Scott didn't feel like answering. "I mean, you'd have those jutting bones coming at you," he added. "She could put an eye out."

"I'd take my chances. Did you know she's from around here? I forget which place, Blue Springs, Liberty…"

"Independence," Scott said.

"That's it. Good memory."

"How can you forget? The local news runs a profile on her every time she blows her nose. And have you ever heard her speak? She's as dull as a broadcast on C-SPAN."

"I'm not interested in her rhetoric," Tug said, his mouth hanging open as scenes from Tifani's latest action flick flashed across the screen.

"Come on, a woman doing kung fu in a catsuit and stilettos?" Scott asked. "Is that all Hollywood can give us, a dated male fantasy?"

"I call it a classic male fantasy," Tug countered. "But I guess you touchy writer types have higher standards. Otherwise, I'd be questioning both your manhood and sanity right now."

Scott turned away from the TV and swallowed some beer, but he about choked it up when none other than Waverly Marks and Leslie Stoneburner came through the front door. Together. How could it be that all these mistakes from his past are coming back to haunt him just minutes apart? The pair acknowledged Scott from across the way, gave him a collective finger wave, and then Waverly whispered something to Leslie before they broke out into chortles and slithered off in the other direction.

Tug had noticed them as well. "What are they, twelve years old?"

Scott felt like the bar had shrunk to the size of a cupboard. He gulped down the last few swallows of his Guinness and settled his tab, his friend understanding the sudden need to leave.

~

Back at home, the dark shell of Scott's apartment reflected his inner mood, at least until he spotted the blinking red light on his answering machine, a beacon of hope, like the lighthouse in *The Great Gatsby*. Maybe Brook had called, wanting to give him another chance. He crossed the room in two strides and hit the replay button, but got nothing but a click and dial tone. Switching on the kitchen light, he checked the caller ID log, but the call came up as a blocked number. Had it been Brook? If so, why didn't she want him to know about it? He didn't dare call her to find out. He knew she needed her space.

Scott tuned in to the jazz show on the local NPR station and thinking back to the job tip Tug had passed along, booted up his obsolete Macintosh and accessed his résumé, a document he hadn't looked at since interviewing for his job. Scott reviewed his credentials. Grade point 3.5 (rounded figure). Ad Club member (meaningless organization). Social Coordinator for the Langley Theatrical Guild (Cookies and Punch Provocateur for his Drama II class). Scott chuckled at his past efforts to pad his résumé and began typing his revisions. He struggled, however, for the best words to describe his job. Media Buyer: Paper Pusher, Number Cruncher, Subservient Slave, The Man's Number One Bitch. Scott delved deep into his brain for more professional and politically correct phrasing to help his cause. His qualifications barely took up a page and he narrowed the margins ever so slightly to fill in the blank space, disheartened that he hadn't come that far since his days at the University of Missouri-Kansas City. Nonetheless, it felt good to take action. Pursuing this lead would mean he'd be committing himself to a career at Pendleton Scrubb, and Scott harbored some reserve about that concept, but it was time for him to step up to the plate, become a bona fide adult and make some real dough. Perhaps he should also ask himself whether he liked writing, or simply the romantic *idea* of being a writer. Maybe if he focused more on attainable goals instead of getting caught up in dreams, he could make something of his career. Even if the lead didn't pan out at Pendleton, he'd have his résumé ready to go and could possibly move to another ad agency since sometimes switching shops was the only way to get ahead. The growing alliance between Waverly and Leslie further solidified Scott's determination to alter his current situation.

Adding one last trumped-up phrase to describe his contribution to the company, Scott saved his résumé a final time and shut down his computer. To reward his work, he popped off the top to a bottle of Boulevard Pale Ale, but when he took a drink, an interesting thought occurred to him. Just as Scott was ready to toss out the notion of becoming a novelist, it had required some of his best efforts in creative writing to take him down another path. Convinced he was heading in a more prosperous direction, it brought him satisfaction to finally put his skills to good use.

CHAPTER TWENTY-THREE

Water trickled down the river stone fountain while music that sounded like the score from *The Joy Luck Club* played softly on a stereo. If only a calming water feature and songs from the Orient could diminish the certain pain that Tifani Diamond would have to endure during her treatment. Dimly lit in orange hues, the room glowed like the inside of a lava lamp and Tifani wondered how Frances, her specialist for the task at hand, could possibly see what she was doing. She inhaled a deep breath as the woman applied warm goo to an area Tifani normally required at least three dates and a stiff drink for someone to gain access to. She reminded herself that she was in the hands of a professional and hoped that the exorbitant amount of money she had to shell out for her day at Sorenti Spa was based more on expert skill than its high-profile status among the London elite.

"Now here we go, love," Frances said.

Tifani bit down on her knuckle and waited for Frances to let it rip. SHWEEET!

Holy Mother of Pearl.

Upkeep was a bitch. No matter how many times she'd been waxed, Tifani still couldn't take the pain, the anticipation of it just as tortuous as each rip of the cloth strips. She gulped back a scream, only allowing herself a pathetic whimper. One had to act refined in such a posh establishment, especially a movie star with a public image to protect.

It was Chaz who had a problem with hair. This day of blissful treatments was for her, but the Brazilian was for him. He wanted Tifani slick and smooth all over, groomed in places no one but he would see, even though Chaz sometimes went days without a shower. Whenever she complained about his funk, he'd scoff at her, tell her that Americans were too obsessive about cleanliness and germs. He was going through one of his dirty cycles right now. He never took a shower during an opening weekend. It had brought him good luck when he directed his first big-budget picture and he had adopted the practice ever since.

Tifani, on the other hand, chose to cocoon herself in the spa while the rest of her camp fretted over receipts and dollars. She had done her part—the junkets, interviews, and photo shoots. Now, it was up to the American public. And that was all Hollywood cared about, the good ol' U.S. of A. If the picture didn't do well in the States, it was a failure, even if it recouped its expenses overseas.

Tifani was relieved to be on the other side of the Atlantic. After wrapping up the U.S. installment of their grueling publicity tour, she and Chaz flew to London where Tifani's assistant had secured them a flat in Notting Hill. There, they were taking a break before kicking off the European leg of the tour, giving Tifani the time to begin her voice training for Chaz's next picture in which she'd be speaking with a British accent. Watch out, Gwenyth!

SHWEET!

Jiminy Christmas.

Christmas. Not too far away. She and Chaz would be spending the holidays in Prague this year. More travel. Tifani loved spanning the globe, but she did grow homesick every now and then, for her real home, not her place in Beverly Hills that sat empty half the time. And no matter where they went, the Hollywood bubble seemed to surround them, one of the pitfalls of dating within her profession. Chaz was a cutting-edge and successful director, but could be so wrapped up in himself and his work that Tifani sometimes felt invisible, at least until she did something to his displeasure and he promptly brought it to her attention. Just the other day she had let egg yolk dry on a dirty dish, and he'd acted as if it was a crime against humanity. "It will take a jackhammer to get this off! I will not have the hotel staff suffer for your carelessness!" So he shattered the dish instead, slicing his hand when he gathered the shards. And people thought actors could be over the top. Directors were far worse in her opinion. They like to be in control, puppet masters of their own little universe.

SHWEET!

God Bless Santa Claus.

Tifani clenched her fists and gasped, glad she'd scheduled the waxing for her first appointment since it'd require a deep massage to work out the tension which intensified with each application. By day's end, Tifani will have been waxed, plucked, scrubbed, dipped, wrapped, baked, soaked, tinted, tanned, and rubbed down until her muscles felt like jelly. She planned to leave the spa floating on a cloud and looking as luminescent as an angel. Her mind would be oatmeal, unable to even fathom the concept of box office numbers.

Purgatory Patrol had been Tifani's big break, a dark action thriller that had become a surprise cult classic. It was also the beginning of her career beating up the bag guys in tight leather catsuits. Soon after her success, she quit her ensemble television gig and landed more high profile roles in big budget pictures—a couple of sci-fi films, a video game adaptation, and her latest, *Über Spy*, what the studio hoped to be the next great franchise. But Tifani had yet to get out of those suffocating catsuits. And an actress could only get away with the look for so many years. She planned to break out of her rut with her and Chaz's next collaboration, *A Pocket Full of Posies*, a tragic period piece set during the years of The Great Plague and Great Fire of

London, a risky departure for them both. Tifani welcomed the challenge. She had been waiting her whole career for a meaty role she could sink her teeth into and now she had one that would launch her to a whole new level. She would show her critics that she had the acting chops, establish herself as a serious actress with depth and range.

SHWEET!

Mommy…I want my mommy.

A watery bubble formed over Tifani's eyes and spilled out onto her cheeks. If only she could have summoned such waterworks for her pivotal scene in *Draco's Dungeon* she wouldn't have had to use fake tears. She had felt like such a failure for having to rely on eyedrops, the old Hollywood standby.

SHWEET!

"No more!" Tifani barked. "I've had enough!"

"Hold still, love. We're almost finished. If you can do all those karate moves, you can finish your waxing."

"But that's all pretend!"

"Leg up!"

SHWEET!

FuckshitfuckshitfuckshitFUCK!!!!!

"See, all done. Now that wasn't that bad."

Tifani felt as if flames had flared up in her groin and vowed to never get waxed again, even though she knew she'd be back once bristles began to show. She sat up and covered herself with the white sheet, not wanting to see her prepubescent baldness. Frances offered her a steaming cup of herbal tea. Tifani took a sip and its essence drifted up her nose, a potent mixture of lemons and fresh cut grass. Although Tifani had embraced the English ways, including a blossoming obsession with tea, the warm beverage did little to soothe the sting.

CHAPTER TWENTY-FOUR

Brook pulled on her tattered Levi's, relieved that they still fit her as old jeans seemed to have a way of shrinking in the closet. Her favorite pin-striped oxford, one of her dad's office tossaways, had softened with wear through the years, but it would still do. Her artist's apron completed the ensemble. All items were splattered with hardened blotches of color, remnants of Brook's past creations. She gathered a bundle of paintbrushes and filled her pockets, then secured her old paint palette under her arm. Before going to work, she shifted the beret on her head so it was slightly askew.

"Nice," Danielle commented in the break room at the office. "You look like you're on your way to Montmartre."

"Don't I wish."

Dressed in a dove grey pant suit, Danielle wore a magician's hat on her head which Brook gave a tap with one of her brushes as if to make a rabbit appear. "I know, it's lame," Danielle said. "But this is as far as I can take Halloween. I'm meeting with a big client today, and he's got to take me seriously." Danielle began to elaborate on the details of her upcoming pitch, but stopped short when a man's voice carried down the hall. Someone was belting out a "Gar-oovy, baby!" which could have shattered what few windows they had at the office. Both women visibly stiffened.

"Is that?" Brook asked.

"Who else," Danielle replied.

Perry Sinclair apparently couldn't find a Bonnie to go with his Clyde so he showed up as Austin Powers, giving everyone the peace sign as he strutted down the hall. "Oh, bee-have!" he purred at one of the assistants.

Danielle put her hands to her ears. "Please, make it stop."

"You're the magician. Just say Abracadabra."

As if he'd heard Danielle's plea, Perry snapped out of character once he saw Brook and marched over to her. "Hey, you've got a beret! You could have been my Bonnie!"

"Forgot I had it," Brook claimed. "I buried it when Monica Lewinsky ruined the look." He eyed her with a suspicious scowl.

"Your wig's on crooked," Danielle told Perry, diffusing the moment with a welcome distraction. He adjusted the mousy-brown synthetic lump of hair, only to make matters worse, but neither of the women suggested another correction.

Later that afternoon, KCXT's third floor was summoned to the black and orange festooned conference room for the department's Halloween party, as well as Barb Myer's twenty-fifth anniversary celebration. A stout, full-figured woman who wore a lot of jumper dresses with socks (including that day as she had not dressed up), Barb worked in Traffic, not those who reported on street conditions for the news, but the overtaxed workers who cleared and placed the ads for air. To kick things off, pictures were passed around of similar gatherings over the past twenty-plus years, and Brook was astounded at not only some of the hairstyles, but also how many people were still in the same jobs. Such visual evidence of corporate stagnation depressed her, and she didn't contribute much to the party, keeping mostly to herself as she picked at her cake and ice cream until the latter had turned into a puddle on her plate.

"Everything okay?" Danielle asked her. "You look like your computer just crashed."

"My brain's fried," Brook said. "Been swimming in numbers all day." Danielle gave her a sympathetic nod.

Brook then glanced across the room at Patricia decked out as the Wicked Witch of the West, her face painted the shiny color of a green bell pepper. Amusing herself with a game of Remember When with some of the senior staff, her boss pounded the table with her fist as she threw her head back in a cackle.

"They didn't even get a new conference table," Brook added in a hushed tone.

"Huh?" Danielle asked.

"Perry got naked right here where everyone's now eating cake." She nodded to where the others were sitting, Brook and Danielle having positioned themselves on the margins of the room.

"They should have replaced the table. The office was way overdue for one anyway."

"Please, you know how cheap the station is. Look at this party."

"I know. Perry should have paid for it. It would have served him right for defacing company property."

Danielle shrugged in a you're-right-but-what-can-you-do manner.

After a half hour crawled by, it came time for Barb's gift, and she opened her package with great attention and care, as if to save the wrapping paper for another use. As she did so, a handful of coworkers resumed with their gabbing. The room fell silent, however, when Barb pulled out a fire engine red gumball dispenser from the box. It was made out of metal and glass, as opposed to plastic, probably top of the line among its kind, but it was a gumball machine. A gumball machine. And everyone knew where it had come from…the dark recesses of the sales closet, promotional junk kept on hand to give out to clients. A hasty afterthought at best. This was how KCXT marked twenty-five years of dedicated hard work, over fifty thousand hours of an employee's life, not including overtime. It might as well have had a big

SCREW YOU! stamped on the globe instead of the station's logo. Patricia hadn't even provided any gumballs to fill it.

"Oh," Barb noted in a deflated voice.

"It will be a nice decoration for your desk," Patricia said.

"Um, I don't really have the space, but I guess I'll figure something out."

"You know, we would have liked to go all out for you," Patricia added. "But we're having to scale back around here."

"It's the thought that counts," Barb said, her ears turning as red as the paint on her gift. Setting the gumball dispenser aside, she helped herself to another hunk of cake and stabbed it with her plastic fork.

At quitting time, Brook happened to follow Barb out of the building and could overhear her talking to one of her Traffic colleagues. "I have to think of the benefits," Barb said. "We have health, dental, a 401(k). Not everyone gets that."

"It was a slap in the face!" the other spat. "They could have at least given you a gift certificate to the Plaza. Those sales guys get them all the time and for what? Doing their job that they get paid too much to do in the first place. Patricia didn't even bother to organize your own party. She pulled that combo bullshit, tossing it in with Halloween. If I were you, I'd throw that damn thing through her office window. And make sure she's in there when you do it."

Barb let out a bark of a laugh, but then batted away the suggestion. "No, I set it out in the break room. That way, everyone can help themselves to a gumball when they feel like it." She crossed her arms on the shelf of her bosom. "But I'll be damned if I'm going to be the one to fill it."

The following morning, Brook arrived early at the station. By the time everyone else arrived, they found that the gumball dispenser had been filled to capacity. Someone had also set out a Dixie cup full of shiny pennies.

CHAPTER TWENTY-FIVE

The sound of a gunshot jerked Brook out of her sleep. She waited a moment and listened, thinking she must have been dreaming, but after hearing another crack, followed by a loud thud, her heart began to pound in her ears. Just then, a dark figure charged through the bedroom door, cloaked head to toe in some form of wrapping, and Brook let out a shriek, convinced that Death had come to claim her.

Her sister screamed as well and drew back the blanket from her head.

"For the love of God, Mel, don't scare me like that!"

"Who else would I be?"

Brook kept her misconception to herself. "Nevermind. What the hell's going on out there?"

"It's the trees." Melissa pulled back the comforter and joined Brook in bed. "They've iced over. And now the power's out so we've got to hunker down and create as much heat as possible."

"I thought we were only supposed to get a little freezing rain."

"Forget that. This is an ice storm. So much for KCXT's accurate forecast."

They remained quiet for a short time as pellets beat against the window. "It's only November," Brook noted. "It was in the fifties just a couple of days ago."

"Take it up with Mother Nature."

Brook pictured the frenzy that would be taking place at the TV station, the late shift scrambling to assemble a special report. ICE STORM: 2000. She was glad to be cozy in bed with her sister. But with the encroaching chill and intermittent snap, crackle, and pop of the tree limbs outside, she dozed at best for the remainder of the night.

When they rose to assess the damage, the shade trees, a source of pride for Brookside, had turned their street into a disaster zone with piles of fallen and splintered branches. A Bradford Pear blocked their driveway, having just missed Melissa's Saab when it split in two and toppled to the ground. Trapped in their drafty, old house for the day, the two bundled up in layers of winter gear to combat the cold. Fortunately, the gas stove still functioned so they could heat up whatever food they had on hand and make hot beverages. For an afternoon treat, Brook prepared some cocoa and carried the mugs into the living room where she and Melissa spiked them with rum before nestling in on the couch with their books in front of the roaring fire and an array of flickering candles.

After a few sips though, Melissa slammed her Grisham shut. "You know those California yahoos from the cruise are probably riding bikes on the beach right now. Lucky bastards. I wish you were a guy."

Brook gazed up from her book, wondering where this random comment was coming from. "Oh?"

"Then this would at least be incredibly romantic." She gestured toward the army of flames.

"Sorry to disappoint you, Mel. And since when do you care about romance?"

"Hey, I'm a sucker for candles as much as the next girl." Melissa added more rum to her mug and slurped her drink. "I'm bored," she whined, kicking her feet under the pile of blankets. "The one time I leave my work at the office and we get iced in."

Brook ignored her sister and returned to reading *Le Divorce*. About halfway down the page though, a hand seized her ankle and even through thick thermal socks, it felt as if spiders on speed danced on the bottom of her foot. Brook convulsed with involuntary giggles and struggled to wriggle free from Melissa's evil claws. "Stop…tickling," she gasped. Her sister's screwed up face only took on a more sinister look as the intensity of the attack grew.

Desperate, Brook reached behind her for a pillow and launched it across the couch, hitting Melissa in the head and knocking off her pompom stocking cap. The tickling ceased and her sister's normally perfect, smooth hair stood on end. Brook erupted with laughter and the pillow came soaring back at her, knocking her in the face. She bent over and faked a nosebleed, but Melissa didn't take the bait as Brook had done the same bit a thousand times when they were kids, and another pillow slammed into the side of her head. Both girls then scampered out from under the covers and the tussle escalated into a full-scale war. Off came the robes, mittens, socks, anything that could be used as a weapon. As they walloped each other silly with their scarves, the fringe of Melissa's caught fire on one of the candles and they both screamed as the cashmere ignited. Melissa doused the flames with her cocoa, but the fire swelled. "Shit! I forgot about the rum!" Grabbing the scarf by its safe end, she ran into the kitchen, threw it in the sink, and turned on the faucet. Melissa looked on the verge of tears when she brought the sopping, singed piece of cashmere back into the living room, but both were soon shaking with a fit of hysterics.

After calming themselves down, the sisters fell back onto the couch to catch their breath. As silly and childish as their display was, Brook experienced a cathartic release, as if she had just laughed off twenty pounds. Moments later, she noticed the fading embers of the fire and went over to add a log and stoke the flames with the poker. Once it came back to life, Brook got an idea and shuffled off to her room.

"Is that what I think it is?" Melissa asked when Brook returned carrying a scrolled piece of paper, her engagement ring secured around its middle. Taking a seat on the arm of the couch, she slipped off the ring and unrolled the sheet now soft with wear, Chip's handwriting scrawled across their watermark monogram.

"I thought I was going to explode when I found this."

"I remember. You would have shattered every piece of your china if I hadn't stopped you."

Brook used the corner of her sleeve to wipe the fresh dampness off her cheek. "I was so consumed with rage that I didn't notice something else going on."

"What was that?"

Brook paused before speaking. "I felt…relief. There was only a hint of it, but it was there. I didn't have to be Mrs. Chip Kincaide. I was off the hook. But I was so wrapped up in the anger, betrayal, and humiliation, the relief didn't even register." Brook crossed the room to the mantle and watched the flames intermingle with one another.

"Do it," Melissa urged. "You can't pass up a poetic moment like this."

Brook crumpled the note in her hand and let go, watching it catch fire and disintegrate. She thought the gesture would bring her a satisfying sense of comfort, yet she still felt a needling sense of discontentment. Brook opened her palm cupping the engagement ring, an emerald-cut diamond with a yellow gold band, and wondered if tossing it in would bring greater reward.

"Bad idea," Melissa said as Brook held the ring out over the flames.

"Right." Brook closed her hand and dropped her arm at her side.

Drawing in a breath, she turned to face her sister. "I cheated on him." For once, Melissa was at a loss for words; the only sound was the crackle of the fire. "And I'm not talking about a kiss or heavy petting. It was…it was only the one time. It happened a couple of weeks before Chip and I graduated from college. I'd gotten a no-thanks letter from a job interview at an insurance company. I didn't even want the damn job. I went more for the practice, but I still freaked out about the rejection. I hopped in my car and drove into Topeka all alone. I don't know why I went there of all places. I was consumed by this need to get away and break out my shell. Anyway, I spotted the capital from the highway and ended up in some bar across the street. Don't even remember the name of the place. Don't even remember *his* name. I snuck out of his apartment around four in the morning. Then I went to a Denny's and cried over a stack of pancakes."

"Shit," Melissa said, breaking the silence that followed. "Sounds like something *I* would do. It's so out of character for you."

"I know. By the time I was back in Lawrence, it already seemed like it had happened to someone else, and I pretended that it did. Chip never knew a thing, but in the end, it caught up with me, I guess. I wouldn't go unpunished." Brook sent her sister a resolute look to quell any argument otherwise. She didn't want to debate the matter to death; she just wanted it off her chest. "I've never told anyone, and I don't ever want to talk about it again." Brook deposited the ring into the pewter dish on the coffee table and sat back down on the sofa. "My dark little secret is back in the vault, and there it stays."

~

By Monday, a neighbor had taken a chainsaw to the Bradford Pear and cleared the driveway. Kansas City returned to normal fall conditions and began to thaw, creating a soupy mixture of de-icing solution and muddy sand on the streets. By the time Brook pulled into the KCXT parking lot, the mess had turned her Jetta into a Pollack painting. Running behind schedule, she parked her car in haste and shoved her stuff under her arm before scrambling out of the driver's seat. "Bad weather is no excuse for tardiness," Patricia liked to say. "It's business as usual." Despite her hurry, Brook had to take care as she traversed the asphalt still treacherously slick in spots. As she did so, a chunk of ice fell off a tree branch and landed on the roof of the station's carport, sounding like a clap of thunder as it hit the corrugated aluminum sheltering upper management's Mercedes, BMWs, and Lexuses. The underlings, along with their Hondas, Toyotas, and Saturns, were exposed to the elements. It bothered Brook to feel like she needed a hard hat to survive the trek to her job, and she quickened her pace as fast as possible without slipping and breaking an arm.

Brook came to a stop, however, when she heard something hit the ground and felt her load grow lighter. She turned around and spotted her steno notebook of sketches lying open in a pile of sludge. It must have slipped out of her leather satchel she now realized she'd crammed under her arm upside down. Rushing over, she bent down and picked it up. To her relief, only the cover and some of the corners of the pages had been soiled. The integrity of her art remained intact. They were only sketches, but to see them ruined would have been an upsetting start to the day. Brook slid the notepad back into the side of her bag and gave the outside a pat, as if to reassure her drawings of their safety. Grabbing the handles properly this time, she straightened up, but just as she stepped forward, an icicle spear fell from the sky, crashing on the sidewalk a few yards ahead of her and shattering to bits.

Brook turned as rigid as a corpse, and a chill ran through her that could have refrozen the entire city. With no trees overhead, she knew the ice had plummeted who knows how many stories off the sky-high TV tower, The Needle. It would have been a crushing blow. If she hadn't stopped to pick up her sketches…Brook had read about such freak accidents, icicle daggers killing on contact. She looked around to see if anyone had seen her near brush with death, but the lot was deserted, eerily muted and calm, as if she had lost her hearing from the shock. Somehow, she managed to put one foot in front of the other and with building momentum, rushed towards the station.

Still rattled with aftershock by the time the elevator reached Brook's floor, she dumped her belongings in her office and went to the kitchen to make herself a calming cup of chai tea. She filled one of the KCXT's promotional mugs with water, and as she waited for it to heat in the microwave, Barb Myer's red gumball dispenser caught her attention. As Brook approached, her eyes zeroed in on its globe where she pictured her future, one where she had grown old in her job, her face sour with bitterness, her hair a Brillo pad of wiry gray curls. Stooped over, she'd scrape her orthopedic shoes on the industrial carpet as she delivered her ratings reports. "Hot off the presses!" she'd announce in her granny voice, but none of her colleagues would acknowledge her. Shaking off the image, Brook's vision morphed back into the handful of gumballs that remained in the dispenser, candy that would probably stay put until they were rock solid as no one had bothered to replenish the Dixie cup with pennies. And that was all Brook needed to see.

Less than a half hour later, she marched into Patricia's office and squared herself in front of the desk. Her boss flicked up her eyes from her pile of papers. "Now's not a good time."

Brook almost defaulted to an apology and a promise to return later, like she always did when Patricia blew her off, but not today. "I need to speak with you. It's urgent."

Copperhead whacked her pen down on the desk. "I know about the ice."

"Yeah, but-"

"What do you expect me to do, climb up the tower with a hair dryer? It's out of my hands. And people should be used to it by now. It happens every year. Anything else?"

Brook felt all the better about what she had come to do. "I'm leaving," she announced, her tone firm with commitment.

A pair of headlight eyes peered up at her. "Pardon?"

Brook presented her resignation letter. "Here's my two week's notice."

Copperhead snatched the paper out of her hands, sucking in air through her fangs as she read the text. A flush of scarlet began to spread across her face, bringing out the harsh, brassy tones of her dyed hair. After a span of quiet, she set the sheet down on her desk and folded her hands on top of it. "Do we need to conduct another assessment, Brook? If you're not happy here, maybe we can do something about it. Is it the money?"

Knowing she was one of the lowest paid Research Directors in the market, it incensed Brook that it took the threat of her walking out for the issue to finally be addressed. "There's more to it than money," she said.

"Did one of the other stations lure you away? Was it Gerald over at KTLU? That jerk makes sport out of snatching my staff away from me."

"No one is snatching me away," Brook insisted, but Copperhead sent her a suspicious scowl. "You see, an icicle nearly killed me out in the parking lot, making me question what the hell I was doing with my life. I process TV ratings for people who only talk to me when they want something. And it bores the hell out of me. Maybe I come across as condescending because I'm forever stifling a yawn. So eat my dust, bee-yatch!"

Brook would have liked to go off like this, but knew to never burn bridges. "I'm taking your advice from our last pow-wow. Never allow yourself to rest or rust."

"I think you misunderstood my meaning."

"I'm rusting here. It's time for me to move on."

"Doing what?" her boss spat, a shower of spittle raining on the resignation letter.

"Um..."

"Don't tell me you don't have a backup plan."

"I'll come up with something."

"This is a bad time for you to leave. We're in the middle of the November sweep."

"It'll be over by the time my two weeks are up."

Copperhead pursed her lips before speaking. "I'm not going to allow that. It's not your leaving that troubles me, Brook, but your vagueness. You could have something cooking for the competition and I can't have you sneaking around here, gathering information for whoever you're going to work for."

"I told you, I don't have another job. This is something I decided this morning."

"No one's that foolish to quit a good job without another opportunity lined up. If you haven't noticed, the economy isn't going gangbusters anymore. I'm surprised at you, Brook. You have more sense than this."

Brook started second guessing herself, thinking about the security and benefits she would be leaving behind. Then that icicle would crash in front of her all over again.

"I tried my best to make something of you," her boss went on. "I made an investment in your career and this is the thanks I get."

Brook crossed her arms and said nothing.

"Fine," Copperhead clipped. "You'll get paid your two weeks, but I want you cleared out of your office by lunch. You'll need to drop off your ID badge at Human Resources and I'll arrange to have Security see you out of the building."

"Nice to know that you trust me."

"I'm watching out for the station. It's nothing personal, it's business." She returned to her paperwork, acting as if no one was even in the room. Brook longed for something more, a note of sentiment, expressed appreciation for her work, happy wishes for her future, anything to kill the tension and bring the conversation to the conclusion it deserved. Brook had dreamt of quitting her job many times, imagining the scenario in hundreds of ways. Never did it end in such an anticlimactic fashion. On the plus side, her boss's paranoia had given Brook two extra weeks of paid vacation. With that realization, she found that as she left Copperhead's lair for the last time, she was finally able to don that sunny smile at the office. No crazy hat or magic trick required.

~

As marvelous as it felt for Brook to leave her mind-numbing job, quitter's remorse caught up with her at home that night. Slouched in one of the chairs at the dining table, she only stirred to refill her glass with more Shiraz. Brook didn't even notice when her sister walked in the door, but came to when Melissa shook her by the shoulder.

"What is with you?" she asked, picking up the almost empty wine bottle. "Please don't tell me you're regressing in your recovery. How long have you been sitting here?"

Instead of responding, Brook slid down further in her seat.

Melissa pried the wine glass from her hand and set it aside. "What's going on?"

"I called my own freakin' pow-wow."

"Huh?"

"I quit my job."

Her sister shrugged off her trench coat and draped it over a chair. "Good. You had no viable career path at that place."

Brook bolted up. "How can you be so casual? I. Quit. My. Job. What am I going to do? I have no plan. I have no savings." Melissa arched an eyebrow. "Well, I do have some money put away," Brook admitted. "Not much after our trip, but one's supposed to have three months of expenses saved before they do something like this. And that was back when we had a healthy economy." She put her hand to her forehead. "What have I done?"

"Something you should have done a long time ago. Patricia talked *at* you and gave you ridiculous guidance. I would never have put up with her bullshit." She sat down and slapped the table. "So what was the straw that broke the camel's back?"

Brook explained what happened: the icicle spear, her life flashing before her, Patricia's reaction to her resignation, security ushering her out of the building by the elbow.

"That doesn't surprise me," Melissa said. "Businesses guard their documents and secrets like they're the CIA. But you're getting paid for those two weeks, right? If they try to stiff you, I'll be all over them."

"I'll get my money," Brook said. "But thinking back, I should have waited until January to quit. I could have gotten another week's paid vacation. And no one's hiring right now with the holidays coming up, except places at the mall. I didn't think this through."

"Sometimes you have to take a leap of faith." Melissa gave Brook's arm a reassuring squeeze. "Don't worry, I'll help you. I'm an estate attorney. It's not like I need your rent money."

"I don't want to be a charity case."

"You can keep the house tidy. That'll earn your keep."

"I do that now."

"So we step it up a notch. Maybe you can learn to cook."

"Maybe," Brook said. Although she wanted to be strong, tears filled her eyes.

"Hey, I know you're having a tough year," Melissa said. "But look at the silver lining here. You're now free of not only a lousy fiancé, but also a dead-end job. I'm proud of you. Not everyone could do what you did today."

"That's because they have common sense."

"But you have courage. Too many people spend their lives working in monotonous jobs they can't stand, yet they choose to be there. I see it all the time with my clients. They are so beaten down, they can't even enjoy their money."

Brook swiped away her tears with her finger, collecting her thoughts before telling Melissa about another decision she had made that day. "I'm going to stay at Mom and Dad's for a few weeks, extend my Thanksgiving visit."

Her sister dropped her gaze.

"What?" Brook asked.

Melissa met her eyes. "That's fine, Brook, but I know Mom. With you out of a job, she's going to try to get you to move back to Tulsa. She'll probably greet you at the door with a stack of want ads and the phone numbers of all the single sons of her bridge friends."

Brook chuckled, knowing Melissa wasn't too far off the mark. "I won't tell her until we get there."

"Don't stay too long. Remember, I'm offering free rent as well."

"You just don't want to lose your housekeeper."

Melissa knitted her brow. "Is that what you think, that I'm that shallow? That hurts."

Brook regretted her jab. Sometimes she forgot that her sister had a softness beneath her tough and frank exterior. "Sorry. That was a mean thing to say. I'll be back soon, I promise. I just need a change of scenery, a little time to regroup and come up with a sound plan."

"If you're not here for the New Year, I'm coming down to kidnap you."

"Won't be necessary," she assured Melissa. Her sister's rare expression of attachment touched Brook, and she would no doubt miss their everyday companionship, but nothing at this point could diminish her resolve.

CHAPTER TWENTY-SIX

Scott lumbered into his apartment, tossed his keys across the room, and rubbed the back of his neck, what felt like hardened wax. Kyle Harding had indeed left Creative Services to pursue a career in photography, but there wasn't going to be any job opening. Pendleton Scrubb instigated a hiring freeze, and a restructuring was to take place, "necessary evils" according to the fellas in charge. It didn't escape anyone's attention that the announcement came on the same day that Kiesler Advertising let go a third of their staff. The Scrubbs were supposed to feel lucky and blessed to have their jobs.

Scott never felt so despondent and trapped. And he wasn't the only one. Morale at the office had sunk to a new low. Leslie had locked herself in her office and avoided her team the entire day. Some leader she turned out to be, but without her looming overhead, most of the media buyers could spend the afternoon contacting headhunters. Tug decided he should finally buckle down and send in his application to grad school. Everyone in the bullpen seemed to be preparing themselves for an inevitable change. Scott didn't know what to do. It was pointless to send out his newly polished résumé. No one in his industry was hiring right now.

He collapsed into his tattered club chair, picking at the frayed upholstery as he took in his overpriced, pseudo bachelor pad. His mind seemed as empty as his apartment, his bank account, his life. *We regret to inform you that no bonuses will be distributed this quarter.* He needed that money. It's how he squeaked through the holidays every year.

Scott pushed himself out of the chair, headed for the kitchen, and pulled out a chilled Boulevard from the fridge, but the beer slipped out of his grasp and fell to the floor. The glass didn't break, but hit the linoleum with a dull thud that left a dent in the cheap flooring. When Scott picked it up, he could see a swarm of bubbles pushing at the cap. It was the last of his supply so he set the beer on the counter and waited for the carbonation to settle. He planned to relish every last drop as he'd soon have to switch to a less expensive brand. A minor cutback, but a necessary evil.

~

On her first official day of freedom, Brook finished the design for Danielle's save-the-date cards and then busied herself around the house, catching up on her laundry, herding the cottonball-sized dust bunnies under her bed, packing for her respite back in Tulsa. Whenever she started to regret or question her decision to quit, she'd find a chore to occupy her thoughts.

As Brook wiped down the kitchen counter, the phone rang and she rushed to answer it, thrilled to have a caller. "Hello?"

"Did you ever know that you're my hero?" Danielle sang in her ear.

"That's beautiful," Brook said through a wide smile. "Bette Midler had better watch out."

"I don't think so. So what are you doing with your day?"

"Oh, you know, I ended world hunger, saved the environment. Nothing special."

"I'm so jealous. If I didn't have a wedding to pay for, I'd also tell Copperhead to stick it where the sun don't shine."

"It didn't quite happen like that."

"That's not the word around here. You're a legend."

Brook snorted. "Funny that it took my quitting to finally make an impression."

"Well, you certainly make an impression with your cards. And now you can-"

"I know."

"So you're thinking about it?"

"Thinking, yes. I'm still absorbing everything. Hey, are you going to be around tonight? I want to review your design one last time before taking it to the printer's."

"Sure, but there's no rush."

"Actually, there is." Brook paused. "I'm, uh, going to stay in Tulsa for the holidays. I need a break."

"Oh. Okay. When will you be back?"

"I don't know." On the other end, Brook could hear a door crack open, followed by Copperhead barking an order. A shiver trickled down her spine and she felt a renewed sense of justification in her leaving. The door slammed shut, and Danielle sighed. "I gotta go. She's in full attack mode today."

"Sorry if I created a shitstorm over there."

"Don't apologize. She's the one who wouldn't let you finish out your two weeks. We all blame her. But you should see Perry. He's very blue. I think he expected that coffee date the instant you left."

"Yeah, he's been calling me at home," Brook said. "Thank God for caller ID. I haven't been answering them, but that man can not take a hint."

"Then you picked a good time to escape. Hey, keep in touch while you're in Tulsa, okay?"

"Of course. We have more cards to do."

"Right and I expect loads of inquiries after I mail out the announcements. You know, word of mouth is a powerful marketing tool. This is the start of something big, Brook, I can feel it."

"We'll see. The concept of starting my own business is terrifying. I'm going to have to ask you for some serious sales advice."

"I'm glad to help in any way that I can. And I insist on paying you for your work on my wedding."

"I've told you, it's my gift to you and Steve."

"It's too much, Brook, especially for what people charge for custom designs."

"Then we'll figure out a compromise. I'll see you tonight."

Brook ended the call and padded into the kitchen to make herself a peanut butter sandwich, the only substance on hand since they'd tapped out their food supply during the ice storm. She ate in front of the television with the women from *The View*, although their catty jibber-jabber soon set her on edge. When they announced that Tifani Diamond was scheduled to appear, Brook zapped the TV off, relieved to no longer have to dedicate any of her mental energy to television, especially daytime programming. She finished her lunch, loaded a batch of laundry, and then roamed the house looking for something to do.

As she poked around, Brook began to gather a collection of Chip's discards—*Maxim* magazines, ratty sweatshirts, cologne samples, packets of gummy bears he kept on reserve for snacking. All reminders of him, including any pictures of them posing as a bogus perfect couple, were deposited into a cardboard box, a coffin for their relationship Brook buried in the back of her closet...right behind her wedding attire.

Minutes later, she had her dress spread out across her bed.

Brook had combed all of the metro area for the perfect gown, from the discount megastore of David's Bridal to the most exclusive boutiques. Overwhelmed and worn out by the process, she had let one sales clerk talk her into a strapless ball gown silhouette with intricate beading on the bodice, a design more poofy and elaborate than what Brook had envisioned at the beginning of her quest, but it was exquisite in construction and by that time, she didn't even know what she wanted anymore. She remembered her first fitting though and how the dress kept slipping off of her, how baffled she was because it was the same size as the sample which had fit like a glove. Brook had lost weight. Too much weight. The sales clerk had just the right solution to the problem—fake boobs to help fill out the dress, the famous chicken cutlet inserts embraced by flat-chested girls the world over. Brook hated the idea of walking down the aisle with something that resembled raw meat crammed in her bustier, but otherwise, it wouldn't work, even with the alterations. Now Brook could see that the dress was too much for her. The tulle alone could have provided enough mosquito netting for an entire African village. How did she ever think she could pull off such a look? Had the wedding fog seeped that deep into her brain, clouding her judgment? She gathered the dress and stuffed it back into its creamy nylon garment bag, zipping it shut with one swift stroke.

Brook then got out her laptop and after some research on the Internet, discovered the Making Memories Breast Cancer Foundation, an organization that sold donated bridal gowns at steep discounts in shows across the country. The proceeds then helped grant the wishes of terminal breast cancer patients. If Brook's dream was going to be put on hold, she figured the least she could do was help someone else's come true.

By day's end, she had the gown packed and ready to ship.

CHAPTER TWENTY-SEVEN

A bull stared Brook down with a stoic vacancy in its eyes. Its presence was most unwelcome as its wide load crowded the lane of traffic and disrupted the flow of cars. The painted Hereford, the kind you see outside of a steakhouse drawing attention to the specials, was hitched to a trailer so it faced the drivers behind it, obstinate in its stature, taking its time as it passed through the depressed towns of rural Kansas. Brook followed along at a tractor's pace, waiting for the chance to pass, astounded and frustrated that the most direct route between Kansas City and Tulsa should still be a pokey and dangerous two-lane highway. But when traffic cleared and she could finally drive past the bull, her annoyance turned to amusement. Only in the Midwest was one likely to cross such a spectacle, and although Brook had as much country girl in her as Coco Chanel, such quirky touches were part of the fabric of the Heartland that she loved.

A few CDs and a pit stop later, Brook pulled into Oakwood Estates, an established upper middle class neighborhood in south Tulsa with tall trees and classic homes, its cachet still on the rise as its residents stayed on top of upkeep. Driving the route she'd done thousands of times, she recalled all the families who had occupied the homes. Most had moved away, gotten divorced, or down-sized, but some had stayed put, the fixtures of Oakwood who'd been around since the houses were built and would probably never leave, the Hollidays among them. The moment Brook killed the engine in the circle drive of her family's Tudor, her parents came rushing out the door, dressed for the autumn chill in their usual L.L.Bean attire. Brook stepped out of the car and was immediately enveloped in her mother's arms. She milked the hug for all its worth, breathing in the recognizable scent of fresh-baked bread, the best in aromatherapy.

Olivia drew back and brushed a wisp of her buttery hair off her face. "Where's Melissa?"

"She had to stay behind to work."

Her mother set her hands on her waist. "I don't like you girls making that drive alone. Not when you don't have to."

"She'll be here tomorrow."

Olivia's eyes bulged. "Tomorrow!? If this is her way of trying to get out of helping with Thanksgiving dinner, she's mistaken."

"It's a waste of gas," her father added. "You two taking separate cars."

"It couldn't be helped," Brook explained. "There was an estate planning emergency. Apparently someone needed to be written out of a will before the holiday. You know her clients, they expect the world to bow to their every whim."

She popped open her trunk and Jack took in the cargo. "Heavens, Brook, where's the kitchen sink?"

"I'm planning on an extended stay, another reason why I came alone."

Olivia's face brightened and she clasped her hands together. "That's wonderful."

"What about work?" her dad inquired.

"I uh…am taking a vacation."

He furrowed his salt and pepper eyebrows. "You had some left after the cruise?"

"Jack, if she says she has some vacation, then she has some vacation."

Her father nodded and then heaved one of the Samsonites out of the trunk, grunting with the weight. He set the bag down and pressed a hand on his lower back. "Just how long are you planning on being here?"

"As long as she wants," Olivia said. She bent over and picked up Brook's tackle box of art supplies. "As long as she wants," she repeated.

~

Brook and Scott had the Merry Merchant to themselves, twirling and swaying to the faraway sound of steel drums, the sun's rays casting a celestial glow about them, as if the heavens were expressing their approval. Bringing their bodies close together, they moved in to relive that magical kiss, but before their lips could touch, someone wrenched Brook away from Scott's embrace and pressed a cold blunt object against her throat. The scene had shifted into shadow, but she could see that her captor was Chip, dressed as Disney's Captain Hook, his artificial hand sharpened to a lethal point. Brook dared not move or swallow. Scott made a start for her, but Chip growled at him in a snarl. "One more step and I turn her into chum."

Brook woke with a start, and it required a few seconds for her to adjust to her surroundings, the Laura Ashley rosebuds coming into focus as she wiped the sleep out of her eyes. Her childhood bedroom had not been touched since she left the nest and remained trapped in time, just like the flowers that had yet to bloom. Despite its familiarity and comfort, nostalgia failed to put her at ease.

Yanking back the covers, Brook crossed the room to rummage through her suitcase, locating her photos from the cruise. She flipped through the stack fast, knowing exactly which picture she wanted to see. Once she found it, she examined the glossy snapshot. Brook and Scott leaned against one another, their heads touching, and both had a glint in their eyes which seemed to express a shared secret, a thrill to be in each other's company. Long John Silver had taken it aboard the Merry Merchant, and Brook had shelled out six bucks for the photo before leaving the ship, an overpriced but treasured souvenir. She felt better after seeing it, having restored the memories from that day back to their original state. With a sigh, Brook wondered how Scott was doing, how he was spending his Thanksgiving holiday. Was he at his mother's, or at his aunt's? And did he have a new niece or nephew?

Brook put the photo back in its jacket and set it aside. She then crouched down on her knees and reaching underneath her bed, slid out her drafting table, an old friend she had left behind once she decided to pursue a career in business. With its weight resting on her lap, she began to write her name in the years of dust that had collected on its surface. As she finished it off though, a jackrabbit knock sounded on the door. "Up and at 'em!" Jack bellowed. "Time for brunch!" The interruption startled Brook and sent her finger off course. Instead of a tracing a "K" at the end of her name, it had left an exaggerated checkmark in its path.

~

Thanksgiving dinner was Olivia Holliday's time to shine. Everything had to be authentic, exceptional, and made from scratch. No canned cranberries, gravy from a jar, Stove Top stuffing, or green bean mushroom soup casserole with onion crunchies on top. Her mother prepared all week for the feast and on the day of, acted as captain of the kitchen, sounding off orders to her regiment. The family scampered about, pinballing off one another as they tended to their duties, the tempers rising with the heat. But once everything was on the table, the tapers lit, and crystal wine goblets filled with Louis Jadot Beaujolais Nouveau, everyone relaxed, gave thanks, passed plates, and devoured the food.

"Honey, you've done it again," Jack said, scooping out another helping of cornbread stuffing. "It gets better every year."

Their mother beamed. "I couldn't do it without my girls." Her proud look then dissolved into a pout. "I just don't know what I'll do when I have to share you two with in-laws." Brook and Melissa exchanged glances across the table. "Of course I'll welcome the change, but I think your dad and I will just order pizza when that happens."

"Won't be anytime soon," Melissa said, wiping her mouth with a linen napkin and pushing her plate away. "So much for the weight I lost getting sick on the cruise. That was delicious, Mom."

Everyone sat in a state of quiet contentment, giving Brook the perfect opening for breaking her news, but she gulped down some liquid courage before making her announcement. "I, uh, have something to tell you," she began.

Olivia tilted her head. "Oh?"

"I quit my job."

Jack's jaw dropped to reveal a mouthful of stuffing. He quickly closed it to chew and swallow before speaking. "What? When?"

"This past Monday."

"You mean you could have come home sooner?" her mother asked.

"That's not the point," Brook replied. "I hated my job, and now I don't have to do it anymore."

"How much do you have saved?" her father asked. "What's your plan?"

"I've got some money socked away. Not as much as I'd like, but you taught me how to budget, Dad."

"That's an understatement," Melissa said.

Jack's brow creased into a "V". "This worries me, Brook. The economy isn't what it was when you graduated from college. People are out of work again, just like in the eighties. That job was safe."

"So was Chip and look how that turned out." Brook paused, letting her words dangle in the air. "I'm sick of safe," she added.

A heavy silence fell upon the room.

"Maybe you could find something here," Olivia suggested.

"Brook's going back to Kansas City," Melissa said. "I'll help her out until she gets back on her feet. Her stay here is temporary."

"I can speak for myself, Mel."

"Then do it," her sister retorted.

"You're not giving me a chance." Brook stood, scooted out her chair, and headed for the stairs.

"Honey, come back," her mother beseeched as Brook darted up the steps.

After fetching a stack of her notecards from her bedroom, Brook rejoined her family and fanned out her favorite designs on the corner of the table.

"Are these *all* yours?" Olivia asked.

"Yes."

Her mother rifled through them. "They're lovely."

"Thank you. I hope others will think so and pay me for them."

"This is your plan?" Jack asked.

"So far."

Her father let out a sigh. "Brook, hobbies are nice to have, but they don't pay the bills."

"Who says?" she shot back.

"Listen, I don't mean to be a downer, but I'm a realist. Heck, most of the people at my office have an inner desire to do something else. Linda plays the banjo. Stewart collects and trades old watches. It's hard to turn those things into a well-paying career."

"People love my cards. And more importantly, I love doing them. This is what I want to do."

"That's great," Jack said. "Maybe it's something you can pursue on the side, provide you with some supplemental income. Once the holiday season passes, you can begin hunting for a real job."

"I can't go back to that life, Dad. Nobody even knew who I was at that place. Nobody cared."

"You have to let them know who you are, Brook. *Make* them care."

"For what? Do you know what the station gave an employee for twenty-five years of service? A gumball dispenser. For twenty-five years! It was insulting. I was ashamed to work there." Brook also told them about the icicle spear, elaborating on how absurd it was to work in a place that would put her in danger, only to reward her years later with something like a cracked snow globe or broken clock.

"Your paycheck is the reward," Jack said. "And don't forget the benefits. I think you just had the wrong job."

"But I'm not like you or Melissa. I'm no good at the corporate dance."

"It's a matter of making the system work for you," Jack said. "If you put up a fight or resent it, then yes, you'll be miserable." He tapped his finger on the stem of his wine goblet. "Nobody said life was a laugh a minute. It's called work for a reason."

Brook plopped down in her chair. "I don't think it has to be that way. I want to do something I enjoy, create a product I'm proud of." She stared down at her plate, the bone china becoming a blurry disc.

Olivia reached over and rubbed Brook's arm. "Don't get upset, sweetie. You know your father, he's a man of logic. The whole Holliday clan is that way. That's why they're all bankers and accountants." She brought her hand back and straightened in her seat. "You get your creative genes from my side of the family."

"I'm just trying to protect our daughter. Look at your brother, he does nothing but suffer as an artist. He's always on unemployment."

"My brother is also a frustrated anarchist who sculpts historical figures in questionable repose. His is a niche audience." Olivia looked over at the cards. "Brook's work is much more…palatable. She is a true artiste."

"I've never liked you indulging this side of her. It's just not practical."

"I never liked you pressuring our daughter into settling on a business degree."

"We were paying out-of-state tuition. She needed to make a decision."

"And I stand by my decision," Brook said, rising to her feet again in an effort to illustrate her determination. "I'm simply taking myself in a different direction. I'll actually be putting what I learned in school to better use. My old job was just pushing numbers and meeting demands. It didn't challenge me or offer any opportunity for growth. And I want to be the one in charge. I want to make my mark."

"And your father and I will support you in any way we can." Olivia sent Jack a stern look that silenced any protest. "We will be your patrons," she added with an air of pride.

Brook looked to her father whose face remained clenched. "This isn't about shunning responsibility," she said. "If anything, I'll be taking on more."

Jack's rigid expression softened. "I know, honey. And I'm not questioning your abilities. It's just so tough to make it on your own. I see it all the time at the bank. Most businesses fail in the first year."

"But you know what the number one rule is in business," Brook prompted.

"What's that?"

"No risk, no reward."

Jack gave her a wan smile. "You've got me there."

~

The next afternoon, Olivia recruited Brook to help her in the kitchen with the post-Thanksgiving turkey chili, a tradition in the Holliday home to jazz up the leftovers. After her mother cued up some classical tunes on the kitchen's CD player, she handed Brook the recipe card.

"Read it," she said, rolling up her sleeves to get ready for action. Brook scanned the ingredients and instructions. "Done?"

"Yes."

"Good. Now tear it up."

"What?"

"You heard me. Tear it up."

"But this is one of your best recipes."

"We don't need it. We've got the general idea. Now let it rip."

Brook did as she was told. It felt like destroying a prized family photo.

"Don't look so distressed. It's all in here." Olivia tapped her temple with her index finger. "The chili is different every time I make it. Once you have the basics down, you can improvise. That's the fun of cooking, the experimenting. It's like your art. You take something familiar and add your own touch. Hopefully, the results will create a positive reaction. Sometimes it fails, but hey, no risk, no reward," she finished with a wink. Olivia's enthusiasm over the greeting card venture helped Brook feel like she just might be able to make a go of it.

"Luckily, you girls were young when I was still learning how to cook," she continued. "I'm embarrassed to say that back then, we had our share of Kraft Mac and Cheese and beenie weenie."

Brook set her hand on her mother's shoulder. "Somehow we turned out all right," she joked.

Olivia shook her off. "You all tease me about being so fussy in my kitchen, but this is how I express myself. It's like I said yesterday, the artistic drive is a Chandler trait. My brother's a misunderstood sculptor…" She picked up a wooden spoon and held it up like the Olympic torch. "I'm a fastidious gourmet."

"Hey, that could be the name of your cooking show."

They shared a chuckle as Jack entered through the door of the mud room just off the kitchen. "Your Jetta's clean as a whistle, Brook," he announced.

"Thanks, Dad."

He stepped in to join them. "I found this in your backseat." He held up a blueberry-colored foam mat coiled into a roll. "What's it for?"

"Yoga. Danielle gave it to me right before I left. It was her fiancé's, but he never used it. She's been singing its praises for years so I thought I'd give it a try. I've also got her collection of DVDs to get me going."

"Danielle is such a sweet girl," Olivia said.

"Yes, she is. I feel bad leaving her behind at the station. We were each other's life preservers. But she understands. Plus, her paycheck would be tough to give up."

Jack tossed the mat over into the mud room, and it landed on the washing machine with a thud. "Back to your car," he said, crossing his arms and setting his weight against the counter. "In the future, you should wash it right away after a winter storm. Salt is murder on a paint job."

"Got it," Brook said.

"And don't neglect the undercarriage. Pay the extra dollar at the car wash to give it the attention it needs. And when was the last time you waxed the finish?"

"Enough!" Olivia said, shooing Jack out of the kitchen with her wooden spoon.

Mother and daughter returned to business, standing side-by-side at the counter. Olivia diced the vegetables with expert speed and precision while Brook had the much easier task of shredding the turkey. When Vivaldi switched over to Debussy, Brook spoke. "I saw on your calendar that you're hosting your bridge club next week. Maybe I could come."

"I'm afraid we don't need any subs this time, honey. Besides, you don't like bridge."

"I'm not talking about playing." Brook set down the turkey leg she'd been tearing apart and wiped her brothy fingers on a dishtowel. "I would like to show your friends my stationery, hold a sale right here at home."

Olivia continued her dicing without missing a beat. "I don't see any problem with that."

"Thanks. I appreciate it. And I promise I won't be obnoxious about it. It'll be a no pressure deal."

"Oh, don't worry about that. Do you know how many Mary Kay and Pampered Chef parties I've been to for those ladies?"

"I don't want people to feel obligated to buy my cards."

"I understand that, Brook, but if you're going to succeed at this business, you have to put yourself out there, get in people's faces a little bit."

"I know. It will all depend on how well I market myself. I just…well, after working with such self-absorbed, pushy sales people and being around Chip who was always in networking mode, I've soured on the process. I don't want to be that person people avoid at parties."

"You make it sound as if you're pushing Amway products. And you will not only be a welcome addition to any party, but also the person who designed the invitations."

Brook's insides warmed at that thought, but her uncertainty didn't leave her completely. "What if no one wants to buy my stuff?"

"Then you learn from the experience and move on. But I think you'll do fine. Your creations are inspired and well-crafted." Olivia stopped her dicing and a look of pleasant surprise flashed across her face. "Who knows, Brook, you might get a strong customer base right here in Tulsa." She continued with her chopping, the smile still on her face. "Now wouldn't that be something?"

CHAPTER TWENTY-EIGHT

Scott balanced his load as he made a grab for the door handle, unable to see around the cardboard box which had grown to feel as if it was full of Kryptonite. He located the knob, turned it, and stumbled into the room, banging his hip on the corner of the pool table. Cursing to himself, he slammed down the box on the felt top and rubbed his side as he took in his new digs. Here he was, back in Fairway, Kansas, although life hardly seemed fair to him right now.

The basement was like most which served more as a catch-all than a living space—disarrayed, dark, damp, and dated with a dusty rose and hunter green motif. Old *Good Housekeeping* issues resided in a corner, stacked as high as Scott's waist. Fake flowers filled the pockets of the pool table and jumbles of woven baskets seemed to be everywhere, all on the verge of toppling over. Finding room for Scott's stuff was going to be a challenge, but he'd have to make do. His former bedroom upstairs had been converted into an exercise studio and Rebecca's was now set up as a nursery and playroom for his nephew. The basement was Scott's only option, shelter for his waning confidence and bruised ego. He had only lived a few miles over on the Missouri side when out on his own, but his Plaza apartment had been his. And even though his life there always had a beyond-his-means, fleeting aspect to it, Scott had the best of both worlds and didn't want to leave. At least in the basement he'd have some sense of separation and independence. He had his own entrance off the side of the house, basic cable, a mini fridge, a full bath, and a room with a full-sized bed and desk.

The deal was that Scott could live in the basement provided that he cleaned up the place and applied a fresh coat of paint to each room. "This is not a free ride," his mother had said. "You have to earn your keep. I would have redecorated years ago, but I can never find the time." In actuality, Scott looked forward to the renovation. Nothing like a home project to make one feel useful.

He plucked the silk arrangements from their braided leather flowerpots and cleared off the top of the pool table. Although Scott also planned to start his novel during his hiatus from the corporate rat race, he would still need his fun time. His skills would be rusty. He hadn't held a cue stick since he played with his ex-girlfriend. Leaning against the wood ledge, Scott shook his head in bewilderment as his mind drifted off back to that time. Tiffany thought she was so damn cute, giggling and tossing her hair, assuming provocative poses whenever she took a shot. She always made such a display of herself, as if the cameras were rolling each and every moment. What a sucker Scott had been. Most of the time, they had ended up messing around before they could even finish a game.

Scott came back to the present when he heard the stairs creak, alerting him to a visitor, a house quirk he had always appreciated. Katherine entered the room wearing her signature crisp white oxford shirt with a wispy floral scarf tied around her neck. "Did you find the quilts?" she asked. "I can't for the life of me remember where I put them."

"I'll use my own bedding."

His mother slipped a hand in her pocket. "Are you going to be okay down here? It gets chilly in the winter. We could switch out the guest bed and my exercise equipment."

"I'll be fine," he insisted. "I don't want to be a bother."

She mussed his hair. "Not possible, kiddo. And it's nice to have someone in the house again. It'll make the holidays all the more special this year with you here, not to mention little Nicholas." Katherine tutted. "I still can't get over this happening to you right before Christmas. That company has no class."

"That about sums it up," Scott agreed. "But I should have saved more money. I got lucky that my landlord let me out of my lease."

"Sure he did. He wanted you out of there so he could charge the next person more rent."

Scott smiled. "And people wonder where I get my cynicism."

"Hey, the Plaza was just as chic and expensive back when I lived there, relatively speaking of course." She glanced around at the boxes and plastic crates. "Can I help you unpack?"

"Nah, I'm keeping most of it contained. No offense, but I don't plan on being here for that long."

"Well then, how about I order us Chinese for dinner?"

"Sounds good."

"Holler if you need anything."

"Thanks, Mom."

Needing a breather from schlepping his stuff, Scott took a seat on the couch, recalling the last time Leslie Stoneburner had invited him to do the same in her office. In that case, however, his back had yet to touch the cushion before she told him the news. "We regret to inform you that Pendleton Scrubb can no longer afford to keep you on staff."

"But I'm one of the top performers in this department," he'd argued. "This doesn't make sense."

"We appreciate your time and service with the agency, but current market conditions require us to make cutbacks." Leslie gave her canned speech with a tired and pained expression, providing Scott with a glimpse of the woman he used to like, the one who was approachable and human. "I'm getting a raw deal here as well," she'd added. "My team is stretched too thin as it is. This is just as hard for me as it is for you." She averted her gaze to her view of the Plaza.

Scott rose to his feet. "No, it's not as hard for you. You're still getting a paycheck."

She set her lifeless, dull eyes back on him. "I'm more than happy to provide you with a reference."

"Thanks, Leslie. That would be swell."

Back in his cubicle, bitterness boiled within Scott and he considered marching into Human Resources and filing a claim that he was being punished for not wanting to date his boss. But he would have been laughed out of the building, especially after carrying on with not one, but two coworkers. And upon further thought, Scott knew the decision to let him go wasn't one that Leslie could have made alone. Pendleton Scrubb's department heads had the ultimate say, and it didn't require a genius to piece together their logic. Scott was the most seasoned media buyer below management level, and had the highest salary in his job category. The layoff wasn't about seniority or performance; it was about cutting costs. Pendleton kept the cheap employees, the pups of the bullpen, people Scott had trained. Management, of course, hadn't been touched. At least not yet. On his way out the door, his belongings and disgruntlement in tow, Scott passed Waverly Marks, one of the safe employees full of smug superiority and false sympathy. "Good luck," she'd called out.

"Bite me," he shot back.

Change is good, Scott reasoned, pushing his dead weight off the couch, reminding himself how much he loathed his job and the way Pendleton Scrubb operated. He had gone into advertising because he wanted to reach people in a surprising and memorable way. Media buying was supposed to be his foot in the door, but he had lingered there for way too long, never achieving the results he wanted. Now that door had been slammed shut…with his foot still in it.

Scott noted the mess about the basement, his belongings blending in with his mother's castoffs. The pool table beckoned, but he turned his back on it and headed for the bedroom. The room/office was not as inviting as a sidewalk café or panoramic view of a lake, but it had a desk and plenty of quiet solitude. Scott figured it was best to let go of his romantic delusions about writing anyway. A novel required hard work, and he could be easily distracted so a sparse, functional space might do the trick, force him to create other worlds in his mind. Scott opened the box with his Macintosh packed inside and dug out the components to his computer.

Change is good.

CHAPTER TWENTY-NINE

Brook straightened her arrangement of cards one last time just as the doorbell rang and the first of Olivia's bridge club arrived. While coats were taken and perfumes and voices drifted down the hall, her heart banged in her chest, and the heat from the fireplace in the den seemed to radiate all the way into the kitchen. She tugged at the folds of her cowl neck sweater, fluttering it out to fan her body, and wondered if this was how artists felt at gallery openings.

Brook used antique plate holders, a thrift-store find, to display her work and set up shop on the kitchen island next to Olivia's to-die-for Christmas treats, a powerful lure. Snowflake confetti dotted the speckled granite countertop and a mug tree hung with Christmas ornaments served as the centerpiece. "Selling is just like cooking," her mom had noted, pleased with the result of their collaboration. "Presentation is everything."

Having no idea what demand would be like, Brook kept the sale small, assembling a couple dozen sets of holiday cards and thank you notes, bundling them with twine for a tasteful and rustic look. Brook also had samples of her other work, including her Sadie Paskahonie series, clipped to grosgrain ribbon hanging on the walls in the foyer. By the time the women entered the kitchen, they were already talking about her cards.

"How charming!" Carol Frost crowed. "I can look like Martha Stewart without the work!" Brook wished people wouldn't automatically refer to Martha when it came to all things crafty, but since these ladies worshiped the domestic deity, she took the remark as a compliment.

"Every year I get my cards from Hallmark only to receive two or three of the same ones myself," Patsy Walker said. "But that's not going to happen this year," she sang.

"Brook, you should get a booth at my country club's annual craft fair," Sally Coolridge suggested. "You'd make a killing!"

One of the ladies, who Brook had never met and looked like an owl, clutched Brook's arm with one of her talons. "Do you have a website? No? Oh, you just have to get on the World Wide Web!"

Brook's concerns about lack of interest and demand evaporated as the women continued to gush over her merchandise. The packaged cards sold out and the women crowded in to fill out order forms. If Brook had the time to do so, she would have pinched herself because it seemed too good to be true. Moving product was supposed to be harder than this.

Later, once the bridge society had sat down to drink wine and play cards, Olivia stole a moment alone with Brook. "You're a smash."

Brook relished in the sales and her mother's praise. "I think I found my target audience: Empty Nesters with disposable incomes."

"Just wait until word of mouth gets going," her mother said. "And do these ladies know how to spread the word!"

Carol Frost let out a chortle that China could hear and declared, "Marcy, your stories are priceless! But listen to this…"

Olivia lifted her brow to show that her point had been proven and again commended Brook on a job well done before leaving to join her friends. Brook gathered her papers and money and headed up the stairs, ready to get to work.

But the cards didn't feel like work. The hours flew by for Brook and even when she felt overwhelmed or panicked about completing her orders on time, she kept her focus. Transforming her old bedroom into her own Santa's workshop, down came yesteryear's party pics and sorority composites, replaced with sketches of holiday insignias: Christmas trees, menorahs, gift boxes, reindeer, snowmen, doves, nutcrackers, and of course, a partridge in a pear tree. Brook had also cleared room for her stockpile of papers, ribbons, packaging, and adhesives, developing an assembly line for her labor intensive cut-out designs that had to be pieced together by hand. She had a system and tackled the cards in order of urgency and difficulty, keeping on top of her numbers and staying in close contact with her printer. All cylinders were cranking away, both creative and organizational.

Although the bridge sale had given Brook the validation and encouragement she needed to get her business started, once demand tapered off after the holidays, she'd have some catching up to do. Coming up with a name for her new company would be first on the list. Holliday Greetings seemed like the natural choice, but that's exactly why she didn't want to use it. Plus, people who didn't know Brook would always be telling her she'd spelled it wrong and she didn't want to risk looking like an amateur. She also needed to research ways to cut her supply costs, reevaluate her pricing, figure out taxes, create a logo, develop a website, etc. etc. Until then, Brook worked at a steady pace, sipping her chai tea and listening to holiday classics, enjoying the comfort and luxury of a home office, albeit her parents' house for the time being. The new lifestyle suited Brook as she didn't require a boss to crack the whip, not when her output had a direct effect on revenue.

Naturally, there came that time in the day when Brook ran out of fizz, and in one such case, she went downstairs for a yoga fix. She would have normally inserted one of Danielle's instructional DVDs, but today Brook wanted to draw on what she had learned and take a stab at her own routine, especially since she had the house to herself and could concentrate without interruptions. Assuming the mountain pose, Brook stood tall with her eyes shut, gluts in, abs contracted, knees soft. She pressed her palms together in front of her heart and zoned in on the sound of her breathing, banishing any poisonous thought tainting her mind. Brook then moved on to her sun salutations. *Inhale. Exhale. Stretch. Bend. Breathe in sunshine.*

As she held herself erect in a push-up plank, an idea popped into Brook's head and she dropped to the floor. *Sunshine Salutations.* It would be the perfect name for her company. She could even picture the logo—a squiggly, rough sketch of a sun with two intertwined S's scrolled on the face. Although Brook would have liked to have evolved to the point where she could stay in the moment and finish her routine, she knew to jump on a hot idea and picked herself up off the floor. After bowing and sending the universe a quick Namaste salute, she rushed up the stairs to jot down the image now ablaze in her head.

She was on fire.

~

Scott sneezed and grabbed the last tissue from the Puffs box, but the lotion-infused fibers did little to soothe his raw nose which stung as if it had been scraped across a cheese grater. He hadn't caught the flu that was so rampant that season. It was allergies. Cleaning out the basement kicked up so many aged molecules of mold, mildew, and dust that Scott felt like he needed a gas mask. But before he was to coat the walls with colors like Cornflower Blue, Honeywheat, and Key Lime Pie, the rooms needed to be stripped down to the bare bones. As anxious as Scott was to begin painting, an overhaul had to happen first.

He and his mother sorted everything into piles— Keep, Recycle, Trash, Donate, and Sell on Ebay—although Katherine took a while to warm to the idea. "I just wanted to update and brighten things up down here, not turn my life inside out." Scott urged her to be ruthless in what made the cut to stay and eventually, she embraced the project. The goal was to have the rooms cleared out and painted by New Year's. Once that was done, then Scott could get serious about writing. One might call it procrastination, but he reasoned that cluttered space cluttered the mind. Besides, decades had been stashed away in the basement, and he had plenty to keep him busy.

With a pair of scissors, Scott slashed through the packing tape sealing yet another unlabeled box which turned out to be a time capsule of his childhood belongings. Pausing for reflection, he picked through his old Star Wars toys, fantasy books, baseball cards, and jigsaw puzzles, and the sniffle which followed had little to do with his aggravated sinuses. These were the pleasures of his youth, diversions from homework, chores, and his parents' arguing. Digging deeper, Scott unearthed a Hush Puppies shoebox and pulled at the frayed rubber band holding the lid in place, the stringy rubber disintegrating with his touch. Inside, he found stacks of photos he either vaguely recalled or had never seen before. Pictures of his father. With the wistful spell now broken, Scott set the box down as if it had bitten him.

"What's this doing in my stuff?" he asked his mother, pointing to the droopy Basset Hound pictured on the side of the shoebox.

Katherine brushed her hands and set them on her hips as she noted the snapshots. "Oh, I put your father in there," she said in a flippant manner.

"Huh?"

"Those are the pictures I took out of the photo albums. I didn't want to look at them, but didn't feel right getting rid of them. Rebecca doesn't want them either so do what you will."

Scott placed the lid back on the shoebox, a Pandora's Box in his mind, and pushed it aside, starting a new pile of his own. If a marker had been within his grasp, he would have drawn a big question mark across the top.

CHAPTER THIRTY

Christmas morning, the Hollidays gathered in the kitchen, everyone bundled up in robes and yawning over their coffee mugs. Gone were the days when the girls couldn't wait to upend their stockings and tear into their presents. It was a Christmas for grownups. Olivia served gooey, homemade hazelnut cinnamon rolls and the egg nog added such a wonderful flavor to the coffee, even Brook indulged in a second cup. The family took their time eating their rich breakfast and afterwards, opened gifts one at a time. The highlights: a PalmPilot for Jack to consolidate all his lists, the standing Kitchen Aid mixer Olivia had been pining for, a spa package for Melissa, and for Brook, a gift certificate to a yoga studio…in Tulsa.

"Why did you give her lessons *here*?" Melissa asked. "Brook's coming back home for New Year's."

"Not according to her," Olivia replied.

Brook met her sister's confounded look. "I'm going to stick around a bit longer," she announced. "I've got a great setup here and I still have orders to fill."

"Why can't you do it back in Kansas City? That's the beauty of art, Brook, you can do it anywhere."

"It would save me a bundle in shipping costs to finish them before coming home."

"If you are coming home," Melissa mumbled before moving on to her next gift. Brook pretended not to hear her.

After all the presents had been opened and cleanup conducted, Melissa followed Brook up to her bedroom and closed the door behind her. "Don't you see what's happening?" she asked. Brook wasn't in the mood for one of her sister's lectures and began to shelve her new books. Melissa refused to be ignored though and frogmarched her over to the bed. "Mom is sucking you in here. She's not even being subtle about it."

"You're making this a bigger deal than it is. The yoga lessons will be good for me. It'll add to my repertoire and get me out of the house."

"You're supposed to already be out of the house, remember? You moved out years ago. Why are you going back in time?"

"I'm not. I'm moving ahead with my life. I've gotten a great start to the business and the yoga's helping me manage the stress. I should have taken it up years ago."

"That's great, but what do you do for *fun*? When was the last time you went out?" Brook opened her mouth to speak, but her sister didn't give her the chance. "Beyond delivering your cards," she added.

Brook shrugged to display her nonchalance on the subject. "So I don't have much of a social life. None of my friends are in town right now. The solitude has been good for me. It builds character." Brook didn't understand why Melissa was giving her such a hard time when she had been the one to hint at her co-dependency on men in the first place. *You go from one boyfriend to the next.* Sometimes Brook wondered if her sister argued with her for the mere sake of it.

"Your life is back with me," Melissa said. "You can't avoid it forever. Come back home."

Brook stood up and crossed the room to the window, taking in the tangle of stripped trees in the backyard. "I moved to Kansas City because of you and Chip. Both of you already had your own lives established there, and it was easy for me to tag along. Maybe I need to stay away for a while to see if it's where I belong. I still need to figure out some stuff and it'd be nice if you'd back off."

She felt her sister's hand on her shoulder. "Brook, I know it's tempting to stay here. Mom makes you wholesome meals and there's always someone around to keep you company. All you have to do is make your pretty cards. But if you're going to make this business work, you have to expand beyond your friends and Mom's bridge club."

"I know. I need to get a solid plan in place, but I've been so busy with orders I haven't had the time."

"But don't you see what you're doing? It's the wedding all over again."

Brook jerked away. "What do you mean?"

"You tackle a project with all your energy, but you also block out the rest of the world in the process."

Brook sniffed at the accusation, and although she knew there was more than a nugget of truth to it, it was harder to hear from someone else. "That's the pot calling the kettle black," she retorted. "You've used your job to keep plenty of men at bay, including your husband."

Melissa pursed her lips and tightened the sash on her robe with a quick yank. "Don't even begin to give me advice on marriage," she replied. "At least my groom showed up." Her sister turned, flung open the door, and skulked off down the hall.

"Yeah, but it didn't take!" Brook yelled after her. "It doesn't count if it didn't take!"

CHAPTER THIRTY-ONE

With *The Nutcracker* ballet spinning its annual magic and mayhem, Katherine had been swamped at work and, as she did in Christmases past when she agreed to host, ordered the family dinner with all the fixin's from the Holiday Ham Company, sending Scott out to pick it up. No, he would not be escaping Brook's name, not this time of year. To help with the feast, his aunt and uncle volunteered to take care of the sweets and showed up at the house carrying enough goodies to send even a Sugar Plum Fairy into diabetic shock.

"Just a little something," Helen said.

"I told her she was going overboard," Al added, the Nordstrom's shopping bag in his hand straining with the weight of its contents.

Soon after their arrival, Rebecca trundled through the front door as best as she could with an infant car seat hanging on her arm. Setting the carrier down, she blew out a gust of air, as if both relieved and surprised she had made it. Although his sister's face had the puffy appearance and tired glaze of the sleep deprived, her new choppy pixie cut gave her a sophisticated touch of chic mommy. "Sorry we're late," she said with breathless urgency. "I'm never on time anymore."

"Relax," Katherine urged, rubbing Rebecca's back to soothe her own child. "You're right on time. Now let me see my grandbaby." Rebecca bent down and lifted back a fuzzy blanket to unveil Nicholas, and everyone crowded in to admire the sleeping newborn dressed in a red and white knitted stocking cap and matching sweater. When Paul traipsed in, they all turned to Rebecca's husband as if an unexpected guest had intruded on the moment. A lanky guy who was all arms and legs, being bogged down with cumbersome baby gear made him especially awkward.

"Need some help?" Scott asked.

"He's fine," Rebecca said. "Just set it over there," she ordered Paul, pointing to the couch, but just as he did as instructed, she noted the haul and asked, "Why did you bring in the Pack 'N Play?"

"It was in the car. You told me to bring in everything. And you're welcome."

"You know Mom has a crib set up for us."

He grabbed the tote bag by its handles. "Fine. I'll take it back out and get the…damn it!"

"What?"

"I forgot the gifts."

Rebecca turned to her family and rolled her eyes.

"I heard that," Paul snapped before lumbering out the door.

Parenthood. It put even the best of couples to the test. And if a structural engineer like Paul could forget to load Christmas presents during the transport process, it didn't bode well for those with less attention to detail. Scott wondered if he could ever be a parent. It looked like such taxing work, and he questioned if he'd be capable of the unselfishness and devotion required, not to mention the patience. He also lacked a model father figure to draw upon. On the other hand, considering the fondness and attachment he had already developed for his nephew, he could only imagine how much more he would care for his own child.

Even with the moments of awkward strain between Rebecca and Paul, it was a good Christmas. Because of Scott's unemployment, the family had overcompensated when it came to the gift exchange, acting as if he had bought them blocks of gold instead of his lame bargain-bin offerings. And he scored big-time on his end: CDs, clothing, books, *tons* of books. Rebecca gave him a whole library of writing texts to help him compose his best-seller. Scott didn't have the heart to tell his sister he hadn't written a lick since losing his job. He hoped his new collection would change that.

"Scott, did you hear me?" Aunt Helen asked from across the dinner table. He looked around the room to find his family staring at him with curious expressions. Scott had apparently missed the point where the conversation moved past the baby, a rare occurrence when everyone gathered nowadays.

"I'm sorry, what?"

"I was talking about the nice girl you brought to the Chiefs game," Helen responded.

Rebecca curled her lip. "You took a date to a football game? Oh, Scottie, have I taught you nothing?"

"What's wrong with going to a football game?" Paul asked. "It beats dinner and a movie."

"Thank you," Scott said. "That's exactly what I thought."

Rebecca shook her head. "Maybe if you've been on a few dates and are in your comfort zone, but not when you're just getting started."

"What was her name again?" Helen asked. "Brook Holloway?"

"Holliday. Brook Holliday."

"Yes, that's easy enough to remember. Are you two still an item?"

"Leave him alone, Helen," Al grumbled.

Scott pushed his peas across his plate. "We just had the one date."

His aunt tutted. "Oh, I see. We liked her."

"I did too, but what can you do?"

Nicholas began to wail and Rebecca poked Paul in the arm. "Your turn," she commanded.

"He's probably hungry," Paul said, bringing up his hands in surrender. "I'm not qualified to nurse him."

Rebecca did a combination sigh and roll of the eyes. "I just fed him. And that's not his hungry cry, it's his poopy diaper cry."

"How can you tell a difference in his cries?" Paul asked.

"A mother just knows," she clipped. Katherine nodded in agreement as the crying intensified. Paul stood and whisked his red-faced son away in his baby carrier, a look of panic spreading across his own face. "Don't forget to wipe front to back!" she shouted after him.

"Rebecca Leeann," Katherine reproved. "Not at the table."

"Sorry. I've become inoculated."

"And sweetheart, ease up on your husband," Katherine added in a lowered voice. "You're making him a nervous wreck."

Rebecca lowered her gaze. "He just…he doesn't…he doesn't get it."

"Few men do," Katherine said. "It's best to accept it."

Rebecca nodded and once the crying subsided, she turned to Scott. "So what happened with this girl?" she asked. "I never even heard about her."

"Nothing happened. It didn't work out."

"I'm surprised," Helen said. "You two seemed like a good pair."

"Helennn," Al warned. "Mind your own beeswax." His uncle served himself another helping of mashed potatoes and smothered them in gravy.

"I hope me telling her about Tifani Diamond didn't scare her away," Helen said, slicing her ham. "I guess some girls can be intimidated by such a history. But Brook didn't come off as the insecure type."

Scott balled up his napkin in his fist. He had to make an effort to keep his voice civil. "What did you tell her about Tifani?"

"I just gave her the overall scenario, how you proposed and how cruel she was to you."

Katherine huffed and crossed her arms. "She disappointed us all."

"I was trying to make you look like a stand up guy," Helen added meekly. "Should I not have said anything?"

Al bowed his head and shook it side to side.

"I wish you hadn't," Scott said. "We were still getting to know each other. It was bad enough that I sprung my family on her on our first date. I think it all freaked her out."

"Gosh, Scottie. I'm so sorry." Helen looked painfully apologetic. "Leave it to my big mouth."

"It's okay," Scott told her after a few quiet beats had passed, even though he hardly felt so. But he knew the end to his brief courtship with Brook was not Helen's fault. "There was something else going on with her," he added. Everyone put their elbows on the table and leaned forward. "Brook was supposed to have gotten married just weeks before we met." His family exchanged surprised glances. "The timing wasn't right anyway. I doubt you telling her about my past made any big difference."

"Honey, we've got a crisis in here!" Paul shouted from the den. "Help!"

Rebecca threw her napkin on her plate and scooted out her chair. "You've got to be kidding me. It's a messy diaper, not a state of emergency."

"Be nice," Katherine advised as Rebecca marched out of the room in a huff.

"Dogs," Helen said in an apparent effort to diffuse the overall tension. "So much easier and they never talk back."

Later that afternoon, while the women gushed over the baby and the men snoozed in front of a bowl game, Scott took a plate of pecan pie down to the basement where the mustiness had been replaced with the smell of fresh paint. Only one more room left to refurbish, the bedroom, but today was his day off. No work. He sat down on the newly slip-covered couch and turned the TV on to the Discovery Channel. Scott knew he was watching too much television in his spare time, but at least it was educational programming. He wouldn't technically call it loafing...not as long as he was learning something.

~

"Did I tell you we got a Christmas card from Chip's parents?" Olivia asked.

Brook looked across the backseat of her parents' BMW to share her shock with Melissa, but her sister stared out the window, the air remaining frosty between them since their argument. She hoped that the festive atmosphere of the Walkers' annual holiday open house might restore relations as neither sister excelled at making concessions and heartfelt apologies. "How decent of them," Brook finally responded, taking on her most sarcastic tone.

"Tell her the rest of it," Jack said to Olivia.

Brook's mother turned around in the front passenger seat, the leather upholstery groaning underneath her. "They sent us a check to help with the money we lost on the wedding. It didn't cover quite half, but it was a nice gesture. They wrote a letter saying how sorry and embarrassed they were about how everything turned out."

"Yes, the Kincaides hate to look bad," Brook said.

"Now Brook, they can't control their son."

"They always tried to. His dad put an enormous amount of pressure on Chip. No wonder he wanted to get away."

Olivia regarded Brook as if she had something to add, but then shifted to face the front. "Well, let's be thankful you didn't marry him."

"Yes," Brook said. "Let's rejoice and be happy."

The Walkers' colonial, one of the larger and more prestigious homes in Oakwood Estates, was outlined in classic white lights. Inside, the house smelled like deep roasted coffee and fresh-baked cookies, and the decorations were a tasteful array of items straight from Pottery Barn—pewter reindeers with tea lights incorporated in the antlers, crystal bead wreaths, sugar berry topiaries, candles with cinnamon sticks and sprigs of pine embedded in the wax. Always culturally sensitive, Mrs. Walker had also placed a menorah on the mantle for the few Jewish families sprinkled about the neighborhood.

"Hey everyone, it's the Hollidays!" Mr. Walker sing-songed.

"Does he have to say that every year?" Jack murmured to his family and Olivia elbowed him in the side. Brook and Melissa exchanged smiles, their impasse softening.

Mr. Walker came over and took their coats, his jovial hospitality punctuated by his Santa cap and snowflake sweater. "Jack, your girls grow more beautiful each year," he said. "Especially you, Olivia." Their mother waved him away and patted her angel food cake hair. "And your daughters," he added, leaving with their coats and yelling over his shoulder, "they won't be on the market for long!" Olivia smiled and set a hand on each of their shoulders.

"Where's the eggnog?" Melissa asked, making a beeline for the refreshments while Brook got trapped into polite mingling with some neighbors she didn't know. When at last able to break away, she helped herself to the boxed rosé and headed for the living room where the neighborhood "kids" had gathered.

Angela Walker sat on the bench of the ebony baby grand, speaking with such grand gestures that Brook feared her red wine might splash onto the plush beige carpet. Brook and Angela had graduated in the same class at Landon High, having both survived its Advanced Placement courses, dance committees, and Student Council seminars. An implicit undercurrent of competition had always existed between them so they had never been super close, but Angela was pleasant enough, and their families had known each other for years. Brook made her way over to say hello.

"Hey there, so glad you came!" Angela said, rising to her feet and giving Brook a hug.

"Good to see you," Brook replied. "Your family has outdone themselves, once again."

"Thanks, but I'm surprised we don't kill each other in the process. And nobody can beat your mom's cooking. She sets a high standard here in Oakwood."

"Well, everything looks wonderful."

A beat passed and then Angela set a hand on Brook's arm and squeezed. "Hey, I'm sorry about what happened with your wedding." Brook plastered on her survivor smile. "I was looking forward to a trip up to Kansas City," she added.

"Another time."

"Sure thing. I'd love to check out that Plaza. I've heard it makes our Utica Square look like just another strip mall."

"It's nice," Brook agreed. Another beat passed.

"Soooo, you're the talk of the bridge club," Angela said. "I saw the cards my mom bought from you. They're super cool."

"Thank you."

"You know, I'm doing pharmaceutical sales now, and I'd like to send personalized notes to my clients, something different than the standard junk my company gives me. I think it'd give me that extra edge."

"I'd love to show you my work. I can even come up with a custom design for you."

"Great. It'd be nice to do a rendering of a prescription pad or something to that effect. Hey, do you have a website?"

"No, not yet."

"You gotta get one going."

"Yes, it's on my list."

"You know who you should talk to?" Angela asked. "Tom Bixby. He does web design."

Brook hadn't heard Tom's name in years, but it quickened her pulse. "Tom? He's a blast from the past. I haven't seen him since graduation."

"He's here tonight." Her interest piqued, Brook craned her neck to get a look around the party. "He's like me," Angela went on, "still in Tulsa. He looks as cute as ever. Didn't you two used to go out?"

"No. Almost, but it never happened. Whenever either of us was available, the other was always taken."

"Yeah, you were that girl who *always* had a boyfriend." Angela tilted her head in an inquisitive manner. "How did you manage that?"

Brook shrugged. "Must have been my bodacious ta-tas."

Angela broke out into raucous laughter, full on Julia Roberts style. Once she composed herself, she said, "Anyway, you and Tom are both single now." She poked Brook in the ribs. "I think he's over at the buffet table. Go talk to him."

Brook smiled. "I think I will." She set up a time to meet with Angela later that week, wishing she had a business card to pass along, another pressing item among her to-dos. Brook then excused herself to go check out the buffet…and Tom Bixby.

As she worked her way through the crowd, however, the sound of Chip's voice snuck up on her. *You've got to network twenty-four-seven to get ahead.* As much as Brook hated to admit it, Chip did have a point. Her sales so far had been based on friendships and family connections, and she was counting on those relationships to help grow her business. Chip's approach, however, always had an aggressive greediness to it which he couldn't conceal, and from Brook's standpoint, that's why he struggled to close the big deals. Clients could sense his desperation, his lack of confidence. Brook saw it all the time at the dinners and functions Chip had asked her to attend—the beads of sweat on his brow and upper lip, the pulling at his tie, the bitter bite in his voice when prospects brought up reasonable questions or objections. She should have suggested he back off a little, but surmised that if she did so, he'd cover up his ears like a child and tune her out. He was fooling no one. Chip had been sinking in his job, but would rather run away before admitting any weakness.

Shifting her thoughts back to the party, Brook spotted Tom Bixby just as he tossed a jalapeño popper into his mouth. No longer the squeaky clean, All-American suburbanite, he had the hip, disheveled look of someone who didn't comb his hair or tuck in his shirt, but still looked stylish and put together. She imagined him frequenting cyber-cafés, pecking away at the latest in streamlined notebook computers, wearing vintage jeans and an Adidas zipper jacket with piping down the sleeves. Brook made her way over and tapped him on the back. Tom spun around, swallowed his food, and gave her a boyish grin.

"Hey there, Holliday." He placed a hand over his heart. "Now that you're here, my night is complete."

"Hi, Tom. It's been a long time."

His eyes conducted a quick scan of her body. "You look fantastic."

"Same goes for you. I'm surprised to see you. Doesn't your family usually head east for Christmas?"

"Yeah, but my mom didn't want to make the trip this year. She's had it with my aunt and her constant appraising of her possessions, so we stayed in good ol' T-Town." He bumped her arm with his fist. "So what are you doing now? Where are you living?"

"I'm technically in Kansas City, but I've been home since Thanksgiving. It's, uh, been a rocky year."

Tom blinked with the appropriate concern and sympathy. "I know. I heard. Good riddance to bad rubbish."

Brook nodded. "Exactly. But I also quit my job."

"Stickin' it to The Man, huh?"

"Actually she was a woman, but I guess you could say that."

"Do you know what you want to do?"

"Well, I've been designing greeting cards."

Tom popped in another fried jalapeño and gulped it down. "Being your own boss is the only way to go," he said.

"Yes, I'm loving it, but I'm just getting off the ground. I still have a lot to put in place."

"You have a website, don't you?"

Brook shook her head. "That's what I wanted to talk to you about. Angela told me you do web design."

"Yep. Business isn't what it used to be, but I'm managing. It's not like the Internet is going away."

"I was wondering if you could help me start my own site. I'll pay you, of course. I'm not expecting any favors."

He lifted a brow. "You think you can afford me?"

Brook hoped she wasn't insulting him. Tom probably got paid a hefty sum for his services. "Oh. Right. I won't be able to pay much. You know, I should probably just sign up for a quickie course at a junior college. I don't want to waste your time."

Tom gave her another friendly punch on the arm. "I'm messin' with ya, Holliday. Of course I'll help you. What are old friends for?"

She relaxed, but still felt compelled to argue her worth. "I'm pretty good with computers," she offered. "That's all I did at my old job."

"I don't doubt it. I remember what a smartie you were back in school. Why do you think I was so scared to ask you out?"

"Oh?" Brook's cheeks warmed at the flattery. "I thought it was bad timing."

"I think it had more to do with me being a chicken," he said. "I was a mediocre jock who struggled to get B's, and you always had your ducks in a row." Tom zeroed in on her with an intense gaze which seemed to come out of nowhere. "But that was then."

Brook smiled. "Ages ago. And now we know better." She lifted her rosé for a toast and over the crockpot filled with Li'l Smokies swimming in a pool of barbeque sauce, they knocked their plastic glasses together.

~

Never able to stay mad at each other for long, Brook and Melissa managed to get back on speaking terms by the time her sister left for Kansas City. "I just want you back home," she told Brook as they hugged good-bye.

"I know," she replied. "Soon. I promise."

The Walkers' open house had resulted in another batch of orders for Brook, but work had slowed down since the holiday rush, leaving her time to develop a business plan with her dad and collaborate with Tom on her website. "I don't want it to look junky," she told him at their first meeting. "It should be polished and professional." Within a week's time, Brook had selected a host provider, domain name, layout, and color scheme and was pleased to find out that publishing a website had a lot in common with the ratings presentations she used to do at her old job. Tom also turned out to be an excellent teacher, giving her just enough guidance without getting too technical. Sunshine Salutations was gaining ground in both structure and design, and Brook couldn't have been more pleased.

One afternoon, as her web design lesson drew to a close, another development took place. In addition to his instruction, Tom gave Brook something else as she tapped away at the computer—a shoulder massage, followed by a gentle kiss on the back of her neck.

CHAPTER THIRTY-TWO

Kevin passed the bong, and the haze of sour smoke transported Chip back to the Phi Lambda Chi house. Back in school though, he had to smoke pot in secret. The officers of the fraternity, especially the Pledge Trainer as Chip had once been, were supposed to set an example for the freshmen. He could have been kicked out of the house if the more uptight members decided to enforce the rules. Brook had also disapproved of his using marijuana, claiming that he zoned out whenever he did so. "You act like a space zombie," she'd said. Chip took a hit, losing himself in the gurgle of the bong water. The intake burned his lungs and throat, but it was the good kind of burn.

"Whoa, man, take it easy," Kevin said. "You have to pace yourself if you want to last past midnight." Chip nodded through a cough and handed the bong to the guy next to him, whatever his name was. Kevin always had a host of acquaintances trickling in and out of his apartment, and Chip could never keep them straight. Tonight, they were all gathering to celebrate the New Year, what would be the toughest holiday for Chip.

Christmas had been pure bliss—no listening to his father carrying on about the business, his mother gossiping about the neighbors. Chip had called his parents to wish them well, but once his mother had established that he wasn't living on the streets or harmed in any way, she'd hung up on him. She didn't even respond when he told her he'd gotten a job painting houses; apparently, the Omaha Steaks he'd sent as a gift had done little to get them to embrace his new choices. On the day of, Chip had been invited out to dinner at the Rockhill home in Lake Forest, one of the premier suburbs of Chicago. A liberal and academic set, Kevin's family talked about art, music, and travel and they didn't judge Chip for being in professional limbo. If anything, they seemed to admire him for it. The Rockhills supported dreams. Each of their four children had been allowed to pursue whatever their hearts desired, and with their kind of money, they could afford to. It was never said out loud, but Chip could tell Kevin had a trust fund to finance his lifestyle. How else could a math teacher, even one who worked at a private school, afford a two bedroom apartment in Lincoln Park with stylish furnishings? Not only that, but Kevin ate out most of the time, had his clothes professionally laundered, and took his dates to concerts, plays, and exotic restaurants. Chip came from a family that was well off, but the Kincaides had to work themselves to the bone to maintain their status. The Rockhills were loaded, part of the leisure class, a dying breed. And if their hospitality wasn't enough to brighten his spirits that season, Chip had been seated next to Kevin's sister at the table. Nothing but a beanpole brat when he first met her years ago, Lauren Rockhill had since blossomed into an articulate knockout. She'd majored in European Studies at Northwestern and spoke French, Italian, and German. Lauren was also uncertain about her career path so they had plenty to discuss. She considered his quitting the family business to be an act of bravery, admiring him for defying the status quo. Rubbing elbows with her had been a privilege and a treat, the best Christmas he'd had in a long time.

New Year's Eve, however, had a distinct association to it. Last year, Chip had spent most of the night pacing the men's room at the Royals Stadium Club, rehearsing how he was going to propose, mistaking the quiver in his stomach for giddiness instead of anxiety. Tonight, Chip wanted to be in a fog, mask the past, and with each hit off the bong, he grew numb and tingly all over.

Phish tunes accompanied the pre-party tokefest and being a fellowship of men, Kevin began to recount the summer he spent following the band on tour. "So I meet these two local girls in Boulder, and you know how hard they party in that town." He said the last part with a wink, and the group nodded as if they'd been there themselves. "Anyway, we're talking, making polite conversation, and they invite me into their minivan to take some acid. So there we are, trippin' in a mom-mobile, discussing philosophy or some junk like that. Next thing I know, they're taking turns kissing me and off come my clothes." Kevin sucked more smoke from the cobalt glass tube. "It was wild."

"You're my idol," one enraptured friend proclaimed as the audience sat in a stunned and respectful silence, all except for Chip who got up to stretch his legs. He had heard the minivan story before, as well as many adventures like it as Kevin didn't seem to go a week without getting some serious action. Chip envied his buddy at first, even wanted to be like him, but he was starting to find Kevin's ways repulsive, especially since Chip was the one who had to cover for his buddy when he wanted to blow off one of his female admirers. It was the price he paid for a free place to stay.

As the party began to swell with more guests, the pot ring disassembled and mingled. Kevin lit some incense, set his high-tech stereo on CD shuffle, and began to make his rounds. Chip recognized a handful of his host's recent overnight guests and wondered which one would be at the breakfast table the next morning. Kevin always made pancakes, bacon, and French-pressed coffee for his girls. He gave them a tasty and memorable sendoff.

Chip said a few hellos, then stepped into the kitchen to get an Amstel Light out of the fridge, but when a wave of dizziness made him swoon, he grabbed a can of Pringle's and snarfed down the contents, tipping his head back as he inhaled the crumbs. When he returned to the throng of the party,

Chip's queasiness instantly dissipated when he spotted Kevin's sister standing next to the fireplace mantle. With dark chocolate brown hair and matching eyes that hooked you from across the room, Lauren stood out from the crowd even though she was less made up than the other women. And unlike them, she didn't need a plunging neckline, over-the-top heels, or a complicated cocktail to look hip and sophisticated. When she noticed Chip, she sent him a shy smile and waved. He stepped forward to make his way over, but another pushy guest beat him to the punch and cornered Lauren. Chip would have to wait his turn, leaving him time to track down Kevin and usher him aside.

"You didn't tell me your sister was coming."

"She's here? I didn't think she'd show. She was supposed to have a date tonight. Guess it didn't work out."

"Sooo…she's available?"

Kevin exhaled as if he'd been holding his breath. "I was afraid you were going to ask me about her after seeing you two at Christmas. Listen, I'm glad you're finally showing an interest in women, but why my sister?"

"She's fantastic."

"Forget it. You're on the rebound."

Chip figured his friend was right, that he should be playing the field, testing the waters before taking a plunge, but nothing could temper his attraction. "I'm done being single. It's gotten old."

"You haven't even been single. You've had what, two dates since you've been here? And they went nowhere."

"Right, which is why you can trust me. I'm not on the prowl for a one-nighter." *Unlike you, Mr. Cassanova.*

"What about all that talk about your freedom?"

"Hey, when you're with the right person, you never feel trapped."

Kevin stroked his chin as if to check for the smoothness of a fine shave. "I don't think you stand a chance. Lauren's wicked smart and super tough on guys, but you can give it a shot." Kevin's lack of faith only made

Chip more determined. He'd show him. He would get the girl. He'd done it before with Brook. She had caught the eye of plenty of guys, but Chip had beat them all out and won her over.

"I'm warning you, Kincaide," Kevin said, clenching Chip's arm. "Treat her wrong in any way, and I'll have you castrated." Chip thought it ironic that such a careless womanizer would threaten him like this, but knew how siblings protected one another, an experience he had never known.

Chip promised Kevin that he had nothing but the best of intentions and left to go to the restroom. Before he could try to woo the enchanting Lauren, some Visine was required to clear up his eyes, as well as a splash of ice cold water on the face. He was baked, no doubt about it, but there would be no zoning out for him tonight.

CHAPTER THIRTY-THREE

Über Spy tanked. The critics destroyed it. The audience rejected it. The studio didn't even think it'd have a chance to redeem itself on DVD. And Chaz…he'd blamed Tifani for its failure, despite the fact that he ignored her comments during shooting. "You just do what I tell you, my darling. Leave the hard stuff to me." Patronizing prick. She had told him that they needed to reveal more about her character's backstory, but he wanted to devote the screen time to chases and fights. And those fight sequences…too drawn out and unbelievable, but he insisted on pushing the realm of plausibility and wouldn't cut back on the slow motion shots. "You look fabulous in this scene. I don't want the audience to miss it." They'd missed it all right.

It had killed Tifani to do so, but she backed out of *A Pocket Full of Posies*, or rather she was strongly urged by both her and Chaz's camps to "pursue other projects." That was the last time she'd begin prepping for a movie months in advance. The English accent she had fine-tuned would have to be put on a shelf, right next to the empty space she had reserved for her future Academy Award. Although she mourned her dream role, Tifani was glad to be rid of Chaz. She was tired of waxing her nether region to please him, and they'd done nothing but fight since *Über Spy's* numbers came in. "Take your skinny ass back to where you came from!" he'd yelled during one of their nasty rows. Funny enough, she was doing what he'd told her, but not in the sense he had meant. She would not be returning to Los Angeles. Not yet. She needed to make a stop along the way.

"Can I get you anything else, Miss Diamond?" The flight attendant spoke with a southern drawl and Tifani locked away the sound of her voice. She liked to inventory people's dialects and incorporate them into her everyday speech. Always on the job, she was.

"More champagne, please," Tifani requested, still speaking with her English lilt as she had spent weeks perfecting it.

"Coming right up, but before I go…" The attendant glanced over both her shoulders before leaning forward and crowding out Tifani's neighbor, an overweight woman who looked as if she'd been shoe-horned into her aisle seat. Tifani had a hunch that the cocktail napkin being handed to her wasn't for the champagne. "I'm not supposed to do this, but would you mind?" the attendant asked in a hushed tone. "I have a niece who adores you. She started taking karate after she saw *Judo Jane* I don't know how many times." She pulled out a pen from her vest pocket.

Tifani took the napkin. "What's her name?"

"Siena. Just like the city."

"And how old is she?"

"Seven." Tifani's hand slipped as she scrawled out her signature. A seven-year-old had seen *Judo Jane*? It wasn't right for a kid to witness all that violence. What was wrong with the girl's parents?

"Thank you so much," the flight attendant said when Tifani gave her the autograph. "She'll be pleased as punch to get this. Now I'll be back in a jiff with your champagne."

As she waited, gazing out the window at the winter browns of quilted farmland, Tifani marveled at the vastness of America. Everything had been so squashed together in London. It was part of its charm, but it had begun to suffocate her. In the States, people had room to breathe, to spread their wings.

She pushed her seat back as far as it would go and tuned in to the hum of the cabin.

"I like the way you talk." It was the heavyset neighbor who had been trying to conceal her sidelong glances ever since Tifani removed her dark shades and Burberry wool bucket hat. The woman snacked on almonds from a brown paper sack and spoke with her mouth full. "It's very classy."

Tifani felt she'd done enough PR for the day with the autograph and wanted to keep to herself, but then recalled her publicist's lectures about improving her people skills. "Treat every fan like they are someone special, no matter how obnoxious they are. It's not about you, it's about them. They buy the movie tickets, and it's part of your job to get their butt in that seat."

"I've been living in London," Tifani said. "Guess I brought back the accent."

The woman eyed her up and down. "How do you actresses stay so thin? I try to eat what they tell me, like these almonds here that have the good kind of fat, but I can't lose weight."

Tifani thought the woman should probably eat a handful of nuts a day, as opposed to a half-pound bag, but she didn't like it when others advised her on eating and wasn't about to do the same.

"You want some?" the woman offered.

"No, thanks."

"Come on, they're organic." She dipped her pudgy hand back into the bag and rummaged around, bringing another fistful to her mouth. She at least swallowed this time before speaking again. "I guess you movie stars never eat. I see on this flight that you've only been drinking the champagne. You should try the steak. This is Midwest Airlines. Their food's not like the others. It's first class for everyone."

"I had a big meal on my first flight," Tifani lied. Like she could afford a splurge. What would start out as a steak today would turn into a lasagna tomorrow, followed by a plate of onion rings, a pepperoni pizza...next thing, she'd be featured in one of those vindictive pieces *US Weekly* liked to run on fat actresses. No thank you. Tifani's occupation required her to stay fit, and that meant exercising control at all times.

"So what brings a celeb like you to our neck of the woods?"

I want my mommy, Tifani thought. "My family's here," she said.

"Nice to see that you stay true to your roots. My daughter lives in Manhattan and never comes home anymore. That's who I was visiting, my Mandy. We did New Year's in Times Square. It was too noisy and crowded for my taste, but she loved it. Mandy's like you, skinny as a rail. It's not healthy." The woman brought the brown paper sack up to her mouth and poured in the last few almonds.

Bending over to reach in her Gucci satchel for the latest batch of scripts her agent had sent her, Tifani set them on her lap and her neighbor's face lit up at the sight of the bound papers. "Ooh, is that for your next movie?"

"Possibly. I get a lot of scripts." *And they all stink!*

"Well, I'm a very fast reader if you need some help…"

"Thanks, but I'm not allowed to show them to anyone. Studio rules."

"Oh. I understand." The woman switched from all smiles to a hoity demeanor, then cracked open a Janet Evanovich book as if she had her own private business to tend to.

Tifani slipped on her reading glasses and dived in, but she couldn't get past the script's first ten pages. It was the same with the second, and the one after that. It incensed her that no matter how much she griped to her agent, she kept getting handed the same shit—action flicks with no substance. Hollywood was jammed with screenwriters. Where were all the good stories? In the hands of Gwenyth, Drew, and Uma no doubt. What did *she* have to do to get the killer scripts, write one herself?

Tifani felt a spark of excitement ignite in her belly. That was it! She'd write her own story. Surely she could come up with better material than the pile of garbage that had been handed her. How hard could it be? She had read enough scripts to get the general idea and had the benefit of her own experience with character development. The more Tifani pondered the possibility, the more she liked it. It wasn't enough to just act anymore. Movie stars had to develop other skills like writing, producing, and directing if they wanted to stay in the game long term. She would do it!

The flight attendant brought the champagne, creating the perfect moment for a private celebration, and Tifani smiled to herself as the bubbles tickled her nose. If she could fake kung fu moves while wearing constricting outfits and stilettos, then writing a screenplay would be a cinch. And the peace and quiet of her childhood home would be the perfect place to do it. She could put Hollywood on hold and return to work on her terms, a masterpiece in hand. Then, she'd be a force to be reckoned with.

CHAPTER THIRTY-FOUR

It was a frigid January night outside, and Scott warmed himself with an Irish coffee in the vacant café of Union Station, listening to the loungy jazz tunes spilling out of the bar. The train station had been given a good scrubbing over the last few years and was now restored to its original grandeur back when it was the hub of Kansas City, and Scott had a prime seat to admire the results. The hundred-foot high baroque ceiling was painted in varying shades of sky blue, mauve, and gold to accentuate the details of its floral bas-reliefs and ornamentation. So dreamy in its decoration, he wouldn't have been surprised to see cherubs flying overhead, chasing one another around the enormous iron chandeliers dangling from sturdy chains.

Unlike the golden days of the locomotive, however, the atmosphere of Union Station lacked an energy and sense of occasion. The voices which echoed off the stone walls and marble floors, creating a backdrop of white noise like that in museums, seemed out of sync with the sparse traffic, as if they were everlasting reverberations from the past. Scott had read in the paper that more than a year after its highly touted reopening, the station was operating in the red. The building housed a theater district, restaurants, shops, traveling exhibits, and a science center, yet failed to bring in a crowd large enough to pay the surely astronomical bills. One could almost hear the money being sucked through the vents just to heat the vast Grand Hall. It worried

Scott to see the space not living up to its potential. It wasn't enough to preserve a historical landmark. People needed to support it.

Glancing up at the Roman numerals on the clock hanging above the building's central arch, Scott noted that the ever punctual Rebecca was fifteen minutes late. The old saying was true, a baby does change everything. By the time his sister finally rushed in, he had finished his coffee. "Sorry I'm late," she said, carrying herself in her usual breathless fashion. "Thanks for meeting me on such short notice."

"Hey, a pauper like me isn't about to say no when his sister offers to buy him dinner."

"I'm surprised this place isn't more happening," she observed, shrugging off her coat. "Oh, well. I'm just glad to be out. I love my baby to death, but, boy, did I need a break." Rebecca plopped down in her seat, removed her wool cap, and gave her pixie cut a quick fix with her fingers. "Nicholas had a major case of diarrhea today," she added, tossing her cap on the table. Scott winced in what he intended to be a purposefully visible way, but she seemed oblivious to his squeamishness. "You wouldn't believe it, Scott. The stuff shoots out of him like a cannon. But I think the situation was under control before I left. If not, Paul can deal with it for a change." She sighed and gave him a tired smile before setting her mobile phone on the table. "Just in case."

"How are you and Paul doing?"

She paused before speaking. "It's getting better, but we're both cranky all the time from lack of sleep. And I just don't understand him sometimes. The man knows how to design a skyscraper, yet a newborn seems to stump him. The other day, he actually tried to reason with the baby."

"Well, you did marry an engineer."

"Don't I know it. And I know I don't do *everything*, but it sure feels like it. I love being a mom, Scott, but you never know how much hard work it is until it happens to you. I read all the books, prepared myself the best I could, and it's still overwhelming." Rebecca stopped, shaking her head as if disgusted with herself. "Listen to me. I shouldn't be complaining. Some of my girlfriends have been trying to get pregnant for years and are going out of their minds with frustration. I'm lucky to have a beautiful, healthy baby and although Paul might be clueless at times, he's dedicated and has a good heart." She seemed lost in thought for a moment, and Scott wondered if his sister was thinking about their own father and how undedicated he had been. Rebecca then whipped out her napkin with a flourish and spread it on her lap. "So, I wanted to take you out because I know I've been a terrible big sister to you lately."

"You've had a lot on your plate."

"It's no excuse. It's been too long since we've had one of our heart-to-hearts. How are things? Any luck on the job front?"

"I've sent out my résumé to a few places, but it's bleak out there. A lot of hiring freezes going on right now."

"Maybe things will pick up now that the New Year has passed. Can you believe it's 2001? It just seemed like yesterday the world was freaking out about Y2K. All that panic seems so silly now."

"We can thank the media for that. Armageddon and widespread mayhem make good news stories." Rebecca nodded in agreement.

Their server, a trim man dressed head-to-toe in designer black, set down a basket of bread and a ramekin of olive tapenade. Rebecca ordered a bottle of Pinot Noir for them to split. "I'm done nursing for the day," she announced with joy. "It's party time." She reached for a slice of bread, but grimaced when she saw the mash of olives, garlic, and capers. "Oof. I can't eat that stuff." She pushed the ramekin in Scott's direction. "It reminds me of what Nicholas pooped out this afternoon."

"Geez, Rebecca, ruin it for both of us."

"Sorry."

"How about we wait thirty minutes after a meal before discussing anything related to diapers? Like the rule with swimming."

"Fair enough, but it's hard. I live in a world where my baby's bodily functions affect what kind of day I have."

"Please, let's change the subject," he insisted.

Rebecca widened her eyes and rubbed her hands together. "Okay, how is the writing going? Have you read those books I gave you?"

Scott didn't say anything.

"Wasn't your resolution to write at least thirty minutes a day?"

He picked up his menu and perused the items. "No one ever keeps their resolutions."

"I kept mine. I've lost three more pounds of my baby weight," she boasted.

"I commend you on your achievement."

"Well, nursing burns loads of calories. And Nicholas has a hefty appetite. Plus, I'm up and down the stairs all day."

The server brought the wine, went through the whole presentation bit, and filled their glasses. After telling him they needed a few more minutes to decide on their order, he gave them a patient nod, winking at Rebecca before he left. Her cheeks nearly turned the color of the Pinot Noir.

"I think he likes you," Scott teased.

Rebecca swatted the air. "He's just working on his tip." She couldn't hide her smile though as she scanned the menu. "It is nice to draw attention," she added. "I still feel like a frump."

"You're talking crazy."

Rebecca let out another weary sigh. "No, I'm not. A pregnancy changes your body in ways that's not appropriate to discuss with one's brother."

He held up his hand. "I won't ask for the details, but I think you look great." Scott wasn't used to this shaky confidence of Rebecca's and wished she would stop reading all those women's magazines which attempted to disparage society's impossible standards on the female form, yet simultaneously promoted and glorified them.

The server returned as soon as they set their menus aside, and Scott noticed the man sneaking a peek at his sister's cleavage while scribbling down their order. Rebecca must have been aware of the server's wandering eyes as well because she set her elbows on the table and clasped her hands so her wedding band was on prominent display. After he collected their menus and scurried off, Rebecca reclined back in her seat, swirling her Pinot Noir in its glass. "Did I tell you Paul has a cousin who just moved to town?"

"No…"

"She's single," Rebecca sang.

"Not gonna happen," he answered in his own song. "The last girl you set me up with couldn't stop yakking about her Atkin's diet and had the breath of a rhinoceros."

"And how many rhinos have you kissed?"

Scott looked up and counted on his fingers.

"Okay, so she didn't work out. That was months ago. I have a whole new crop for you now."

"I might not have much of a dating life-"

"Try *no* dating life."

"But I refuse to be set up again."

"So you're perfectly content to just waste your life away playing pool and watching the History Channel?"

"I don't do that," he shot back.

Rebecca sent him a pointed look. "Mom and I talk every day."

He squirmed in his seat, searching for a rebuttal. "It's the Discovery Channel I like," he corrected. "They aired a fascinating special about leaping monkeys the other night. You'd be amazed at the height they can spring. I think I might use them in one of my stories someday. So you see, I'm conducting research. And the pool helps me unwind. I've been busy working on the basement."

"But you're finished now."

"I'm recuperating."

"Scott, you've got to do something with yourself, *anything*. And what about this Holliday girl you took to the game? Helen told me you seemed really into her."

"Our aunt needs to learn to shut her trap."

"You know she doesn't mean any harm."

"She certainly didn't help matters." Scott refrained from criticizing their aunt any further, knowing he was more angry at himself than Helen. "It's like I said at Christmas," he continued. "The girl's not interested."

"Maybe she's changed her mind."

"The ball's in her court."

"And how would she reach you? You've moved out of your apartment and left your job. She doesn't know you're living with mom."

"Thank you for the happy reminders."

"I think you should give her a call."

"Yes, I can imagine how that would go. 'Hey, Brook, wanna give things another try? I have no apartment or money to take you anywhere nice, but maybe we could hang out in my mom's basement and play a nice game of Scrabble.'"

"You have to be resourceful, Scott. Get creative."

"I'd like to get my act together first."

"By that time, it may be too late."

"Your vote of confidence is staggering."

"I'm sorry. That came out wrong."

Scott spotted the server carrying a tray of food in their direction and unrolled his napkin. "I'm going through a rough patch right now," he said, bringing the topic to its conclusion. "Dating someone would be a bad idea."

The server set down their dishes, averting his eyes from Rebecca this time around. As they ate, Scott picked at his sun-dried tomato pasta, but his sister inhaled her Thai chicken pizza. "Slow down," he said. "You're going to give yourself indigestion."

Rebecca finished her slice of pizza and took a gulp of her wine. "I know. It's hard to shift out of mommy commando mode." She paused before reaching for another slice, resumed eating at a normal pace, but after a few bites, once again devoured her food as if rushing to catch a train.

"I've, uh, been meaning to talk to you about something," Scott said, glad to have a new topic to give his sister pause, although it too could upset her stomach. "Mom gave me those pictures of our father."

Rebecca stopped mid-bite and set her pizza down. "Have you looked at them?"

"Just enough to know what they were. Have you ever?"

"Once, a couple of years ago. That was all I needed to see. He certainly put on a good show in front of a camera. A picture may say a thousand words, but it's not always the truth."

Scott hesitated before speaking again. "I've thought about writing about him and all we went through," he revealed. "Do you think that's a good idea?"

Rebecca turned away as if looking to someone else for her answer before setting her eyes back on him. "I can't tell you what to write."

"Why? You tell me how to do everything else." They shared a chuckle, but Scott didn't stray far from the serious nature of the conversation. "I'm afraid it would hurt Mom."

"That's thoughtful of you, but I wouldn't worry about Mom. She wrote him off years ago and never looked back."

"But the absent father figure seems so overdone in literature."

"So is every other story line, Scott. Only you can write about it in your own way."

He stared into the flickering flame of the candle votive on the table. "I guess. Sometimes I wonder if I need to explore that part of my life, get it out of my system. Maybe purging myself of him would help unclog my brain. But I also hate the idea of devoting any of my time to his memory."

"I don't know what to tell you," she replied. "They say to write what you know. Tap into your pain. The material is certainly there. Our father was an immature, selfish bastard who didn't deserve us. Now that I'm a mom, what he did just pisses me off even more. I mean, what kind of fucker doesn't call his kids on their birthdays?" Rebecca placed her hands on the table as if to steady her nerves. She drew in a breath and continued, "Don't worry about what your writing will do to others. It's your life experience, and you shouldn't have to censor the past or dip it in sugar to please others. I'd let go of your reservations. You never know where it could lead."

Scott soaked in the advice, pondering whether he had the guts to explore his own reality instead of escaping into fantasy. The last time he had written a contemporary piece had been the one-act play he composed for Tiffany back in school. But when she rejected him, he took it as a reflection of what she thought of his work. If he had been talented enough, she would have asked him to come with her to Hollywood. Ever since then, it seemed safer for Scott to distance himself from his material and write tales of dragons and knights, although he didn't read those kinds of stories anymore—problem number one. Now Scott preferred novels grounded in everyday life, along with the classics of Hemingway, Salinger, Fitzgerald, and Maugham. But no way could he stack up to such literary giants so he avoided even trying—problem number two.

The server refilled their glasses with the last of the Pinot Noir. Scott took a sip, and as the velvety liquid ran down his throat, he once again drank in his surroundings. Union Station would have been thriving back when Hemingway lived in Kansas City. Working as a cub reporter for *The Star* before fighting in World War I, the young Ernest would have spent a lot of time hanging out in the Grand Hall, keeping tabs on the traffic of people, dashing across the expanse of marble to chase down an interview. Even legends had to begin somewhere, learn their craft before fulfilling their destinies. Nothing happened overnight. Scott too often forgot that for every book that stood on the shelf, there was a process behind it. Keeping that in mind, he imagined himself absorbing some of Hemingway's spirit still alive in this building, his voice forever echoing off the walls.

~

The next time Scott sat down to write though, discouragement, an all too familiar foe, soon set in. He tried to channel his favorite novelists, reminding himself that a rocky start was better than no start, but only ended up staring at the blank computer screen. The cursor seemed to taunt him as it blinked on and off. *LO-SER, LO-SER, LO-SER.* When the phone rang, its shrill cry penetrated Scott's temples, but he welcomed the distraction.

"Hello?"

"Hi there," a man's voice said. "May I speak to Scott Webster, please?"

"Speaking."

"My name is Trenton Sikes. I'm a writer." Scott perked up and wondered if Rebecca had passed his name along to someone who shared his interest. Maybe something good would come of the day after all. "I'm conducting research for an article and was wondering if I could interview you." The excitement began to fade. "You'd be paid, of course."

"What's the article about?" Scott asked, although he already knew the answer.

Trenton cleared his throat. "Tifani Diamond."

"Never heard of her," he snapped.

"Now we both know that's not true. I know you two were involved back in college." Scott heard the rustling of papers, "My sources tell me she really did a number on you."

"So naturally I'd want revenge," Scott said.

"I can make it worth your time."

"I take it that Tifani won't give you the time of day."

"Movie stars like to maintain an air of inaccessibility. It adds to their mystique."

"If that's what helps you sleep at night."

"Hey, I'm just giving the public what they want. Magazines fly off the racks when Tifani Diamond is on the cover."

"They do? I didn't think she was *that* big."

"When you've dated a director like Chaz Finglehausen, you're a player. Now, are you in?"

Scott considered the proposition. This Trenton clown wasn't the first to ask him to dish the dirt about his past with Tifani. *Inside Edition*, *Access Hollywood*, E!, VH1, they had all approached him for interviews since his ex made the A-list. He turned every one of them down. This guy had some timing though, calling when Scott was out of work with no appealing prospects. And he had to be honest with himself. A bitter, spiteful part of him did want to get back at Tifani, to cash in on her fame. She had asked for it after all, leaving him behind to chase after the spotlight. Scott found that he was struggling to take the higher road this time.

"How about it?" Trenton pressed.

There was a long pause. "My answer's no. I'm no fan of Tifani's, but I don't believe in kissing and telling. You know, you've got some nerve to call yourself a writer."

"Dude, a guy's gotta pay the bills. I'm telling you, you're passing up some serious greenage."

"Maybe, but my answer's still the same."

"Don't be a-"

"Goodbye." Scott hung up the phone and paced the room, telling himself that no amount of money could replace the loss of his integrity. And since he didn't have much else going for him, he had to stick to his principles now more than ever. Scott glanced over at his Macintosh, the cursor still blinking at him from across the room, but he felt too agitated to write anything now. He went into the den, grabbed the wooden triangle off its hook on the wall, smacked it down on the felt surface of the pool table, and began rounding up the balls.

CHAPTER THIRTY-FIVE

"Valentine's Day is coming," a man whispered to Brook. Floating between states of consciousness, she searched to place the owner of the voice. At first, it sounded like Chip and she thought a lingering memory from the past was toying with her. Then a much more pleasant possibility came to her in the form of Scott Webster, the most frequent star of her dreams nowadays. But when an arm wrapped around Brook's torso, reality presented itself and her awareness sharpened as a naked body pressed up against her own.

"Hell-o. Did you hear me?" Tom asked.

Brook stirred, creating some distance between them as she woke. "Sure," she said through a yawn. "How could I forget about Valentine's Day? It's been keeping me busy."

"I think we should go out. Do something special."

Brook turned to face him and propped herself up on one of the bed pillows. "I'm supposed to be the girl here, not you."

He frowned, picking at a loose nylon thread of the comforter. "I'm sick of this sneaking around. We're not in high school anymore." Brook looked around her childhood bedroom and even with her work setup, the rosebuds and Princess furniture screamed teenage frill. "I have my own apartment," Tom continued, spooling the thread around his finger. "We could work on the website over there and not have to be so secretive about our…extracurricular activities."

"But all my stuff is here. And you have two roommates."

"It beats your mom and dad." He let go of the thread, pushed himself up, and rested against the headboard. "Are you embarrassed to be seen with me or something?"

"No." And Brook wasn't ashamed of Tom. But she didn't want to go public with him either, to be coined "an item." Of course she couldn't tell him this. "It's just…cozy here." Brook nestled deep into the covers and hoped he would drop the subject.

"Well, I made reservations for us at The Duck Club for the big day," he announced with a firm tone. "This isn't a torrid affair, Brook. We have nothing to hide."

She gathered some covers for warmth and sat up with her legs folded underneath her. "I'm going back to Kansas City. Probably sometime soon. The website is almost finished, my business plan is coming togeth-"

"So you've got your website and now you're done with me?"

Brook sighed with frustration, refusing to justify his accusation with a response. "Listen, I've told you all along that my stay here is temporary."

"Yes, but…" he paused. "Plans have a way of changing."

Don't I know it, Brook thought, her eyes and attention drifting elsewhere until Tom fastened a gaze on her which couldn't be avoided. His youthful smile, usually bestowed with a hint of mischief, now had a cheekiness behind it that she didn't find one bit charming. Did he actually expect her to alter the course of her life for him? Didn't he know this was a fling and nothing more? Isn't that what most guys wanted?

Before she could form a rebuttal, the garage door rumbled open, signaling that someone was home. She and Tom scrambled out of bed, threw on their clothes, and arranged themselves in front of the computer. For a last minute adjustment, Brook cracked open the door to authenticate the scenario.

Minutes later, Brook's mother knocked and pushed the bedroom door open. "Hi, Tom. I noticed your car outside. Again. How's the website going?"

"Your daughter's pretty much got it down," he said.

"Yes," Brook added, facing Olivia. "The ordering system just needs some more testing."

Her mother stood there for a moment, regarding them with what seemed to be a hint of disapproval. "Can I get you guys anything?" she finally asked.

"Thanks, but we're fine," Brook replied.

"All right." Her mother turned and walked off, leaving the door wide open behind her.

Brook swiveled back around to continue with her posturing at the computer, but could sense Tom's eyes on her. "What?" she asked.

"I think she sees right through you. Your voice raises about five octaves when you're putting on an act. Makes me wonder what else you've been faking with me." He got to his feet and yanked his jacket off the bedpost.

Brook stood, took Tom by the arm, and pulled him towards her. "So what time do we need to be at The Duck Club?"

His eyebrows lifted. "You changed your mind?"

She nodded. "And I insist on paying. It's the least I can do."

"We'll discuss that later, but I'll pick you up about a quarter til seven."

"Looking forward to it," Brook said, keeping the pitch of her voice in check. They shared a brief kiss before she walked him to the door.

In the kitchen, Brook found her mother perusing a Spiegel catalog at the dinette, flicking her eyes up from the comfortable leisure wear when she entered the room. "I think we need to have a talk," Olivia said. Distracted by hunger, Brook crossed over to the refrigerator and opened the door. "Did you hear me?"

"Can I get something to eat first? I'm starving." She bent down and searched for Tupperware containers. "Where's the ginger chicken from last night?"

"Your father had it for lunch."

"What else have we got?"

Brook heard the scrape of a chair across the kitchen tile. Olivia joined her at the fridge, shut the door, and led her over to the table. Her mom then retrieved a box of Triscuits from the pantry and slammed it down in front of Brook. "There. Feast on those."

"Why are you so moody? Bad menopause day?"

Brook hadn't seen the look on her mother's face since the time she snuck out with her parents' car and drove it into the neighbor's mailbox. When Olivia sat back down, however, her expression softened. She folded her hands in front of her, studying them before speaking. "Brook, I think you might be getting too comfortable here."

"What? You're the one always trying to get me and Mel to move back. How can you be saying this?"

"I know, I'm surprised at myself. I've always wanted you girls in Tulsa. Don't get me wrong, I still do, but only if it's what's best for you."

"Are you kidding? Being home has been great for me. I have no distractions. Look at all I've done."

"But the only time you leave the house is to deliver your cards or go to yoga. Your heart's not into establishing a life here. And cavorting with Tom Bixby doesn't count. He's simply convenient."

"We're just friends."

Olivia gave her a stern look. "Your shirt's on backwards, dear."

Brook looked down at her chest. Sure enough, her v-neck sweater had turned into a crew neck and she was suddenly aware of the tag poking at her throat. She pulled at the collar.

"What's going on with you?" her mother asked. "You used to be so social, always out and about in the center of action."

Brook shrugged. "I've got to watch what I spend. And my energy needs to be focused on growing my business."

"I'm afraid you might be overdoing it, honey. I'm proud of what you've accomplished, but making improvements and changes doesn't mean you have to give up your life."

"Okay, so I'll get out more. In fact, Tom and I have plans to eat at The Duck Club on Valentine's Day. Does that make you happy?"

"Does that make *you* happy?"

Brook wanted to scream. Why did everyone have to be on her case all the time? Melissa, Tom, her mother, they all seemed to know what was best for her. What irritated Brook even more was that she couldn't figure out what the hell she wanted. Just minutes ago, she had told Tom she was planning on packing her bags; now she was practically hanging on to her mother's skirt. Some days Brook felt secure with herself, ready to conquer the world, then her confidence would dissolve into crippling uncertainty. She almost expected to find another note cluing her in to how things stood. *Who do you think you are? Go get a proper job like everybody else.*

"I know you might not want to hear this," her mother continued. "But I held my tongue about Chip and it did you no good."

Brook met her mother's eyes. "You? Held your tongue?"

Olivia drummed her fingers on the table. A few ticks on the clock passed before she spoke. "We were never all that crazy about Chip."

"You could have fooled me."

"We didn't *dislike* him. He was always polite and respectful towards your father and me. It's just that…well…he seemed to be putting on a…performance. You dated him for years, but he never opened up around us. And your dad thought he was a spoiled rich kid."

Brook arched an eyebrow. "Mel and I didn't exactly come from the sticks."

"But we taught you girls the value of a dollar, how to work hard and stand on your own two feet. And now look at you two. Chip was handed his daddy's business on a silver platter. He had it easy. He never struggled for anything and when life got sticky, he didn't know how to handle it. I know it's been painful for you, but his leaving was a blessing in disguise. I think you two would have had an unhappy marriage."

Brook sat in quiet contemplation, wondering if her mother possessed a sixth sense when it came to matters of the heart. Olivia Chandler had only known Jack Holliday for seven months when they tied the knot. How did her mom know that Jack, who had simply looked good in his Oklahoma State basketball uniform, would be a good father, a stable provider? His average grades and college pranks couldn't have provided any assurances. And how did her dad survive being the only man in the house, living with all that estrogen and moodiness for all those years? It astounded Brook how such a model marriage, one that had withstood both lean and mean times, could produce two daughters who were complete failures in matrimony.

"Okay, so Chip and I probably wouldn't have been happy together. I realize that now. But it's easy to say all this in hindsight."

"Yes, but I know you're still searching for answers about him. You have to deal with the possibility that you might not ever get them." Olivia paused. "Regardless, I think you might have better luck finding closure back in Kansas City."

"I can't leave yet. Dad and I are still putting the final touches on my business plan."

"Your father thinks you've developed a sound strategy. Now you have to execute it."

"But what if I missed something?"

"So what if you did? You'll figure it out."

Brook swallowed back a lump. When she spoke, her voice was barely above a whisper. "What if this is like the wedding? I could be living in a dream world and not even know it."

Olivia got to her feet and set a hand on Brook's back. "Listen to that little voice inside your head. It will never steer you wrong." Her mother gave her a soft pat before leaving.

Little voice. The slice of Brook's conscience that deserved more attention than she had given it over the past couple of years. It had once told her to reconsider marrying Chip Kincaide, but she charged ahead with her wedding plans anyway. It had also urged her to quit her job, but it took an icicle spear to get her to listen. Brook had blocked out her inner voice at times when she shouldn't have. It had scared her with its brutal honesty. It told her the right way to take her life, but not the easy way. And it never offered any guarantees. What was it saying to her now? Brook closed her eyes for some insight and wisdom, but could only hear the hum of the refrigerator. Her little voice seemed to have shut down, as if it had grown angry with her for being ignored all that time, denying her access to its guidance as punishment.

~

Brook carried on with her routine, gradually growing her client list, staying on top of demand, delivering her orders. Having landed a rush order for a baby shower given by a procrastinating aunt, Brook had to go to Kinko's to print the invitations since her boutique printer had closed for the day. Still, Brook felt like a traitor when she walked into the store to pick up the final product, feelings that were soon overcome with amazement when a person from her past served her at the counter.

His hairline had shifted back a couple of inches over the years and he'd grown out the rest of his graying hair long enough to tie back into a curlicue ponytail. His girth was wider, his face more swollen, and the harsh lighting accentuated the shadows under his eyes. Straightening his Sears tie, he spoke. "Name, please." His voice still sounded like he had a bubble clogging his throat, and the name tag identifying him as a senior manager left no doubt that he was Mr. Sweeney, Brook's high school art teacher.

"Name, please," he repeated.

"Uh, Holliday. *Brook* Holliday," she added for emphasis. "Two l's."

A flicker of recognition seemed to register on his face, but with an indifferent nod, he plodded off to retrieve her materials. When he returned, Mr. Sweeney wouldn't look her in the eye and rang her up with detached efficiency. She paid with her credit card, keeping her eyes trained on him, waiting for some acknowledgment when he matched her signature on the receipt to the back of her Visa. Nothing.

He handed over her order, and Brook flipped through the invitations to make sure they were up to snuff, stretching out the moment. As she did so, he leaned forward to take a look at the artwork, a simple graphic design with a striped border and teddy bear motif. It was then that he re-established eye contact. "Cute," he quipped with a crooked smirk.

"No, I'd say they're more Neato Frito," she retorted, stacking the cards in a neat pile. Satisfied with his baffled expression, she turned on her heel and sauntered out the store with her head held high. Cue the sassy Aretha Franklin music to mark the dramatic exit.

Once in her car, Brook dialed Tom on her mobile. "You will never believe who I ran into at Kinko's."

"Garth Brooks? Amber Valletta?"

"No."

"I'm running out of local celebs."

"Mr. Sweeney."

"Who's he?"

"The art teacher at our high school."

"I didn't take his class."

"I know, but everyone knew him. His tyranny was legendary."

"Sorry. The name's not ringing a bell."

"Trust me, he was terrible. And now he's managing a Kinko's. There's justice in the world."

"Listen to you, Brook. You're relishing in what had to be a step down for him. It's sad."

"No, what's sad is that he was ever allowed into a classroom, and that he's probably making more money as a manager than he did as a teacher. But thankfully, he's no longer tainting impressionable minds. Don't you see the beauty of it?"

"Beauty? At a Kinko's?"

Brook didn't continue as she became suddenly aware that the person she wanted to tell about her encounter the most was Scott Webster. He would be willing to speculate on the subject and understand just how huge the moment had been for her. He would get it.

"So I made our reservations for The Duck Club," Tom said. "My dad knows the owner so I was able to reserve us a primo spot by the window."

"Great," Brook replied, her voice rising in the way Tom had called her on the other day, and she had to temper her inflection before continuing. "I'll be sure to wear my best duds." Brook ended the call, feeling trepidation about her upcoming date, what felt more like an obligation than a fun outing. How did this happen? How did she end up in the same place when she was supposed to be working on her autonomy? *You were that girl who always had a boyfriend.* It's what Angela Walker had said at the party, backing up what Melissa had once claimed.

But Angela and her sister were wrong. Brook went plenty of years without a boyfriend. Shy and flat-chested, she didn't draw much attention in junior high, and although Brook wasn't a total reject, she never got invited to the cool kids' make-out parties. While the "developed" girls were getting hickies, she stayed at home with her books and drawings, waiting out the awkward years and focusing on her studies. By her sophomore year of high school, Brook had secured her place on the honor roll, belonged to all the right social clubs, and at last came into her looks. The chest never blossomed, but she did. She took care in how she dressed, discovered a hair gel to help control her frizzies, started speaking up more in class, and stopped holding other people's popularity against them. Bolstered by a sound GPA, she developed the confidence to hold her own, and when a boy she liked talked to her, she no longer choked. Perhaps Brook's delay into the dating world made her overcompensate once it came to fruition, seizing every chance at a relationship she had, whether it was good for her or not. As Brook gazed out her car window at the composition of red roof tiles of the Tuscan-inspired strip mall, she began to string together her history.

  Trey Rogers was her first official boyfriend, the warm up who had introduced her to the basics, but it had never progressed past that level before they both lost interest. Drew Kentworth came next. A year older than Brook, she feared he might pressure her into sex before she was ready, but to her surprise, he had turned out to be more of a prude than she was. Despite her advances, all he wanted to do during their darkened hours together was watch old movies. To no surprise, she'd later heard that he'd come out of the closet. Senior year was Justin Braddock, president of the student body, the perfect candidate to abolish her virginity. Their relationship took shape, reached its peak, but once they decided to go to different colleges, things tapered off into more of a friendship. She had graduated with her chastity in tact.

  Freshman year at the University of Kansas presented a plethora of opportunities, and she had kissed her fair share of guys before she started dating Matt Berry. Unfortunately, he was such a lush that even when they ventured to do the deed, he hadn't been up to the task. Plus, he'd pissed in her bed on more than one occasion, and Brook could only take so much. She moved on to Dan Simmons, a studious type who wanted to be a pediatrician. Brook respected him for his serious pursuits, but he ended up being more devoted to his books than to her. Enter Andy Wheeler, a rich semi-hippie from Denver, the one who would finally deflower Brook at his parents' ski cabin. He was fun, good-looking, clean, knew how to balance partying with his studies, and had great taste in music. Brook fell so hard for him she couldn't see straight. It was the first time she had ever been in love, and when she ventured to tell him so, he'd replied that things were getting too intense for him, that he wanted to see other people.

Chip Kincaide was supposed to be a rebound. After Andy shattered her heart, Brook picked up the habit of drowning her sorrows at The Bull, a ramshackle, frat-infested bar within stumbling distance of her sorority. There, she found safe refuge since Andy preferred to hang out at the more alternative bars in downtown Lawrence. There, through the magnification of the oversized chalice of a schooner glass, Brook spotted the fuzzy outline of the super-prep she knew from her Psychology 101 class. Her future fiancé. Chip approached and took a seat next to her on the wooden bench marred with the etchings of drunks. He bolstered her spirits with devoted attention and a host of compliments, coming right out and admitting that he'd had a crush on her since their freshmen year. His unguarded flattery came at a time when Brook was in a wounded and fragile state, and she responded to him. Before long, he had her laughing, and although Brook knew there was no chance of Andy walking through the front door, she pretended that he could see her enjoying the company of another man. By night's end, she'd agreed to go with Chip to the Phi Lamba Chi pajama party where they had danced under a rain shower of Natural Light. And that was that. Chip Kincaide was supposed to be a rebound, but he made Brook feel beautiful and desired, and she wasn't about to pass him up.

So yes, there had been a chain of boyfriends, as well as other guys in between the principal players, first dates and fillers that didn't go anywhere. Brook had been fixed up, stood up, fed up. She'd had her share of variety and never felt sheltered or naïve when it came to love. But Chip changed that, made her doubt her approach to both men and life. This was why she had to break her pattern, why there could be no Duck Club for her on Valentine's Day.

CHAPTER THIRTY-SIX

After a night of Anti-Valentine's Day debauchery among the lounge lizards at the Velvet Dog, Tug dropped Scott off at the house. It had been good to see his old pal again. Their hanging out was the one thing Scott missed about work. Tug had also left Pendleton Scrubb since the Big Layoff, although his departure had been by choice. He now worked in his dad's plumbing supply store, making better money while he saved up to go back to school to get a Master's in psychology. He even had a date lined up with a cute girl who had come into the store complaining of a leaky faucet. Scott was happy for his friend, but also a tad jealous and as a result, drank too much in an effort to soothe his ego.

He staggered around in the basement, knocking his hip against the pool table. His head pounded, and although the room was cloaked in darkness, it seemed to swim around him. Lumbering over to the mini-fridge, Scott wrenched it open, and the sudden burst of light seared his eyeballs. He took out a Pepsi and cracked open the can, but he needed something else to satisfy his appetite and trudged up the stairs to go on the hunt. He stopped, however, when he heard a faint creak coming from outdoors. Although the incessant ringing in his head made it difficult, he cocked an ear to listen for more. A few seconds of silence passed. Scott then wavered, and the stair croaked underneath his hiking boot as he shifted to regain his balance. Steadying himself on the guardrail, he pressed his foot on the step to confirm the source of the noise, putting his mind at ease.

He tiptoed up the rest of the stairs so he wouldn't wake his mother, angry with himself that he still had to think of such a matter. But he intended to get back with the program soon. After tonight, no more messing around. Scott made his way into the kitchen, grabbed a bag of Fritos, and crept back downstairs.

Back in the basement, he detected a hint of clove cigarettes hanging in the air, what must have been traces of bar smell he had left behind moments before, even though he didn't recall anyone smoking cloves around him at the Velvet Dog. The type of cigarette had such a distinct spicy, sweet smell, it never escaped his notice. And something else seemed off. The dynamics of the den seemed to have changed, as if a gust of cool air had blown through the room. He reasoned that it was the nature of basements to contain volatile ecosystems and odd smells and headed for the couch, ready to settle in with his junk food and Discovery Channel.

Scott collapsed into his favorite spot and the indention in the cushion molded to his backside, but he quickly shot back up when he noticed a shadowy figure sitting in the nearby recliner. He stumbled backwards, ramming his back into the wet bar and spilling his Pepsi and Fritos. Hit with a thunderbolt of sobriety, Scott flipped on the light and rubbed his eyes, convinced the alcohol must be playing tricks on him. When they came back into focus, however, the intruder was still sitting cross-legged in front of him. Tifani Diamond shook her pointy-toed, stiletto-heel as if Scott had some nerve to keep her waiting.

"What the fuck?" he asked.

"Surprise," she said in an arrogantly cheerful manner.

He put a hand to his chest where his heart hammered inside, and not in the good way. "Why are you-? How did you-?"

"You still keep the spare key in the garden lantern," she stated in an affected, upper-class English accent.

"Have you ever heard of a phone?" He shifted his weight, crunching the spilled Fritos underneath his boot.

"I'm an actress. I like to make a dramatic entrance."

"Mission accomplished."

Tifani stood on her twig legs, her shredded mini-skirt hitting her mid-thigh even though it was still February. She wore a silky, lingerie type blouse with a low neckline, showcasing her toned pectorals. When she stepped forward and wrapped her praying mantis arms around Scott's neck, he kept his own plastered at his side. "Bloody good to see you," she said. "It's been ages."

"I see you all the time. Is there a magazine cover you haven't been on?"

Tifani pulled back and tossed her auburn hair over her bony shoulder. "You always knew how to flatter me."

"What's the deal with your voice?"

"I've been living in London."

"So you're British now?"

"I've been perfecting my accent for work. Besides, it's natural to pick up on the local dialect when you spend some time in a country, especially for an actress who's sensitive to people's ways."

Scott massaged his temples with his thumb and index finger. "Whatever. Tifani, what do you want?"

She returned to the La-Z-Boy and crossed her legs. "*Über Spy* bombed."

"That doesn't surprise me. It looked like a piece of crap."

Scott meant for his words to sting, but Tifani's chiseled face lit up. "See, that's what I need, someone who will be straight with me. I get nothing but a bunch of yes-men in Hollywood. And they're the first to turn on me when the movie they insisted I do doesn't break box office records."

"So your movie flopped. Big deal. I'm sure you got paid well. You always manage to land on your feet."

Tifani picked at her manicure. "My career is in trouble, Scott. Chaz and I are over."

"And he is..."

"Chaz Finglehausen. He's only like the hottest director right now. But our collaboration has come to an end." She heaved an exasperated sigh.

Scott folded his arms. "If you've come here for tea and sympathy, you broke into the wrong basement. How did you even know I was here?"

"My assistant tracked you down. You probably know him as Trenton Sikes."

Scott recalled the tabloid reporter who had offered to pay him for information on Tifani. "You were behind all that?" he asked.

"He's good, isn't he? An out-of-work actor, of course, but surprisingly dependable. I had him call to check you out, make sure I could trust you. I wanted to get in touch, but I thought you might have it out for me."

"You still haven't answered my question. What are you doing here?"

A smile alighted Tifani's face. "I'd like you to write me a screenplay."

"You've got to be joking."

"I'm quite serious." As if to let her proposal sink in, she picked up her pack of Djarums. "Mind if I light up a fag?"

"You know the answer to that."

She tossed the pack aside. "So you're still psycho about the smoking thing."

"If this is your way of buttering me up, it's working like a charm."

Tifani crossed her arms and sulked. "Blimey, Scott, you should see the screenplays that come my way. They're pure rubbish. The meaty parts go to a handful of actresses and I get handed the sloppy seconds. If that's not bad enough, I've been pigeonholed into these catsuit roles. I liked them at first, even found them empowering, but an actress can get only so much mileage out of them. The gig has gone stale."

"I'm sure Hollywood has something for you. And I'm sure there are hundreds of screenwriters out there who know what they're doing. Hire one of them to write something for you."

"Right," Tifani chided. "You'd think the place would be oozing good material, but it's like the smog clouds everyone's imagination and good judgment. Just look at Mattie and Ben and their *Project Greenlight* competition. They're turning to nobodies for ideas and they got a bloody Oscar for their screenplay!"

"Is that what I am, a nobody?"

"I could turn you into a somebody."

Scott considered the idea, the seduction of Hollywood seeping into his system. He supposed he should be flattered that Tifani came to him, but working with her was absolutely out of the question. "Again, I'm afraid you've broken into the wrong basement," he told her in the firmest tone he could muster. "But here, take these Fritos." He offered her what was left of the bag. "You look like you could use some fatty food."

Tifani rose and stamped her foot. "Scott, I need you."

He lifted an eyebrow.

"I mean, I need your talent. You did interesting, edgy work back in school. Remember the monologue you wrote for me about the hipster coffee shop girl with the prosthetic foot? She was vulnerable, smart, witty, and STRONG. The whole package. She didn't have to put on a catsuit to prove herself to the world."

Scott smiled in spite of himself. "I spent a lot of time on her, blowing off my own studies in the process."

"It got a standing ovation from my class. Your writing almost outshined my performance. I need material like that, Scott. I've taken a stab at writing myself, but I'm not too proud to admit that I need help."

He scratched his head. "I'm rusty. I haven't written anything substantial in a long time."

Tifani picked up a Gucci satchel. From it, she retrieved about a half dozen manuals, all of which looked slightly used, and held them out at arm's length. "Here. Read these."

Scott scanned the titles: *Writing Screenplays That Sell, 500 Ways to Beat the Hollywood Script Reader, How NOT to Write a Screenplay.* "No," he said, pushing the books back at her. "I don't want anything to do with you, not after the way you treated me."

Tifani held the books to her chest and rolled her eyes like a peeved schoolgirl. "Scott, this is business. Don't let your resentment towards me keep you from the opportunity of a lifetime. I have the connections. Now you just need to come up with the story. And I've got some great ideas to get us started. I only have one rule." She paused for dramatic emphasis. "No. Leather. Catsuits. I'll do corsets, hoop skirts, even partial nudity, just no more bloody catsuits. Oh, and my name gets top billing in the writing credit. We'll want to take advantage of my recognition factor."

"You're wasting your time. I'm not interested."

"I'll pay you twenty-thousand up front. Another thirty when it's completed."

Scott found that the word "no" wouldn't pass his lips so easily now.

"That's a standard deal for a novice," Tifani continued. "And I can help you land an agent. You don't even have to live in L.A. like most screenwriters. This could be the start of something *huge* for you. You have the talent. You should be putting it to use instead of watching late night telly and eating crisps." He turned his back on her, but Tifani pulled him towards her and got right up in his face. "Are you going to tell me this is what you want out of life?" Her eyes swept the room before locking back on him. "You and I are so similar, whether you like it or not. An ordinary life will never do for us. Come on, this is your chance to stand out from the pack."

"You act as if I should just forgive and forget. I'm not that big of a person."

She backed off and produced a pen from her satchel, clicking it open with her thumb and scribbling a number on the back cover of one of the books. "I'm staying at my mum's out in Independence, laying low while I'm in town. The media bothers her enough and she's an extremely private person so we'd have to meet here."

"Did you lose your hearing in London? I said no."

She again offered the books to him, the one with her phone number stacked on top. "Give me a ring."

"I once gave you a ring, remember?"

Her plump lips formed into a smile. "See…you're clever."

Scott shoved his hands in his pockets. "I'm going to bed. You can show yourself out."

CHAPTER THIRTY-SEVEN

Whether it could be blamed on global warming or not, a sixty-degree day in February was to be embraced and it left Brook with no choice but to get outdoors. She rented a pair of Rollerblades for a glide in Tulsa's Riverside Park where the path was flat, smooth, and easy, perfect for the once-a-year inline skater like her. In case of an unfortunate tumble or collision, she had her mobile on her, and when her jacket pocket began to ring, she tilted back her right foot to activate the skate's break, glad to have an excuse to catch her breath. "Hello?"

"Have you started my invitations?"

"Hi, Danielle. Um, no. I still have plenty of time."

"Well, don't worry about them because we're eloping."

Brook stepped off the path onto the bleached and brittle winter grass. "No, you're not. You've said this before so I'll come up there to talk you out of it."

"I'm serious this time. I can't take it anymore."

Danielle's voice cracked and Brook could tell her friend wasn't kidding around. She found a nearby bench and had a seat. "What's wrong?"

"I've been holding out on you, Brook," Danielle began. "I thought my problems seemed silly compared to what you've been through. But I'm losing my mind over this wedding, and I need someone to talk to."

"I'm all ears."

"Are you sure?"

"Yes. Danielle, you were there for me. Now it's my turn to listen." Brook didn't say so, but she felt relieved not to be the one struggling for a change. "Tell me what's going on."

"Four months! We've had the church reserved for four months and now Steve's mother is making a fuss about us not having a Catholic ceremony. She won't even come out and say it, but keeps dropping these snide hints about how we're basically going to hell. Steve hasn't even been to mass in years!" Brook thought back to Chip's mother and all the trouble she had caused during the planning, contradicting Brook on almost every detail, but now wasn't the time to share her own horror stories.

"And the florist and I aren't seeing eye-to-eye at all. She's pushing baby's breath on me, claiming that it's so out, that it's in."

"Wait, are you using Sophia over at Krandall's?"

"No, Sophie over at Warner's."

"Uh oh. Red hair? Always wears it in braids?"

"Yes."

"She's the same one I butted heads with. She must have switched shops. Or got fired."

"Wonderful."

The list of grievances went on. The credit card bills were mounting, the band had broken up, a friend refused to attend the wedding because children weren't invited, and a selfish bridesmaid wanted to make the day all about her and Danielle didn't know how to tell her that she'd been demoted to Guestbook.

"Why is it all so hard, Brook? You know what my mom did? She got married in her tiny Korean church and they had punch and cake in the rec room. I think the whole deal cost a hundred dollars and took a month to plan. My parents didn't even have a honeymoon."

"Is that what you want?"

"No."

"What do you want?"

"I just want to spend the rest of my life with the guy and have his babies."

Brook experienced a catch in her throat, touched by her friend's conviction. Although she now wanted more than just a husband and kids, a part of Brook longed for the days when that was enough for her. And she knew she still wanted marriage. Someday.

"It's all the decisions," Danielle added. "It's driving me nuts."

"Maybe eloping isn't such a bad idea. The fairytale wedding is a myth."

"But you went after it. Isn't it worth it?"

"I don't know. I didn't make it to the finish line."

"What would you have done differently?"

"Tons, but you can't afford the phone bill."

"Come on. You can give me something."

Brook paused to think, taking in the view of the power plant across the river. She would have paid better attention during her engagement, that's for certain. Surely there had been signs that all was not well, probably right under her nose, only she had missed them. But Brook had no doubt that Danielle and Steve belonged together. "Just focus on the marriage, not the wedding," she advised. "I know it's trite, but it's all I got."

After a short stretch of silence, Danielle spoke. "I get what you're saying, but I want to share this day. I want to celebrate our commitment."

"Then that's what you should do. It's not going to be easy, nothing worthwhile ever is. And Steve's mother sounds like she's going to be a pain regardless of what you do. Just think, if you did elope, you'd probably never hear the end of it."

Danielle gasped. "You're right. When I think about it that way, it's not even an option. Thank you, Brook. That's exactly what I needed to hear. And I'm sure it'll all come together in the end. I'm just having a meltdown and needed to vent. I miss you. I wish you were here so we could talk face-to-face. It's not the same over the phone. Haven't you had enough of a break? I'd go crazy living in my parents' house for so long."

Neither said anything for a few seconds.

"I'm sorry," her friend continued. "I know being there is a part of your healing process, but I'm telling you, Brook, there's this great guy at Steve's work I want you to meet."

"A blind date is no way to get me to rush back."

"Okay, but I think it's time you get yourself out there."

"I am out there. I just broke it off with Tom."

"Oh yeah, the website guy. I forgot about him. How did he take the news?"

"Not so well. If a hacker sabotages my website, I know who to blame."

"All the more reason to get out of there, distance yourself from the situation."

"Ah, the Chip Kincaide approach."

"It's different and you know it. You love it here. I've never heard anyone go off like you do when someone disses our town."

Brook assessed the scene before her—the murky Arkansas river, the power plant, an artless steel bridge—not a fair or representative snapshot of Tulsa, but for the first time since her arrival, she felt the pull of Kansas City. Brook missed the nights drinking wine and watching movies with Melissa, her long lunches with Danielle, her therapeutic walks in the Brookside neighborhood. There would be no avoiding her past. Memories of Chip would be scattered all over the place, but Brook had changed since she left and felt the city could hold new meaning for her.

"Your silence is encouraging," Danielle said. "Is my nagging going to work this time?"

Brook opened her mouth to speak, but it took a couple of moments before she could provide a solid answer.

CHAPTER THIRTY-EIGHT

Enchanted with the fluttery notes of Irish merriment, Brook forgot where she was until she felt someone grab the soft part of her upper arm and give it a painful squeeze. "Ow!" she yelled, wheeling around to find a stocky, tow-headed man with a sheepish grin. "Hey, no pinching," she snapped, pointing to the shoulder of her celery green sweater. "See the green?"

"Doesn't count if it's not Kelly Green," he said in a fake brogue accent.

"You're making that up."

"No, I'm just a purist. You are in violation of St. Paddy's Day code." Brook thought the man's pungent aftershave was the true and more offensive violation and began to back away for some air, but he moved towards her, his eyes rolling across her body as he gave her a suggestive look that made her skin crawl.

To her relief, Danielle came to the rescue. "Come on," she urged. "Let's go watch the band and do a little jig." Brook followed as her friend pushed her way through the crowd at Harling's Upstairs. Thankfully, people tended to part like the Red Sea when the beautiful Danielle Swan approached.

Harling's was one of Kansas City's most popular Irish bars on any given day. On St. Patrick's Day, a crush of people clad in festive green attire fought to be seen and served. Occupying the second floor of an art-deco building in Midtown, the bar had the feel of an old church rec room with its wood construction, cafeteria-style seating, and stained glass windows. Only here, folks worshiped Guinness. Brook and Danielle made their way to the spillover room where a barrel-chested Irish singer, a ruddy Santa Claus in street clothes, belted out pub sing-a-longs and filthy limericks from a platform stage.

Danielle hooked her arm through Brook's. "See…if you'd stayed in Tulsa any longer you'd have missed all this."

"Glad to be back."

Despite their cheerful moods, Danielle's face drooped. "Work stinks without you there, not that it's ever been a bed of roses. Last week Patricia called me Dana during a staff meeting. I've been there for three years and my supervisor calls me Dana! I wanted to jab her with my pen, but there were witnesses." Brook patted her friend's hand. "I'm looking for another job as soon as I get back from the honeymoon," she added.

"Sounds like a wise move. Any idea what you want to do?"

She gulped down her Guinness before answering. "Haven't a clue."

Returning from the retro arcade situated in a corner of the bar, Melissa caught up with the two of them. "There you are stranger," Brook said. "You shouldn't be spending such a happening night playing Space Invaders."

"Oh, yeah?" Her sister fanned out a collection of business cards like a skilled poker player. "Look at all the numbers I scored."

Brook widened her eyes. "I stand corrected."

Melissa handed her a card. "Here, take one. The guys are so sloshed out of their minds they won't be able to tell the difference. All they'll remember is that they talked to some blonde."

Brook glanced down at Melissa's exposed cleavage. "Right," she quipped. "I'm sure that's all they noticed."

The three of them took in the music as Mr. Claus strummed his acoustic guitar, a fiddler and flautist providing the accompaniment. Melissa had volunteered to be the designated driver for the night so Brook and Danielle braved the bar in shifts, making it easy to lose track of how many beers they drank. After a couple of hours, the crowd, including the girls, grew rowdy. Folks linked arms and formed swaggering chains while attempting to kick like Rockettes. Beer splashed everywhere and on everyone, and no one seemed to care as they all chanted, "Olaaayyy, olay, olay, olaaaayyyy. O-laayy. O-laayy." The place vibrated with so much music, stomping, and carrying on that it was a wonder the stained glass windows didn't shatter.

Brook didn't know what the heck they were singing, but relished in the good time. Breaking away from the chain, she moved to a clear patch of floor and with her arms stiff at her side, started flailing her legs about as if performing in *Riverdance*. Pleased with the laughter coming from her companions, she quickened her steps until her feet went out from under her and she took a comic spill. Melissa and Danielle helped her up, and the three of them were in stitches. Brook collected herself, however, when she noticed someone standing in her periphery, demanding to be acknowledged.

It turned out to be Cassie Drumwright, the wife of a surgical resident and a key player in Chip's circle of friends. In her alternate universe, Brook would have spent her married life with Cassie. They would have played Bunko together, exchanged recipes, organized a play date circle for their kids. Heck, they might have even started a book club. Brook hadn't seen Cassie since her and Chip's couples shower. She had buffed up since then, and her dirty-blonde hair had been brightened with flattering highlights.

"Holliday, I thought that looked like you...sort of. Nice dancing."

"Thank you, but please, no tips." She extended her arms to behold the crowd. "I dance for the people."

Cassie laughed, and they stepped away from the revelry to talk. "So how are you, Brook?"

"I'm doing all right. How about yourself? Still selling pharmaceuticals?"

"No, not after my product started killing people. The drug's been recalled, and there are thousands of lawsuits. It's a mess, and I'm glad to be out of the business. So now I'm a rep for Boulevard Beer."

"One of my favorites," Brook said. "Mark must be loving that."

"Oh, he is. The free beer makes up for the cut in pay."

"How is Mark?"

"Good. Busy. I hardly ever see him, but that'll change once he's finished his residency. Only two more years," she said with forced brightness.

An awkward pause followed.

Cassie at last spoke. "You know, I feel like a jerk for not calling you, Brook. But Mark told me not to get involved in other people's breakups. And no one knew what had happened between you two. Chip wouldn't talk to anyone."

"Including me," Brook said.

"You're kidding."

"Afraid not."

"What a shit," Cassie spat.

"Yep."

"And now you have to deal with this other news."

"What news?" It was a reflex response, one Brook wasn't sure she was prepared to ask.

"You haven't heard?" Cassie looked as if she'd just bitten into a raw onion.

"I've been out of the loop," Brook said. "Is it that bad? Has he joined a cult or something?"

"Chip's getting married."

Brook's stomach plummeted, and the room began to swirl around her as the fiddler's playing penetrated her eardrums with an unbearable shrillness. Overcome with the shock, she could only catch snippets of the rest of the story. "Chicago…Kevin Rockhill's sister… whirlwind romance …" Brook tried to repress the feelings, but started to burn with jealousy and rage. Would Chip Kincaide receive no retribution for his actions? The bastard did not deserve a happy ending, especially before she got hers.

"Please, tell me she's pregnant," Brook managed to say once Cassie had finished. "She has to be."

"That's what we thought too, but Nicki talked to Mike who talked to Kevin. There's no baby."

It took a while before Brook could speak again. "I'm…stunned. No, beyond stunned. This is unbelievable. This is insulting! Did our relationship mean nothing to him?" Brook didn't expect Cassie to answer her, nor did she want her to. She just needed to think out loud.

"It always seems to happen like this," Cassie said. "My older sister broke up with her boyfriend of three years, and he married someone else six months later. It's like once they find out the single life isn't all it's cracked up to be, they panic and propose to the next person who comes along. And Chip used to be such a sensible guy."

After digesting the news for another few seconds, Brook tossed her hands in the air in surrender. "You know what? Nothing he does can surprise me anymore. The man is a mystery to me." As hard as it was to hear about the engagement, it felt wonderful for Brook to admit that Chip was beyond her comprehension. She realized that trying to make sense out of him would only hold her back from moving on with her life.

Cassie was next to speak. "Well, apparently Chip thinks he's Mr. Chicago now, acting like he discovered the place."

"Let him think whatever he wants."

Cassie set a hand on Brook's shoulder. "Sorry to be the one to tell you."

"No, I'm glad you did. I don't like being in the dark."

"Hey, if you're up for it, how about we go out for a couple of drinks next week? I'd love to catch up with you."

"Sure. I'd like that."

"Great. What's your number?"

"Here. Let me give you my card."

"Are you still at the TV station?

"No, thank God. I've started my own business doing stationery design."

Brook handed her a card and Cassie nodded in approval as she looked it over. "Excellent. I'd love to check out your stuff."

"I'm holding a home sale next month if you'd like to come."

"Count me in!" Cassie slipped the card into her Kate Spade purse. She then tipped her head, hesitating before continuing. "You know, don't take this the wrong way, but you always seemed kind of wound up around Chip. Like you forgot something back at home and were lost without it. When I spotted you across the room tonight, my first thought was how much more relaxed you look. I'm sorry about the news. It's tough to take, but it's more proof that you're better off without him."

Brook's spirits warmed at Cassie's words. "I agree. I only wish I'd seen it coming."

"Hey, if you want, I'll be more than happy to introduce you to one of our doctor friends."

"Or maybe one of your Boulevard Beer friends," Brook suggested with a Groucho Marx lifting of the brow.

Cassie nodded. "I'll get working on it. I'll call you!"

After saying goodbye, Brook rejoined her crew. "So what did one of the Stepford Wives have to say?" Melissa asked.

"Not much," Brook said in a nonchalant manner. She then smacked her palm against her forehead in mock surprise. "Oh, wait, I forgot. Chip is engaged."

Melissa's smirk evaporated. "Let's get you home."

"No," Brook insisted, shaking her head in protest. "What that man does no longer influences my life." She crossed her arms for finality. "I'm not leaving. Not until I'm ready."

Just then, a beer bottle flew through the air, shattering against the wall, and the women watched with their mouths agape as two men lunged towards each other in a scuffle. "Okay, I'm ready now," Brook said.

~

In bed that night, darkness engulfed the room and a drunken exhaustion weighed heavily on Brook. She should have slipped into a deep sleep once her head sank into her pillow, but instead, squirmed about like a fish flopping on a dock, her covers wrapping her up in a cocoon. Her mind refused to be still, mulling over what ifs, how comes, and deep regrets. As she lay on her back, she felt moist streams trickle down her temples and seep into her hair.

STOP IT! she told herself, pounding her fist on her duvet. *There will be no more crying over Chip Kincaide!*

Brook sprang up, flung back the covers, threw a robe on over her sunflower patterned pajamas, and retrieved the box full of Chip's crap from the back corner of her closet. She had kept his stuff around just in case he decided to show up, as if holding it hostage might lure him back, give her the chance to interrogate him and get some answers. But that was never going to happen, and she was no longer willing to give him space in her life.

The trash wasn't scheduled to be picked up for a couple of days, but Brook set the box out anyway. The man who had once turned her into a pity case was now officially vanquished from her life. She had kicked him to the curb.

CHAPTER THIRTY-NINE

Scott paced the basement, wearing a path in the berber carpet. He guessed what would be the excuse for the day—a highlighting job gone bad, a long line at Starbucks, an unexpected run-in with an avid fan. It was always something, and he never bought the stories. Scott might not have much else going on in his life, but it didn't give his employer license to disrespect his time.

Just when he was about to give up and make a grab for the TV remote, Tifani waltzed through the door, still letting herself in with the key kept inside the garden lantern. Scott made a mental note to change its hiding place. "Hi there," she chimed. She had on a tight-fitting Hello Kitty t-shirt with army green cargo pants. On most people in their late twenties, the outfit would look like a ridiculous throwback to their childhood, but Tifani looked hip as usual.

Keeping his scowl in place, Scott tapped his finger on his watch.

"Dude, sorry I'm late. Killer traffic." Judging by her speech and attire, Scott guessed that Tifani was playing a surfer girl that day. Her dialect changed as much as her hair color which had blonde streaks added to it since their last meeting.

"Traffic?" he responded. "Remember, this isn't L.A."

"A water main like, burst man. The whole street looked like that bad flood movie with Christian Slater. Now *Über Spy* was a masterpiece compared to that stinker. Anyway, I had to follow a detour and then I got lost."

Scott took a seat at the drop-leaf table littered with dozens of their drafts and notes. "Whatever you say. Let's just get to work. We don't have all day."

"That's your deal, not mine. You're afraid to let your mommy know about me."

"Oh, she knows about us. She just wants to pretend she doesn't."

Katherine had groaned with disapproval when Scott told her about his new work arrangement. "What in the world are you thinking?" she'd asked.

"This is a great opportunity," he argued. "A springboard for my career."

"You don't need her. You have your talent. And do you want that woman in your life, to have a role in shaping your career?"

"She can get me an agent. That's a big deal. I think she's trying to make up for the past."

"Don't be so naïve. She's playing you, just like she always did. She may be acting like she's doing you a favor, but Tifani's only out for herself. She's just like your father, selfish to the core. I think that's why you were attracted to her in the first place. You wanted to fix in her what you couldn't control with him."

"Please, let's not dish out armchair psychology. Look at it this way, Mom. I have something to gain here, recognition and money. She's actually the one taking a professional risk."

"But you're taking a personal risk. She broke your heart, Scottie."

"I know, but I'm putting that resentment aside. This is strictly business. And it will do me good to branch out and experiment with another form of writing."

"It won't be *your* writing, it'll be *her* writing. Hollywood writing."

"It's better than what I've been doing which is nothing."

Katherine shook her head, still unconvinced. "I don't trust her. She could end up giving you a raw deal or worse, steal your ideas and pass them off as her own."

Scott sighed. "Mom, I did my research and she's paying me a standard novice fee. It's good money. Listen, I know I'm living in your basement right now, but I'm still an adult. I can watch out for myself. If this is a mistake, then I'm prepared to accept the consequences."

Katherine huffed and crossed her arms. "If you're going to do this, so be it. I hope you prove me wrong." She raised a finger for one last point. "But I don't want anything to do with her. I don't even want to see her." Scott agreed to respect his mother's wishes, and since Tifani couldn't meet in public without attracting attention, she came over while Katherine was at the office. His mom's words needled his conscience, though, as she had made some valid arguments.

Tifani smoothed her tiger-striped hair before tossing her Gucci satchel onto the pool table and hoisting herself up on its ledge. She chose to conduct all their meetings this way even though it couldn't possibly be comfortable. Scott didn't like her sitting there, perched above him in a position of power, but he would have felt silly asking her to get down since doing so might indicate that he was thinking about the other activities they used to do on that table. Tifani set her spiral notebook with the hot pink glitter cover on her lap and thumbed through its pages. "Now, I know we made some great progress the other day," she began. "BUUUUUT…I have some suggestions."

Scott looked down at his own papers and pinched the bridge of his nose with his fingers, once again reminding himself that other wannabe writers would kill for the chance to work with established talent. That was why he had changed his mind and agreed to go through with this plan in the first place. Otherwise, he'd just be a glutton for punishment. Scott braced himself for another marathon session of notes, his shoulders already working their way up to his earlobes.

~

With the benefit of time and distance, Brook could see how she had behaved too rash with Scott. Severing relations with him had done no good in getting him off her mind, and her little voice said he deserved reconsidering. Dating didn't mean Brook had to sacrifice her independence. If she could leave a stable job to start her own business, she could find the discipline to never lose herself in a relationship again. On top of that, Scott's past wasn't so scary to her now. If anything, his proposal to Tifani Diamond showed he possessed a willingness to step up to the plate and put his heart on the line. Brook shouldn't have held his history against him. She had acted like a coward, like her ex-fiancé, and it was time to set matters right.

Praying that Scott was still available and willing to see her, Brook dialed his home number, but it had been disconnected. She then rang Pendleton Scrubb, only to discover that he didn't work there anymore. "Do you know where I could reach him?" she asked.

"I don't know where he's working," the snooty receptionist replied through her gum chewing. "But I did hear that he moved in with his mom. Even if I had that information, I couldn't give it to you."

Brook dreaded the thought of having to reach Scott through his mother, but there was a bigger problem. She couldn't remember the woman's name, and there were enough Websters in the phone book to require it. But Brook did recall a couple of things about that day at the Chiefs game. Scott's mother liked a good bratwurst and worked for the ballet. In minutes, Brook booted up her computer and logged on to the Internet. One search engine later, she was on the ballet's website. A couple of mouse clicks after that, she found a webpage with the staff listings. And just like that, she had it. Katherine Webster, Director of Development. Brook returned to the phone book where the listing seemed to jump out at her in bold type, and her heart raced as she scribbled the information on a Post-It note.

Before Brook could talk herself out of it, she found herself in her Jetta. Anyone could make a lousy phone call. It was the safe way to get in touch. A personal visit would make a statement, express how serious she was about wanting to see Scott. It would be like sending one of her cards as opposed to an electronic greeting. Her nerves tingled with a mix of excitement, anticipation, and anxiety.

Please be home. Please be home, she pleaded in her head. *Please be home and please be single.*

~

"I think we should go in a different direction," Tifani said, swinging her legs so her clunky Doc Maartens knocked against the pool table.

"Okay…"

"The heroine, that's my part."

Scott looked up and blinked. "Yes, I know."

"Now, I'm thinking we could ugly her up a bit. Maybe give her a bad nose or saggy eyes. They can do amazing things with prosthetics nowadays. Or we could make her mentally challenged in some way. The Academy eats up that shit."

"She's an overachieving former homecoming queen," Scott replied. "None of that would make sense. The premise of the story is that she seems to have everything: the grades, the looks, the hunky boyfriend. She supposedly has her act together, but she's just as confused and lost as any of us. You were crazy about this idea just a couple of days ago. I've got fifteen pages for you to read."

"Right," Tifani droned. "And I'm sure you've come up with some cool stuff."

"At least review it before you change your mind."

She grabbed the eight ball from off the pool table and lay down on the ledge, talking to the cottage cheese ceiling as she rotated the ebony sphere in her hand. In the old days, with Tifani sprawled out in such a suggestive manner, Scott would have pounced on her for a ravishing, but now she just looked like such a poser. "I don't need to read it," she said. "I'm no longer stoked about the story. The vibe…it's just not there for me."

"I stayed up late polishing these pages for our meeting today."

"And you're getting paid for that work. Remember, this is a collaboration."

"This is bullshit!" he wanted to shout, but he only slouched in his chair and said, "We can't keep going on like this."

"What do you mean?" Sitting back up, she tilted her head. "Are we still talking about the script?"

Tifani had mentioned at their first writing session that nothing physical was to happen between them. Scott told her that wasn't going to be a problem, and she had seemed offended, as if upset to be denied the opportunity to turn him down. Even if Scott wanted to make a pass, to exact his revenge by having empty sex with Tifani, her bad accents and even worse manners quelled any desire for her. Despite his lack of interest, she never missed an opportunity to turn a phrase or take something out of context to make it seem as if he was dying to jump her bones.

"We're getting nowhere," he clarified.

"Oh. Right. I know. Who knew it'd be this hard. Just when we think we've got something, I have another radical epiphany."

"You're all over the place," Scott said. "First you want to do a serious Victorian piece, then a romantic comedy, and now that we've outlined the homecoming queen story, you want to chuck it like yesterday's news."

"It's too pretty of a role. All of them are. I want ugly. Ugly and gritty."

He tapped his pencil on his notepad. "If you fashion a story to win an Oscar, people will see right through it. You have to respect your audience. It's as basic as starting with a well-rounded character in a challenging situation." Scott leaned forward and shuffled the papers. "We've got a ton of ideas. We just need to decide on one and stick to it."

Tifani pouted and resumed swinging her feet. "It all seems like it's been done before."

"We're not trying to break ground here and stop doing that!" He pointed to her Doc Maartens. "You're going to scuff the wood. Please, sit down at the table with me like a normal person."

She hopped down off her perch, but didn't take a seat. "I can't. Standard work practices block the chi of my creative juices."

"What?"

"It's all about feng shui, Scott."

"O-kay...you've lost me. Anyway, what I'm trying to say is that the stories have been the same for centuries. What we need to do is take one and put our own spin on it." Scott paused as it dawned on him how much he sounded like his sister. "I think our goal should be simple, to entertain."

"Easy for you to say. You're just the writer. I'm the one whose career is at stake. If I have another flop, I'll go from the fringes of the A-list right down to the C-list." She made a nose-dive gesture with her hand. "And I refuse to go back to television. It's all over when that happens."

Scott wrung his hands under the table. He wanted to wring Tifani's neck. Since they started working together, he had come to realize how much he had changed from the days when they were a couple. Back in school, Tiffany Peterson could do no wrong, and Scott had worshiped her despite the criticism from some of his friends and family. They lived in their own world where all they needed was each other. Now he could recognize it as an unhealthy infatuation. Towards the end, her leaving for Los Angeles seemed inevitable, and his proposal had probably been a desperate attempt to hold on to what they had. He had to give her some credit. She seemed to have known back then what was obvious to him now. If they had gotten married like he wanted, it would have been an utter disaster. Scott was beginning to think any partnership between them was a bad idea. Tifani tested his patience and tolerance every time they met. But then he'd wonder if this was another instance where she knew something he didn't. Showbiz was her world, after all.

"I think your agenda is getting in the way of the story," he said, sticking to his guns. "That's why we're having so much trouble."

Tifani's expression hardened. "Your job is to write for me. *I'll* do the thinking."

Scott bolted up out of his seat, sending his chair backwards. "I don't have to take this shit," he snapped. "I don't care how much you're paying me." He stomped over to the wet bar and grabbed his car keys. "I'm going out. When I come back, you will have decided on a project, or we're done here."

Scott didn't even wait for her reaction. He charged out the door and expected that when he returned, Tifani Diamond would be gone and out of his life forever. And he wanted it that way. The woman had done enough damage already.

~

After ringing the doorbell, Brook pressed her hand against her stomach to calm the fish swirling around inside. *Sunshine. Breathe it in.* She took in a cleansing breath, inhaling the fragrant lilac blossoms bordering the porch, and sneezed.

During her wait, Brook began to think she was crazy to surprise Scott on his door step like this. Who dared to show up unannounced anymore? She would never conduct a sales call in this manner, why should her personal life be different? And would he be insulted that she'd presumed he'd be home instead of working at a job, that he'd still be single and glad to see her? Not a sound came from the house, but just as Brook began to think she could make a getaway, she heard the crank of the deadbolt. There would be no chickening out now. Straightening her posture, she smoothed her skirt and smiled, wishing there was a glass door to check her reflection. The person who appeared before her, however, was not at all who Brook expected to encounter. At first, she thought it was a teenager, as the shrink-wrapped Hello Kitty t-shirt and striped hair would indicate. Then Brook noticed the bothered look on a recognizable face...that of Tifani Diamond.

"How did you find me?" the actress demanded.

"I...uh..."

"Really, you people are relentless. You have no respect for privacy."

"Um..."

"Why so star struck? You're the one stalking me."

"No, I-"

"You know, I have a website. That's how I prefer to reach out to my fans." Tifani rolled her eyes and sighed. "I suppose you want an autograph."

Brook felt like the air had been sucked out of her. She understood there was a chance that Scott could be seeing someone and she'd have to accept it. But Tifani Diamond!? Why did it have to be *her*? And *how?* The woman lived all the way out in Hollywood! What was she doing here, ruining Brook's big moment?

"Do you have a pen?" Tifani asked, taking on an air of impatience.

Brook gathered the fortitude to cast aside her astonishment. "No," she replied, reaffirming her posture so as not to be intimidated. Tifani Diamond put on her pants one leg at a time like everybody else, probably Prada pants in a size zero, but they still went on the same way. "Actually, I'm here to see Scott. Is he around?"

"He's out."

"Do you know when he might be back?"

Tifani planted a bony hand on the doorjamb as if to block Brook from going inside. "We're extremely busy, Scott and I." She sent Brook a stony stare, a venomous look she probably practiced in the mirror while delivering her lines. "He's not available," she added with loaded enunciation.

Brook didn't need to be beat over the head with a stick to understand Tifani's meaning. But she wasn't going to let her visit go entirely to waste. "Could you tell him Brook Holliday stopped by?" She reached into her handbag for a business card. "Here's my information. Scott, uh, wanted to see my work."

Tifani took the card, reading it with a smirk. "Sunshine Salutations. How...*cute*." She then slipped the card into her back pocket. "I'll see that he gets it." Brook figured peace in the Middle East stood a better chance at happening, but she had made an effort. "Ta-ta now," Tifani said, stepping back into the house and shutting the door.

Standing face to face with the lion's head of the brass knocker, Brook cursed the universe for such lousy timing. Like Chip, Scott had also moved on and she couldn't blame him, even though she hardly approved of his choice. Brook had taken a risk in coming here and knew it might end in disappointment, but the actual weight of it pressed down on her heart with an unexpected heaviness. She ambled back to her Jetta and folded herself into the driver's seat. Before starting the engine, she picked up her mobile and called Danielle, intending to let her friend know that yes, she wanted to meet this guy she'd been trying to set her up with ever since she got back in town. But Brook hung up before the call connected. A filler date was not the answer. She did not need to go looking for a substitute for Scott, not when she had plenty else to keep her occupied.

CHAPTER FORTY

In the weeks that followed, Brook worked diligently on expanding her client base and in one such effort, found herself waiting in a plush chair in the coffee bar of State Line Books & Café, a well-appointed gem tucked amongst a row of chi-chi antique stores on Forty-fifth and State Line Road. What the shop might have lacked in book sales was surely offset by the café which did a steady business, requiring Brook to arrange her meeting during the lull of a weekday afternoon. The window seat, where one could watch ladies-of-leisure stroll from one high-end store to the other, was empty except for a pile of newspapers and a stack of board games. The couch in the back had sags in its cushions from frequent use, but it was currently unoccupied. Besides Brook, the only other patrons included a gray-haired couple playing chess on one of the checkerboard tables and a rumpled man nestled in a corner with his laptop. Brook liked to see others out on their own in the middle of a workday, those apparently free from the nine-to-five drill, if not every day then at least for the time being. Was the couple retired and playing chess to pass the time? Had they paired off early or late in life? Were they even a couple? What history and circumstances had brought them there on a rainy spring day? And the disheveled man, was he answering e-mail, composing poetry, or plotting to put Bill Gates out of business? She enjoyed guessing at their lives and situation.

Brook looked over at the concrete gargoyle squatting on a pedestal next to her armchair. The creature had a mischievous look instead of a sinister one with its elbows propped on its knees, chin resting on its paws, tongue sticking out, and she pressed her finger on the knobby protrusion as if to push it back into its round mouth. "Rub its head and it'll bring you good luck," a woman said. Brook hadn't noticed the attractive brunette who had joined her. "I do it every day," she added. "Right before we open. I like to think it keeps the big guys from putting us out of business."

Brook smiled and gave the gargoyle a quick rub on its bald head. She then stood and offered her hand. "Nancy Powell?"

"Yes, and you must be Brook."

"Thank you for taking the time to see me."

"Hey, anything for Melissa. Your sister handled my inheritance so I could make this place happen. She's a real pro and a mighty hard worker."

"That she is," Brook agreed.

"She says the same about you. Must run in the family."

"Well, I hope to have the chance to prove myself to you. Where would you like to talk?"

Nancy stretched out her arms. "Welcome to my office." She took a seat across from Brook and pushed up the sleeves of her cable knit sweater. Brook's nerves settled a bit as she sat back down. Despite her sister's assurances, she had expected the worst—a prim and proper snoot who would regard this meeting as an inconvenience. Instead, her prospective buyer had a relaxed, warm demeanor and carried herself with an air of poise and professionalism. This was someone who Brook would have liked to work for, as opposed to Patricia, the corporate chump.

"Your place is so cozy and chic," Brook said. "I love all the European touches. There's something to see everywhere you look."

"Thank you. My partner has a design background. I stock the place and do the bookkeeping. She takes care of the décor and displays."

"Sounds like a nice arrangement."

Nancy nodded. "It works for us. You should see it at Christmas. She goes nuts." The owner leaned on one of the armrests. "And speaking of Christmas, Melissa sent me one of your cards last year. I thought it very eye-catching, and I'm anxious to see what else you've got."

Brook couldn't have asked for a better opening so she reached for her linen covered album. Inside, she had samples of her work displayed in plastic sleeves and arranged by occasion. She handed the collection over for Nancy to peruse.

"I think my line would be a perfect fit for the shop," Brook said. "I noticed you hang local artwork on your walls. My cards would be another way to foster Kansas City talent."

After leafing through a few pages, Nancy spoke. "I have to say, you're not the first to approach me about carrying handcrafted cards, but this is some of the best I've seen. Your work has a professional polish the others lack." Nancy slipped out one of the samples and turned it over. "You use recycled stock. I like that."

"It's the only way to go," Brook said.

The owner continued turning the pages and studying the designs. "I've been wanting to increase my selection," she said. "And I'd prefer to carry someone from around here…besides Hallmark. But I've had some bad experiences. Shoddy work, unreliable delivery. If these cards do well, how do you expect to keep up with demand?"

"This isn't a hobby for me. I've dedicated myself to this full-time."

"Good for you. I worked at Sprint for way too long."

"As far as demand, I use a printing shop to help with production. If you run out of stock, I could have it to you the next day." Brook handed over her pricing sheet. Nancy scanned the copy, nodded, and then flipped through more of her work.

Brook set her elbows on the armrests and intertwined her fingers. "I see this as a partnership," she said. "If you do decide to carry my line, I can list you on my website with a link to your own, if you'd like."

"More exposure never hurts," Nancy said. "We rely mostly on word of mouth."

"I'm also working on getting local TV coverage."

Nancy shook her head and clucked her tongue. "Good luck. I've been trying to get on the news ever since we opened."

"Well, I used to work at KCXT and the V.P. of News is keen on featuring local entrepreneurs. I can't guarantee anything, but he's shown some interest. I used to spin the ratings so he looked good. He owes me."

Nancy tilted her head back to regard Brook with what she wanted to interpret as respect. She then closed the album and set it on her lap. "I do have one problem," she said.

Here it comes, Brook thought. These meetings were never easy. People seemed determined to say no. "What's that?"

Nancy drummed her fingers on the linen cover. "I have to start small, and it's going to be nearly impossible to decide which ones to order."

Brook relaxed and felt a smile spread from ear to ear. She had to practically sit on her hands to keep herself from lunging forward to hug Nancy. Having experienced a series of fruitless sales calls, it felt wonderful to secure a deal, especially in a shop with such style. "If you'd like, I could browse the books while you decide." Brook didn't want to leave and give Nancy the chance to change her mind. She had learned that lesson after meeting with a boutique owner who seemed all hopped up on her product when they met, but then backed out when Brook followed up later. Plus, a book purchase or two might fatten up her order.

"I won't be long," Nancy said.

"Take your time. My top sellers are the ones marked with the silver stars. And the seasonal items are featured up front." She got up and smoothed her pants. "Just let me know if you have any questions."

With some extra bounce to her step, Brook headed for the book section and after browsing a couple of aisles, had a stack of paperbacks in hand. With so much of her attention focused on her business, she had fallen way behind in her reading. During her perusal, Brook froze in place when she spotted Scott Webster bent over one of the book displays. She watched as he arranged the books, his strong hands working with dexterity and care, and the only part of her that seemed to be functioning was her heart beating triple-time. How could someone make such a simple task look sexy, make a casual gray t-shirt and jeans appear so debonair? It was Scott's intensity which made him so irresistible, his absorption in his work reflected in the crinkle in between his brows. It took her a minute to rally the courage to go up to him and tap him on the shoulder.

Scott turned to her with a slight start, widened his eyes in surprise, and smiled. "Brook. Hello."

She dipped her head towards the display. "I hope they're paying you for your time."

His face reddened. "No. I just don't like it when one book tops another's stack, especially if it's a bestseller. I like them all to get equal exposure. One pile each. I guess it's my way of creating good book karma." A paused followed, and since Scott didn't mention Brook's visit to his mother's house, she thought it safe to assume that her business card never left Tifani Diamond's back pocket.

"So, how's the writing going?"

Scott ran a hand through his hair. "Yes, the writing. It's going okay, I guess."

"Found your muse, have you?" Brook wanted to say in a biting, sarcastic tone, but she held her tongue and reminded herself that it was she who had chosen to stop seeing him.

"I'm no longer at Pendleton Scrubb," he told her after a couple of beats had passed. "Layoffs."

"I'm sorry," Brook said. "There's plenty of that going around right now."

"True, but I never liked it there."

"I left my job last fall," she revealed.

"Oh, did they have layoffs as well?"

"Um, no. It was just time to leave. I'm actually here on business."

He lifted his brow. "Are you doing the cards?"

Brook nodded. "I just met with the owner about carrying my designs. I'm killing time while she decides on her order. But it takes a lot of cards to earn a decent living so I'm also looking into picking up some freelance design gigs on the side."

His smile broadened. "Wow, that's terrific." But his happiness for her seemed to subside as he dropped his gaze and studied the checkered floor.

"So, what have you been up to?" she asked.

Scott looked up, but wouldn't meet her eye. "Let's see, I moved in with my mom where I get a daily helping of humble pie." He let out a nervous laugh. "I've been sprucing up the house for her. It's been a lot of work. Not much time to-"

"I'm sorry, but I've gotta run," Brook interrupted, noticing Nancy flagging her down over Scott's shoulder. "I need to finish this deal," she added.

Scott glanced back into the café and nodded. "Oh. Sure."

Something seemed to hang in the air, awkwardness mixed with traces of their attraction, but Brook thought it pointless to elaborate on either of their lives or make a promise to get in touch. Scott was with Tifani Diamond, and no way could Brook compete with a rich movie star who could surely provide him with the means and access to the writing life he wanted. Scott was probably only buying time at his mom's so he could get ready for a move to L.A. where they would live a charmed life among celebrities and artists. As if to create a tactile souvenir of what was sure to be their last meeting, Brook touched his arm. "It was good seeing you, Scott. Take care."

Leaving to tend to her business, Brook felt relieved to have an excuse to end the torture of seeing someone she wanted, but was out of reach. She hadn't allowed herself to get close to Scott in any fashion, not even as friends, and now she was paying the price. *Home improvements.* So that's what he liked to call his carrying on with Tifani Diamond. Brook supposed she should suck it up and be happy for him. It would be the well-adjusted thing to do. But Scott didn't appear happy. If anything he looked…uncomfortable. But wasn't that typical for a guy when he ran into an old flame?

"Someone you know?" Nancy asked.

"Just an old friend," Brook replied, tucking a ringlet of hair behind her ear. She produced an order form from her portfolio folder and poised her pen for action. "Now, let's see what you've selected."

~

Scott watched as Brook rushed off, aching at the idea that it could be the last time he'd see that funny walk of hers. Resting his hand where hers had just been, he wondered if her touch was a gesture of pity, or simply, "Have a nice life." He knew business had called her away, but it was obvious she was anxious to leave. Just as well. Scott wanted more from Brook Holliday than polite conversation and if he wasn't going to get it, then it was better this way.

He continued to place the books back in their proper piles, stealing the occasional glance over into the café where the two women talked, admiring Brook for being so proactive in her pursuits. Not one to talk or think things to death, she took action while Scott reacted to outside forces beyond his control.

She must think he's the biggest loser on the planet. And he did his part to solidify that image, hardly painting himself as the catch of the year. No wonder she wanted to get away from him so fast. No one wants to hear about a guy with no job, no apartment, no direction.

Scott did have the screenplay. Why hadn't he mentioned it? Thanks to his ultimatum, Tifani had finally settled on an idea and he had written almost half the story. The script was the one thing in his life that could pass as an accomplishment, yet he'd dismissed it as nothing. He supposed he was ashamed, not only because he was less than proud of the material, a girls-gone-bad heist story which did indeed feature Tifani in a catsuit, but also because it took someone else, and her money, to get him to buckle down and commit a story to paper. Scott had also been disappointed to find out that he didn't enjoy writing scripts. Although the text was sparse and screenwriting sounded glamorous, he struggled to connect with the mindset and technique required to follow industry standards. Nothing was supposed to go on the page that couldn't be seen on screen. Sounded easy enough. But Scott kept wanting to get inside the characters' heads, to explore dimensions that couldn't be filmed. He understood that the rules existed for good reason and for an unproven writer to bend them, it would expose him for the amateur that he was. Still, he wished to have the freedom for creative experimentation. But above all else, Brook knew about Scott's past with Tifani, and he didn't want to risk her forming a connection. She might see his writing a screenplay as an attempt to win back his ex, especially since Brook knew his true desire was to be a novelist. Scott needed something in his life to call his own.

Hit with an idea, he sidled up to the counter. "I'd like to apply for a job," he told the clerk with eager cheerfulness.

A scrawny man with buck teeth nodded and brought out a form from underneath the counter. "We're only hiring part-time."

"Works for me." Scott began filling out his information. This shop would be the perfect place for him. No cubicles. No ratings. No Leslie

Stoneburner. Plus, he'd get to interact with customers and tap into what readers wanted. The literary atmosphere and café crowd was sure to inspire him, and he'd still have the time and energy to write at the end of the day. Right then, Scott decided he'd no longer be someone with a day job who writes only when the mood strikes him. He'd be a serious, dedicated writer, who just happens to work another job to pay the bills. Working here would mean less Discovery Channel, but that would be a good thing. And Scott just might happen to bump into Brook Holliday from time to time when she comes to call on the owner—another bonus. Then, he could hold his head high and feel good about himself.

"Do you have many writers on staff?" Scott asked.

"Almost everyone," the clerk replied. "I dabble in mystery sci-fi myself. The owners are super supportive. They understand what it's like to have a dream. We even have a writers' group that meets here after we close on Sundays. We get free coffee and you can't beat the space."

Scott loved the idea of these meetings and hoped to be invited as a member, picturing it as a secret society huddled together in a back corner of the store, wearing knitted scarves and fingerless gloves, poring over their words and exchanging ideas as they guzzled good, strong coffee. He finished the application and handed it over.

Scott didn't linger. He wanted to return home and make some headway on the script. The sooner he was done working with Tifani Diamond, the better.

~

Filled with a surge of productivity, Scott polished the first act of Tifani's caper film, knowing his "partner" would be upset at him for revising some of her dialogue, but he absolutely refused to have one of the characters say, "Let's do this thing." He then composed a first draft of two more scenes before running out of steam. Rising to his feet, he retrieved a can of Pepsi from the mini-fridge and cracked it open, pacing the basement as he drank, waiting for the caffeine and sugar to kick in for another writing session. He ran a hand along the smooth wood of the ledge of the pool table, tempted to engage in a round of practice, but it would be too much trouble to clear the debris scattered about its top, the very reason why he had let it all collect there. Distractions were deadly to his progress.

Scott headed back towards his room, resting against the doorjamb as he admired the lemon cream paint job he had given the walls. Dreading the thought of getting back to Tifani's pet project, he zoned out for a period of time. When his eyes came back into focus, they settled on the Hush Puppies shoebox sitting on top of the oak filing cabinet. Scott could see the jumble of photographs contained inside as if he had the x-ray vision of Superman, and he took a contemplative gulp of soda.

Begin in your own backyard. Brook had suggested Scott do so on their date; seeing her that afternoon must have refreshed his memory. With her words reverberating in his head, a magnetic force seemed to pull Scott forward as he stepped beyond the threshold and crossed the room. Standing over the mopey Basset Hound, he removed the warped lid to the shoebox, eased himself back into his chair, and began picking through the Kodak moments. In one, his dad was teaching him how to play the piano and he recalled how his father pounded the keys in anger whenever Scott messed up a note. He had been seven years old at most. In another photo, Scott sat on his father's shoulders in a swimming pool, and he shook his head in amazement at the image. Even when he swam, Owen Webster smoked a cigarette. There were about a dozen or so pictures like this, that of a father and son who resembled one another and supposedly shared a bond. But it was a snapshot of the entire family which Scott reflected on the longest, one where they posed as a nuclear unit in front of the horsemen at the J.C. Nichols fountain. Was this why Scott was so drawn to the landmark? Had this brief moment of family togetherness planted itself in a deep recess of his psyche, only now resurfacing when faced with its physical manifestation? Scott remembered that afternoon.

His family had gone for a walk around the Plaza after an Easter Sunday brunch. He had been forced to wear a beige leisure suit, hating every suffocating minute of it, and Rebecca kept pulling his striped tie whenever their parents weren't looking. Scott would have voiced a complaint, but his mom and dad were doing their own bickering so he punched Rebecca in the back to defend himself. In the snapshot, however, all was sunny and bright with everyone dressed in their Sunday best. Scott could understand why his mother and sister wanted nothing to do with these photographs. They depicted an artificial history. No one's clicking the camera when a parent loses his temper, yells at the kids, or throws a dinner plate at his wife. No one takes a picture when a father marches out the door with his suitcase.

Begin in your own backyard.

Most of Scott's memories of his father had either been diluted through the years or intentionally erased, but the few which remained washed over him with a poignant intensity that created a tightness in his chest. Scott looked down and noticed that he had crushed the empty Pepsi can in his hand. He tossed it aside and swiveled around to face his computer. As Scott's fingers began to dance across the keyboard, daring to write things he hadn't even allowed himself to think before and not caring a lick where it would take him, some relief eventually came.

CHAPTER FORTY-ONE

Snug on the couch with her chai tea and Sunday paper, Brook was just about to dive into the lifestyle section when she heard Melissa's door open and a man's voice carry down the hall, the same baritone that had boomed through the house late the previous night. Brook readjusted herself and bloused out her pajama top, unnecessary, but it made her feel more comfortable about being seen in her bedclothes with no bra. "Hi," she croaked when they entered the room, her voice not yet warmed up for the day. Melissa and her guest both jumped, either at the roughness of Brook's throaty greeting, or the mere surprise of it. The two of them looked as if they had been tossed about in a tornado.

The man smiled. "I'm guessing you're the sister."

Brook cleared her throat. "That I am."

"I'm Bryce."

"Brook."

An awkward silence followed. "So, I'll call you," Melissa told Bryce, slapping him on the back and pushing him towards the door.

Bryce looked over his shoulder as he left. "Nice meeting you." Brook returned his smile and waved.

Melissa gave her guest a quick peck good-bye and collapsed against the door after she shut it. "I'm getting too old for this."

"So, are you going to call him?"

Melissa shrugged and crossed the room, plopping down next to Brook. "He's fun enough, but I don't know if I see it going anywhere. He's too…I don't know. Too something."

"You amaze me," Brook said. "Your disposable contacts last longer than your men…and receive better care."

"Ha, ha. Aren't you hilarious."

Brook sipped more tea, turned the page of the lifestyle section, then spat out her drink, giving the paper a rain shower.

"What the hell?" Melissa said.

Brook pointed to the splotchy page listing the wedding announcements. In a grainy black and white photo, her ex-fiancé nuzzled a toothy woman wearing a strapless gown and poofy veil. Lauren Rockhill. The two looked like Donny and Marie Osmond with their All-American smiles, shiny cheeks, doe eyes, and dark lustrous hair. Brook stared at the picture, slack-jawed. Although she had some time to grow used to the idea of the engagement, seeing the woman who had supplanted her made Brook feel as if someone had sunk an iron fist into her stomach.

"They didn't waste any time," Melissa said, moving in close to see the paper. Both remained silent as they read the text. "Are you sure he didn't knock her up?" her sister asked when they were done.

"Not according to Cassie and she has reliable sources. I'm surprised Chip's mom wanted to advertise a quickie marriage. It screams scandal." Brook crumpled the announcements on her lap. "I wonder if his new bride knows what he did to me."

"My guess would be no, at least not the whole story. You should write your own note, clue her in to the kind of man she just married."

"If she doesn't know, she'll discover it eventually. He may be living in Chicago now, but he can't erase his past. And when she does find out, I'm sure he'll talk his way out of it. He's gifted that way."

"I give them six months, tops."

Brook wadded the paper into a ball and lobbed it across the room. "I sold the engagement ring."

"About time. How much did you get?"

"It was a nice chunk of change."

"I think that calls for a frivolous shopping spree."

"Too late. I gave the money to a women's shelter. It felt like the right thing to do."

Melissa nodded in agreement. "Just be sure to write the donation off your taxes."

"Of course." Brook waited some time before speaking again. "You know, Chip's not entirely to blame for what happened between us."

"He's the one who skipped town."

"Right, and I'm not justifying what he did by any means, but I should have called off the wedding, Mel, long before he left. I should have never accepted the ring in the first place."

Melissa didn't say anything.

"I knew deep down something was off." Brook swallowed before continuing. "I didn't love him anymore."

Finally coming to terms and voicing what had plagued Brook for months didn't distress her as she had feared; rather she felt as if a boulder had been lifted off her chest. "I don't know when it happened, but instead of dealing with it, I coasted along on auto-pilot, obsessing over my damn checklists. I was living a delusional existence." Melissa listened with an open, accepting expression, as if she'd been waiting for this moment, expecting it. "I didn't want to get married, not to Chip, but I was too scared to let him go until he gave me no choice. I'm embarrassed that it took such an extreme act for me to grasp reality." She fiddled with the edge of her nightshirt before continuing. "I knew something was going to happen the day I found the note. I knew it was over…and that it was long overdue."

The two sat in silence until Melissa spoke. "Seems like all that yoga has worked some magic. I'd say you've had a breakthrough. Oprah would be proud."

Brook sighed. "Possibly. One thing for sure is that Chip and I didn't shine as a couple. I guess that's about all the closure I'm going to get with him."

Melissa rubbed Brook's arm for a stretch of time before tending to herself and massaging her temples. "Oof, this hangover's killing me." She lifted herself off the couch.

"Please, stay. I need to tell you something else."

Melissa paused before reclining back against the cushions. "Did you take another trip to Topeka?"

"No, nothing like that. And remember, that's in the vault," Brook warned before going on. "I ran into Scott at Nancy's shop the other day."

"Is that all?"

"No, that's not all." Brook explained Scott's past with Tifani Diamond and her run-in with the actress at his mother's house.

When she finished, Melissa let out a heavy exhale. "Wow. That's crazy. Tifani Diamond?"

"All ninety pounds of her," Brook confirmed.

"You should have called first."

"Yes, thank you. Anyway, it was torture seeing him at the store, like having a chocolate cupcake dangling in front of me."

"You still have a thing for him, huh?"

Brook nodded. "I thought it would go away, but it hasn't. I haven't been able to get him out of my head, especially after seeing him. I shouldn't have cut Scott off like I did."

"I think it was a wise choice at the time. You weren't ready."

"But why did it have to be all or nothing? Now I've lost him for good."

Melissa knocked her leg against Brook's. "Come on, a movie star dating an average Joe?"

"Scott's not average."

"You know what I mean."

"Yes, well, it happens."

"Did Tifani actually say they were a couple?"

"Not in so many words, but her message was clear."

"Brook, I'm a lawyer. Wording is everything. Now tell me exactly what she said."

"I don't remember *exactly* what she said. It was something like, 'We're busy,' and 'He doesn't have time for you.'"

Her sister shook her head. "You need to hear it from Scott before you jump to conclusions."

"The woman was at his place in the middle of the day."

"Don't let her intimidate you. Her movies aren't even that good. And she probably won't be around for long. Actresses have to keep working to stay hot."

"Yeah, and she'll probably take Scott with her to Hollywood this time."

"Again, you're assuming too much based on this one encounter."

"Two encounters. He was acting all shifty and awkward when I ran into him."

Melissa positioned herself to face Brook head on. "You can't give up because there's a complication. Get the whole story. They could just be friends. Even if he is seeing her, it doesn't mean he's in love."

"They have a history together."

"Okay, worst case scenario is that Scott is back with Tifani and they're packing their bags for Tinseltown. He should at least know where you stand. Let him have a choice."

Brook shifted on the couch. "That sounds selfish and manipulative."

"All is fair in love and war." Melissa set her hand on Brook's. "Hey, I know I act detached when it comes to men, but if someone got under my skin like Scott has with you, I'd be all over it. I'll make a deal with you."

"The lawyer in you never rests."

"I'll give Bryce another chance if you do the same with Scott."

"You're equating my connection with Scott to that of someone you just met and kicked out the door?"

Melissa pressed a hand against her forehead. "Geez, Brook, I'm only trying to give you incentive. Things are easier when you have a buddy."

"Oh. Sorry."

Her sister hoisted herself up off the couch. "All I'm saying is this: Talk to him and tell him how you feel. That's it."

"Easier said than done."

"Well, *I'm* done. I've given my big sister speech for the day."

"No day would be complete without one," Brook teased.

Melissa flicked Brook's arm before shuffling away. "I'm going to sleep off this headache. Keep me posted on any developments." Her sister stopped just before disappearing into the hall. "But do call ahead next time. If he's not interested, at least you'll be spared some embarrassment."

CHAPTER FORTY-TWO

Tifani hovered over Scott's shoulder as he typed in the latest of her ludicrous suggestions, her hot breath wilting the hairs on the back of his neck. *Just a couple more lines,* he told himself. *And then you can get back to your real work.* Scott hit the Enter key, punched in the letter which cued up the character's name, and typed the closing line for the scene. There. They had finished the second act of the screenplay. He thought the day would never come. Scott conducted one last save and stretched.

"Thank heaven," Tifani said, smoothing her platinum blonde hairdo and speaking as if she came from the Deep South. "I thought you'd never get done."

"*I* was done a couple of days ago," he said. "These were all your changes."

"Well, it wouldn't have taken so long if you weren't always fighting me. Sometimes you act like a bronco being strapped by the heels."

Scott bit back a rebuttal, having learned to pick his battles with Tifani. And since they were now in the final stretch of the project, he could see the light at the end of the tunnel.

"So, this is huge," she said. "Only one act left. We should celebrate." She pulled him up out of his seat and dragged him into the den.

Scott was too tired to resist, having been up most of the night working on what he hoped would be his new book.

Tentatively titled *Floor Sample* and inspired by a visit to the JC Penney Home store with his mother, the story follows an isolated and desperate furniture salesman whose past involvement in a corporate scandal caused his professional, financial, and personal ruin. While other men his age are retiring into golf and leisure wear, he still has to put on a suit everyday and make sales to pay off his legal bills. He and his son don't speak, his upper-crust sommelier daughter looks down her nose at him, and his ex-wife has a new husband and granite countertops. As he sets out to redeem himself and patch up his relationships, his efforts only expose more of his weaknesses. Scott felt good about the story and his writers' group from the book store had a positive reaction to his work so far. For once, he had direction, purpose, and above all, a beginning and an end. As far as Granier, Falsafett, Brewshire, and Lockheed were concerned, he hadn't found a place for them yet, and didn't feel they belonged in this book. They would have to wait their turn. And that was okay.

Doing his own work created gratification for Scott, making his time with Tifani easier to take, offering him hope that he could one day sever the chains to her coattail. Tifani let go of his hand and pranced over to the wet bar to pull out one of his mother's merlots from the wine rack. "Bingo!"

"Just like old times," Scott said, recalling the way she used to raid his mom's liquor back in college.

Cocking her head, Tifani wagged a finger at him. "Now, we've talked about this."

He waved her away. "I didn't mean it like that."

"Oh. Pardon me. I'm just used to guys always hitting on me. You got a corkscrew 'round here?"

"It's not even two o'clock."

"Don't be such a stick in the mud. We've reached a mile-marker."

"I need to stay sharp. I've got other writing I want to get done today."

Tifani approached him with the wine bottle still in hand and set her fists on her waist. "Not another screenplay, I hope."

"God, no," he said with more vinegar in his voice than he intended. "I'm working on my novel. And I've got that part-time job, remember? I'm closing tonight."

"That's fine that you've got other projects in the mix."

"I'm not asking for your permission."

"I just worry that you might get stretched too thin. I don't know why you even need a job with the money I'm paying you."

"I'm not doing it for the money." *Unlike with you,* he added in his head.

"I see. Well, best of luck on your other stuff. It looks like us working together has been good for you. And now we have two reasons to celebrate, the screenplay and your future bestseller. Come on, one itty-bitty drink won't hurt. Now, fetch me a corkscrew."

Scott caved in, thinking it'd be quicker to just have the damn drink with Tifani than to continue arguing with her. He went behind the wet bar, pulled open a junk drawer, and picked through the assortment of butterfly ties, coasters, and matches until he located a corkscrew. Just as he was about to close the drawer, however, a flash of yellow caught his eye. Brushing aside a tangle of paperclips, he saw that it was a drawing of a sun with two intertwined S's scrolled in the face, a business card advertising Brook Holliday's services for Sunshine Salutations. When Scott picked it up, his heart kicked against his chest, but soon after, an unsettling idea set in and he marched over to Tifani to show it to her. "Do you know anything about this?"

Tifani regarded the card with nonchalance. "Some Ann Taylor type dropped it off."

Scott experienced a mix of elation, confusion, and then finally, anger. "What?! When? And answer me in your normal voice before I lose it."

"I don't know," she said, dropping the Southern belle accent. "I think it was the day you threw your temper tantrum and stranded me here."

Scott placed both hands on his head as if to keep it from exploding. "Why didn't you tell me?"

"I meant to. Must have slipped my mind. Anyway, you don't need any distractions right now."

He jabbed his finger at his chest. "That's for me to decide."

"Come on, Scott, relationships have a way of clogging the brain."

"You don't even know the nature of our relationship."

Tifani rolled her eyes. "Puh-lease. I'm an actress. I know how to read people. I could see the disappointment on her face when I answered the door. It didn't even faze her that she was face-to-face with a celebrity. She just wanted to see you."

"And what did you tell her?"

"The truth. I said you were busy."

Scott threw his hands up in the air. "Great. She thinks I'm with you." Tifani lowered her gaze and wiped the dust off the neck of the wine bottle. "And I imagine you didn't give her any indication to think otherwise," he added. "No wonder she acted so weird when I saw her."

"I had a good reason. You need to focus. You get a little obsessive when it comes to women. I should know."

"No, you were being selfish. It's what you do best."

Tifani set down the merlot. "Okay, so I screwed up. I'm sorry. I didn't do it on purpose."

"So the card just jumped into the drawer and buried itself under a pile of junk?"

"I was going to tell you about it…eventually. Don't let this ruin what we've got going."

"No. *We* don't have anything going. Not anymore. We're finished here." It felt wonderful for Scott to say this.

"Don't be stupid," she cautioned. "Don't let this silly matter get in the way of your career."

"It's not silly to me."

"Jesus, you can be so touchy and stubborn. You always were." Scott glared at her, and Tifani held up her hands as if to backtrack. "But I'm fine with that. I'm used to dealing with difficult personalities. You know, some of the best Hollywood teams fought like bandits behind the scenes."

"We're not a team. We've never been a team, even when we were going out."

She smirked. "Funny you should say that. You were the one who wanted to trap me in a marriage."

"I was young and didn't know any better. Now please, just leave."

"But Scott-"

"Go."

Tifani plodded over to the pool table and picked up her Gucci satchel. "Okay, it's obvious you need to cool down. I'm going to go home, and tomorrow we'll pick up where we left off."

"I said, we're through."

"Scott, you're making a huge mistake."

"No, the mistake was letting you back in my life. You do nothing but muck it up."

She narrowed her eyes. "I think you do a fine job of that on your own."

"Get. Out."

Tifani sulked with dramatic emphasis before heading for the door. "Wait," he called after her. Turning around, a coy grin stretched across her face. Scott held out his hand at arm's length. "The spare key. Give it to me."

After the smile left her face, Tifani reached into the outside pocket of her satchel, holding the key in her hand for a few seconds before hurling it across the room. Scott ducked and the key just missed his head before it clanged off the mirrored tiles behind the wet bar. Tifani then stormed out, the smell of clove cigarettes leaving with her.

Scott picked up the spare key and tossed it into the junk drawer. He then planted himself on the couch, collecting his thoughts as he examined the business card, rubbing his finger across the raised lettering. *Brook Holliday.* Despite the setbacks in his life, she had tracked him down and come to see him. In person. That meant something. Scott kissed the card with relish and then leapt to his feet.

CHAPTER FORTY-THREE

Brook cradled the cordless phone in her palm, her fingers shaking as she pretended to dial the number and rehearsed the conversation in her head.

Scott, I made a mistake. I'd like to have you in my life in whatever capacity I can, even if it means we're just friends. Too stiff and rehearsed.

Scott, I'm hot for you. Now let's get it on. Too direct.

Tifani's all wrong for you. You need a woman with substance. Too arrogant.

Brook figured it was best to just say what sprang to mind. Besides, a full-on confession about her feelings would hardly be appropriate over the phone. All she had to do right now was make some small talk and ask if they could get together. Still, her heart boomed just thinking about it. She felt like a schoolgirl asking a boy to her first Sadie Hawkins dance.

Brook inhaled a deep breath and punched in the numbers. On the first ring, however, there came a knock at the front door. Melissa was gone so Brook hurried out of her bedroom to answer it as the line continued to ring. When she opened the door, she nearly fumbled the phone when she found Scott Webster standing before her.

"Hello? Helloooo!?" a woman's impatient voice called from the receiver.

Brook put the phone back up to her ear. "Uh, hi. Is, um, Scott there?" She met his eyes and they both smiled. He pointed to himself and raised his brow as if to ask that it was him she was trying to call. Brook nodded.

"He can't come to the phone right now," Katherine said. "May I take a message?"

"No, that's all right. No message. Thanks." Brook clicked off the cordless. "Hi," she said, both surprised and pleased with the coincidence.

He said hello back and they stared at each other for a short stretch of time. Brook then glanced down at the phone. "So…that was your mom."

"So it was." Their eyes expressed a shared understanding. They had exchanged the same words on their first date, but now they held different meaning.

Another beat passed.

"Would you like to come in?" she asked. "I could make us some tea."

"Sounds great," he said, stepping inside.

Brook didn't know where the British hostess bit was coming from, but seized the opportunity to steal a moment for herself. In the kitchen, she clasped her hands, sending a thank you up to the heavens before filling the kettle and setting it on the stove. When she returned to the living room, Scott was holding out a business card. Even from a distance, she could see that it was one of her own. "I just found out about you stopping by," he said, tucking the card into the pocket of his rumpled oxford. "I'm sorry you had to run into Tifani like that."

"So am I."

"I wish I'd been there. I've been thinking about you."

A delightful tingle spread from Brook's heart to every fiber in her body. "Same goes for me," she said. Consumed with fantasies would be a better way to describe it, but Brook didn't share that part. "About you, I mean, not me. That would be narcissistic. Although we're always thinking about ourselves, aren't we? It's only natural..." her rambling ceased when he moved in close.

"The whole matter with Tifani, it's-"

"You don't need to explain. It was presumptuous of me to surprise you like that. And I couldn't expect you to be available just because I changed my mind about us."

Scott's face brightened. "You've changed your mind?" She nodded. "That's...when I saw you at the store, I thought you wanted nothing to do with me."

"I thought you were taken. Then I realized I was thinking in the extreme. I was calling you now because, well, I wanted to hear your side. I thought that if you are with Tifani, maybe we could at least be friends."

He shook his head. "I am very much *not* with her." Scott took hold of her hand. "And I want to be more than your friend." Brook's spirits soared, and any trace of inhibition or doubt vanished. "Things seem to come into focus when I'm around you, Brook. I'm not where I ultimately want to be in my life, but I'm working on it. And I think it'd be much more interesting with you in it. I don't believe in making false promises. Life has no guarantees..." He paused. "But I've put my past behind me." His warm, earnest eyes searched her face. "And you?"

Brook set her hand on his. "What matters is the here and now."

Scott pulled Brook in and kissed her. The kettle started whimpering with ghostly noises, but she barely noticed it. Breaking away to savor his full presence, Brook gazed up at a man who seemed to be just the right complement to her. Her little voice trusted this, and Brook was prepared to embrace the unknown since she had learned it's more important to be engaged in one's life than to a man. She nuzzled in close to Scott's chest and they wrapped their arms around each other, both ignoring the kettle as its whistle escalated into a wail.

Brook basked in the moment and breathed in the sunshine.

Other fiction by Kristin Dow:
LIBERTY & MEANS

ACKNOWLEDGEMENTS

I'd like to thank my husband for his support, especially when I left my day job to dedicate more time to writing. He never asked me to prove myself worthy of such a step. I'm also grateful for my family, constructive readers and spirit boosters. It's hard to say if this book would have ever been completed if not for the various writers' groups I've belonged to over the years. Thank you for your commitment and feedback.

And many thanks to you, the reader.

Made in the USA
San Bernardino, CA
31 October 2015